THE SECRETARY;

OR,

CIRCUMSTANTIAL EVIDENCE.

A DOMESTIC ROMANCE.

"What demon prompted you to this?"

LONDON:

PUBLISHED BY E. LLOYD SALISBURY-SQUARE, FLEET-STREET.

PREFACE.

THE Romance of "THE SECRETARY; OR, CIRCUMSTANTIAL EVIDENCE," has been written to show how, step by step, it is possible that, for a time, the greatest excess of villany may succeed in compromising the happiness, and even the lives, of the most innocent persons, at the same time that the intricate web of dissimulation by which the false testimony is sought to be supported is at the mercy of the slightest accident that may arise to unmask its insidious aspect.

For the credit of human nature we will believe that there are few such men as John Oxley, and few such women as Mrs. Lerew and Miss Wicks; but that there are such, however grievous such opinion of the great human family may be, experience is a sufficient proof of.

With many thanks to the press and to the public for the many eulogies passed upon the work, and the great success that has attended its production, the Author presents it in a complete form to the public.

London.

THE SECRETARY;

OR, THE

VICTIM OF CIRCUMSTANTIAL EVIDENCE.

A ROMANCE OF DEEP INTEREST.

THE LITTLE CRAFT RIDES GALLANTLY THROUGH THE WATERS WITH THE CORSE.

No. 1.

CHAPTTER I.

MORRIS COURTLEY IS HUNG ON SOUTH-AMPTON COMMON.

On Southampton Common, one bleak day in July, Anno Domino 1751, such an assemblage of persons had collected, that, when you looked from an elevation at the monster gathering, it seemed to extend for miles into the open country, while from every road and lane, fresh contingents were each moment arriving to swell the concourse.

The best elevation to look at the monster crowd from, was a scaffold, that was erected some short distance from the high road across the common to Winchester.

There was that day a man to be hanged.

A sharp north-east wind, that now and then brought with it an army of frosty particles, that cut like knives, careered over the immense space; but the curiosity of the thousands there assembled upon that awful day of storm and wretchedness, as it turned out, was proof against all inclemencies of the season; and the great mob swayed to and fro with excitement, while now and then the fierce roar of many voices would rise upon the air, as some *melee* took place amid the assemblage, from some real or fancied cause.

From Southampton—from Winchester—from the Isle of Wight, and from the towns bordering the New Forest, as well as from Portsmouth, had come throngs of sight-seers.

Yes, there was a man to be hanged!

A fellow-creature was to be strangled according to law upon Southampton Common; and it was not likely that human nature, in its ordinary variety, could resist the attraction of such a show as that.

What to them was the cold and biting air from the frozen regions of the north? What to them were the icy particles that hung upon their beards, and cut their faces as though millions of little needles were dashing through the air? What to them was the fact, patent to them all, that the clouds were gathering over the sky, and that a snow-drift or a torrent of hail might be expected soon?

There was a man to be hanged, and that was such a grand attraction that it outweighed all events that might be encountered in the course of seeing such a sight.

Now, it will be remembered that all this was one hundred years ago, and many things took place then, that would not take place now. To be sure, now, as then, crowds collect to see a fellow-creature sent to his long account with all his sins upon his head, but the affair, as regards the authorities, is conducted rather differently.

We shall see how they did those things in the old times. It wants a quarter to twelve o'clock, and the sky is getting darker and darker each moment. The dense clouds are coming up per favour of some independent current of air from the south, and they would bedew the earth with plentiful showers, if that north-east wind did not meet them, and nip up the soft drops into hail and snow.

Many feathery particles of snow are already in the air, floating hither and thither, as if enjoying a gambol before they plunged down upon the sea of upturned faces that crowd the old common.

And now a cry arises from ten thousand throats—

"They come! They come! Here they are! They are coming now!"

Oh, what a striving, and trampling, and pushing there was now for a better place than those who strove and pushed though they already had. The mob seemed to be having throughout its length and breadth a fight of its own, for no other earthly purpose than to celebrate the arrival of the malefactor, who, then and there, upon that spot, and on such a day, was to make reparation with his life for the evil he had done to society—that society that had come, roaring and shouting, to see him die.

Poor wretch!

But there is the scaffold. It is worth a word or two. It had been the custom to hang criminals on what was called a gallows-tree. That gallows-tree consisted of an upright piece of wood stuck firmly in the ground, with the traditionary piece at right angles from the top of it, and the slanting strengthening band of timber beneath. On this occasion, however, an attempt had been made to construct a scaffold.

It was, to be sure, a very rude attempt.

A quantity of planks had been brought from the town, and placed on the tops of some half dozen carts, as nearly of a height as possible, so that a kind of platform was made, loose and shifting certainly, but still tolerably secure.

In the middle of this platform, where the boards were left open for the purpose, rose up the awful gallows, with its cross-tree at the top, and the rope dangling from it. The hangman, who was a bit of a genius in such matters, had so managed, that by the removal of one board, the victim of the day would be suspended in a tolerably satisfactory manner, and from underneath he could remove that board with ease.

A black cloth was laid over a portion of the extemporaneous platform, so that the erection looked something like the proper sort of thing, and had more of a professional look about it than the ordinary rough mode of shuffling poor mortals into eternity.

That ordinary mode was, to bring them in a cart under the gallows, and when they were suspended, to move the cart from under them, so that the last words the criminal usually heard, were from the carter to the horse, and consisted of " Come up !"

The parson did not like that, as he wanted the last say, and so all that is altered now.

Well, we have spoken of the gallows, and now we will say a something of those who are upon it. By-the-by, it was reached by a pair of steps that were lashed firmly to the wheel of one of the carts that formed the substructure of the whole concern.

Upon the platform, there was the Sheriff of Southampton, conversing with a gentleman from London, who had come down to see the sight in a kind of amateur capacity. Around the scaffold were a company of mounted yeomanry, with their heavy jackboots and huge bearskin helmets and drawn swords. They shook again with the cold.

A small knot of some eight or ten officers of the police stood close to the steps that led up to the platform.

The sheriff took out his watch (it was not much larger than an ordinary saucer) ; and, as his nose turned bluer and bluer from the cold, he said to the gentleman from London—

"Confound them, they are late! It is only a quarter to twelve, now. Why don't they bring him and hang him at once?"

"Ye-e-yes!" stuttered the gentleman from London, whose teeth went like castanets from the cold. "If they don't come and turn him off quick we shall not have a bit of feeling left."

"Not a bit," said the sheriff.

What sort of *feeling* did they mean? Was it for themselves or the poor belated wretch who was being brought out shivering to die?

Well, it was just as the sheriff and the gentleman from London had made these feeling remarks that the cry arose from the crowd of—

"They come—they come!"

"Ah, there they come," said the sheriff.

"Yes," said the gentleman from London, as he rubbed his hands together. "I see them. By-the-by, Mr. Sheriff——"

"Yes, sir?"

"Have *you* any doubt of the guilt of Morris Courtley?"

"None in the least."

"Oh, you haven't?"

"Oh, dear, no. Didn't the judge put on his black cap, sir, and didn't he solemnly pronounce the sentence of the law?"

"Oh, yes, he did."

"Then, sir, it would very ill-become a sheriff to have any doubts after that. I mean to say, sir, that it would be setting a very bad example, indeed, to the lower classes, if the authorities were to be wrong ever. Better that the man should hang, right or wrong, innocent or guilty, than that the majesty of justice—that is to say, if the law should not be a—a—that is—you understand, sir?"

"Oh, yes, it's quite clear."

A shout from the mob now interrupted all further discourse, for the cavalcade with the condemned man was close at hand. Yes—there it turns by the old clump of trees, and now it is fully visible to all present.

First of all there came some mounted officers of police, with cutlasses in their hands, and pistols in their belts; then there came the governor of the old jail of Southampton, and then there came an open cart, in which was the chaplain of the prison, and a coffin, and the hangman, and the criminal !

Another troop of yeomanry followed this procession, and on each side of the cart rode a mounted police officer.

This was rather a brief cavalcade, but it was terribly significant.

The executioner had his coat off, but he had tied it on his back by the arms round his neck, he felt so cold. The clergyman was bare-headed, and appeared to be much more deeply affected at the situation of the prisoner than at the cold, which must have cut him deeply—or the piercing wind that played among his thin white hair.

There was a look of firm and dogged resolution about all the officers, and the governor of the prison was as pale as death itself, as he rode along.

But now for the prisoner—the one poor shrinking human soul, concerning which all this parade and racket was made. Let us take a look at him.

Imagine a young man of about twenty-three years of age, of rather fair complexion, but with hair approaching to the darkest of browns. He has blue eyes, that seem full of gentleness. The contour of his face is all that can give promise of nobility of soul. There is not one feature that can be carped at. The brow is clear and expanded—the mouth rich in intellectual beauty, and the whole carriage and demeanour of the man is such as could only belong to a being of the very highest order of mental culture.

He is dressed in a plain suit of black, but he wears no cravat. With his arm flung over the coffin, to steady him as he stands in the cart, and the white fingers of the delicately formed hand quivering with agitation, this youth, for after all he is little more, comes on to die.

His name is Morris Courtley, and his crime is *Murder !*

Now look at him again. Is that a murderer's face? Are those eyes the eyes of a murderer? Is that soft, melancholy aspect such as you would picture to yourself as belonging to one who would commit a foul, dastardly, cowardly murder? for such were the characteristics of the deed for which he came there to die.

Now the clergyman speaks to him—

"Courtley— Morris Courtley—oh, ease this poor heart of the world of woe that sits at it, and tell me, even now that you see the dreadful insignia of death, did you, oh, did you, Morris, do the deed?"

"No!"

"You still say no?"

"I still say no. I am as innocent in thought, or action, or complicity of any sort, of the deed, as you are, sir."

"Oh, but this is terrible—this is too terrible!"

"Hush, my best and kindest friend. Let *me* comfort *you!*"

And now the crowd saw a strange sight, indeed, for they saw the man that had been brought there to be hanged holding the clergyman by the hands, and soothing him, and trying to comfort him in his deep affliction.

A groan burst from the assemblage.

"Morris, Morris," said the old clergyman, "if you had been guilty I could have soothed you."

"Yes, but I am innocent, and so, my dear friend, you suffer more in the pang of seeing me suffer innocently than I do in so suffering. Is it not so?"

"It is—it is, Morris! It is!"

"My poor friend, you will—be kind, I know, to my mother—she will not live long—and my little brother, Ned, poor child!"

The old clergyman could not speak. The 'yes' that he would have said, stuck in his throat; but he looked it, and that was quite enough for Morris Courtley; and with a faint smile, he said—

"I think, after all, my dear old friend, that the bitterness of death is past for me."

"Thank Heaven!—thank Heaven!"

"Yes, I do thank Heaven that has given me constancy and courage to bear the death without much misery, although I am innocent of the crime laid to my charge. But, sir, so sure as the bright and beautiful summer will succeed this sterile time—so sure as night will follow day, and day succeed to night, the time will come when my innocence will be apparent."

"Morris!—Morris!"

"What would you say to me?"

"This must not, shall not be! It is murder!—murder! I say to all here, it is murder!"

The old clergyman stood up in the cart as he spoke, and held up his hands above his head, and his voice arose to shrieking accents, as he screamed out that word—

"Murder!"

All was confusion and dismay. The cavalcade was stopped; and the governor, turning his horse's head towards the cart, called out—

"What has happened? What is this? Officers, be alert. What is the meaning of all this?"

A yell arose from the crowd, which, for the moment, effectually prevented any one from giving a reply to the governor. And yet the crowd knew not what they yelled at, except that it was at some undefined idea that there was something amiss in the proceedings of the authorities conducting the procession of the condemned man.

"Hear me!" cried the clergyman. "If this execution proceeds, it will be a murder; for Morris Courtley is innocent, I tell you! He is most innocent of the crime for which he is condemned! He is no murderer; and

if you take his life, you will be the murderers! We shall all be slayers of the innocent that have hand or part in the deed! He is innocent!"

"Sir," said the governor, "this is insanity."

"No—no! He is innocent! I declare it to you all—to the world, I declare it! He is innocent!"

"Upon what grounds, reverend sir? I suppose he has told you so?"

"He has."

"Forward, officers! We are late already. It is now twelve o'clock. Forward! Clear the way, there! Forward to the scaffold, will you?"

The mounted officers pressed forward, striking the people right and left with the flats of their cutlasses, as they impeded the progress of the cart; and it was quite a fight towards the scaffold.

And now a tall, stalwart man came battling through the crowd, and upon his shoulders he bore a lad of about ten years of age; who now and then raised a shriek, and clapped his hands together with despairing gestures.

The long, fair hair of the child floated in disordered masses down his shoulders; but those who looked him in the face could see that there were the same blue eyes that gave so remarkable a feature to the condemned man; and then a cry arose from the crowd of—

"It is his brother!—it is his brother!"

"Morris!—Morris!" shrieked the boy, and his face grew scarlet with the exertion he made to scream loud enough for his poor brother in the condemned cart to hear him.

How the tall, stalwart man fought forward; but as soon as the people found out what he meant, they made a lane for him to pass through; and with shouts and cries they welcomed him, and cheered him on.

"Bravo, Roots!—bravo! It's Roots, the poacher! Go it, old fellow. Bravo! Make way for him!"

And so the man, with the boy upon his neck and shoulders, got through the crowd, and approached the cart. And then Morris Courtley saw that it was his young brother, Ned, who was upon the shoulders of the tall, strong man; and stretching out his arms, he cried—

"Come—come, let me hold you to my heart once more before death parts us, my poor Ned!"

"No!" shrieked the boy, "they shall not kill you, Morris! No—no! Oh, they shall not!"

"Keep back!" cried the mounted policeman who was by that side of the cart—"keep back!"

"What!" shrieked Roots—"would you place yourself in the way of the poor lad taking a last embrace of his dying brother? Why, I know you, John Appleby—you have children of your own!"

The constable hung down his head, and

rods on a pace or two, and in another moment the brothers were in each other's arms.

"Go home, Ned," said Morris—"go home. I don't ask you to forget me, my poor brother, for that would be impossible; but go home, my dear Ned, and grow to be a man, and comfort our poor mother: she will need all that you can do for her!"

"Morris—Morris—my brother, Morris!" shrieked the boy, as he clung to the neck of the condemned one.

"Roots, old friend, take him away!"

"Ay, ay, Mr. Courtley. God bless you!"

Courtley shook hands with the tall, stout man, and then the governor called out, in still louder tones—

"Forward—forward! Clear the way, officers! Forward!"

CHAPTER II.

THE SNOW FALLS UPON THE DEAD BODY.

THE shrieking boy was carried away from the side of the cart, and Morris Courtley, for a few moments, covered his face with his hands, and wept.

The clergyman was kneeling, and appeared to be completely absorbed in prayer, and insensible to all that was going on around him. It is possible that, in the abundance of his faith, he yet looked for some miracle by which the innocent should be saved from the death of the guilty.

The mounted policeman resumed his place by the side of the condemned cart, and said, in a voice which showed that he was much affected—

"I pity you, Morris Courtley, from my soul. I did not stand in the way of Roots and Ned. I am glad he saw you."

"Thank you, John Appleby. You have been a friend to me from the first to the last. I thank you."

Morris shook hands with John Appleby, and then the crowd raised another shout. What it was they shouted at, though, it is highly probable not one of them could have told satisfactorily.

Now, the sheriff, who had, at some risk to his neck, tottered along the unsteady platform to that end of the scaffold which was the nearest to the approaching cavalcade, stood with his huge watch in his hand, and shook his head at the governor of the prison, who, as he wiped the sleet and the snow from his face, just said—

"I could not help it, sir. There have been all sorts of delays."

"Well, well—be quick, now. We shall have a snow-storm, as sure as fate."

"Not a doubt about that, sir—with a little hail, too, to keep it company."

"Yes—yes—no doubt. Now, Mr. Crackles."

This was to the hangman, who jumped from the cart on to the scaffold.

A howl of execration burst from the mob at the sight of that unpopular functionary of the law, and several stones were cast upon the platform. The sheriff got alarmed, and turned round three or four times, as if he did not know what to do. The yeomanry looked fierce.

"Down with Jack Ketch!" roared a hundred voices.

"Oh, get along with you!" growled the hangman, as he sidled along towards the projecting gallows, and began to adjust the rope.

"Back—back!" said the governor, as the crowd now swayed to and fro, and pressed the yeomanry closer each moment to the scaffold. "Keep the mob off, Captain Singleton."

The captain of the yeomanry gave the necessary orders, and the heavy, lumbering horses began to tread upon the toes of the foremost of the people, and for some few minutes a scene of great confusion arose, all of which the hangman looked at with quite a grin of satisfaction, for several stones had struck him, and he was glad to see the people harassed by the burly yeomanry.

But, after all, the hearts of the bluff farmers who composed the troop of county cavalry were not with the business they had in hand, and the people knew it, so they did not much heed the demonstration of the horses after all.

"Hats off! Hats off!" suddenly was the cry that arose from many throats, and the multitude at once uncovered as Morris Courtley appeared upon the scaffold. Oh! what a strange unearthly flush was upon the face of the young man! How his eyes now sparkled, as if lit up with an intelligence that was not of this world.

"Now, sir," said the executioner.

He started at the touch which the minister of the law laid upon his arm.

"No—no!" he said. "No—oh, God—no!"

"My dear sir," said the sheriff, "really this is, permit me to say, a kind of a—a—you see."

"I am ready," said Courtley, and the flush was gone from his face, like mist before the blaze of a noon-day sun. He was now so white, oh, so white! The mob gave a great sobbing kind of groan, and then one voice cried—

"Did you do it?"

The doomed man started as though electrified, and throwing all his strength into his voice, he shouted—

"No, I did not do the deed for which I am condemned!"

It was frightful now to hear the shouts from the mob. The governor of the prison got alarmed, and caught hold of the captain of the yeomanry by the shoulder as he said—

"You will have to charge!"

"I'm d——d if I do," said the captain.

The sheriff, in dumb show, urged the hangman to more expedition; but Morris Courtley stepped forward to the front of the scaffold, and raised his hand.

"No—no," said the sheriff, "my dear sir, this is no time for a speech. Besides, after all, dear me, what is the good? I beg that you will consider, my good sir, the peace of the county. Now don't—don't, I beg of you."

"Now, sir," said the hangman.

"Hear him—hear him!" yelled the mob. "Hear him first, if you hang him afterwards! Hear him!"

The rage of the vast assemblage terrified the hangman, who crouched at the feet of Morris Courtley as he shook off the odious grasp that had been laid upon him by those dreadful hands.

The sheriff shook so that he actually stopped the watch that he held in his hands, and then, as Morris Courtley still held up his right hand for silence, a universal shudder came over the multitude, and all was in a few moments as still as that grave to which the doomed man seemed so fast to be hurrying.

"I have little to say," began Morris, "very little; but that little I feel that, for the sake of those whom I leave behind me, and who claim kindred with me, I ought not to leave unsaid."

"Hear him—hear him!"

"Oh, dear," said the sheriff, "be quiet!"

"I stand here to meet death," added Courtley, "a shameful death in the face of hundreds, perhaps thousands, who know me, for an alleged offence that I never even dreamt of. I am innocent. I leave the legacy, not of vengeance, but of justice, to all those who love me. The day will come when my innocence will be apparent; and that it may come the sooner, let all who know me, and who hold out the right hand of fellowship to me in this world, do their utmost——"

"Now—now," said the sheriff.

"I am ready," said Morris, and his hand dropped to his side.

"Don't hang the man if he didn't do it," cried a voice, and then, as with one will, the crowd cried out—

"Save him—save him!"

"There, you see," said the sheriff to the governor, "that comes of these sort of people making speeches."

"It could not be helped," said the governor. "God help us all, if he be innocent!"

"Innocent, my good sir? Why, you saw the judge's black cap as well as I, and if that will not convince you that it is all according to law, I don't know what will."

"I die for the alleged murder of Lord Francis Bloxdale," said Morris Courtley. "But I loved him; I never lifted my hand against him, so help me, Heaven!"

Now the sky got darker and darker still, and the wind was hushed, and the snow began to come down in large frothy flakes—

the people swayed to and fro, and the yeomanry looked grim and sulky; but they did their duty so far that they kept the people from actually pressing on to the scaffold, which otherwise they would have done.

Had there been anything like unity of design among the mob—had there been a leader, who, with a full knowledge of the populace, could have given expression to it by a judicious use of the immense force there collected, the execution of Morris Courtley might have been stayed in a moment; but a mob is but a mob, and whenever did on achieve any great or useful purpose?

The people yelled and shouted, and the snow now came down in a dense drift in their upturned faces; but the yeomanry and the constabulary kept their ground.

A couple of constables had come upon the platform, for the sheriff was quite unnerved, and the executioner was trembling perceptibly.

"Come," they said to Courtley, and one took his right arm and the other took his left, and they tied his wrists, and then they led him beneath the gallows. The hangman approached to perform his hideous office. The sheriff looked about him restlessly.

"The clergyman! Good gracious! where is he?"

"He has fainted away in the cart, if you please, sir," said one of the constables.

"Dear me, how very wrong. How could he think of such a thing just now? Oh, dear—oh, dear, what can be done?"

"I am here," said the clergyman; and he tottered up the steps to the platform.

"Well, my dear sir, now do say the prayers for the defunct, you know, and let us get this job over."

"Oh, Heaven! is there no hope?"

"No what? No rope?"

"Hope, sir, I said—hope!"

"I beg your pardon, there is such a noise. No. All we have to do, is our duty. Now, reverend sir, for goodness gracious sake let us get this job over."

The clergyman fell upon his knees on the scaffold, and beat his breast.

"Just Heaven!" he cried, "acquit me of any part or paticipation in this deep iniquity."

"Amen!" said the sheriff, who did not hear what he said.

"Oh, let not the innocent perish."

"Amen! Goodness gracious, Crackles, be quick."

The rope was adjusted around the neck of Morris Courtley; and then you might have heard his heart beat, so still did the mob become. One voice only had called out—"They will do it!" and that voice seemed to have fallen like a spell upon every heart. The horror, however, of the scene, appeared as though it had deprived all present of the power to interfere by word or action.

"Are you ready," said the sheriff.

"Yes, sir," said the hangman, as he dropped from the scaffold to go underneath it, and get hold of the shifting board.

"Innocent!—innocent" cried Courtley, as getting one hand free, he tore the night-cap from his face, and cast it at his feet. "I am innocent!"

"Now, Crackles, if you please. Amen! Yes, good-day—I mean, now for it."

"Yes, sir."

The clergyman made a dart forward to catch Morris Courtley, but he ran against the sheriff, and they both fell.

There was one shriek from the crowd, and the body of Courtley swung by the rope, as the board was dragged from beneath his feet.

The snow fell fast and thick, and the scaffold, the body, the multitude, the common, and all beneath the influence of the dense drift, were powdered with the white particles.

And so they hanged Morris Courtley, on a cold day in February, Anno Domino 1751, on Southampton Common, for a murder, kind reader, that he no more committed than you or I.

_____

CHAPTER III.

THEY HANG MORRIS COURTLEY'S BODY IN CHAINS.

NOBODY who thought at all about the matter considered that young, handsome, brave, and accomplished Morris Courtley would, after all, be hanged upon Southampton Common.

Those who came to see the sight, perhaps, were not of the most thinking class. And, indeed, some of them of the very lower order, indeed, felt a secret satisfaction at the idea that the civil law, as they called it, sacrificed the rich and the educated, as well as the poor and the ignorant.

This they thought, before they saw poor Morris Courtley upon that temporary scaffold. But when they looked in his noble, handsome countenance — when they heard his few candid and earnest words, they could not think him guilty; and so it was with anguish that all in that great swelling multitude saw him die.

Swinging to and fro in the keen wind, covering up fast with snow, till scarcely an outline of the human form was visible, the body hung.

Horrible!—oh, most horrible! What potent spell will restore motion and sensation to those limbs again?—what medicament —what skill of learned men?—what subtle secrets of science will open those eyes again upon the world? All, all is over! The pure spirit has gone surely, with all its wrongs, to its God, there to find no false accusers—no fallible judges, but that holy calm—that exquisite serenity which is not of this world, and which the turbulent spirit, vexed by the strifes and the collisions of life, may not comprehend.

The snow-drift and the north-west wind— it was only the merest trifle westerly—came on savagely now; and amid a whirl of snow,

sleet, and misty vapours, the dense multitude took its way from the Common.

To and fro gently swayed the body. The carts and the temporary platform had all disappeared. The hangman alone, with a strange, wild-looking lad, whom he called Jokes, no one knew why, for his appearance was anything but provocative of a joke, remained.

The lad was about sixteen years of age. He was preternaturally tall for his age, and his limbs, and body, and head appeared to be so much at variance with each other in his attitudes, that if the hangman had picked him up by fragments in some churchyard, and had the art to put them together, and then to imbue the hideous creation with a strange vitality, he could not have contrived a more odd-looking specimen of humanity than Jokes.

An immense shock of red hair covered the head and shoulders of this lad; and what with the snow and the cold, his eyes were bloodshot and watery; and he made the most hideous grimaces as he dodged round the gallows-tree to protect himself as much as it was possible to do from the cutting blast.

The hangman had a sack over his head and shoulders, and squatted upon the ground, smoking a short, black pipe, and looking tolerably composed, as his work was all but done for the day.

"Jokes," he said.

"Yah!" howled Jokes, "it's in my eye again."

"Hold your row. Look along the road, and see if you can see Tom Miller, with his donkey-cart."

"Shan't!"

"How dare you? Now, for half a pin I'd—But no matter. The time will come. We shall see, my boy—we shall see how much you will make by such behaviour to me—Ha! we shall see."

"I don't care whether we see or not," said Jokes.

The hangman now rose, and shading his eyes as well as he could with his hand, he said—

"Ah, he is coming. I can just see the glimmer of his pipe through the snow-drift. What would a man do without his pipe on such a day as this?"

"They will fit me, I know," said Jokes.

"What are you talking about?"

"His boots. The boots of the dead man. When you cut him down you must give me his boots."

"Idiot, don't you know as well as I do, that he is to be hung in chains?"

"Oh, is he? Ah!"

"Oh, is he, ah, indeed? I thought every fool knew that, but it appears that you didn't, so I tell you he is. That's the sentance. Do you think I would have stood here in all this rain, and snow, and hail, and sleet, and I don't know what beside, if it wasn't my duty to do so, eh, stupid?"

"Go along!"

"I tell you what it is, young fellow, I am bringing you up to a profession that will make a man of you, and if you don't behave yourself a little more genteeler, I'll let you go, and you will be a vagabond. Do you hear that?—a vagabond!"

"Oh, don't bother."

"Ah! that's all very well, when you have —Oh, here is Tom Miller at last—I can't take up my time with you; but I tell you what you will have to do, Jokes."

Jokes shook himself like an angry bear, and growled out something quite unintelligibly.

"You will have," continued the hangman, "to climb up to the top of that tree."

"What, up there?"

"Just so, and then you will have to put the mask on him."

"What mask?"

"Why the iron—But I forgot, poor infant—he don't know nothing, yet. He never saw a man hung in chains—poor infant.—Ah, he don't know."

"Oh, go along!" cried Jokes, shaking himself, and blowing upon his blue fingers, for blue they were, with the nipping cold. "Go along, do!"

By this time, a man in a fustian coat, and a moleskin cap on his head, leading a donkey, to which was harnessed a cart of the roughest and rudest construction, reached the foot of the gallows-tree.

"Woa! Woa, will you!"

The donkey paused, and flapped the snow out of his ears as well as he could.

"Well, here I am," said Tom Miller, "and the sooner this job is over the better. Here's the irons—Woa, will you!"

The man let down the tilt-board of the cart, and there rolled out of it on to the snow-covered ground a quantity of black iron bars, with chains and loose pieces hanging to oddly-shaped long ribs of metal, an huge rings of the same, for the purpose of encircling the body of the dead man.

"They ought to be welded," said the hangman, rubbing his chin in a thoughtful manner.

"So they ought," said Tom Miller, "but the smith wouldn't come, and so, what was to be done? He says they can all be hooked on easy enough, and he said that if he did come there would have been no such a thing as bringing a pot of fire with him thus far, in such a snow as this; and I don't suppose as there would."

"It's awkward."

"Rather; but the sooner it's done the sooner we shall get back to the Black Lion."

"Ha! ha!" laughed Jokes, "they won't let me and master into the Black Lion. Ha! ha! they——"

"Hold your tongue, will you!" shouted the hangman. "I have a house of my own to go to, and I don't want to cross the threshold of ever a house in all Southampton, not I. Come, if we are to do this piece of work,

let us set about it now at once, and get it over, as you say. Jokes?"

"What now?"

"Get up. You can climb like a squirrel, when you like."

"Shan't!"

"What's that you say?"

"That I shan't; so don't bother. Go along with you, do.'

The hangman caught up a piece of iron, and advanced on the boy.

"Say that again, will you?"

"Give me the boots, then. Don't hit a fellow. Give me the boots, and then I'll do it."

"You wretch! You have no more feeling than a pig. So you want the dead man's boots, do you? You unfeeling reprobate! You hard-hearted wretch!"

"Get along, do."

"Well, well, if you have the heart to take his boots, take them; and, Jokes, as you are taking his boots, which is one of the coolest and unfeelings things as I know of, why—I—I—think I'll have his stockings, and——"

"Hold hard!" said Tom Miller. "I have a eye to his coat."

"His waistcoat!" screamed Jokes. "I'll have his waistcoat. Mind, master, I said his waistcoat first."

"Confound your impudence, what do you mean by that?"

"Hold hard! Woa!" cried Mr. Miller. 'Somebody is a coming."

Scarcely making any sound upon the snow, although the horse was at a gallop, a mounted man made his way to the spot upon which this horrible wrangle for the habiliments of the dead was going on. They all knew him. It was the chief constable of the district, and as he reined in his horse, he cried out in a sharp voice—

"What, ain't this job done yet? Come, my men, look alive about it. It's a matter of form, but the law says do it, and it must be done."

Upon this the three set to work without making any further remark. Jokes sulkily clambered up to the cross-tree of the gallows, and, with some assistance from the hangman and Miller, placed the rough irons upon the figure, connecting them by chains and hooks, which the smith had made for the purpose.

The body now presented a strange appearance in the irons, but it hung much more steadily, as the additional weight resisted the keen air that before had driven it from side to side. It was only occasionally now that it swayed a little, and then the irons would jingle together with a terrible significance.

The snow-drift which seemed for awhile to have paused, came on afresh now with such a fierce and mad vehemence that the officer's horse could hardly stand against it; and setting his teeth, he muttered a few hearty curses, and then calling out, "Is it done?" he turned his horse's head towards the town.

"Yes, sir. All's settled now," said the hangman.

Without another word the officer set off at a full gallop.

"The boots!" cried Jokes.

Even as he spoke the sky darkened.

Dense masses of clouds, fringed with an ominous yellow-looking edge, covered up the southern sky, and seemed to pause over the common. For a few moments the air was so still that the cutting wind which had made itself so very manifest only a little time before, seemed to be completely stopped in its progress.

Then there was a strange rushing sound, and down came the snow like a white mantle over all things.

The common was devoted to the dead.

The snow piled itself up a foot high at the foot of the gallows-tree. It piled itself up upon every ridge and inequality in the dress or the chains in which the mute figure was hung. Into a conical shape it heaped itself on the cross-tree of the gallows; and gradually then, as minute after minute passed, the strong upright piece of wood to which hung the body, appeared as though it were slowly sinking into the earth.

It was the snow which was piling itself up around it. A few frightened birds screeched past the dismal spectacle. The dense shower of white flakes hardly permitted the sound to vibrate through the air; and so for the space of four hours the snow came down upon the common, till the shrubs were all but concealed, and the trees looked short and stunted, as they rose black and wiry and dead looking from the pure white surface around them.

As for the swinging figure upon the gallows, it seemed as though there would have been no difficulty in standing below and touching it with your hand, so much lower had it seemed to drop to the earth.

And now the dim twilight of that winter's day had come. The brief sun had set, and although the snow-storm had abated, still great quantities were caught up by a fierce wind that had risen, and dashed hither and thither with mad vehemence.

A dull, heavy booming noise would occasionally, too, make itself heard in the air. It was the roar of the waters of the Solent, and of Southampton Water, as they were dashed about in wild frenzy by a north-west gale.

Oh, that was a fearful night!

The wind was now fearful enough to swing the body to and fro upon the gallows-tree; and the chains rattled and jammed against each other. A carrion bird hovered round the head of the hanging man. It was the eyes of the victim that it wanted, as a delicious morsel ere it tried to roost in the depth of the woods across the water. But as often as it flapped its wings almost to the touching

of the face of the hanging man, it flew off again with a scream of disappointment.

There was some strange instinct which prevented that bird of prey from touching Morris Courtley.

The twilight died away quickly, and a dark night shrouded the face of nature. There was quite, for a time, a strange reflected radiance from the snow, and then all was gone like a dream; and earth and sky appeared mingled together in one black confusion.

As the wind set with a sudden gust from the town, the old clock of St. Mary's Church struck the hour of seven.

A faint light showed itself some distance off in the intense darkness. It moved along some two feet from the snowy surface, casting a strange halo around it. After a time it stopped; but it was not far from the gallows when it did so.

There was a faint murmur of voices, and then the light came on again; and suddenly some one cried—

"It is here. God help us all, it is here!"

A loud shriek rang upon the night air, as the beams of the lantern, for that was what it was, was held up; and the furthest spreading of its beams fell upon the hanged man.

"There he is! Oh, there he is! My brother, Morris!" shrieked the voice again. "Oh, Morris—Morris!"

Those who had heard the voice of the boy who had hung for a brief space round the neck of the condemned man, as he went to death, would have known those shrieking, wailing tones to be the same.

"Don't, Master Ned—don't," said a rough voice; "you said you wouldn't, and here you are a-doing of it."

"Brother Morris!—brother Morris! Come down—oh, come down to me!"

"There you go, again, Ned; and you promised me as you wouldn't. Come—come, do you want to frighten my two pals here, who, all for the love of me, have come upon this errand?"

"No—no!" sobbed the boy, "but—I wish I were dead, like poor Morris. Is he dead, Roots?"

"Ay, dead enough, my poor boy."

"But—but he was so strong, and so handsome, and he loved us so."

"Like enough—like enough; but he's gone his way, for all that."

"And we, too, loved him. Oh, how we did love him! We used to look up to Morris always since father died; and what he said was always right; and now he—he will—never, never say a word more!"

"Never, my poor Ned—never! But come, now; you wait here, while me and my pals go and do the job."

"Yes, I will wait. Oh, God!—oh, God, kill me!"

"Now, there you go again."

"No—no! I won't—I won't, Roots! You

are very good to me—you are, Roots! Oh, so good!"

"That's worser," said Roots the poacher. "Don't you be a-going on in that way. What did I tell you you ought to swear to do, when you growed up in a year or two to be stout enough, and old enough to do it?"

"Ah, I know—I know!"

"To be sure you does; but if you goes a-bellowing, and a-crying in that ways, you will never be able at all for to do it."

"You told me that I ought never to forget, night or day, that I had to clear the fair fame of my poor brother, Morris, by ferreting out who really did the murder, for that he was innocent of it."

"That's about it. Now, you keep that in mind, Master Ned, and keep steady, and quiet, and don't make a noise, and you'll do it."

"And you will help me, dear, good Roots?"

"Hold again: don't speak that-a-ways."

"Have I offended you, Roots?"

"No, not that, neither; but don't say anything to me about what I does. I does it 'cos I likes, and there's an end on it. You stay, now, will you?"

"Yes. But, Roots, you are good. Didn't you, when it was all settled that they were going to kill poor Morris, take mother and me across the water to the New Forest, and didn't you give up your own little cottage to us, and didn't you bring us all we wanted? Oh! yes, Roots, you are good; and now—oh! yes, now you are going to bring home poor, dear, dead Morris!"

———

CHAPTER IV.

THE DEAD TAKEN TO THE REFUGE OF THE LIVING.

"THERE he goes agin," said Roots, as a fresh burst of grief which the boy could not control came from his heart. "There he goes agin. I say, mates, we must just get this job over as soon as we can, you see, or it will be the death of that lad to go on for long this-a-ways."

"So it will," said one of the two rough-looking men who were with Roots. "Poor fellow! Well, I means to say, if so be as Morris Courtley didn't do it, it's hard lines for him, poor fellow, to be hanging here—isn't it, Joe?"

"That's my opinion, exactly," said Joe. "But, come on. Here we are, half-way up to the waist in the snow, and the old hammock is friz as stiff as tin."

"Don't you stray, Ned," said Roots.

"Na—a!"

The boy flung himself down in the snow, while Roots and the two men went up to the gallows-tree.

Roots, from a broad belt which was round his waist, took a woodman's axe, and casting a glance up and down the upright beam of wood, he said—

"Let him come gently, Joe: lay hold of him when you see the consarn on the go."

"All's right."

"There you go, then," said Roots, as he swung the axe once round his head, and then sent its blade deep into the solid timber.

Another blow, and the gallows slowly bended over, crackling into splinters at the spot where the axe had made its deep indentation. Joe and the other man caught it, and in another moment Morris Courtley lay upon the ground, half hidden in the snow.

"Hold the light," said Roots, as he now knelt by the figure, and by the aid of a knife, cut away the rope. "A little closer with the light, Joe. They haven't rivetted these irons."

"Not a bit of it. The smith told me he couldn't do it this weather. There they come."

A very few minutes sufficed to free the body of all the insignia of the gallows, and then they opened a hammock which they had brought with them, and laid it in it, and lashed the sides together with cord, so that the body was completely hidden.

"Thank the fates for that!" said Roots. "It's done so far. Do you know, mates, I wonder Ned has been so quiet."

"So do I. Come on. You go on afore us with the light, Roots: we'll carry the burthen. You know the nighest way to the boat in the little creek, I take it?"

"I do. But if either of you get tired, I'll take a hand at it in a moment."

"Ay—ay: that's all right."

"Ned!" cried Roots—"Ned! Where are you?"

There was no answer.

"Why, what's become of him? Ned, I say! Hulloa! my boy—it's all done, now, and right as it can be."

By retracing his steps, which showed sufficiently distinctly upon the snow, Roots got back to where he had left the boy; and there he lay, in a state of the most perfect insensibility. Whether it was the intense cold, or the reaction of his highly-wrought sensibilities, it is hard to say; but certain it was, poor Ned was, for the time being, dead to all external sights and sounds—ay, dead as the poor insensate brother that the two rough seamen carried in the hammock!

"Why, the young 'un hasn't slipped his cable, too, has he?" said Joe.

"Oh, no," said Roots. "But he would come, and it's too much for him—that's all. I tried all I could to get him to stay away, but he wouldn't; and so here he is, done up, as I expected. Well, perhaps it's all for the best. Come on."

Roots lifted Ned from the snow; and holding him partially over his shoulder with his left arm, he strode on, carrying the lantern in his right hand, and followed by the others with the body of Morris Courtley.

It was a strange and sad-looking procession, that!

There was the tall, stout, stalwart poacher of the New Forest, striding along, at each step up to the knees in the snow, bearing what appeared to be the dead body of a boy in his arms, and now and then turning back a moment to hold up the lantern for the others to follow him without losing a step by any deviation.

Then, likewise, following him were the two men, in their rough pilot coats and oil-cloth hats, bearing between them the hammock with its terrible burthen; and the lantern shed a sickly halo upon them all; and as their footsteps in the snow made no noise, they looked like spectres moving slowly across the common!

Instead of going direct into the town, down the avenue, they turned off to the right, and by a slightly circuitous route reached, after half an hour's hard work—for the snow impeded their progress much—the edge of the water.

As they neared the point upon the beach where they knew their boat was waiting for them, all conversation became next thing to impossible, except they were very close to each other, indeed; for the sea kept up such a roaring and breaking of huge waves upon the shingle at that spot, that the noise was deafening.

Those who have not had an opportunity of seeing as much can hardly believe what a commotion a gale in the Channel can produce, even upon such a land-locked piece of water as that which runs up to Southampton; but there are times and seasons when the pent-up water seems absolutely furious.

This was one of those occasions. A high tide was rolling in from the Solent, often vexing itself against the iron-bound southern coast of the Isle of Wight; and such a gale was blowing as the inhabitants of inland cities and towns can have no real conception of from mere description.

It was with difficulty that Roots, powerful and heavy as he was, could keep his feet upon the margin of the water. The two sailors were more habituated to the violent gusts of wind, and did not feel the like inconvenience. One of them placed his hands to his mouth, and shouted with that prolonged tone which goes so much further than a sudden and sharper note—

"Cricket, a-hoi!"

In the pause that followed, a faint "Hilloa!" came upon their ears.

"All's right," said Joe. "Come on. The Cricket is in the creek, up this way. I thought Bobbins would have to work her in there out of the gale."

"It is a gale, indeed," said Roots. "I suppose we shall get across the water?"

"No fear of that, Roots, though it may be a little longer and a little rougher job than we looked for."

"Well, old friends, it's kind of you to take all this trouble on my account, and I am not the sort of fellow to forget it."

"Don't say a word about that," said Joe. "Haven't you hid more than one of our sort in the forest, when the Philistines had hard pressed 'em, just for landing a keg or two of cognac on the coast? We will be glad any day or night, too, Roots, to lend you a hand."

"Thank you—thank you. Hilloa!—there's the wind again!"

The wind, which had lulled for a few moments, seemed only to have done so to collect fresh power; and it now roared and battled over the water and along the shore most terrifically.

The men staggered on; but one of the seamen now held the lantern till it was fairly dashed out of his grasp by a sudden gust of wind; and then they went on in the dark, as well as they could, stumbling through the deep snow.

It was well they were all so well acquainted with the route they took, as a false step or two would have precipitated them into the water, and upon such a night as that, so benumbed by cold as they were already, if such an accident as that had happened to them it must have been fatal.

After thus struggling on in this way for a quarter of a mile, they descended a rather steep declivity, and arrived at a little creek, that was, in a great measure, protected from the gale. There rode freely by a kedge anchor a little skiff. A light was at its prow, which, as the little vessel tossed in the agitated water, bobbed up and down dazzlingly.

"Cricket, a-hoi!" said Joe.

"Cricket, it is," said a voice from some one on board of the skiff.

"All's right," said Joe. "Now, Roots, you take the body, and we will haul in the skiff as close as we can, here."

This was done, and with some difficulty the party embarked, the body of Morris Courtley being laid in the stern, upon the under planking. Roots laid Ned by the side of his dead brother.

"Poor boy, he hasn't recovered, and it's perhaps as well,' he said.

The seamen consulted with each other for a few moments, and then they determined upon trying to cross the water by the aid of a small jib sail, which Joe took charge of, keeping it loose and ready to slip in a moment if he should find too great a strain upon the little craft from the gale.

The other seaman took the tiller and flung himself at full length to stern, keeping his head just above the gunwale.

"Let go," said Joe.

The man who had had charge of the boat drew up the kedge anchor, and away they went out of the creek, dipping rather ominously, and shipping a sea or two.

Roots looked ahead, and strove to pierce the darkness by half closing his eyes, and se concentrating his vision; but all was foam and cloud.

Suddenly the skiff rounded a promontory, and shot into the open water. For a moment the little vessel shivered from stem to stern, and then almost careening over from the violence of the gale, it began to dash through the water amid a cloud of foam and spray, which in a few moments drenched every one on board to the skin.

"Keep her head a little more to windward," said Joe.

"Ay! ay!"

Even as the steersman spoke, a tremendous sea rose like a wall, and would have swamped the boat at once, but that it was cleverly steered; but as it was, it shipped a great deal too much water to be at all safe.

"Bobbins!" cried Joe, "bail away, old fellow!"

"I am at it; but you won't be able to carry the sail."

"I'm afraid not."

"Hold on, it's coming now!"

A gust of wind seemed to lift up the water as if by an invisible hand. The boat dipped its starboard bulwarks right under water, and the little sail, with a sharp crack, flew to ribbons and disappeared in the darkness.

There was one wild cry, and Joe then shouted—

"He's over! he's over! Hilloa! God, he is gone!"

The man who had had charge of the boat had been swept over to starboard, and amid the seething roar of waters had disappeared. Any attempt to look for him would have been as futile as to hunt for a particular grain of sand upon the sea-shore.

"Lost!" said Joe. "One gone. Roots, where are you?"

"Here, in the water."

"In the water?"

"Yes, at the bottom of the boat. What has happened?"

"Never mind, old feller, it can't be helped. We are going across, I think, somehow, with wind and current; but I can't take upon myself to say where we shall land, or when."

The skiff did better now without her sail than she had done with it, for the current took her across as she was steered a point or two against it, and a wave dashed the little vessel high and dry upon the snow on the shores of the New Forest.

Another wave might have dragged the skiff back again, but the two sailors secured it quickly, and then they lifted the dead body from the boat, and Roots took Ned in his arms.

"Now," he said, "I am on my own ground, in a way of speaking. Follow me, and we shan't be very long before we meet the cart; and then, away for the present."

They all struck off at a right angle from the bank of the water, and were soon amid the trees, that modified the progress of the wind, and whose brave branches dashed wildly together in the storm.

CHAPTER V.

SHE LOVES THE SECRETARY.

THREE months before the events recorded in our last chapters, a rather brilliant assemblage of the rank and fashion of the county of Hampshire had gathered together at Bloxdale Park, one of the most considerable estates in the immediate vicinity of Southampton, and nearly adjoining the old ruins of Netley Abbey.

The residence, familiarly known all over the county as Bloxdale, was one of those old palatial buildings which the nobility have either not the money now to build, or the taste and spirit of magnificence to inhabit. Its turrets, towers, wings, and extensive outbuildings, made it, from any elevation from which it could be well viewed, one of the most imposing features in the surrounding landscape.

A dense wood protected the whole domain from the keen influences of the east winds; and sloping towards the Southampton Water, were meadows, and woods, and gardens of surpassing richness and beauty.

The stern winter, however, o our churlish climate had made in-doors at Bloxdale much more desirable than out; and so in the magnificent grand saloon of the mansion, we find some twenty or thirty guests assembled, who were on a visit to the lordly owner of the domains.

That visit had a special object, too.

Lord Francis Bloxdale, the only son and heir to the estate and title of the earl, his father, was about to return from abroad, to take up his permanent residence at the park.

This young scion of nobility had, in consequence of great weakness of constitution, been compelled to pass a year or two in a more southern latitude than England. But now he was returning, strong and well, and as he himself said in his letters, entirely free from the constitutional delicacy that had beset him.

The inhabitants of the Park were: The Earl of Bloxdale, verging upon his sixtieth year.

The Countess of Bloxdale, aged forty, and a woman of what is generally, in the world, considered to be of strong understanding.

Lady Fanny Bloxdale, aged seventeen, of whom we shall soon hear more, and Morris Courtley, the secretary librarian and cherished friend and companion of the old earl.

These persons, with Mr. Oxley, the steward and general manager of the estate—a man much respected for his unostentatious mode of life and his seeming integrity, so everybody said—made up the most important of the inhabitants of Bloxdale Park.

A host of servants, who had a very easy and idle time of it, indeed, and an army of game-keepers and grooms, made up the state and dignity of the household.

We prefer to let our puppets speak for

themselves, and so show the reader what they are, to any laboured description of them and their peculiarities.

The hour is six, and the dinnner at Bloxdale Park is to be on table (by order of the countess) at seven precisely. Some time during the day Lord Francis had been expected. Every invited guest had arrived; and it would have been very difficult, indeed, to find an apartment in which so much of the gorgeousness of still life, united to so much of the beauty and fashion of animated existence, made up such a spectacle as that grand saloon at Bloxdale Park presented at a little past the hour of six.

Of course, at that time of the year, darkness had crept over the face of the country long before that hour; and the grand saloon was brilliantly illuminated by three immense chandeliers, which sent down a glorious flood of soft mellow light upon the assemblage below, almost obliterating all shadow, and making the rich carpets and the profuse gilding and silken hangings glitter again with the refulgence of that artificial illumination.

A heap of piled-up logs of beech wood, in the ample grate, diffused an agreeable warmth throughout the apartment; and there was that gentle murmur of conversation, which, in spacious rooms, where there are many, but not too many people, comes with such a subdued cadence upon the ear.

Truly the scene, take it for all in all in that room, was such as shrinking poverty, at such a cold and sterile season, might have dreamt of, but never fancied could be realised, except in fairyland. It looked too rich, and warm, and soft, and dazzling, to be real.

An elderly gentleman, in a plain evening dress, with a star upon his breast, stepped across the soft-yielding carpet to the back of Lord Bloxdale, who sat near the fire in a low chair with an immense high back, apparently looking at the embers, and smiling.

"Bloxdale," said the distinguished-looking person with the star upon his breast. "You quite expect your son, I suppose?"

"I do, your grace—I do—that is, I think I do."

"My love," said the Countess of Bloxdale, who was close at hand, "you mean, you don't think at all, but that I have informed you Lord Francis will be home to-day."

"Oh—ha!—ha! Yes," said the earl. "I only said——"

"Silence!" whispered the countess in his ear, as she swept past him, and she said it in such a tone that the old earl jumped again. "Silence! You are more than usually silly to-night."

"Ah! ah!—I—am!—I—my dear, I—am!"

"Your grace," continued the countess, treading at the same time violently on the toe of the earl to induce him to be quiet. "Your grace asks if my son will return to day?"

"I did, madam."

"Then I beg to state that I expect him, and so there can be no doubt."

"Oh, none in the least," said the duke, for a duke it was, as he bowed himself out of the conversation.

"Mr. Courtley," said the earl. "Ah! ah!—where are you? I should like—ah! ah!—to know why——"

"Silence!" said the countess.

"Oh—ah—I only—said—y-e-s—I only wanted——"

"Silence! You only expose the fact that you are silly."

"Ah—I do—I do—but I only wanted to know how it was that——"

"Dear father," said Lady Fanny Bloxdale, advancing and leaning upon one arm of the tall-backed Elizabethan chair upon which the earl sat, while her long wavy ringlets fell in a shower of beauty on the old man's neck and shoulders, and strayed across his breast. "Dear, dear father, can I get you any book you want to refer to from the library?"

The old, imbecile earl turned his eyes to the fair young cherub-looking face by his side, and a gleam of joy lit up his eyes. With a trembling hand he smoothed the long silken ringlets, as he said—

"My darling—my little darling fairy child—my Fanny—my own pretty—pretty child!"

"My lord!" whispered the countess. "Do you know where you are?"

"Ah—ah—yes—I—am——"

"Hush!"

"Oh, dear! I—only—ah—I—yes, my dear. I want a book, and I thought that Morris Courtley——"

"You are always thinking what you ought not," said the countess.

"I—know it—I—yes—but you were so good as to—ah—ah—think for me! Ain't it kind of your mother, my pretty little Fan? He! he! and so you love the old man yet, my own diamond?"

"Oh, father, do not speak so; our guests will remark that—that—you—perhaps rather spoil your little Fan! Ah, you do—no—no—you shall not say you don't—you do, dear pa."

With one little child-like hand she stopped him from speaking, by placing it over his mouth, and with the other she held him round the neck, and added—

"Don't answer ma when she says unkind things."

Tears gushed from the eyes of the old earl, and the countess, with one jerk at the chair, wheeled it right round, so that the back of it was towards the guests.

A slight scream from Lady Fanny testified to the fact that the countess, in the exercise of her imperious will, had done that without caring or looking to see if Fanny were in the way or not. The chair had struck her severely on the arm.

The guests all rose.

"What is it? Lady Fanny!"

The earl sprang to his feet, and stepped

from the side of the chair, and confronted his wife for a moment with such a look as his face had not worn for many a long day.

"Madam!" he said, "how dare you!"

The guests looked at each other, and shrunk back from what they thought was about to be the scene of a domestic *fracas*, but it was but a momentary glimmer of lost faculties that animated the old earl. His tall and once commanding-looking figure, which for a moment had assumed its former height, seemed to shrink up again, and his head drooped.

"Pray heed him not," said the countess, turning with a smile to her guests. "You are well aware that the earl has not, for some time, been just what all his friends would wish him."

The guests bowed, and muttered some civil nothings.

"Be seated," said the countess, "I pray you."

They resumed their seats again; and then she stepped up to the earl, and laying her hand upon his arm, she whispered—

"Sit down, idiot!"

"Ah! I am—I am. My dear! I——"

"Sit down."

"Yes—yes, anything you like. I was only going to say——"

"Nothing!"

"Ah—ah! yes, my dear, nothing, I—I—nothing. Where is Morris Courtley, my secretary? A good youth. I told him to come and sit by me."

"And I, sir," said the countess, "told Morris Courtley that his place was not in this apartment on such an occasion as the present."

"Eh? His place not—eh?—here! I thought——"

"How dare you think when I have spoken?"

"No I—only—well, I won't."

Resting his head upon his hands, the old earl lapsed into silence; but Fanny whispered in his ear—

"Dear father, I will go and get you anything you want from the library. Shall I not go for you? Ah, yes; your own Fan, you know."

"My pearl—my pretty Fan, yes. He! he! She don't hear me now—she is a wonderful woman, your mother is, Fan; such a—he! he!—such a mind, such a spirit—a fine woman—a wonderful woman. But she has gone away now, and so my pretty pearl of a Fan, you will go and get mo—he! he! that book about the butterflies, do!"

"I know it; you were showing it to me, father, to-day."

"Eh? I was. Go. It's a great pursuit to inquire—he! he!—into the family history and the habits of a butterfly. From them I shall make a transition to—he! he!—earwigs!"

Struggling against the tears that were trembling in her eyes, Lady Fanny Bloxdale, the fine and beautiful being—that innocent and lovely girl, with a heart as ingenuous and open as the day—glided from the grand saloon, and made her way along a corridor hung with portraits of the illustrious dead of the Bloxdale family, towards the library.

But wherefore is the colour heightened upon the cheek of the lovely girl?—and wherefore does she pause at the door of the old gothic room, upon the shelves of which lie enshrined the wit and the learning of past ages? Why does the little hand shake and slide over the handle of the door for some moments ere it can take a firm enough hold to open it? Why does she catch her breath, and then turn from red to white, as she, at length, does open the oor, d and glides gently into the room?

We shall see.

In old, very old times, the library of Bloxdale had been a chapel appended to the mansion. But since the Reformation, the family had given up private worship, and the chapel had been converted into a library, for which purpose it answered magnificently.

The gorgeous carved roof, the richly grained walls, and the deep old stained-glass windows, all adapted it beautifully and peculiarly for its present purpose. There was an air of sanctified repose about the place, that of itself was favourable in the highest degree to calm study, and deep and earnest reflection.

The library was lit by a huge bronze lamp, hanging from the ceiling, the shaded glasses of which shed a soft and chastened radiance upon every nook and cranny where a book could be placed.

In the very centre of this splendid depository of literature, past and present, was a huge circular oaken table, covered with writing materials, and reading stands, and all the litter of a library. The huge fire-grate, with its seats on each side of carved oak, sent forth a ruddy glow from the piles of burning wood.

Sitting listlessly by the fire, with a book carelessly in his grasp, was a young and noble-looking man. A half-smile was upon the lips of this young man, as if some pleasant and happy thought had just crossed his mind; and his eyes were bent on the fire, although one glance at him would have been sufficient to convince any one that his thoughts were far from that room, or anything that it contained.

That young man was Morris Courtley, secretary to the Earl of Bloxdale. So slight had been the noise made by the Lady Fanny in opening the door of the library, that he had heard it not; and still he sat, as like some fair vision sent on an errand of goodness direct from Heaven, the young girl stole gently forward.

Suddenly, then, the secretary clasped his hands over his face, as he exclaimed—

"Oh, if I only had the power to tell her how much I love her!—if I could only find language in which to depict the real and true affection that I have for her, I should be more content. I know I am not worthy of her. Who can be? for she is all beauty—all goodness—all gentleness. She is such as we picture to ourselves the angels to be, without one thought that is not good, and sweet, and gentle, and dignified, and all that Heaven can make it. I shall never be able to let her know how much I love her. God bless her!—bless her! Bless her sweet smile, and her sparkling eyes, and her little fairy hand, and the soft dimpled mouth, and the happy laugh. and the tones that thrill through me as I listen to them!"

"Morris!" said Lady Fanny, in a low, soft whisper. "Morris!"

He sprang to his feet.

"Oh, God!" he said. "In the height of my fond ecstasy I have conjured up a vision!"

"No, Morris. I—your own Fanny. And so, my poor Morris, you do, indeed, love me so well?"

With a gushing cry of joy he sprang towards her, and clasped the little hands in both his own. He drew her gently to the old fire-side; and how he trembled as he placed her in the ancient gothic chair! And then he knelt at her feet, and still holding her hands in both of his, he looked up into her face; but he could not speak.

"Oh, my poor Morris. And do you, indeed, love your little Fan so well?"

"My darling, you are so good, so kind—so all that is beautiful and true. Oh, this is joy, indeed!"

"I tremble, Morris.—It is now only one month since you told me that you loved me, and—and——"

"A month of such joy!—Are you not happy?"

She smiled, and placed one of her hands that she had disengaged upon his cheek, as she said—

"I won't tell."

"Ah, yes, your eyes tell."

"Wicked eyes!"

"No, no—not wicked, but full of heavenly light and love. I was thinking of you, my darling."

"And—and—I—was thinking of—butterflies. No—no—you mustn't! No—no!"

Fanny said "No, no!" but, somehow, Morris hastily kissed both the pretty eyes and the cheeks; and, trembling with joy, and exultant in the purity of his love—for it was as pure and sinless and holy a feeling as could be dreamt of—he folded his arms around her, and the fair girl let her head repose upon his breast, and peeped up in his face and smiled; and then Morris kept lifting the long masses of the silken hair, and pressing them to his lips, and he could not speak for the joy that sat smiling at his heart.

"Naughty Morris," said Fanny; "so, he makes love to earls' daughters, does he? Is he not afraid?"

"No, no. I have but one fear in all the world, and that is that such pure joy as I have known for this past month cannot last."

"Then you think you won't go on loving me long?"

"Oh, Fanny, my darling! it is because I do love you so well, and know, and feel that I shall ever love you so well, that I turn sick at the idea that we may be separated."

"Oh, that would be sad."

"I should then fret like the poor summer butterfly, who——"

"I came for a book about butterflies for pa—the book he had this morning.—Give it to me, you bad Morris, and let me go.—Indeed you must, and—and, dear Morris, I do believe that you love your little Fan; and, so she will try to come to you again if she can; so give me the book about the butterflies, do, there's a good Morris, at once."

CHAPTER VI.

LORD FRANCIS BLOXDALE ARRIVES AT THE PARK.

A TRAVELLING carriage dashed up to the main entrance to the mansion just as seven o'clock was pealed forth from the clock tower.

The domestics of the house were all on the alert in a moment. The arrival of Lord Francis, whom they had none of them seen for the space of three years, now, was to them a most important event, for the health of the earl seemed to point to the fact as not now very far distant that Lord Francis would be master of the earldom and estates.

To be sure, the imperious character of his mother sufficiently convinced them, that as long as he permitted her to do so, she would rule with the most despotic sway at Bloxdale; but they had yet to discover what sort of disposition the young lord came home in.

When Lord Francis had gone abroad, it had been as an invalid, and he was so young then, being but eighteen, that he had hardly acquired the right to have a will of his own in the house, or exhibited sufficiently marked traits of character to enable the domestics to discover whether or not he was likely to assert one.

Hence it was rather an interesting inquiry with everybody connected with the family, to know how the young lord and his imperious mother would get on together.

The hall was a complete blaze of light, and the servants, in their state liveries, lined it, as a tall, thin, rather pale young man alighted from the travelling carriage, and crossed its threshold.

"Welcome, my lord! Welcome, Lord Francis! We are all glad to see you, my lord! God bless you, Lord Francis!"

Such were the salutations which the young heir to the princely estates of Bloxdale was salute with by the servants, who had grown gray in the service of the family; and who considered that its dignity wa o the full as great as that of any royal line.

"I thank you, my friends!" said Lord Francis, in a clear, firm, decided voice; and the ease with which he slightly bowed and removed the travelling-cap he wore, showed at once that the boy of eighteen had been a very different personage to the young man of twenty-one.

"My son!" cried the countess, as she made a rush forward, and folded Lord Francis in a voluminous embrace that went very near to smothering.

"Dear mother!" he replied. "How are you? Why, you are looking exceedingly well."

The fact was, that the countess had increased to about double the width she had been during the absence of Lord Francis.

"Yes, my love, I am pretty well, though weak.'

"Weak, mother, did you say?"

"Yes, my child. But come in. We will excuse your travelling costume. Come in, my dear. All your friends are here."

"But, my father and dear little Fan. Where are they? Ah! I did think that they would have welcomed me."

"Your father is an idiot, Francis."

"Madam!"

"Well, well! I don't mean to say that; but you know the earl was never very bright, and he has not improved."

"But here is the little Fan, if you please, my lord," said a soft voice, and in a moment Fanny was in the arms of her brother.

"Ah, Francis, still the old smile; you still love me?"

"Love you, Fan? Indeed, and in truth I do. But—but you have grown from a child to a what shall I say? A real pretty—presentable—nay more than pretty——"

"I don't wish to hear any more of that," said Fan. "You are a man, I declare; and you don't look like my brother Francis a bit."

"Don't I, indeed?"

"Ah, yes, you do. When you smile I know you again. Come, I can't let go your arm now. Come with me, and we will both go into the grand saloon together, dear Francis. Oh, what lots of things you will have to tell me, of all you have seen and heard while you were away."

The countess stalked on majestically before the brother and sister, and the servants shrunk from her path; and Francis whispered to his sister—

"Our dear mother seems to have taken a new lesson of pride and harshness; she spoke of my poor dear father in a way that made my blood boil. How is he, Fan?"

"But poorly. He loves me, though, as ever, and he will love you."

"Then he is no worse. While the affections last, the mind cannot be wholly gone; but for our mother to call him what she did—it is too bad it is unwomanly—unfeeling!"

"What was it, Francis?"

"It will shock you."

"Oh, dear, no, it won't, Perhaps I have heard it before."

"I hope not. The term was idiot."

"Oh, was that all?"

"All? Do you mean to say that she is in the habit of using such expressions towards him? Is it possible that she can so far have lost all affection—all respect for him as to speak so of him or to him? Oh, no, no, you must be mistaken, Fan."

"I wish I was."

"Then, Fan, it must not be. Oh, Mr. Oxley, is this you?"

The old steward—he was not so very old either—pressed forward, and a gush of tears relieved the heart of the faithful servant, as he was styled, as he strove in vain to say something to welcome the young lord.

"Come—come, my old friend, Mr. Oxley," said Lord Francis, "you must not be so affected at my return. I hope you are quite well?"

"Oh, my lord, I am; but never better than now that I have the joy of seeing you recovered as you are."

"Thank you—thank you."

In another moment the grand saloon was thrown open by a footman out of livery, who called himself a groom of the chambers, and the countess preceded her son and daughter into the gorgeous apartment.

In a few moments Lord Francis had shaken hands with some dozen or two people, and then making his way through the throng, he fell into the arms of his father, who cried and laughed by turns, as he patted him on the back and kissed him.

"My little boy Francis," said the old earl. I—ba!—dear me, he is not so little. How you have grown! The family grow. You get tall, and so does my pretty Fan, and your mother gets wide——"

"My dear!" said the countess.

"I—ah—I only—did I say wide? I meant—fa—Ha! ha!—I was saying something wrong again."

"Silence!" whispered the countess in one of her energetic asides.

"Y—e—s—I—will—I am."

"And you too, dear father," said Francis, "you look pretty well. You have a colour, I declare."

"The fire has caught my nose a little, my boy, that's all. But when I look at you, I feel so well, I could dance—dance? Ha! ha! I could——"

"Hush!" said the countess.

"Ye—s, I will. I—only forget at the moment, my love."

"As you always do."

"I know it—I—know it."

A deep-toned bell at that moment announced that the dinner was upon the table in the huge dining-room, which was only separated from the grand saloon by a couple of doors and a short corridor; and then there commenced all that soft subdued bustle, and that rustle of silks and satins, and those silvery speeches, and those little gentle laughs, incidental to the movement of some well-dressed and courtly-mannered people from one apartment to another.

The dinner at Bloxdale Park, upon that occasion, was a splendid banquet. The board was loaded with costly gold plate, and the beaufets blazed with a countless show of tankards, vases, cups, and candelabra of the same metal. Everything in the room, and connected with the banquet, was upon a style of princely splendour; and even, at times, the poor Earl of Bloxdale managed to look something like the master of the house, as he faced his imperious lady at the table, and found himself surrounded by such a goodly company.

The arrival of his dearly beloved son, too, had given a spur to the flagging faculties of the old man; and he was several times as nearly rational as he could ever hope again to be.

Heaven only knows what species of mental blight has come over the mind of that man. He had never been a brilliant individual; but he had only lately sunk into that species of fatuity, which we have been at the pains to depict to the reader. It is possible that the constant alarm the imperious conduct of his wife had kept him in for so many years, had had the effect of overturning his faculties. But certain it is, that but little of the intellect of the earl survived but what was contained in his affections. His head had gone woefully astray, but his old original kind heart was yet in the right place.

It was his love for his two children that saved him from utter fatuity.

The dinner passed off as such dinners usually do, in a murmur of small talk, a faint clatter of silver plate, a few courtly challenges to wine, and then a general move of the ladies to the drawing-room, and the introduction of unlimited claret for the gentlemen.

Lord Francis watched, with terrible anxiety, every movement of the earl, his father. He dreaded to own to himself that the look of health and content which the countenance of the old nobleman had arose from the mind having ceased to exercise any wearing influence upon the body; and every time he opened his lips, Lord Francis dreaded that he was about to give utterance to some strange comment, that would open the eyes of the company to the fatuity of its utterer.

Poor Francis! The company was as fully aware, and, perhaps, more so, of the state of the earl than he was. That news, which affection and delicacy had kept from him for the past years, had become well known to them.

The melancholy fact was, that as the countess had grown in arrogance, and violence, and domineering propensities over her husband, he had lapsed into that state which we found him in, when he shook at her bursts of rage, and was ready to drop when she cast upon him one of her withering glances.

In fact, the poor earl, to use a popular expression among his servants, " dared not call his soul his own."

We may imagine the painful situation into which the gradual discovery of these facts plunged Lord Francis. He well knew, from the experience of his earlier years, that his mother had always been an imperious, domineering woman; but he had not observed, or there had not been exhibited, such open and avowed power over the wreck of his father's mind as he now saw exercised with such utter want of even common delicacy or tact by his mother, the countess.

Such a course as she was pursuing, Francis was old enough to feel, could only bring disgrace and ridicule upon the whole family; but yet how difficult his task would be to alter such a state of affairs! How sad the task of stepping between his father and his mother!

We shall see how Lord Francis, with the assistance of his sister, did make an appeal in the right direction.

"Now, gentlemen," said the earl, "pass the wine, if you please. Ha! ha! I feel quite happy now, with my little boy at home again."

" Do you go to Oxford?" drawled a dandified personage to Lord Francis.

"I think not; but I don't know, my lord," said Francis.

" It's uncommon slow.'

" So I have heard."

" Are you much troubled by poachers, my lord?" said a ruddy-faced gentleman, addressing the earl.

" Poachers? Let me see. Yes, they disturb the game, poor souls."

" Poor souls, my lord! You don't pity poachers? You have one of the finest sporting estates in the country."

"I don't sport," said the earl. " I let all upon my grounds live free. I don't think— Ha, ha!—there has been a shot fired at bird or beast here for a long time."

" And, besides, father," said Lord Francis, " I think if Roots is still with you at the head of your foresters, you need not be afraid of poachers."

" Roots! Roots!" said the earl, touching his forehead. " What did Roots do? What did he do?"

" Saved my life, father," said Lord Francis, " when my favourite pony ran away with me, and threw me into the lake, when I was only five years old. Don't you recollect, father?"

" Ah! And they sent that man out to starve, branded with the name of thief. I will not have it. I say, Mr. Oxley, it shall not be done!"

The earl had risen to his feet, as he uttered

these words, and the guests all rose in confusion.

"Father, father," said Lord Francis, "what is all this? To what do you allude, father?"

"Ha! ha! I—only—nothing.—Yes, my ove, I am a—goose!"

The guests shook their heads.

"Can any one explain the meaning of this to me?" said Lord Francis. "If any one here can, I beg of you, gentlemen, as we are all friends, and at a social board, that you will do so. There is some painful remembrance upon my father's mind regarding this man Roots.—Who knows of it?—Ho! Mr. Smithers!" addressing the butler, "do you know what has become of Roots, the gamekeeper?"

"Yes, my lord. I—that is, my lord, Mr. Oxley, my lord, found out that Roots used to take the pheasants and—and—a—the—the other game my lord; so he was turned away about eight months ago, my lord—turned adrift, my lord, by Mr. Oxley, my lord."

The eyes of Lord Francis flashed again, as he cried—

"What! the man who saved my life at the risk of his own, turned adrift for taking a few head of wild birds.—Impossible!—impossible!"

"It shall not be!" cried the earl, rising again. "Am I the Earl of Bloxdale or am I not. I tell you, woman, it shall not be! You may foam, and rage, and think, but it shall not be—ha! ha!—only—it is nothing—Yes, my love—yes—I——"

The earl fell back in his seat, fainting, and at the same moment one piercing scream rang through the mansion, which was echoed by a cry from the earl, who fell to the ground in a swoon.

That scream came from the lips of Lady Fanny Bloxdale.

CHAPTER VII.

LADY FANNY FINDS AN UNEXPECTED VISITOR IN THE LIBRARY.

THAT artful, scheming, little Fan!

When the ladies, along with the pompous, and we fear, not very amiable Countess of Bloxdale retired from the dining-room, Lady Fanny Bloxdale managed to give them the slip, and to dart across the corridor in the dark, and make her way, breathless and flushed, to the door of the old library.

She had promised to see Morris Courtley again, if by any means she possibly could, upon that evening, and she had come to redeem that promise.

Yet the fair and gentle girl felt rather agitated, and she stood at the door, and, for a moment or two she was half inclined to follow her mother and the ladies to the drawing-room, instead of venturing upon compromising both herself and Courtley, the young secretary, by seeking another meeting; but she loved him, and when did prudence, in all

its cold, chilling solemnity of form, ever wage a successful war with love? Lady Fanny opened the door.

The library was very dark now—the wood fire, which alone lent a flickering, uncertain radiance to it, was very near expiring, so that it was only now and then that it sent out a little bright flickering flame to play upon the ancient carved walls of the old stately abode of learning.

But in the arm-chair, by the fire-side, there was the same seeming figure that she, Lady Fanny, had seen when there upon her former visit. There was her lover.

With a few bounding steps she came across the floor of the library, and in childish glee, she dropped upon her knees before the chair, and holding out her hands, she whispered—

"Dear Morris?"

In an instant the person who was seated on the chair clasped her round the neck, and roughly tried to kiss her, while a voice which she knew not said—

"By Jove!"

Lady Fanny, with a cry, sprang to her feet in time to save her lips from the desecration of that kiss, and turning swiftly, she darted towards the library door, and rushed against Mr. Oxley, the steward, who was just at the moment entering that apartment.

"Oh, gracious!" cried Oxley.

"Do not stop me, sir!"

"Lady Fanny?"

Poor Fan burst into tears, and darting past the bewildered Mr. Oxley, she ascended the grand staircase, and springing like a hunted fawn along the gallery that was on that floor, which she now reached, she soon gained her own room, and hastily entering it and bolting the door, she fell to the floor in a paroxysm of tears.

Poor Lady Fanny!

The room was quite dark, and it was quite a quarter of an hour, at the very least, before she could sufficiently recover herself to think with anything like precision upon what had taken place in the library. When she did try to think, however, she only felt how hopeless it was to attempt an explanation of the circumstance.

Who could it be that occupied Morris Courtley's chair? Who could it be that so audaciously tried to take advantage of the mistake she had made?

These were perplexing questions; but there was another which poor Fanny put to herself, of what she had said while still under the mistake that it was Courtley she addressed.

"Did I name him?" she asked herself. "Did I place, by one fatal mistake the secret of our love in the keeping of one of whom I know nothing, but that he was ungenerous enough to take a dastardly advantage of a mistake?"

This was a question which, in her agitation, Fanny found it quite impossible to answer. At times she thought that she had uttered the name of Morris, and she trembled to think of what might be the result; and then again she tried to calm herself with the idea that she had only thought the words that she had a reminiscence of having uttered.

The state of perplexity that she was in, was most fearful, but her ruminations were suddenly interrupted by some one trying to open the door of her room.

Fanny listened to the sound with breathless attention, and she heard the voice of her own maid, Ann, say—

"Bless me, the door won't open."

Fanny fancied that Ann might give an alarm in the hall, so she quietly went to the door, and unbolted and opened it, saying, as it swung upon its hinges—

"I am here, Ann."

"Oh, dear—oh!"

"What is the matter?"

"Oh, my lady, you gave me a turn, that was all."

"Come in, Ann."

"Yes, Lady Fanny; but, bless me, here you are in the dark. Why, how very odd, to be sure. Shall I get a light? Well, I really did think you were in the drawing-room along with the countess, and the lady visitors. Oh, what a fine, good-looking man the duke is, now, is he not, Lady Fanny?"

"I am not well."

"Not well? Oh, my dear mistress! why did you not tell me that at once. Oh, why did you not ring for me? How cruel of you! You know that, though I am only a—a very poor girl, I love you very—very truly, and it was that odious Mrs. Wicks, as she calls herself, your mother's maid, who kept me talking, or else I should have been here before."

"I know you do love me, Ann."

"Indeed, and in truth I do."

"Get a light. I am not well, but I am not very ill."

Poor Ann, quite in a fright at the news of her young mistress's illness, lit a couple of wax candles that were upon the toilette-table, and as they burnt up, she looked in the now very pale face of her young mistress with startling eagerness.

Ann idolized Lady Fanny. In fact, it was impossible for any pure and good spirit to come into contact with her without doing so. The poor girl's colour fled when she saw how pale her young mistress looked; but Fanny then smiled, and held out her hand to Ann, saying—

"My good girl, I don't think I am ill at all. It is only that I am a coward, that is all. I have been alarmed."

"Alarmed? Oh, who has alarmed you, Lady Fanny?"

"I don't know."

"Some wretch?"

"Well, I'm afraid I cannot say he was a gentleman. But have you seen any stranger about the house, Ann? I don't mean any one who could be a visitor of my father's, but any one who could be—in the library, for example, and—and sit down

there, and then act and speak as no gentleman could possibly do?"

"Oh dear, no."

"It is very strange."

"But won't you tell me how it was, Lady Fanny? Won't you, indeed? Not your own Ann? Ah, you do not think that I am faithful enough to you—or if you do, you think that I am too foolish to be trusted; and so you keep such a silence and such a reserve to me that you almost break my heart. You forget that my poor dear mother nursed you when you were such a weak little thing that they all said you could not live, and when the countess would go to London because it was the season."

"I have heard that," said Lady Fanny, with a sigh.

"Yes, dear lady—it was so, as I have heard my mother say a hundred times. The countess left you to die, but my mother saved you; and when she came back from London, you were placed in her arms, and my mother said to her, ' Madam, this child is yours, for God gave her to you: but I am its mother, so far as affection and attention to it goes.'"

"Yes—yes: it is all true, Ann."

"And then you know that the countess pretended to faint."

"She did faint, surely, Ann?"

"Oh, no—no."

Lady Fanny commenced sobbing bitterly, as she faintly articulated—

"It is all—all true! I never knew the real love of a mother. Oh, Ann, I ought to be dead!"

"Dead?"

"Yes. I am afraid that—that I have done very wrong, indeed, and this circumstance that I have told you of has opened my eyes to that truth."

"Oh dear! But you have not told me, dear Lady Fanny."

"Have I not?"

"Not a word. You asked me only if there was any one in the library who was not a gentleman—that was all."

"My poor brain is so confused, Ann, that I hardly know what I say; but I have now made a sudden determination, and I will take you, my dear foster-sister, into my entire confidence. But you must not call me Lady Fanny any more."

"Good gracious!—why?"

"Because you know me now well enough just to call me plain Fanny, and so I beg that you will do so. You used to call me Fanny years ago, you know."

"Yes, but your lady mother gave me such boxes on the ears for it, that she soon frightened me out of it; and she used to make my headache for a whole day sometimes."

"Then you shall call me Lady Fanny to others and when others are by, and Fanny when we are alone."

"Ah, yes, that will do well. But—but—you said that you would trust me."

"I will. Ann, I—that is, Mr. Courtley, my father's secretary——"

"Yes, Lady—I mean, Fanny."

"He—he, I think, loves me!"

"Oh!"

"Yes, Ann. I think—that is, when I think, I am pretty sure that he loves me. Morris Courtley loves me!"

Lady Fanny evidently found a secret pleasure in having some one to utter those words to.

"Oh, miss, there is no doubt about it," id Ann.

"Oh, no! He does love me! Dear, noble, generous, gifted Morris!"

"He is a very nice young man. But is that all, Fanny?"

"All! Yes, to be sure it is."

"Oh, I thought—that is, I expected you would say whether or no you loved the secretary, that was all."

Fanny was silent.

"Ah, dear Lady Fanny—no, Fanny, I mean," cried Ann, as she knelt at the feet of her young mistress, and placed her arms round her waist, "you do love him, and he may well be loved; for he is handsome and brave, and young, and honest, too, and his voice is so soft and gentle, and he looks more like a real gentleman than any of the grand folks who come here, that he does."

"You think so, Ann?"

"Think so? Oh, I know it. Only look at him with his fine, open, manly face, and his gentle smile. But, it wasn't a secret!"

"Not a secret? What can you mean?"

"Oh, no!"

"Speak, Ann, you alarm me."

"I mean, that I knew all about it."

"Oh, impossible!"

"Yes, Fanny, it is impossible, very like but it is true for all that. Ah, do you think that you could keep such a secret from me? Didn't I see it in your eyes—didn't I see it when there came just a little more colour to your cheeks when you saw Mr. Courtley? Didn't I see it, too, in him, when he looked as if he were ready to die of joy when he saw you in the garden, or upon the grand staircase, or in the library, or the dining-hall, or anywhere? Oh, yes, I saw it."

"And others too?" gasped Lady Fanny, as she clasped her hands over her face. "And others too!"

"No, I don't think that," said Ann, "for who but Mr. Courtley himself ever looked at you, and watched you, because of loving you as well as I did?"

"My dear Ann!"

Tap! tap! came to the door of the room, and Fanny started to her feet.

"Who is that?"

"Hush," said Ann. "I will go and see."

She opened the door, and discovered Mrs. Wicks, the waiting-maid of the Countess of Bloxdale.

Now, Mrs. Wicks had gone considerably past the prime of life, if her life ever had a prime, and she had lapsed into not the *sere* and yellow leaf, but the *sour*; and besides, Mrs. Wicks was a little evangelical. She was quite the confidential woman of business of the countess, and as cordially detested Lady Fanny and her maid Ann as they detested her.

There was a whining, conventicle-like tuning about the voice of Mrs. Wicks, and a cringing affectation of Christian charity; and, like all affectations, it had not the smallest reality.

"It's Mrs. Wicks," said Ann.

"Yes, my dear Lady Fanny," said Mrs. Wicks. "Providence be praised always, I have found you."

"Do you want me, Mrs. Wicks?"

"Yes, dear lady, mother is very anxious to know where you are."

"You can go and tell her then, Wicks."

"Hem—yes. Thank you. Shall I say that you will soon be down stairs?"

"Yes, Wicks."

"God bless you, my dear, I will."

"Oh, the wretch!" said Ann, when the door was closed upon Wicks. "I hate her I do."

"Hush, Ann, hush! Hate no one. We certainly have found, upon several occasions, that Mrs. Wicks has no regard to truth, and that she is a hypocrite and a spy; but still, she may have some good qualities in her which we know not of."

"Oh, well, of course, Lady Fanny, I will say no more. You never will think half so bad of people as they deserve, that I am certain. But now, don't you go down to the drawing-room at all; but let me go and find Mr. Courtley, and tell him there was somebody in the library that you mistook for him."

"Yes, Ann, go. Yet, no—no—I think—I don't think. Oh, Ann, perhaps it will be better not, after all."

"Oh, yes—let me go. Who knows but he may be able to find out who it was?"

"Yes: it would be a great relief to know who it was. Go, Ann—go."

Ann left the room; but Mrs. Wicks, who had been indulging herself by listening at the keyhole, managed to get away in time to escape being observed by the young girl.

Ann thought it was now more than likely that she should find Morris Courtley in the library, and she accordingly made her way down one of the several staircases of the mansion in that direction.

She had hardly been gone a moment, though, when Fanny began to regret that she had let her go at all upon such an errand; and with that instinctive dread of appearing too forward in her love for the secretary—which was a feeling inherent in her nature—she would fain have called Ann again.

Hastily stepping out into the corridor, Fanny ran to the head of the stairs, and called, in a subdued tone—

"Ann—Ann!"

At the moment, some one passed an arm round her waist, and whispered to her—

"I know your secret. Whether I keep it or not depends upon yourself!"

It was then that Lady Fanny uttered the scream that had alarmed the guests.

CHAPTER VIII.

MR. OXLEY DISCOVERS WHO THE INTRUDER IN THE LIBRARY IS.

ACTING upon the impulse of the alarm that had been given by the sudden cry that Lady Fanny Bloxdale had uttered, the young Lord Francis was the first person who reached the foot of the grand staircase. He was quickly followed, though, by some half-dozen of the guests who were the most quick in their movements, and the least apprehensive of any personal consequences from anything that might be amiss.

Some bewildered-looking servants were in the hall.

"Where was that cry from?" cried Lord Francis.

"Up stairs, my lord. It was from some one in the picture-gallery, up stairs, my lord."

"And it was the voice of my sister?"

"It sounded like it, my lord."

Three steps at a time, Lord Francis bounded up the grand staircase of Bloxdale House, and the moment he reached the picture-gallery—which, in point of fact, was nothing more nor less than the long and wide corridor at the top of the staircase—he called out aloud—

"Fanny!—Fanny! Where are you? It is I, your brother! Speak to me, Fanny, if you can!"

"Here, brother—here!"

Fanny darted forward, and clung to her brother's arm, trembling with alarm; and then she burst into tears.

Those of his father's guests who had hastily followed the young nobleman, now, too, reached the gallery, and several of the servants followed them, so that Lady Fanny was soon surrounded by a sufficient number of defenders.

"Tell me, Fanny," said her brother, earnestly. "What was it that so much alarmed you?"

"I hardly know."

"Well—well, cheer up. Come, now, you are quite safe. Will you not confide in me, Fanny? Gentlemen, I am much obliged. I suppose this is some false alarm."

The guests made some civil speeches, and then left the brother and sister together, on their being requested by Lord Francis to state to the earl that all was well.

"And now, Fanny, that we are alone, what was it that made you scream so, if it was really you?"

"Oh, yes, Francis—it was poor, silly I."

"Then what alarmed you?"

"You see, Francis, that there is a very dim light here, indeed; and what with the portraits and the old armour on the walls, and the odd shadows, you see, Francis——"

"Yes, dear?"

"Well, I thought I saw somebody."

"Was that all?"

"Oh, but I am sure I saw somebody."

"Well, dear Fan, might it not be one of the servants."

"Oh, no—no."

"Come—come, we will think no more of this. It was these old portraits, and the armour, and the shadows, and the dim light that, combined, made up to your imagination a something terrible. But you ought to be used to the old house by this time, Fan."

"Yes, I am; but——"

"But yet you tremble. Why, I love the old place so, that at any hour, by night or by day, it would not really matter which to me, I would traverse its most silent and gloomy chambers, and feel as if every one were an old friend."

"Yes, brother; but you are brave and a man, while I——"

"Ah, Fan, but you used to be brave."

"Indeed, used I, brother?"

"That you used; but come, now, I will escort you to the drawing-room, and we will say no more of this alarm."

"No, Francis. I am, to tell the truth, not over well, and I will go to my own room. Oh, here is Ann. You recollect Ann?"

"To be sure I do. Your pretty foster-sister. Well, Ann, do I hold no place in your remembrance?"

"Oh, dear, yes, Mr. Francis—Lord Francis"—dropping a low curtsey—"I ought to say."

"Well, Ann, you used to give me a kiss in old times, and you shall not refuse me one now?"

"Oh, my lord—oh! Well I never."

Lady Fanny laughed, and ran off to her own room, followed by Ann, while Lord Francis, with a smile upon his handsome features, made his way back to the drawing-room.

"You have seen *him*?" said Fanny.

"Yes, dear Fanny, I have, and he says he was only away from the library about ten minutes to the conservatory, and he can't think who could have been there."

"It is very strange indeed. But I have had another alarm. Did you not hear me scream?"

"Oh, no."

"I did, then, for some one on the landing, just at the top of the grand staircase, placed an arm round my waist, and whispered in my ears,—'Your secret is known. It depends upon yourself whether I keep it or not,'—or some words to that effect."

"You terrify me, Fanny. Some one who ought not to be, is in the house, that is quite clear. Oh, Fanny, what shall we do?"

"What can we do?"

"I will run back to Mr. Courtley."

"No—no. It was in trying to prevent you from going to him that I went into the gallery, and for the second time to-night encountered the man, for it was the same person who was in the library."

"No doubt. But how did you know that?"

"There was a particularity about the voice that can never be mistaken if it be once heard."

"Good gracious We may be all murdered in our beds this very night!"

"Oh, no, no! Not quite so bad as that; but I will yet take an opportunity of speaking to my brother about the circumstances before the guests retire for the night. I am too agitated to do so now. And so you saw Morris—I mean, Courtley?"

"Oh, yes; and at the mere mention of your name, his colour brightened, and he looked so happy."

"Poor, poor, Morris!" sighed Lady Fanny, as she clasped her hands over her eyes. "My poor Morris!"

*   *   *   *   *

We must now leave Lady Fanny Bloxdale in her mingled dream of joy and apprehension, while we take a glance at some of the darker spirited persons of our story.

It will be remembered that when Fanny was hastily leaving the library, after making the sad mistake that she had done in addressing a stranger for Morris Courtley, she encountered Mr. Oxley, the steward, on the threshold of the door.

The sedate and precise Mr. Oxley was stepping out with much greater expedition than was at all usual with him; but Lady Fanny was by far too terrified and occupied by what had befallen her to pay any attention to him.

She was gone almost before he could look at her.

For a moment or two, Mr. Oxley, that gracious and well-to-do exemplary steward, stood rubbing his fat white hands together, and performing several half bows, in mute wonder, at the state of apparent excitement in which Fanny had passed him.

Then with a lip that quivered with emotion and anger, Mr. Oxley at once strode into the library.

"No, no!" he said, as he advanced. "He never could be so imprudent—so mad! It is not to be thought of."

"Hilloa!" said a voice.

It was the voice of the individual who had taken possession of the chair by the fireside.

"Peter!" gasped the steward.

"To be sure," said the person addressed as Peter. "To be sure, and why not?"

"Good Heavens! Did I not tell you not to come down from the gallery?"

"Yes, but the fire looked so provokingly nice, and I should suppose that nothing could be more unlikely than that any one would come into this place, seeing that they are all in the drawing-room drinking their claret, where I should like to be. Ah! and such I will be—eh, father Oxley? Eh, old boy? And you, too, if you behave yourself—eh?"

"Curse you!"

"Ha! that's good. There's a pretty father-in-law."

"I tell you, you will spoil all."

"As how? I am no fool, as you well know. Tell me that I make one false step, and I soon step back again. What's amiss now? Why, your teeth chatter as if you had the ague."

"You will be the ruin of me and yourself, too. Come this way. For God's sake come this way."

"Well, well! I am coming. What's the row, that's all I ask?"

"Come, come, I say; a moment may be fraught with danger."

Mr. Oxley grasped the individual whom he had named Peter by the arm, and led him up a cylindrical flight of iron steps to the gallery that ran round the library, and then he drew a long breath, as he said—

"What, in the name of all that's vicious, tempted you down there?"

"Down the steps?"

"Yes, idiot."

"Come, I say, be civil, father-in-law. It was the fire, if you must know, and then there came a devilish pretty girl."

"Do you know, wretch, who she was?"

"How should I?"

"Lady Fanny!"

"The devil! Why, she all but put her arms round me in the dark, and called me her dear Morris!"

"Dear who?"

"Morris!"

"Morris? Morris? Say that again."

"Dear Morris, that was what she said."

Mr. Oxley laid hold of his step-son by the collar, and in a hissing whisper said—

"Will you on your soul swear it?"

"To be sure I will."

"Then we have her with us—we have her in our power, and we have the secretary in our power. Morris Courtley is my lord's secretary; and now by this happy accident it is past all doubt that she loves him. Why, why, it is an intrigue."

"Looks like it."

"It is. Oh, glorious!"

"Then it wasn't quite so bad a thing for me to go down stairs yonder, after all, Oxley, was it now?"

"Not as it turned out, but you might have encountered Courtley himself, for he sits there for hours together, and, no doubt, Lady Fanny knew it. Oh, this is glorious. You and I are now in possession of a secret that may work wonders for us."

"Well, I ain't sorry to hear that, I can tell you; but I didn't know her, and all I can say is, that she seemed a devilish pretty girl."

"She is beautiful as an angel."

"Ha! I don't suppose, Father Oxley, that you or I will have much opportunity of verifying that fact by comparison; but where's the odds? If I can be made master here, as I hope, then I care for nothing, for I will have plenty of flesh and blood, rosy-cheeked, bright-eyed angels about me, I can tell you. Ha ha!"

"Silence, Peter, silence!"

"Don't call me Peter: I am the Earl of Bloxdale."

"Not yet, Peter, not yet."

"But I shall be. You know that, you old sinner."

"Oh, yes, you shall be; then I shall be the first to congratulate your lordship on your title: the very first, of course."

"You c——"

"Hush—hiss! Ah—come away—come away."

The door of the library had opened, and Morris Courtley walked in very slowly and thoughtfully.

Mr. Oxley touched a spring in the wall, and a tall narrow door that was artfully concealed in the wainscoting opened, and he dragged Peter through it.

The door shut with a slight noise, that made Morris look up.

CHAPTER IX.

LORD FRANCIS HAS A PAINFUL INTERVIEW WITH HIS FATHER AND MOTHER.

THE guests at Bloxdale sat late, and Fanny was quite unable to achieve the interview with her brother that she wanted.

As for Lord Francis himself, he ascribed her fright merely to an imaginative fear, and his whole attention was absorbed in a determination that he had made since he had come home.

That determination was, that before he slept he would have a communication with his father, and thoroughly satisfy himself of the state of his mind, discovering how much of his seeming fatuity was owing to a real failure of his intellectual powers, and how much to the state of nervous dread and excitement he was kept in by the countess.

What a sad task for a son!

This intention on the part of Lord Francis gave him an air of abstraction in his intercourse with his father's guests, that aroused some remark; and those of them who were the least charitably disposed towards the family, did not fail to hint that they thought the intellect of the son partook somewhat of the imbecility of the father.

Of course such remarks were all masked by the courteous civility of the address of such persons, who, in the guise of that politeness, which is thought such an essential of high breeding, took good care entirely to conceal their real sentiments upon any and every subject.

At length, though, the most prolix story-teller and the latest sitter had retired, and Lord Francis found an opportunity of whispering to his father—

"Father I have something to say to you.'

"To me? Oh, dear!"

"Yes; but not here. Can you go to the library and wait for me there?"

"Oh, yes; that is—I——Where is your mother?"

"Not here, father. What I wish to say to you, though, is for your private ear alone, and, therefore, we will not inquire for her."

"No; that is, I—yes. But—but——"

"But what, father?"

"Would it not be better, for the sake of peace and quiet, you know, just to—to——'

"To what?"

"To ask her if we may have a little talk in the library together, you know. Perhaps, she might not approve of it, my dear, and we should not be hasty, you know."

Poor Lord Francis was still more shocked to find what an abject state of subjection his father's intellect was in. He thought rightly that such a condition of things was a far greater disgrace to the countess, his mother, than to the earl, his father. The latter might be pitied for weakness; but she must, by all thinking people, be condemned for arrogance and pride.

"Father," he said, "I shall not ask the leave of my mother to speak to you. If you will come to the library as soon as convenient, you will find me there."

"Yes, I—that is, I will. She is not here!"

Lord Francis could not bear to see the looks of terror that his father cast around him—looks that evidently dreaded to meet the stern glance of his wife; and the young nobleman retired, with a heavy heart, to await the possible—but, he feared, the not very probable—arrival of his father in the library.

The great clock that was in the hall struck the hour of one as Lord Francis reached the library door; and he paused for a moment to listen to the sound.

"I was wrong," he said, "to ask my father, at his age, and in his state of health, to visit me here to-night. To-morrow ought to have sufficed, and so I will tell him, if he should come to me."

With these words on his lips, Lord Francis entered the library, and walked towards the fireplace. He was startled to see some one there, apparently reading, by the light of a small hand-lamp, for the large chandelier had been extinguished.

"Mr. Courtley!" said Lord Francis.

"Yes, my lord," said Morris Courtley, rising. "I am late up, I daresay; but permit an old playmate to welcome you back to Bloxdale."

"I am very glad to see you, Morris Courtley," said Lord Francis, as he shook hands with him. "I recollect what great friends we were when mere boys."

"Yes, my lord; but now——"

"Nay, Morris, you must call me Francis, as you used to do; for we were familiar enough years ago, when we both went to the same school. I, to be sure, was the patrician; but what of that? You always beat me in learning, as you did in athletic exercises. Believe me, it gave me great pleasure to hear that my father had made you his secretary."

"I am indebted, I think," said Morris, "to the generous letter you sent in my behalf from Genoa for my office."

"I spoke but the truth of you, Morris, believe me. To-morrow I should much like to have some conversation with you."

"I am at your service at any hour."

"Let us meet, then, at twelve, in the old copse, where you used to help me out with my Latin exercises so often, Morris. Can you be there?"

"I can, Francis—I can, and will. And now I will wish you good-night, unless you came here for anything that I can get you."

"No—no, Morris. I came here, at this hour, with the hope of having a little private conversation with my father, whom I expect."

Morris Courtley bowed, and went to the door at once. Just upon the threshold of it he encountered the trembling, aged-looking figure of the earl; and he stepped aside to let him pass.

"Good-night, my lord."

"Good-night, Mr. Courtley. I—I missed you at dinner—I—that is, my lady—Oh, yes—Dear me!"

Morris Courtley knew well the good feelings of the old earl towards him, and he was as much distressed to hear him stammering out apologies to him for what, considering the subjection he was under to the countess, he could not help, as the old man himself was in making the attempt to gloss over such obvious facts. It was a great relief to both parties for Morris to hastily retire.

"Come, father," said Lord Francis, as he advanced, and placed his arm within that of the earl. "Come, now, I do hope and think that we are alone, and I have much to say to you."

"Ye-e-s, my dear. I—that is, you have grown quite a fine boy, you have. But where is your mother?"

"Forget her for a little time."

"Forget her? Forget—Oh dear, no! I wish—that is—no, I do not wish anything of the sort. She is a commanding woman, Francis."

"Very."

"And—and a female of rare endowments—a masculine intellect, Francis."

"It seems so, father."

"Ah—yes! I—he! he!—but she is not here, now. Well, my boy, you had something to say to me. Go on, my boy—go on."

Lord Francis led his father to the chair by the fireside, and placed him in it; and then, in a voice at once respectful and firm, he said to him—

"Dear father, who is master of Bloxdale?"

"Master of Bloxdale, my boy, did you say?"

"Yes, father, I want you to tell me honestly and fairly, who rules here in this house with despotic sway?"

"I—that is—Where is your mother?"

"I know not but I beg of you, father to answer me."

The old man trembled.

"Father, I can read the answer in your agitation. You are the ninth Earl of Bloxdale—you have immense properties, large resources—you hold a distinguished position, if you like to hold it—the honour of our ancient family is without a stain, and what are you?"

"What am I?"

"Yes, father. What position do you, the ninth Earl of Bloxdale, one of the oldest nobles in England, hold in your own house?"

"Oh, hush—hush! If she were to hear you! She—she says I am an idiot!"

"I heard her."

"And—and—she says she will put me in a madhouse if I resist her commands. Oh, pity me, pity me, my son!"

"I do, father, from my soul. My mother was, I believe, the daughter of a poor Scotch baronet, and now she is Countess of Bloxdale, and Earl of Bloxdale, likewise, for you have resigned your title to her, and your very intellect, likewise. Oh, father, you are not, you cannot be in the state that she says you are, or you would not feel as you do now."

"Spare me."

"No; it is time that the truth should be told to you. I, as your son—the heir to your estates, and to your title—I am tender of the honour of that name which I bear, and which has ever been associated with honour."

"What—what can I do?"

"Be a man!"

"Yes; but she is so—so—violent. She terrifies me. Besides, my dear boy, she is your mother, you know, your own mother!"

"Father, I am not unmindful of that fact. It is because she is my mother that I would see her act in such a manner as should command my most respectful admiration, and not in a fashion that tends to get up in my heart a war between natural affection and reason. I would have her learn the first duty of a wife—obedience to the judgment of the man with whom she has linked her fortunes. I would have her present the most lovely phase in woman's character—gentleness."

"Oh, dear, yes. I—so would I."

"Well, father, surely it is possible enough for you to resume the reins of power that you have let slip through your fingers. But tell me: do you go through the accounts of the estates now?"

"No—I—that is, your mother and Mr. Oxley manage all that.

"Do you not, then, deal with your property in any way? Do you not know what is done as regards your old and attached dependants? Are you so completely in leading-strings?"

"I—I am! Oh, dear, I am!"

"Who is here at this hour of the night?" said a sharp stern voice suddenly, and the countess entered the library.

"The earl, madam," said Lord Francis, "is here."

"Indeed, and my son, too, I presume?"

"As you say, mother."

Lady Bloxdale walked up to the earl, and in a sharp tone that made him jump again, she cried—

"Sir!"

"Ye—e—s, my love."

"Retire!"

"Yes—I—only—I—yes——"

"To your chamber, sir!"

"I'm going. I—I—only——"

"And you, Francis, go at once to rest. I will have no conferences at such an hour as this at Bloxdale."

"Hold, father!" cried Lord Francis, as the old earl was sidling towards the door of the library. "Hold! Pray be seated again."

"How, Francis?" cried the countess. "Dare you dispute my orders?"

"Oh, yes, mother, I dare do much when I see that you are mad!"

"Mad! Me mad?"

"Quite mad, madam. If madness be to be the thing one ought not, you are quite mad, madam, I say; for in place of being a loving and gentle wife, you are a virago without sense or reason. In place of being a tender and affectionate mother, you would be the domestic tyrant, ruling by force, not love. But I resist you, mother—for your own good I resist. I hope to see you what you ought to be once again."

"Wretch!" cried the countess.

"Mother!" said Francis.

"I—oh, dear!" said the earl. "Don't! I—that is, my dear—let her have her own way. Oh, dear, do! She is rather a violent woman."

"Father, it is your duty to exert your authority. You ought to order the countess to retire to her chamber."

"He order me?" screamed the countess. "He order? Things have come to a pretty pass, indeed. My lord, you will go at once to your own apartment. As for you, Francis, you will set out again for the continent as early to-morrow as possible. I will not have you at Bloxdale twenty-four hours longer, and your return will depend upon the tone of your letters."

"Father, remain where you are," said Lord Francis. "As for me, mother, I have come to stay at Bloxdale, and I do not intend to leave it."

"You do not intend?"

"Certainly not—such is my determination.

To-morrow morning I will send for my uncle, the Duke of Acreston, and my father's cousin, the Bishop of Glouston, and such other friends of the family as I can think of, and we will ascertain who is most mad in this family—the man who has permitted his very judgment to be wrested from him by his wife, or the wife who plays such a part as surely never human being with a woman's heart in her bosom ever played."

The countess staggered back till she reached the table, against which she leant, and looking at Lord Francis in silence, her very lips quivered with agitation and rage.

"On your knees, sir," she shouted, "on your knees, and beg my pardon for this outrage!"

"No, madam!"

"You shall, I say—you shall, if you do not want my curse!"

"Hold, madam!" cried the earl, rising in one of those bursts of sensitiveness and reason that at times relumined the night of his faculties, and made him all that he once had been. "Hold, madam! How dare you, in my presence, speak thus? Would you curse your own child? To your chamber. I command you to retire!"

"You hear, mother," said Lord Francis. "You hear your husband's orders.—It will be graceful to obey them quickly."

"Orders! Graceful!"

"Yes, madam," said the earl. "Begone. I have something to say to my son—to my —my boy—I—He!—that is—Oh, dear!"

He sank back again into the old chair. A slight smile crossed the face of the countess as she said—

"So that is past, and now we will see who has the greater control over this wreck of an intellect."

"Stop, mother," said Lord Francis. "If this is to be a trial of strength between you and I concerning the decaying mind of my poor father, we will have witnesses."

"Witnesses?"

"Oh, yes, madam. You seek to plunge the Earl of Bloxdale still deeper into the degraded mental condition in which it should be your deepest horror to behold him. I wish to raise him up as much as possible to his former state; and as this is a fierce contest between mother and son, in which a father and a husband is the stake played for, we will see what the world around us says of it, madam."

"What would you do?"

"Summon all the servants, and as many of our guests as have not retired for the night, to this spot, to witness this most seemly exhibition. If it is good to do, it is good to witness. Let those who dread the publicity of their actions tremble: I do not. Of course, what you do and wish to do, cannot have had reprehensible motives, for you are a wife and a mother, and it is your husband and your son with whom you are dealing; so, madam, you shall have the full benefit of your reputation."

"Francis, you no more dare carry out your threats than you dare attempt to leap from the topmost pinnacle of this mansion!"

"We shall see, madam. Oh, we shall see."

Lord Francis immediately laid his hand upon a bell-pull, the massive bullion tassel of which was close to the earl's chair, and pulled it violently; nor did he cease until he heard the sound of footsteps rapidly approaching the library.

The countess turned as pale as death.

"Listen to me," she said. "Francis, you have proclaimed open war against me."

"I have, mother."

"Then be it so. I have ruled here long enough to know the secrets of power. I will not resign my sway while I can hold it."

There was a rush of some half-a-dozen servants into the library, and Morris Courtley brought up the rear.

"Oh, Morris," cried Lord Francis, "the countess will have it that my noble father is mad and an idiot, and that he is unfit to move, or speak, or think, without her leave. I differ from the countess. What is your opinion, my old friend Morris?"

Courtley looked amazed.

"And yours, Mr. Oxley?" added Lord Francis, "and yours, John and Thomas? and yours, Phillip—and all your opinions? Come, mother, we will have this affair fairly settled, and there shall be no concealments. There is so much scandal spoken about noble families that for once it is a good thing to give a true domestic story to the world to prate about. Oh, sister, are you here?"

"Francis! Francis! What is all this?"

"Hush! There is no mischief done. There may be some good."

"Oh, dear! oh, dear!" said the earl.

"Mother," added Lord Francis, "my father has ordered you to leave the library and to repair to your chamber."

"Allow me," said Morris Courtley, "to open the door for your ladyship."

"Here's your night-lamp, mamma," said Lady Fanny.

"Way for the countess!" cried the old earl, again rising from his seat, and speaking with energy. "Way for the countess! Why do you block up the door so for?"

The countess looked from one to the other of them for a few moments in silence, and then making a very low curtsey, she said in a mild, soft voice—

"Thank you. Good-night."

In another moment she had left the room.

"You may go," said Lord Francis to the servants; and then, observing that Courtley was likewise retiring, he added—"Morris, I want you."

Courtley paused, and his eyes met those of Fanny, over whose sweet face passed a radient flush of colour. Lord Francis then stepped up to his father, and touched him on the arm.

"Father, the fight is begun. One victory is yours. You have but to continue to do battle for your right, and it will be restored to you. It is not in the nature of things that any woman should ultimately triumph in such an unholy war as this my mother wages against all that is just and proper; and it will be for her peace and happiness that she should not. Always recollect, father, that it is as much for her as for yourself that I struggle."

"Yes, I—that is—oh, dear!"

"He relapses again."

"But, brother," said Fanny, "what does it all mean? What has happened? Oh, tell me!"

"I will tell both you and Morris, if you will listen to me."

CHAPTER X.

MR. OXLEY PAYS RATHER A LATE VISIT.

LEAVING Lord Francis to explain to his sister and Morris Courtley the precise character of the recent *fracas* between himself and his imperous mother, we now place the reader in the society of Mr. Oxley, the steward of the Bloxdale property, who had an expedition in view that night which he dared not miss carrying out, let the hour be what it might.

Nobody in the world, to look at Mr. Oxley, with his smooth, sleek-looking face, and his bald head and respectable-looking rather rotund figure, would believe that he was other than the very beau ideal of a good steward. He looked like a man who had grown respectable and portly in the service of those whom he esteemed and loved.

Mr. Oxley, too, was rather famed for his religious feeling, which the clergyman of the parish said was of the most profound and exemplary character; so that he had reached that height which is believed to be a little above morality and righteous living, and which brought him almost to a level with the saints—namely, piety.

Then when he spoke, it was always gently, and deprecatively, as if he knew how many wild, ungovernable human passions there were always tugging at human hearts, and what a good thing it was by fair words and much gentleness to turn them aside. Oh, yes, Mr. Oxley, the steward of the Bloxdale estates, was a very exemplary man, indeed—very.

But for all that, it so happened, that instead of retiring, and saying his prayers, and blessing everybody, as it would be rather dreadful to doubt, and going to sleep with the smile of an easy conscience on his placid face, he had an appointment for any time between twelve and four at night.

At about a quarter past two, the pious and respectable Mr. Oxley prepared to keep his word. And we will accompany him.

"Lord Francis," said Mr. Oxley, as he coiled a thick travelling shawl round his neck, for he had a great idea of taking care of himself, had this steward—"Lord Francis is no more like the same person he was when he left England than I"—Mr. Oxley paused for a comparison—"than I am like Harlequin."

He had caught a sight of his comfitable-looking figure in a dressing-glass, and it had suggested the comparison.

"We shall have some trouble with him," he added; "but we shall see—we shall see. Ah! we shall see."

The shawl was, by this time, adjusted to the satisfaction of Mr. Oxley; and then he sallied forth from Bloxdale by a small door that led to the flower-garden. Crossing that, he made his way to a little gate, of which he had the key. He passed it, taking good care to lock it after him, and then skirting a meadow by a path that was well kept along its margin, he reached an oaken paling, at which he paused, and listened.

"Nobody stirring in the garden," he said, "and I don't wonder at it, for the wind is enough to cut one in two."

Mr. Oxley crept along the paling, till he came to a door, which he speedily opened by the aid of another key, with which he was provided; and that door led him at once into the garden of a cottage, known as Lime Cottage, and which was upon the Bloxdale estate, and sometimes let to strangers, and sometimes allowed to be occupied by friends of Mr. Oxley. Lime Cottage was in the occupation of the latter class of tenants now.

"Hem!" said Oxley, when he had safely locked the door in the oaken pailing behind him. "Hem! Mrs. Lerew, are you there? Hem!"

"Who's that?" said a female voice.

"Dear me," said Mr. Oxley, "I should have thought you would have known my voice in a moment anywhere, Mrs. Lerew."

"The east wind," said the lady, "is enough to blow any voice past one. But you are rather late."

"No—no. Any time before four, you know; though the fact is, I should have been here sooner, but there has been a regular disturbance between Lord Francis and the countess."

"Come in—come in. Where is Peter?"

"Has he not come back?"

"Not he. Did you not see him in the hall?"

"Yes, confound him, he nearly got me and himself into a scrape. He must not come there again until he can learn to be more cautious, although, as it happened, by mere accident, he got possession of a secret which purchases two of the inhabitants of Bloxdale."

With these words on his lips Mr. Oxley stepped into Lime Cottage after the lady whom he had named Mrs. Lerew. A couple of wax candles, that looked very much as if they belonged to the same stock as those in use at the hall, enabled Mr. Oxley to look about him, and enables us to indulge the reader with a glance at Mrs. Lerew.

Imagine a woman of about forty years of age, rather above the middle height, with staring black eyes like immense bright black beads, a high fresh colour, and long ringlets of a jetty hue depending upon each side of her face, and you have Mrs. Lerew, who was considered by many people to be rather a fine woman.

There is no accounting for tastes.

"Well, Oxley," said the lady, "what is the discovery that Peter has made? I should like to know."

"Just that Lady Fanny and Morris Courtley are on the intimate terms of declared lovers."

"You don't say so?"

"I do, though. I long suspected it; but Master Morris was cunning enough to baffle even me for a time. Now, however, I may fairly say that I have him on the hip. Ha!—ha!"

"A good thing, too. But now about the young lord?"

"Well, there be our trouble."

"I thought you told me that he was only a poor, sickly boy, hovering on the brink of the grave."

"He was; but now he is quite another person."

"Well, if he were ten times what he is, I don't see myself, after the way in which we have agreed to manage matters, what can prevent Peter being the Earl of Bloxdale?"

"Nor I. And at the same time our puppet."

"Just so. What more easy. I am very fond of Peter; but I don't mean to say that I am taking all this trouble just on his account."

"Certainly not, Mrs. Lerew, certainly not."

"Why do you call me by that name, John Oxley, now that we are alone? You know as well as I do that you have married me, and that, therefore, my name is Oxley."

"Yes, my dear Maria; but, you see, if I got into the habit of calling you Mrs. Oxley, I should perhaps do so at some unlucky moment when it would be the greatest possible mischief to all our plans."

"Ah, well, John, there is something in that."

"Everything, Maria, I think."

"Very good. You may call me Mrs. Lerew then, until I announce myself as the Countess of Bloxdale."

"Just so, just so."

"Countess of Bloxdale! Well, that is something for Maria Welch to come to at last. But Peter says it can be done, and you say it can be done, and the more I think of it, the more reasonable it seems to me. But, after all, if we should not succeed with Parson Musgrove?"

"We shall."

"Well, well, and about young Tom Musgrove? How does Peter get on with him, think you?"

"Oh, capitally. I tell you, Mrs. Lerew, that nothing can save Tom Musgrove from being so far in my power that I shall be able to show that old doting father of his, the old clergyman of Bishopstoke, that if he don't do as we wish, his son will hang—hang! Do you hear?"

"Certainly. I am quite willing."

There was a light tap at the door of the cottage at this moment, and Mrs. Lerew cried out—

"That's Peter."

She rose and opened the door, and Peter made his appearance.

"Well," he said, "here you are, old dad Oxley. How are you now? A precious row they have had at the old hall yonder, I should say."

"It's all in our favour," said Oxley; "the more divisions they have among themselves, of course, the better chance we have of conquering them. It is just possible when they feel the serious danger that is impending over them, they may make common cause as against a common enemy; but still it is a good thing they are at variance.'

"How do you mean to manage about your accounts," said Mrs. Lerew.

"I am in hopes that things will jog on as they have been accustomed to do, and if they don't, I shall avail myself of the little secret I now know of Morris Courtley's, to call upon him for aid."

"That will do," said Peter. "Capital, Ah, dad-in-law, you are a knowing old chap, after all, that you are."

"Hush," said Mrs. Lerew, "I hear a footstep in the garden."

"It's Tom Musgrove, then," said Peter, as he darted out of the cottage.

CHAPTER XI.

LORD FRANCIS PUTS A DISAGREEBLE QUESTION TO MR. OXLEY.

OPEN war might now be said to be fairly proclaimed between Lady Bloxdale and her children.

A more lamentable state of things than this could not possibly exist in any family, and in that of the Bloxdales in particular; when we come to consider the peculiar circumstances in which some of its members were placed, it was positively sad to think that there should exist such a want of unity of purpose.

There was, too, about Lady Fanny a feeling of constraint in the presence of her brother, which arose from the consciousness that was always present to her that she had a secret which she dreaded he should discover.

That secret was her love for the secretary.

Morris, too, suffered much, since the return of the young Lord Francis; and every word of kindness that was spoken to him by that young nobleman went like a dagger to his heart; for he, too, felt that the secret of his devoted attachment to Lady Fanny weighed him down, and sat like guilt at his heart.

Morris Courtley passionately adored Lady Fanny Bloxdale; and when such is the case, the cold suggestion of ordinary reason found but little chance of being commented upon.

For a long time he had concealed his love, and probably he would still have let the secret of its existence lie corroding his very heart, except from an accident which had given him both the opportunity and the influence to speak out; and then—oh, blissful surprise!—he had found that there were reciprocal feelings in the bosom of the sweet young girl.

What that accident was, we shall take some more particular opportunity of detailing to the reader.

We have now to do with what took place on the morning of the day following Lord Francis's arrival at his old ancestral home.

Cold, gloomy, and desponding, the sun rose through a misty vapour of snow and sleet upon that morning; although, by its ruddy colour, it gave some promise of breaking through the vigours of the winter as the day advanced, and of presenting some of its gladsome beams to the cold earth.

As it was, though, early in the morning, out-of-door exercise was not thought of.

Lord Francis was early astir, and sent word soon after to the valet of his father, to say that he would speak to that personage; and the valet was soon in Lord Francis's dressing-room.

"Hill," said Lord Francis, "you have been with my father many years, and you were always represented to be a good and honest servant. I am sorry to say that this house is in the position of one divided against itself. I want to know which side you take?"

"Oh, my lord—my lord!" said the old valet, his eyes filling with tears, "I would go through fire and water for you and your father; but—but the countess has discharged me."

"Discharged you?"

"Yes; I am to go at the end of the month. She ordered me to bring her all letters addressed to his lordship that I found in the letter-box, whereas, it is my lord's orders that I should take them all to Mr. Courtley, and so I respectfully told her ladyship, when all she said was, ' Will you obey me?' whereupon I said I must obey the earl, my master, and then she wrote me a dismissal at a month."

"Don't go, Hill."

"No, my lord."

"You will now go to my father, and tell him that I want to see him as soon as he can permit me to do so. I will come to his dressing-room, if he will permit me."

"Oh, my lord, come now! The earl is up, and as he is rather in low spirits this morning, I'm quite sure that the sight of your lordship will do him good."

"I will follow you."

In a few minutes Lord Francis was in his father's dressing-room; and he was shocked to see what ravages a few short years had made in the appearance of the earl, now that he saw him in dishabille, and not got up for the drawing-room as he had been on the preceding evening.

The old earl sat by the blazing fire, in a thickly-quilted flannel dressing-gown. His white hair was in disorder about his face and head, and he was slowly rubbing his shrivelled hands together as Lord Francis entered.

"Father, I hope you are well this morning," said the young man, trying to command the tone of his voice to as much firmness as he could.

"Oh, my boy, is that you? I—I—Come and sit here, my dear. Why, how you have grown, to be sure! And when did you come home—eh?"

Lord Francis uttered a groan, as, by those words, he found how shattered the memory of his father was.

"Dear father," he said, "don't you recollect that I arrived last nght from Naples?"

"From Naples? Oh, yes, my dear. To be sure I do. Oh, my poor head, how it wanders at times. Did you ever see the Fientarini family at Naples?"

"Yes, father."

"They were old friends of mine when I held a diplomatic position at the court. I think the villa by Foscatair the most charming place that I ever saw."

"It is quite a fairy palace, father."

"Yes; and the Terrace Gardens on the side of old Vesuvius. What a world of beauty they contain. There was a dear friend of mine there at the time I speak of—General Baxter; and he and I were never weary of admiring those gardens."

How delighted Lord Francis was now to hear his father speaking so calmly and rationally. The black and shuddering idea that had come across him, to the effect that the old man's memory, if not his reason, was shattered past recall, faded away again, and he had bright hopes yet of rescuing his father from the state of mental lethargy into which he had fallen.

"Ah, father," he said, "perhaps yet you and I will take a trip to the old sweet bay, and climb the side of hoary Vesuvius."

"Yes, my boy; I don't see why we should not."

"We will. But now, father, I have come to speak to you about our home affairs—our domestic matters, you understand? My mother——"

"Ah!" said the old man, as if suddenly heart-stricken at the very sound. "Ah, your mother, the countess. I—I—that is, I leave everything to her. She is a wonderful woman, and—and I am but a poor creature,

so she tells me. I—oh, dear!—he—he! Your mother manages everything, my boy, and—and you mustn't contradict her, whatever you do. She can't bear that. You must just—just let her have her own way. Oh, dear—oh, dear! I—I—yes, to be sure you must. When did you come home, my boy?"

Lord Francis felt faint and sick at the conviction that it was entirely his mother's work that mental fatuity that had come across his poor father. The mere mention of her had been sufficient to put out the spark of reason and recollection that a temporary forgetfulness of her was fanning into a flame.

From that moment Lord Francis felt that he must be the protector of his father; and that it was nothing but the constant dread that the wildly imperious conduct of the countess had kept him in that had had the effect of so overpowering his faculties. She had called him an idiot until she had made him one.

The half-formed purpose with which Lord Francis had come to his father's dressing-room, and which if he had found him mentally stronger would have been abandoned, became now a fixed resolution.

What that was we shall quickly see.

"Well, my boy," said the old earl. "Well, you look sad and weary."

"I am, father."

"Eh? so am I—so am I."

"Father?"

"Yes, my dear, yes; what would you say to the old man? But no, no—say nothing. Go to your mother. Do not anger her. She—she ——"

"Hill!"

"Yes, my lord," said the valet, appearing from the next apartment.

"Bring your master's writing-desk here."

"Yes, my lord."

The old valet placed a writing-desk open on the table by which Lord Francis Bloxdale and his father were sitting; and the old earl looked at it, and then at his son with surprise for a few moments, and then a faint smile crossed his features, as he said—

"I—I can't do it. I—must not. She—she won't have it. My dear, I would if I could, but I can't do it."

"In the name of Heaven, father, what do you mean? What do you allude to as supposing I want you to do?"

"My dear, you want some money. But I can't do it. She won't let me. She took the cheque-book from me long ago; and—I—I—eh?—she made me write to the bankers to honour her drafts for the future only—that is—only—I—I—he, he! When did you come home for your holidays, my dear? I can't do it."

"Oh God!" cried Lord Francis, as he let his head droop upon his hands. "And has it come to this? Is it my mother who has done all this?"

"Come—come, my dear," said the earl.

"Don't you cry. I'll—I'll—borrow some money of Mr. Courtley, or of Mr. Oxley, and let you have it, and you will not tell your mother? He, he! That's a good idea —a capital idea; but—if she should find it out. Oh, oh! I am afraid to do it, that I am, my boy."

Lord Francis looked up, and in the inner room he saw the old valet crying. The young lord beckoned to him to come and seat himself in the room, which the old man did; and then as he paced the apartment twice or thrice to calm his agitation, and passed the old servant, Lord Francis whispered to him—

"Hill, I want you to stay here and be a witness to what passes between me and my father."

"Yes, my lord."

"Hush. Be still till I call upon you to come forward."

Lord Francis now drew a chair close to his father, and touching him gently on the arm, he said—

"Father, will you lend me all your attention?"

"To be sure, my dear. You don't know how wonderfully better I feel while you are here."

"Well, father, I am your only son."

"Yes, my dear."

"And I am the successor to your title, and your landed estates, and all the heirlooms of the Bloxdales."

"I hope, my dear, you will have it all soon."

"I hope not, farther—I hope not. But we will not talk of that, it is too painful to me. But it is quite clear to me that you find the cares of business too much for you. Now, there are the old family solicitors, you know, in the Temple."

"Eh? Oh, I recollect. Your mother made them give up the papers, and got rid of them."

"Got rid of them?"

"Yes, she—she made me sign something —I don't know—your mother is a wonderful woman, though, my dear."

"What shall I hear next?" said Lord Francis to himself. "Well, father," he added aloud, "what I want of you is, a written authority to audit all the accounts of the property, and to deal with it in your name, as I think proper, subject to your sanction."

"Eh?"

"What I want, father, explicitly from you is, a written authority to act for you in all respects as regards the Bloxdale property. As your son, I ask it of you, under the present circumstances, as a right; and I am sure that you will be all the happier, that some one is placed in such a position, for, at present, there can be no supervision of the rentals, and no auditing of the accounts."

"Well I—oh dear!"

"You will sign such a document for me?"

"Oh, dear, I musn't—the countess, you see—she made me sign a something."

"Never mind that, father. You give me, in the form that I shall draw up, a complete authority to act for you, and I will manage everything for your comfort after that. You do not doubt me, father?"

"What, doubt my own boy? Oh, no—no! And you came from Naples?"

"Yes, father."

"And you saw the Fieritosini?"

"I did, father."

"Ah—ah! I recollect the terrace gardens. There were many young people of note at the Neapolitan Court at the time. He —he! There was the lovely Lady Bianca, the niece of the queen, whom all the young gallants made so much about; but to my thinking, she was anything but equal to a real English girl in her youth and beauty. You may go far, my boy Francis, before you find any of the boasted beauties of the Continent even near the angelic loveliness of a real, unaffected, gentle, pretty English girl."

"I think so, too, father."

"He—he! it is true."

Lord Francis was writing rapidly while his father was speaking, and then putting the pen in his hand, he said—

"Now, father, I will read to you what I have written for you to sign, if you will."

The document was as follows:—

"I, John Spencer Algernon, Earl of Bloxdale, hereby make and declare null and void all previous, forms of attorney or authority to act for me concerning my affairs and properties; and I appoint my son, Francis Bloxdale, usually called Lord Francis Bloxdale, as my representative, and bestow upon him complete power of action in all respects over my properties and affairs of every kind and description, and I enjoin all persons to deal with him as they would with me, as witness my hand and seal."

"Will that do, father?"

"Yes, my dear. There."

The earl affixed his signature, "Bloxdale;" and Hill, the valet, at a sign from Lord Francis, stepped forward, and placed a massive family seal in the hands of his master, and the document was duly sealed, and Hill witnessed it.

"This may want something in legal formality, father," said Lord Francis; "but if it should, I will get you to arrange it."

"I will, my boy, I will."

"Now, write to the bankers, and tell them to honour my cheques."

"Yes, my dear, oh, yes; and as regards the Bay of Naples, why the pleasantest time of all upon it is at sunset with your back to the west, you see; but there are times of the year when the sea wind is rather oppressive to those who are not used to it. I—I—think—"

"Write a few lines first, father, to the bankers, telling them to honour my drafts, if you please."

"Oh, dear, yes, my boy."

The old earl wrote the note required, and Lord Francis was armed now for the coming struggle. No one in the world would have shrunk more than young Lord Francis would from getting two such documents from his father, if the urgency of the case had not convinced him of the propriety of the act. It was for the old earl's preservation that the son armed himself with power, and not for his oppression.

It was as if they had both been engaged in battle, and Lord Francis had asked of his father the loan of his sword, on purpose to defend him, not for the purpose of leaving him defenceless.

Hardly had Lord Francis placed the two important documents in his pocket than the door of the dressing-room was opened, and the countess appeared on the threshold of the room.

"Oh, oh!" said the earl, and he made an attempt to slide off his chair, but Lord Francis prevented him.

"Oh, indeed!" said the countess. "A cabinet council I see. The Earl of Bloxdale, Lord Francis, and Hill, the valet."

"Eh—eh! I—yes—I——"

"Silence, father," whispered Lord Francis. "Let me beg of you to leave all to me."

"Oh, speak out, my dear," laughed the countess; "you won't be here long, so say what you have to say at once; and as for Hill, he goes within the hour!"

CHAPTER XII.

MR. OXLEY TRIES AN EXPERIMENT WITH MORRIS COURTLEY'S HEART.

THE imperious attitude that the countess assumed so frightened the old earl and Hill, that the former shook perceptibly, and the latter would have bustled from the room, had not Lord Francis detained him by saying—

"Hill, remain."

"Yes, my lord."

"Madam," added Lord Francis, "the earl declines parting with his old and faithful servant."

"Declines?"

"Yes, madam. Father, you decline to discharge Hill?"

"Yes, I—that is——"

"Yes, that will do. You hear, madam. The Earl of Bloxdale will not cast adrift an old and faithful domestic after twenty-five years of service. The earl will not disgrace himself and his name by such an act."

"How dare you? But no matter. Francis, my orders are that you quit this house at twelve to-day, and go at once to any large city on the continent that you please. You can then advise me of your place of residence,

and when I wish for your return, I will write to you to that effect."

"Mother, I intend to remain here. I thought that I had made that fact sufficiently evident to you."

"You shall not remain. I say you shall not."

Lord Francis only bowed.

"We shall see, madam. And now will you permit me to ask you who has charge of the books and papers of the family; and who audits the accounts, which I know are rather heavy and complicated?"

"That is my business," said the countess.

"No, madam ; mine, if you please."

"How yours, may I ask?"

"It is a duty that I owe to myself to see that my patrimony is not wasted, and I will do that duty. Can you oblige me with the bankers' book, madam, that I may see what money is there to the credit of my father?"

"Insolence!" cried the countess in a high shrieking tone of voice. "This passes everything that I could possibly have imagined. But I can inform you, young man, whom I will no longer call son, that I have taken great care no witnesses from you or from any one can effect my position at the head of this family."

"She is a wonderful woman," moaned the earl.

"And as for you, idiot——"

"Oh—I—yes, I am—I am!"

"Madam, I will not stand by and hear my father addressed in such terms. I warn you that if you repeat that expression, I will summon to this mansion every relative and friend we have ; and I will either by force or shame put an end to this most disgraceful state of things. Oh, mother, be all that you might be, and allow me to love and reverence you ; but shake off this wild and termagant spirit that possess you, and makes me know you not."

"It is you," said the countess, "who must first learn obedience—yes, obedience, that pearl of virtue in a son ; and as for you, my lord——"

"Beware, madam," said Lord Francis, for he saw that the countess was upon the point of expending some explosion of wrath upon the head of his unhappy father. "Beware, madam. I have told you what will be the consequences of goading me too far."

"Goading you too far? What do you mean by such language?"

"Just this, madam. I mean to take the command in this house—I mean to assume the control of my father's affairs—I mean to look into his accounts—I mean to be the Master of Bloxdale, so long as the earl, its real master, will permit me. It is for you to choose what will in your judgment be the most graceful position for you to assume."

The countess sat down and laughed loudly, but the laugh had something strange and forced in it.

"Oh, dear," she said, "this is quite an interlude, Francis. Well—well, my dear, we shall see—we shall see. As for the information you so kindly require regarding the balance at the bankers, I beg to decline giving it." Here the countess rose, and executed a very low curtsey. "Yes, I beg, with all humility, to decline giving it to the Master of Bloxdale. Heigho! what we are forced to hear in this world! But you have had my orders, and you go to the Continent. As for Fanny, who shows symptoms likewise of rebellion, I will to-morrow send her to some rather strict finishing academy in the north."

"She shall not go, madam."

"Oh, indeed!"

"No. I will not permit her to go."

"Well—well," laughed the countess again, hysterically, "we shall see—we shall see all that. Dear me, what we are forced to hear in this world from boys and fools! Hill, you leave Bloxdale in an hour."

"No, my lady."

"No?"

"Oh, dear, no, my lady."

"Francis?"

"Yes, mother."

"Will you allow me to be insulted, even in your presence, by a servant?"

"Certainly not; but in my thinking, the man is perfectly respectful; and if he would consent to go at your orders, he would be grievously insulting his master."

"Ah, well! We shall see—we shall see. We won't get out of temper about it. Oh, dear, no! We shall see—we shall see. Ha! ha! ha! Heigho! Ha! ha! ha! This is quite exhilarating upon a cold winter's morning, I declare. Francis, I shall see you at breakfast. Till then I leave you to think a little."

The countess sailed majestically from the room, and the old earl, with a yawn, slipped off his chair and fainted.

It was half an hour before Hill and Lord Francis could bring the earl to his ordinary condition again; and then leaving him in the care of his old and faithful attendant, Lord Francis, half maddened at the utter heartlessness of his mother, repaired to the library, where he hoped to find Morris Courtley, and he was not deceived, for there was the secretary alone, and resting his head upon his hands in profound thought.

"Morris!"

Courtley sprang to his feet.

"Lord Francis, I—I, that is——"

"Why, you look half scared, Morris. Come, I want to consult you, old friend. Sit down, and let me talk over the state of affairs here. I think you can do me a great and good service, Morris."

"It is a great joy to hear you say so," replied the secretary. "But—but——"

"But what?"

"The countess has sent me this note."

Lord Francis took a note, which Morris held out to him, and hastily read as follows:—

"The Countess of Bloxdale begs to inform Mr. Courtley that his services are no longer required by the Earl of Bloxdale, as librarian and secretary, and that a quarter's salary will be paid him in advance by Mr. Oxley, the steward; and the countess would feel obliged by his removing with all convenient dispatch."

Lord Francis looked very pale; but he twisted up the note and cast it in the fire. It was a fluttering piece of tinder, and flew up the ample chimney in a moment.

"Don't go, Courtley. Read these two papers."

Morris read the authority that the earl had given to Lord Francis, and the note to the bankers.

"You perceive, Courtley, that I have power now at Bloxdale."

"I should think that sufficient; but the countess has a power of attorney, or something like that, which she got prepared by some solicitor at Southampton that Oxley brought to her."

"Indeed! Oxley brought him?"

"He did."

"Well, and now, Morris, do you know who is the family solicitor now? for I understand the old respectable firm, which for so many years managed all our business, has been got rid of."

"I cannot tell you, my lord. I only know that Messrs. Lamb and Co., in the Temple, no longer manage the affairs of the estate. I think, however, that Mr. Oxley and the countess, fancy they get through all the business between them in some way."

"Monstrous! This is worse and worse. Why Oxley, then, to all intents and purposes, has the control of the whole resources of Bloxdale, subject only to the weak suspicions of a woman, who cannot be expected to enter into accounts as a man would."

"It is so, my lord."

"Well, Morris, tell me, do you think the bankers will act upon the letter from my father?"

"Undoubtedly they will. It is, in fact, just nothing more nor less than opening a credit for you."

"Exactly; but if I could find out how much was there, I would draw it all out, and so cut off the supplies from the countess. But I don't see how I am to get at that piece of intelligence, for I don't like to ask the bankers."

"Certainly not; but why not do it in this way, my lord: Your letter of credit is unlimited, and all you have to do is, draw some half-dozen cheques for different amounts, and go on presenting them, until the bankers declare they have no effects. By that means you will get all the ready money, at all events, into your hands."

"A good thought, Morris; I will do it. Oh, what a tangled web my poor, mis-

LADY FANNY BLOXIDALE ENDEAVOURING TO ROUSE THE DORMANT ENERGIES OF THE EARL.

guided mother has drawn our affairs, and I am sick at heart, Morris."

"I feel deeply for you, my lord."

"And now she wants to send Fanny away to the north, somewhere."

"Send Fanny! No—no!—she dares not!"

"Eh?"

"I—I mean, she surely will not. You love—that is, I—I am sure you love your sister too well, to permit that, my lord."

"In good truth I do, Morris. But you look quite ill!"

"Oh, no—no! I have not been very well lately; and—and I have suffered so much mental anxiety on account of the earl, that my spirits are in a low state, I fear.'

"Be at ease, my good friend, Morris. All will be well, I feel quite assured; for well I know that I fight in a just and holy cause. Let me but take care that I keep rather within the step beyond the line of my duty, and I shall be well content. But, oh, Morris, what a sad thing it is that the person I have to fight against is a mother."

"It is sad!"

"But yet I must not shrink, Morris; for, after all, it is better for her that I should make her pause in her career than permit her to go on adding still bitter remembrances for that hour of repentance which, sooner or later, is sure to come."

"That is true."

"So I will not shrink from that which I feel I have to do, Morris. I will make this Oxley give me a full and true account of the moneys that have passed through his hands, and you must help me in that, Morris; will you?"

"You have but to command me, and my life itself is as your service, at any time."

"My kind, good Morris! We—that is, Fanny and I, shall both feel that we have a friend in you. I will meet you here again in a short time."

Lord Francis left the library; and Morris Courtley, covering his face with both his hands, sank back in his large old chair, and said to himself, with a shudder—

"Oh, what will he think of the poor, dependant secretary, when it shall come to his knowledge that he has stolen the heart of his sister?"

Morris did not see an outstretched hand towards him in the gallery, clenched and threatening. It was the hand of Oxley, who had been listening to all that had passed; and now, with stealthy steps, the villain, for a villain was he, slunk from his post of observation through a secret door in the old chapel wall.

CHAPTER XI.

THE BROTHER AND SISTER MEET IN THE GARDEN.

LORD FRANCIS BLOXDALE saw that the sun had broken through the mists of early morning, as he passed out of the old library,

and he was tempted to repair to the sheltered garden of the manor.

That the young noble was much disturbed in his mind it would not have taken a very accurate observer to find out, for the most casual glance at him would have been sufficient to assure any one of that fact.

Under the painful circumstances in which he was placed, it would be quite impossible but that he should feel ill at ease.

"Where will all this end?" was the question that Lord Francis proposed to himself, and it was one to which he could not find, in the list of possibilities and probabilities that presented themselves to him, a sufficient answer.

Would the countess awaken from the kind of proud vanity that beset her like madness, and see more truly her own position and her own respectability? or would she fight the matter out to the last, with the certainty, in the end, of being conquered, and cowered with all the ignominy of a defeat in a bad cause?

Very much, from his knowledge of his mother's character, did Lord Francis fear that the latter would be the wild and mistaken course she would pursue.

"Well, well," he said, "if I must go through with this affair, I will, and nothing shall induce me to shrink from doing that which my judgment and my conscience tell me is right."

By the time he had got thus far in his cogitations, Lord Francis had reached one of the most cheering spots of the old manorial garden attached to Bloxdale.

It was a circular space of about one hundred feet across, and fringed with the most beautiful evergreens that art could secure in this country, so that, even at that season of the year, the place presented an appearance of luxuriant vegetation.

A little fountain, in the centre of this charmed circle, sent up a splashing jet of sparkling water to a height of about thirty feet, and close to that fountain was a small building that the family frequently sat in when the intense heat of summer made such a cool retreat desirable, and partook of some of the cool fruits of the well-stocked garden.

Lord Francis paused, and gazed around him upon the well-remembered spot. It was years since he had looked upon it.

"Ah!" he said, "how well I know each bush and tree in this place. It is about here that Fanny and I have wandered many a sunny hour away, when we were both little children, and long before there was a shadow of care upon our brows. Well, well, it is no use to look for those days to come again."

A slight sound attracted the attention of Lord Francis at the moment, and casting his eyes rapidly in the direction whence it came, he saw a figure half emerge from among the bushes, and, seeing him, draw back, and disappear.

"Why, that was Morris Courtley," said Lord Francis, in astonishment. "What does he here, I wonder? or, rather, why does he shun me? His being here is nothing, as the whole garden is free as air to him. This is very strange. I could not be deceived. It was Morris."

Hastily approaching the spot where he had seen the figure appear and disappear, Lord Francis plunged among the shrubs, and looked in vain for any trace of it. If it were Morris Courtley, he had managed with very great rapidity to effect a retreat.

This circumstance was far beyond the conjectures of Lord Francis to come to any probable opinion concerning, and he racked his imagination to build up some hypothesis upon the matter, which should look like the fact, but all in vain.

"There's nothing but to go and ask him what is the meaning of it," said Lord Francis, as he emerged into the open space again.

But then a new surprise awakened the senses of the young man. He saw opposite to him a female figure, just making its appearance from a narrow path among the evergreens, which he had himself just reached the spot by. One glance at that figure assured him that it was his sister, Fanny.

It would seem, though, that when he glanced at Fanny that she, too, glanced at him, and then, with a gesture of alarm, she hastily turned and fled from him.

Lord Francis was so staggered at this circumstance, that he stood for a few moments perfectly still, not making the least attempt to pursue Fanny, so that she had abundance of time to escape from the spot.

"What on earth can be the meaning of all this?" said Lord Francis. "Why, the very two people, of all others, who, I should say, would seek me, and be quite delighted to meet me, fly from my presence as though it were contamination. Am I mad, or are they?"

With hasty steps the young nobleman was crossing the grass-plot and had just got to the little fountain when he saw a thin wreath of blue smoke ascending from the roof of the little summer-house, and he paused, in surprise, to regard it as another of the mysteries of the garden upon that morning, for well he knew there was no fire-place in that little building; and if there had been one placed there during his absence, nothing could be very well more unlikely than that anybody should be in such a place at that season of the year.

But there was the thin wreath of blue smoke; and as facts are rather stubborn things to get over, Lord Francis was forced to come to the conclusion that there was a fire in the summer-house.

He modified this opinion a little as he approached the door of the summer-house, for then an incontestable odour of tobacco came upon his senses, at once accounting for the wreath of smoke.

"Oh! some of the servants smoking," thought Lord Francis. "It is prohibited in the mansion, so some inveterate lover of the lazy weed has come here to indulge himself with its fumes, I fancy."

"Hilloa!" said a voice, and, at the same moment, a head was popped out from the little door of the summer-house. One glance at the pert, London vulgarity of that head and face, and the meretricious finery of the stock, with its showy pins, and the flaming colours of a portion of a waistcoat that was visible, convinced Lord Francis that is was neither a visitor nor a servant that he saw.

The young nobleman looked at the apparition of vulgarity for a few moments in silence, and then the personage, who was no other than Peter, the individual who claimed the doubtful honour of being step-son to Mr. Oxley, said—

"Nice morning, ain't it?"

"Sir," said Lord Francis, "may I take the liberty of asking who you are?"

"Oh, the liberty? Well, no—you may-dent."

"Are you aware, sir, where you are?"

"To be sure I am. Who are you?"

"That is quite beside the question, sir. Since you do not think proper to account, in any rational manner, for your presence here, perhaps you will not think it very unreasonable a discretion upon my part, if I give you into the custody of a constable?"

"A constable? Oh, stuff! I suppose you are one of the valets—eh? Come, come, you don't know who you are speaking to, old chap. I may be able to give you a good turn some of these days, for all you know. I suppose the great folks don't get up till rather lateish, eh?"

Lord Francis looked about him with the hope of seeing some of the men-servants, to whose keeping he might consign Mr. Peter; and, then, who should make his appearance through the fringe of flowery shrubs that bordered that spot but Mr. Oxley, the steward!

"Oh, here he is!" cried Peter.

"Mr. Oxley!" said Lord Francis.

The steward stopped short at the sight of his young master, and an expression of intense alarm crossed his features as he glanced from him to Peter, and then from Peter back to him again. But Oxley did not effect, as the other persons whom Lord Francis had seen reach that spot had done, a precipitate retreat from it; on the contrary, he came slowly forward, with a distressed kind of smile upon his face.

"Now, my fine fellow," said Peter, "you will catch it. You will find that you have rather put your foot in it; for I am a friend of Mr. Oxley's, I can tell you."

"My lord!" commenced Oxley, with a low bow to Lord Francis. "I—I—that is, my lord, I hope——"

"What," cried Peter, "is this—that is, I mean, this is——"

"Lord Francis Bloxdale," said Oxley in a low tone.

"Oh, indeed."

"And this is a friend of yours, Mr. Oxley?" said Lord Francis.

"I am very sorry, my lord——"

"Yes, I am," said Peter, "though Mr. Oxley pretends he is sorry."

"You must be aware, Mr. Oxley," added Lord Francis, without paying the least attention to Peter, "that this spot has always been a chosen one by my sister and myself; and, therefore, I hope that, for the future, your friends will not select it to smoke in."

Mr. Oxley looked white and flabby as he rubbed his hands over one another; but Peter cried out—

"Oh, very well, my lord; of course those who happen to be masters of Bloxdale, while they are such, or fancy themselves such, can make what regulations they please. Other people may have different notions; and for my part I——"

"Silence!" said Oxley.

"Oh, bother! I don't see why——"

"Fool! Ass!"

"Hilloa! fine names. Well, I never!"

Lord Francis had walked slowly and calmly away, and when he had got some distance off, so that there could not be a possibility of his being overheard, Mr. Oxley grasped the arm of his step-son, and said frantically—

"Do you want to ruin all? Do you want to expose your odious vulgarity too soon? Can you not wait until fortune has raised you to a height that she cannot bring you down from again, before you indulge your petty vanity, and your low disgusting tastes?"

"Hilloa!"

"I tell you what it is, Peter Lerew, once for all, that if you thwart me in the way you have shown a disposition to do lately, I will abandon the whole affair, and leave you to your original obscurity and contempt."

"Oh, lor!"

"I will, I tell you. I thought that by this time you knew that I was not a man to be trifled with."

"Well, but what have I done? You told me to meet you here, and here I am. What have I done?"

"What fiend possessed you to begin smoking here?"

"It was so devilish cold."

"Cold—stuff! And what devil prompted you to quarrel with Lord Francis, eh?"

"I didn't know him."

"But when you did know him, how your vulgar insolence continued—how your tongue ran with the low London slang, which is your proper mode of discourse! Oh, fool—fool!"

"Well, thank you, Daddy Oxley. Upon my life, you can come out a bit when you like. You know as well as I do that you and mother have got up the affair between you; and you want to make me a lord, and all that sort of thing, so that you may have the profit; and now you set to abusing of me, as if I were a pickpocket. I tell you what it is, father-in-law Oxley, I ain't used to it,

and I won't have it. Lor bless you, if any fellow at the Coal Hole or the Cider Cellars in London had said half that to me, I should have thrown a glass of brandy-and-water slap in his face."

"Peace—peace!"

"Oh, it's all very well to say peace—peace! I'll just tell you now of a row I got in with a fellow at Vauxhall."

"No, no, I don't wan't to hear it. I have something to tell you of more importance. You are shrewd enough, Peter, when you like. Your education in an attorney's office has sharpened your faculties."

"Rather," said Peter, placing his finger by the side of his nose, and casting upon his step-father rather a knowing wink.

"Well, then, I tell you that Lord Francis suspects me."

"What a pity."

"He has got some sort of authority from the old man to look into my accounts; and he and that Morris Courtley will, no doubt, be very troublesome to me shortly, notwithstanding all the support I am likely to meet with from the countess."

"Well, but she is the mistress," he cried. "Didn't the old gent give her the power of attorney to do what she liked?"

"Yes; but I dare not refuse my accounts to Lord Francis; and you knew as well as I, Peter, that if the countess thought there was anything amiss in them, she would be the first to turn round upon me."

"Very well, Father Oxley. I forgive you all your robberies, old fellow. I will pass a bill of indemnity for you; and as I am to be the Earl of Bloxdale when the old man is gone, why you are all right. I mean to begin, then, all straight and fair, and to say nothing of the past."

"Yes, Peter; but all that has to be completed first. Of course, if I and your mother make you the Earl of Bloxdale, we will take good care to profit by it, or we will unmake you again."

"Oh—eh! we shall see. But we mustn't quarrel about that just yet, Father Oxley. What do you mean to do?"

"I can do nothing but threaten Courtley. We know his secret, and I think that is a power that will bring him to our feet. Tell your mother that I will manage if I can to run over to the cottage to-night, and let her know how things have gone on; and whatever you do, keep away from here, I beg of you, now."

"Oh, very well. I don't want to come. It's precious cold, that's a fact. Good evening, daddy."

Oxley made an impatient movement with his hand, and they parted—Peter to make his way to the cottage where his mother resided, and Oxley to hurry back to the mansion again.

In the meantime, Lord Francis had reached the house, and the first servant he met he desired to convey his wish to his sister, Lady Fanny, that she would come to him in the Crimson Drawing-room. The message that was brought to him was, that Lady Fanny was indisposed, so that, at that time, Lord Francis had no opportunity of questioning her regarding her mysterious appearance in the garden, and her flight from him.

Poor Fanny, when she found that her brother was on the spot where she expected to meet Morris Courtley, had adopted the most imprudent course she possibly could; for instead of advancing and speaking to him, and passing the affair off with the idea that she, like him, had merely taken a morning's walk, she had fled.

It was not until she reached her own room, and began to reflect that she felt how easy it would have been to have explained her presence in the garden, but how difficult it would be to explain her flight.

When, therefore, the message of her brother was brought to her, she dreaded to meet him, and she had sent word back, as we have heard, that she was indisposed.

Morris Courtley, too, with all his presence of mind, which nearly forsook him, had made the same error of judgment, since he, upon seeing Lord Francis instead of Fanny, had made a retreat; but he was under an impression that Lord Francis had not seen him, or if he had, that the glance had been so slight and trivial as to preclude the possibility of recognizing him.

Such, then, was the state of affairs when Lord Francis, after his disappointment of seeing his sister, repaired to the library.

Morris Courtley was there.

"Morris," said Lord Francis, "were you in the garden a little time ago, by the fountain?"

Courtley felt at once that he had been recognised, and he replied with that truthfulness that was an inherit portion of his character—

"I was, my lord."

"Why did you shun me, Morris?"

A deep flush of colour came over the face

of the secretary, and then he said, in a low voice—

"Lord Francis, an untruth never, to my knowledge, passed my lips; I therefore beg that you will excuse me from telling you."

"Be it so," said Lord Francis, in rather a sad tone.

CHAPTER XII.

MR. OXLEY FANCIES HE HAS THE SECRETARY IN HIS CLUTCHES.

LORD FRANCIS felt very much hurt, indeed, at this conduct of Morris Courtley's; and yet he could not withhold a certain degree of respect for the man who, in preference to telling him an untruth, which would have been easy to concoct, risked his displeasure by a refusal to answer his question.

After a few minutes' silence, he said—

"Morris, I did hope that you would have placed some confidence in your old friend; but I am sure it is not so."

"I dare not."

"You dare not? How so?"

"Oh, do not ask me. God knows how willingly I would tell you all; but yet, I—dare not—No—no!"

"You are distressed, Courtley; and it would be ungenerous of me to press you for an explanation; but rest satisfied that I know you so well, that I feel as convinced as I do of my own existence it is honour that keeps you silent; and that when I do know your secret, it will be found to be one to reflect candour upon your name. Nay, say no more. You are not the man to falsify all that we know of you. You cannot commit a dishonourable act, Courtley."

"Oh, Francis!"

"Ah, that is right. We used to be just 'Morris' and 'Francis' to each other, you know, in old times."

"I forgot—I forgot."

"You mean, you remembered Morris. But come now, do not distress yourself about the matter. I am satisfied. When Morris Courtley declines to speak, I know that it is because it is better, and more generous, more just, and more honourable, for him to hold his peace."

Every word that the young nobleman spoke now, was like a poniard rushing to the heart of Courtley. How had he acquired the confidence that was reposed in him? Why, by receiving the affections of one, who might look for an alliance with the noblest of the land, while he was but the son of a peasant, and a salaried dependant. "Is that noble? Is that just?" asked Courtley of himself. "Is that what Lord Francis expects from me? Oh, no—no!"

"Well, Courtley," added Lord Francis, "I am going to send for Oxley, and to insist upon an inspection of his accounts."

"Yes, my lord—yes."

"Nay, call me Francis, do. You did so just now."

Lord Francis rung for a servant, and sent a message to say that he desired to see Mr. Oxley in the library.

Oxley fully expected the summons, and he had made up his mind that it would never do to shun it. In the course of five minutes he made his appearance, looking quite calm, collected, and serious.

"You sent for me, my lord."

"I did, Mr. Oxley. Take a seat, as it will require some time to answer me what I shall ask of you."

Oxley quietly slid into a chair.

"I am always only too happy to obey the commands of those who have the authority to question me," he said.

"Precisely, Mr. Oxley. To commence then, sir: May I ask if the papers and documents connected with the Bloxdale property are in the hands of any legal firm?"

"Your lordship will allow me to refer to

your noble mother, I am sure, for every particular regarding the property."

"Exactly, Mr. Oxley; but I choose to ask you certain questions, and I expect explicit answers from you."

"With the countess's permission I will speak."

"Why not without?"

"Because her ladyship has condescended to inform me that the earl, your father, has deputed her to be his representative, and to manage all his affairs, for which purpose she holds a power of attorney, giving her every power of action."

"So I hear; but the earl has revoked that, and given me a power of action in his name. Read that, Mr. Oxley."

This was just what Oxley wanted, namely, to read the document upon which Lord Francis founded his right of interference.

"Very good, my lord," he said. "I will, with your lordship's permission, show this paper to the countess."

"No, Mr. Oxley. Do you dispute the signature?"

"Oh, dear, no, my lord."

"Do you allege that it has been procured by fraud?"

"Oh, no—no. I would not presume——"

"Very well; then, Mr. Oxley, as the expressed wish of the earl, I do not see that it leaves you any option but to obey it, unless you can say that you have any other desire than to act according to his intentions."

Oxley saw that he was in what his stepson, the delectable Peter, would have called a fix; but he decided upon his course of conduct in a moment.

"My lord," he said, "I can have but one desire, and that is to do my duty—that duty is to obey the Earl of Bloxdale, and this paper that you show me is a declaration of his orders, therefore, I will bow to it, and am quite ready to act in accordance with its contents. It may not be so strictly legal as the power of attorney given to the countess."

"But that is nothing to you," said Lord Francis.

"Nothing in the world, my lord."

"Very well, then. Why are the old solicitors of the family discharged?"

"I do not know, my lord. The countess discharged them."

"Where are the papers and documents?"

"I do not know, my lord. The countess, I presume, has them."

"What money is at the bankers?"

"The countess has the pass-book, my lord, and I never see it."

"How long has this surrender of his power of action into the hands of the countess upon the part of my father been going on?"

"Two years, my lord."

"Who audits your accounts?"

"The countess, my lord."

"Very well. As her functions are over, I will do so. Of course, you can have no difficulty in satisfying me regarding the in-comings and outgoings of the estate for the last two years?"

"Certainly, no difficulty whatever."

"I presume the solicitors supervised your accounts previous to that time, Mr. Oxley?"

"They did, my lord, and gave me a written acknowledgment of their correctness once in six months."

"Very well. I depute the task of looking over your books and vouchers to Mr. Morris Courtley."

"Very good, my lord."

"Was cash received paid to the bankers or to the countess for the last two years?" said Courtley.

"Ay, how was that?" said Lord Francis.

"To the countess sometimes, and sometimes, by her orders, I sent it to the bankers," said Oxley.

"Very good, Mr. Oxley," said Lord Francis. "You will clearly understand your position. I do not cast any blame upon you whatever, as regards the delegation of my father's power to my mother. All that is required of you is, that you make your accounts clear as between you and the countess and the estate. I now leave you with Mr. Courtley, who will go at large into the affair, and report to me accordingly."

"Certainly, my lord. I have great pleasure in being associated with so worthy a gentleman as Mr. Courtley."

Oxley held open the door of the library for the exit of Lord Francis, and bowed very low as he passed out. Then, closing the door, he walked slowly up to Courtley, and said—

"When will it suit you that I bring my books?"

"Now."

"Good."

Oxley left the library, and making his way up the grand staircase, he made his way to a small room on the upper floor, and tapped gently at the door. It was opened by Miss Wicks.

"Oh, Mr. Oxley——"

"Hush! my dear Miss Wicks. Really, you—a—look quite—charming to-day, indeed, you do."

"Don't! Oh, Mr. Oxley, really you kiss one in such a way, you—you quite stop one's breath. Ah, you wicked man!"

"Wicked, Miss Wicks?—Oh, no."

"Oh, yes. Did you not say you would make me your wife, Mr. Oxley, and you have not yet named the day?"

"But I will name it, my dear Miss Wicks, as soon as these family jars are arranged here. You know how much I admire you, and you know that we are both pretty well off."

"Ah, yes, Mr. Oxley, providence has been pretty good to me in the way of perquisites and little pickings."

"And to me, Miss Wicks."

"Yes, Mr. Oxley, when I see Lady Bloxdale's purse on her dressing-table, and take ten or twelve guineas out of it, which she never misses, I bless and praise the Lord for all his mercies."

"Ah! how charming is that religious fervour, my dear Miss Wicks, that possesses you. But I must see the countess at once, and you must tell her so. Lord Francis threatens all sorts of things; and I need only tell you that if we do not stop him in what he is about, there will be no more little gifts of a benign providence, in the shape of perquisites and odds and ends, to convince you of the propriety of immediate action."

"The wretch!"

"He is, indeed."

"I will go to my lady directly, Mr. Oxley; but the Lord, no doubt, will protect us. Look at this."

"What is it?"

"A diamond pin. I found it—in a stock of the earl's. Take it, my dear Mr. Oxley. It is quite a gift of the Lord."

"I feel it to be such. Providence *does* look after us. But go at once, and te the countess know that I humbly and respectfully wish to see her."

Miss Wicks soon procured the steward an audience; but here we must guard against any impression that the reader might erroneously have, that Lady Bloxdale was in any degree privy to the iniquities of Oxley. She was his victim—his dupe; and the only hope he had for seeing her, was to make the credence to play off her pride and and anger against the assumption of power upon the part of her son.

Oxley well knew the weak points of the countess, and he could in the most respectful manner, mould her mind to anything.

The countess received him in a small apartment adjoining to her own boudoir; and when he bowed very low, she said at once—

"Well, Oxley, of course you have something to say to me about the rebellion in the house. What is it?"

"Your ladyship will be surprised to hear that Lord Francis has demanded of me a statement of my accounts, which I am to submit to Mr. Courtley; and he says that your ladyship's judgment with regard to them is of no moment at all, as you may, from folly or——"

"Or what, sir?"

"I really—I dare not——"

"Speak out, Oxley. I can bear to hear the truth from you. You are an old and faithful servant."

"Oh, my lady—my lady," cried Oxley, taking out his handkerchief, and really shedding a shower of tears, "my heart is almost broken to hear your ladyship, whom I respect and reverence as a queen, spoken of in—in—oh, oh, my poor heart is breaking!"

"Restrain your feelings, Oxley—they do you credit; but I beg of you to restrain them. My own child has raised the standard of rebellion against me in this house, but I will triumph yet. Go on with your story."

"Ye—e—s, my honoured queen—I mean, my lady; but you ought to be a queen, for never was there so much natural dignity—so much grace—so much—oh, oh, my poor heart!"

"Say no more upon that point, my good Oxley; but tell me at once the grounds upon which your accounts were acquired."

"Why, my lady, Lord Francis and Mr. Courtley said, that your ladyship being a compound of folly and fraud, they considered your auditing of my accounts to be nothing at all, as far as accuracy is concerned you might pass anything. Oh, oh, oh, dear! that I should live to say this to my honoured lady!"

The countess's face turned ghastly white, as she said—

"Mr. Oxley, leave me."

"Yes, honoured lady. Oh, yes. But——"

"Leave me!"

Oxley had no resource but to bow himself out; but he had the satisfaction of hearing the countess utter a shriek of rage after he had closed the door.

"He, he!" laughed Oxley. "He, he! We shall see."

CHAPTER XV.

MR. OXLEY SHOWS THE INFINITY OF A WICKED MIND.

THE steward had been in hopes that the countess would have come to some immediate decision respecting the accounts, that would have enabled him at once to avoid the threatened investigation of them; but such not being the case, he was thrown upon his own wits for a little delay.

Returning to the library, he sought Courtley, and said with an air of great candour, and apparent ingenuousness—

"Mr. Courtley, it gives me great pleasure that it is to you I have to make up my accounts."

Courtley merely inclined his head in reply to this speech.

"But," added Oxley, "I fear it will be twelve o'clock to-morrow before I can be ready for you, as I have to get all the documents and vouchers in order, so as to waste no more of your time than may be absolutely necessary."

"There has been one delay, Mr. Oxley."

"True; but, of course, as I wish you to be quite satisfied as regards the correctness of my books, I think I may fairly ask till to-morrow morning at twelve o'clock."

Now, however Courtley might wish the job of auditing Oxley's accounts well over, he found it difficult to say nay to the request; so, after a little consideration, he merely said—

"Very well, Mr. Oxley."

"That hour then will be convenient?"

"I will make it so."

"Thank you, Mr. Courtley. Allow me to say, sir, that I am really very much obliged to you—very much; and if I can do anything to give you any gratification, it will be excessively pleasing to me to do so. Hem!—Good-day, Mr. Courtley."

Courtley again bowed, and when Oxley was outside the library door he shook his clenched fist, and muttered—

"It shall go hard, Mr. Courtley, but I will be even with both you and Lord Francis. I know your secret, thanks to the blundering of Peter, and we shall see whether I cannot make it work so as to entangle you both. Oh, that night were come! I—I would go to the common—yes, to the hut on the common; for it is very strange that what that hag who resides there prophecies, generally comes true. Yes, I will go to her again. I am not superstitious, I am sure I am not; but I will go to her once again."

Now it has been said that pride is the infirmity of noble minds, and certainly superstition is the infirmity of low and narrow intellects; and in Mr. Oxley there was, to all intents and purposes, an under current of that powerful feeling, mingling with and terminating all the actions of his life.

It so happened that amid the thick and tangled mimic forest that lies to the left of Southampton Common, as you leave the town a woman, of apparently great, age had taken up her residence. Of hag-like form and repellent aspect and manners, this woman led the life of a recluse.

In less enlightened times she would have been the reputed witch of the district; and, in all probability, would have expiated the twin offences of age and ugliness at the stake; but as it was, the country people shunned her—the boys pelted her with stones—the dogs barked at her, and she was isolated from all apparent connection with the great world in which she still unhappily lingered.

This woman had met Oxley once on the common, and had followed him, soliciting alms. He had refused her roughly, and she had cast a malediction at him, hoping that before sunset something would happen to him, and that he would then remember her.

Something did happen to him, for before he reached the town, the sure-footed cob that had carried him for so long in safety, shied and threw him.

Mr. Oxley rose with aching, although, as good luck would have it, as far as he was concerned, no broken bones; and the words of the old woman at once rushed to his imagination.

All the superstition that was lurking in his breast was aroused, and he slowly went back to the spot upon which he had left her. He gave her money, and accompanied her to a squallid hut in the wood, where she resided, and the remains of which are still to be seen. There she affected to read to him some of the secrets of the future, and had so far infected his imagination with fears and hopes, that he had communicated the particulars of his visit to Mrs. Lerew, as he called her, although, as that lady had said, he had married her, and she was entitled to the name of Oxley.

Now at first this Mrs. Lerew had laughed to scorn the prophetic powers of the old hag; but then, as if struck by a sudden thought, she had begun to speak in doubt upon the subject, and finally encouraged Oxley more and more in his notion that there might, after all, be "something in it."

It will be found that Mrs. Lerew had her own reasons for this course of conduct.

Twice since then had Oxley visited the hag, and her revelations of the future, whatever they were, had had a great effect upon his imagination.

It was a third visit that he now contemplated to the common, when night should enable him to go with a due amount of concealment, to that spot without the town.

While these thoughts were occupying the politic, but still weak, brain of Oxley, both Courtley and the Lady Fanny Bloxdale passed hours of great suffering, from fear that they should be, as they were then suspected, standing upon the brink of a precipice, which would at once, if they approached it a step nearer, engulph them in destruction.

To them, destruction and the discovery of their love were all but synonymous terms.

The few words that had been spoken to Lady Fanny in the picture-gallery had, as we are aware, greatly alarmed her at first; but upon consideration, they alarmed her still more, and coupling them with the disappointment she had experienced in meeting Courtley in the garden on the spot which they had often before met on, she was truly wretched and full of fears.

Ann, her faithful and attached attendant, found the task of comforting her young mistress beyond her powers; and it was at last only after half-an-hour's tears that Fanny was at all able to look up or converse rationally upon her situation and prospects.

What a relief it was to the young creature, then, to find, in the fact that Ann knew her secret, the consolation of a confidant, and one who spoke no word of disapproval, but one who would go to any extent in serving her.

"Oh, Ann!" she said, "I am so glad I told you all. I feel that my heart is bursting, and that I am not long for this world!"

"Don't say that," said Ann. "You and this world, I'm sure, ain't done with each other by a long while, Lady Fanny."

"But what am I to do?"

"Oh, I don't know. Nothing."

Now this nothing was about the most sensible thing that Lady Fanny could possibly do, for it is by trying to do something which, in ninety-nine cases out of a hundred, people fail in doing, that they make their situations so very much the worse than what they would have been.

Many a little complication of circumstances, which, if left alone, would right itself, is rendered past all mending by some ill-directed effort to alter its complexion. But

LORD FRANCIS LEADING THE EARL, HIS FATHER, TO THE LIBRARY.

Ann did not reason in that way when she said nothing. All the good girl meant was, that she did not know, at that moment, what to advise in the state of perplexity which her young mistress had fallen into.

"But I must do something, Ann," said Lady Fanny.

"Yes; but what?"

"That's what I want to know."

"So do I."

"Ah, Ann, how truly the poet mentioned that

"'The course of true love never yet ran smooth,
But either it was different in blood,
Or else misgrafted in respect of years—
Or else it stood upon the choice of friends;
Or if there were a sympathy in choice,
War, death, or sickness did lay siege to it.'"

"You don't say so, my lady! Did the poet say all that, now?"

"He did."

"Well, I don't pretend to understand it all; but I'm so glad you recollect it, because it has cheered you up a bit."

"Dou you think so?"

"I'm sure of it."

"Alas, my poor Morris! Oh, that you were noble as you deserve to be, and then I might be happy!"

"If you please, Lady Fanny, I don't see why you shouldn't be happy, even if he isn't. I'm sure, he is good-looking, and has such eyes, that if dukes were only made on account of 'em, he would be one before long, I know."

"Yes, Ann; and so you advise me to send you to him with leave to come to the picture-gallery, so that I may say a word or two to him."

"Me, Lady Fanny? Oh, no!"

"I—thought you did."

Ann laughed.

"Oh, lor! I see how the cat jumps—I—no, I don't."

"The cat, did you say, Ann?"

"No, my lady; excuse me, I didn't mean it. I meant that I do advise you to see Mr. Courtley in the picture-gallery, if you please."

"I thought you did, Ann."

"To be sure; and what do you think of me going, and managing to say so to him? Suppose I try at once, if you please?"

"Well, perhaps, Ann, it would be just as well; but, mind, I only do so to please you, as you look so miserable, and as I have a great affection for you, Ann, you know, considering you have been so long with me, and that I have been in the habit quite of considering you like a sister; so you may go at once, and you needn't tell him that I am very unhappy, indeed, and that I must see him as soon as possible; and, above all things, don't say that I shall quite count every minute till he comes, now."

"Certainly not, yes, Lady Fanny."

Well, then, go now—No, stop! I am afraid that—that——"

"Don't be afraid of anything," said Ann, and she left the room at once to seek Morris Courtley.

Now, there was no difficulty whatever in Ann speaking to Courtley, provided he was not actually engaged upon any business for the earl, or for Lord Francis, so she made her way direct to the library, and like a prudent waiting-maid as she was, she listened at the door for a little first, in order to be quite sure that Morris was alone.

All that she heard there was the unmeasured tread of some one pacing to and fro.

"Ah, poor young man," thought Ann to herself, "he is quite as miserable as she is, I'll be bound. Well, they will make quite a sweet couple, and I only hope that young Hopkins, the gamekeeper, and I may be half as happy as I am quite sure Mr. Morris Courtley and Fanny would be if they could only come together; but then, as that poet says that Lady Fanny speaks about,

'Of course, true love isn't smooth,'

and—and—oh, I can't recollect the rest of it."

Ann had pretty well assured herself that nobody was in the library besides Morris Courtley, but still she could not be quite sure, and fully impressed with the idea that the very best excuse she could make for going there would be to ask for a book, she called out as she opened the door—

"The History of England, if you please."

"What?" said Courtley, abruptly.

"The History of—Oh, nobody."

"Ann, is that you?"

"To be sure it is, Mr. Courtley, and I wonder you ain't in hysterics, I do."

"What do you mean?"

"Only that somebody else is very nearly in 'em, though not quite, you needn't look so frightened. Oh, dear, she ain't quite in 'em."

"You do, indeed, alarm me, Ann."

"I meant it."

"You meant it? What can you mean it for?"

"Why, because its quite right and proper, to be sure, and Lady Fanny says — eh? Lady Fanny says—Hush!"

"What does she say? For the love of Heaven tell me."

"She says that—oh, dear!"

"What?—what?"

"You are sure there is nobody here but you?"

"Quite sure, and you. What does she say? Oh, Ann do tell me! You are a good, kind girl, I know, and Lady Fanny loves you, and so do I; so tell me at once."

"Well, I'm sure! you love me?"

"Yes, as the kind, and gentle, and tender-hearted friend of Fanny."

"Well, then, I will tell you; but if you had said I was pretty, I wouldn't have told you a word about it."

"Why so?"

"Because I should have thought, then, that—that, in fact, you were saying what you ought not to say, considering Fanny is in the house."

"You are right, Ann; I should have been saying what I ought not to have said, however strictly true the statement might have been."

"That's almost as bad, Mr. Courtley, so I won't stay another moment, but just to say that it is possible Lady Fanny will be in the picture-gallery, and just expecting to see you. Shall I tell her you cannot come?"

"Oh, no—no! How could you possibly think of such a thing, Ann, as to tell her that?"

Ann tripped out of the library smiling, and Morris hastily made his way to the picture-gallery. Morris Courtley ought, in good truth, to have been a little more careful how he proceeded, for he was watched in his progress to the gallery, and Mr. Oxley gathered yet another proof of the story that had been told him by Peter, his son-in-law.

Poor Fanny was waiting with the deepest anxiety in the recess of one of the bay-windows the arrival of Morris; and yet when he came, and when she fell upon his breast and wept long and bitterly, she had nothing to say to him, but that many griefs, to none of which she could give any denomination now preyed upon her heart.

In good truth she had sought the interview with him, not so much that she had really anything to say to him, as that it was an exquisite relief to hear his voice, and to feel that she was with some one with whom she need have no concealments.

The dread of a thousand evils that might possibly take place, contingent upon this imprudent love, was tugging at the heart of the young girl, and she felt as if a sort of mental retribution had come over her for ever dreaming of uniting herself out of that artificial sphere in which she in her nobility of extraction moved.

Poor, poor Fanny Bloxdale! She was suffering all the pangs which love, at its best and happiest, ever afflicts it votaries with; for, inasmuch as love is so much a thing of imagination, the fancy, when once extended beyond its ordinary action, will prey upon itself.

And so it was, that when Morris Courtley, the young secretary, did, in fact, reach the picture-gallery, and held to his heart the blushing, trembling girl, she had nothing to say to him but that she loved him. But what a world of joy it was to him to hear her say as much! Did he wish that she should say aught else? Ah, no! Sufficient for him was the fact that her young heart was all his own; and in the silent and dim obscurity of that gallery, they both felt that they lived but for each other—and they both forgot that there was a vast world around them, to the decrees and the prejudices of which they were bound as by chains of adamant.

The dusky portraits of the ancient family of the Bloxdales were around them; and from many an old moth-eaten piece of tapestry, and many a rotting panel, the "counterfeit presentments" of the bygone lords and ladies of her ancient race seemed to be regarding the young Lady Fanny with frowns of ill-omen.

She shuddered, as now and then she cast her eyes upon these grim effusions of the past; but she still clung closer to Morris Courtley.

CHAPTER XVI.

MR. OXLEY VISITS THE WITCH OF SOUTHAMPTON COMMON.

WE now leave the young lovers to converse in that low, soft strain, which is so delightful to those who are mutually attached, while we follow Mr. Oxley upon his errand to the Witch of the Common, from whom he hoped to hear such prognostications of success in his villanous schemes as should have the effect of inciting him to pursue them with vigour and spirit.

It was an easy enough thing for Oxley to leave the hall when he pleased, so that he had no obstacles of that kind to encounter upon the threshold of his enterprise.

Mounted upon a rough-coated, broad-backed, short-legged, bull-necked cob from the stables, he defied the dreariness of the road, and well wrapped up against the cold, he took his route towards the river Itchen, which he would have to cross to get to the common, which lay upon the other side of that rather picturesque stream.

The Itchen ferry was not then quite so commodiously provided with the means of transit as it is now; and Oxley, when he reached the banks of the stream, had to shout himself hoarse before the horse-boat, as a broad flat-bottomed barge, half full of litter, was called, came to take him and his steed over the river.

The wind blew from Southampton Water like something bodily with a cutting edge to it, and it carried, too, with it a sharp sleet, that no clothing seemed sufficient to be proof against.

Mr. Oxley was rather uncomfortable.

"Hilloa! The horse-boat!" he shouted. "Hilloa! The ferry, here! Where the devil are you, you rascals?"

"Hoi! Here we are, master," said a rough voice, "but it ain't the best weather to stand out waiting for a fare, sir; so you see, sir, we make ourselves comfortable in the tap of the Duke's Head, hard by."

"Confound you!" said Oxley, "I don't care where you make yourselves comfortable. All I want of you is, that you put me across the water."

"Very good, sir. It's old Oxley," whispered one of the men to the other. "I wonder where he is going to-night."

"To the devil, I hope; and there, too, if I had my will, he should remain."

"Ay—ay, he had no business to discharge poor Roots."

"Not a bit of it. But here is Roots. Perhaps it will be better to tell him it's Mr. Oxley, and so send him back to the Duke's Head."

"Well, I don't know, mate. The fact is, there's a deuce of a swell coming in from the water outside to-night, and another hand, and that such a one as Roots, will be no bad thing when we get into the set of the current."

"That's true, so let him come; but I'll tell him who the passenger is, and then if he don't like it, he can leave it alone, you know."

"True—true. That's all fair."

While one of the ferrymen spoke to a tall man, wrapped up in an old great coat, who had lounged down to the beach, the other got the horse-boat in readiness for Oxley and his steed; and the steward, having dismounted, led the animal into the boat among the litter.

"He'll stand quiet, I suppose, sir?" said the man.

"Yes — yes," said Oxley, impatiently. "Why don't you push off?"

"Waiting for my mate, sir. Oh, here he is."

"Who is that with him? I thought there were but two of you ever at the ferry?"

"More there ain't, sir, in a usual way; but there's a strong current to-night, and this is a friend of ours who will help us to make way agin it, sir, that's all. We shall put you over all the easier, and quicker."

"Very well."

Oxley spoke to the man sharply in a tone of command, and their manner to him was that of men who feared the damaging power of the person to whom they spoke.

The horse-boat was now pushed off into the stream, and Oxley leant upon the saddle of his steed in deep thought, when the boat began to toss in the current, and he cried out—

"Steady, confound you all! Do you think that the horse can keep his feet in such a whirlagig concern as this? I'll have you all sent about your business, and put a new man on the ferry."

"Ah, just as you turned away Roots from his place at Bloxdale, and put a new man in it," said Roots, who now dropped his oar, and folding his arms across his chest looked sternly at the steward by the dim night light.

"Who are you?" said Oxley.

"Oh, you know well enough, Mr. Oxley. You ordered me to send about half-a-dozen heads of the best game the place afforded, some three or four times a-week, to a Mrs. Lerew, who lives in the white cottage, and, furthermore, you ordered me to say nothing about it to any one, but to be thankful that I could do you a favour."

"Hold your tongue, fellow!"

"I won't, fellow! Well, mates, I wouldn't do it, cos, you see, the game isn't old Oxley's no more than it is yours, and so

I got my discharge, and here I am, what Oxley has made me—a poacher."

"Hold your row, Roots," said one of the ferrymen.

"No I won't. I shan't have half so good an opportunity of speaking to him again, because, you see, now he can't very conveniently run away."

"I have nothing to say to you," said Oxley.

"Oh, but I have to you."

"I won't hear you."

"You shall. I tell you, Mr. Oxley, to your face, that you are a villain! a rank villain! A man without common feeling, without honesty, without justice; and I tell you that as sure as you live, and that I am here now, and with a touch could send you shrieking and choking into the boiling surge, I tell you the day will come when you will be paid off for your evil deeds."

Oxley shook with fear.

"Roots," he said, "I—that is—I will think about restoring you to your place again."

"No you won't."

"Yes—I—my good fellow, do be quiet."

"No, Mr. Oxley, you won't restore me my place again; I know you better than that. The fact is, you are half dead with fright now, and you would say anything in the world, or promise anything, you are in such a state of dread for fear I should pitch you overboard."

"No—no, I——"

"Don't say no to me, confound you, or I will do it!"

"My good fellow——"

"I ain't a good fellow. I was a good fellow till you wouldn't let me be one any longer; but I tell you that now I ain't a good fellow, for I poach upon other men's lands, and most of all upon Lord Bloxdale's. You—you, I say you have made me what I am, and I don't know at this moment what stops me from taking you by the throat, and dashing you to destruction, villain as you are."

"Murder!" screamed Oxley.

"Come—come, Roots," said one of the ferrymen, "be quiet, do. We can't have any nonsense here, you know. Mr. Oxley is our fare, and we are bound to put him on shore on the other side of the Itchen, all safe and sound, so we will do it."

"Five guineas a piece for you, my men," said Oxley, "if you protect me from that—that misguided individual."

"Oh," said Roots, "I am only a misguided individual now, am I? Why, I was a ruffian and a scoundrel, and everything else, the last time we parted at Bloxdale. Ha!—ha! What a difference. Well, old Oxley, I won't throw you into the Itchen, but I will let my two friends here do their duty, and put you over the river safe and sound, as they ought to do, and then—ha! ha!—and then——"

"Murder!" cried Oxley. "The man will

murder me! I call upon you both to protect me from that man."

"Oh, no, I didn't say I would murder you."

"Let him alone, Roots," said one of the men. "Let him alone."

"We shall see."

"Take an oar, and let him alone," said the other. He don't know what he's a-talking about, Mr. Oxley, you see; poor fellow, he takes a drop of drink since he lost his place, and that gets into his noddle, and then he don't know what he is about."

"Hem!" said Oxley, who began to feel pretty well assured that the two ferrymen would protect him from Roots, "I am very sorry for you, Roots, and I will speak to Lady Bloxdale to take you on again. Be a good fellow, now, and keep sober. Go back with your friends here, and all shall be well. I forgive you what you have said, I am sure, for I am the last man in the world to bear malice against any one."

"You forgive me!" cried Roots, springing up in the boat, and making a movement to approach Oxley. "You forgive me, villain that you are! I will——"

"Hold hard, Roots," said one of the ferrymen. "Think of your little girl. What is to become of her, poor little thing, if you get into trouble?"

Roots staggered back, and fell upon the tiller in the boat, as though he had been shot.

"My poor little May!" he sobbed. "I did, indeed, forget you! Oh, God, what, indeed, would become of you? My little May—my only one—the legacy of a dying wife and mother—I forgot you! yes, I let my passion get the better of me, and forgot you!"

Resting his head upon his hands, the poacher wept; and Oxley finding the horse-boat grating upon the beach on the opposite side of the Itchen said to the men in a low tone—

"Take him back, and when you come up to the hall to-morrow, you shall have a guinea a-piece; but mind you take him back with you, and don't think of bringing him over to this side. I shall, myself, be here in about an hour or so."

"Very good sir; but it's all right, you needn't be afraid of Roots now; he is as harmless as a baby. Whenever his little May is mentioned, it always takes his equality down, you see, sir. The little thing is only six years old, and it's mother is dead; so you see, Roots takes to it in a sort of way as I never seed afore."

"Ah," said Oxley, as he mounted the cob, "Very good—I daresay you are quite right. Good night."

"Good night, sir."

When Mr. Oxley got some distance from the road-side, and felt quite satisfied that Roots was not pursuing him, he uttered the most awful maledictions upon the head of the poacher that the mind of man could

conceive; and after calming down a little, he said—

"Oh, Master Roots, but I will be avenged upon you for this! I will lay some trap for you, you may depend, and you shall cross the seas, my fine fellow. I am not going to have my life rendered a scene of apprehension from fear of some day meeting you alone. No, no, Master Roots. We shall see—we shall see."

Oxley made his way by the back of the town of Southampton, and soon emerged some distance above the Avenue, as that beautiful walk is called upon the London road. A smart trot of some ten miles' distance conducted him to the common; and then looking carefully for a horse track to the left-hand side of the road, he found it, and plunged in among the trees.

The track that Oxley was now on narrowed so quickly, that he felt himself in a short time compelled to dismount, as the low branches of the trees struck him some rather sharp blows about the head and face.

Leading his horse by the bridle for some time, he suddenly paused, upon seeing a dim light at what appeared to be only a short distance from him in advance.

"That must be the hag's hut," he said.

Even as he spoke, a sort of screaming, derisive laughter came upon his ears, and he fancied that he saw something lying heaped up in a round mass close to his feet.

The fears of Mr. Oxley were very great, and he called out—

"It is I—it is Mr. Oxley! Don't fancy there is any danger. It is a friend."

The round mass at his feet uncoiled itself, but instead of presenting itself like any other human being, all that Oxley could see in the darkness was two feet about on a level with his chest, and he became aware that some imp-like looking being was standing on its head close to him.

"Who are you?" said Oxley, his teeth chattering in his head with fright. "Pray, who are you?"

"Flopperwoftlewoubuskottleinscreach!" said the imp.

"Good gracious, what a name!" said Oxley.

CHAPTER XVII.

MR. OXLEY THREATENS COURTLEY WITH A DISCLOSURE OF HIS SECRET.

THUS, then, another night has passed at Bloxdale Park, and the domestic turmoils still continue. Lord Francis Bloxdale was, if possible, more and more determined that he would rescue his father from the sad state of thraldom in which, to the disgrace of all concerned, he was held.

One of the means to that end was the certainty that the general accounts connected with the prosperity were well kept; for Lord

Francis felt that if he once got hold of the supplies, he should be soon able to convince his imperious mother that it would be prudent for her to come to terms with him, and submit with what grace she could.

For the accomplishment of this object Lord Francis waited, with some impatience, for Morris Courtley's report of the account auditing, which Mr Oxley had promised at noon on the day that had now arrived.

Morris Courtley himself, to tell the truth, felt as anxious as Lord Francis could possibly feel upon the occasion, for he well knew that he had enemies in Bloxdale Hall; and that the steward was one of them he had every reason in the world to think.

We do not mean to say that Courtley wished, for one moment, that there should be anything wrong in the accounts of Mr. Oxley; but he felt so confident that between him and Lady Bloxdale the accounts were anything but satisfactorily kept—that he expected some sort of explosion of the existing order of things, now that they were demanded by the young lord.

At the appointed hour, Morris Courtley was in the library, waiting with some impatience the appearance of Mr. Oxley, who came some few minutes or so after the proper time, and looking as placid and as confident as it was possible for any man to look.

Whatever had passed, upon the previous evening, between him and the witch in the wood on the common, had evidently not had a tendency in any way to impair his courage.

What did pass upon that occasion between the steward and the very cunning female, will be communicated to the reader in due time; but just at this juncture the general tenor of our plot requires that the interview between Mr. Oxley and Morris Courtley should be set forth clearly and distinctly, as contingent upon it ensued a variety of circumstances of real moment to all the parties at Bloxdale.

Who can help, to a certain degree, believing in presentiments? Certainly no one of an imaginative frame of mind can ever hope to protect himself from some lingering belief in them. However the judgment may be called in to set up its cold philosophical dictates against such matters, they will lay hold of the feelings; and so it was that as Morris Courtley had paced the library for some half hour before Mr. Oxley condescended to make his appearance, that he felt as if some terrible crisis was then at hand.

The secretary was not wrong in that feeling.

Mr. Oxley advanced with a world of courtesy towards Courtley; but it was that fulsome civility that an essentially vulgar mind can only dictate to the reader. It was far from being of the right sort, and Morris Courtley merely bowed in acknowledgment to it.

Oxley had with him several very large account books, and a mass of papers tied up with red tape.

"I am very much afraid, Mr. Courtley," said Oxley, "that I have kept you waiting; but, really, I could not help it, and hope that you have not been inconvenienced."

"It is of no consequence, Mr. Oxley; and if I had been inconvenienced, your apology is all sufficient. What you could not help, you cannot be blamed for."

"Thank you, Mr. Courtley. I have no doubt but that we shall come to a perfect understanding about these accounts. The fact is, I felt a little lazy this morning, and that was why I was not here sooner."

This was a calm and insolent defiance.

Courtley made no answer to so insolent and frittering away of the former apology; nor did he allow Mr. Oxley, whom he saw looking keenly at him, to see that he was galled by his insolence.

There can be no doubt in the world but that Oxley, with his high salary, and his tolerable little fortune that he had scraped together in the service of the Bloxdale family, thought himself a very superior person in social rank to poor Morris Courtley, the secretary, who was *only* a scholar and a gentleman.

But when did such qualities ever go for anything with the sordid, base, and ignorant souls that make up the staple of human nature? Never!

"I can't help thinking," added Oxley, "that Lord Francis would do better to go abroad again, as the countess orders him, than be making himself so busy about matters that he cannot possibly comprehend."

"Mr. Oxley," said Courtley, gravely, "it neither becomes you nor me to discuss upon the private motives and feelings of the family whose bread we eat."

"Ah, very likely. I don't think, though, that anybody is listening."

"Listening?"

"Yes; you speak as if you thought one of the family whose bread we eat were listening to you, Mr. Courtley. But I assure you we are alone, so it will do no good to spout about virtue, and all that nonsense."

"Sir?"

"Oh, Mr. Courtley, it is of no use for you to get into a passion with me, I assure you. I am an independent man, sir."

An angry reply was upon the lips of Courtley; but one glance at the object of his resentment had the effect of subduing it. His contempt for Oxley was so great, that he felt at the moment how very much beneath him a quarrel with such a man would be. It struck him, moreover, from the manner of the steward, that he came prepared to try and provoke one; so Morris Courtley was put thoroughly upon his guard, and he said quite calmly—

"Mr. Oxley, as I have been deputed by Lord Francis Bloxdale to look over your accounts, and as I have no desire for your society one moment longer than is necessary, I will trouble you to be as speedy as possible in placing me in possession of the necessary documents."

"Ha! ha! Oh, to be sure. Certainly, sir. With all due humility, of course. Well, sir, here we begin. The total amount I have received on account of the Earl of Bloxdale, from the twelfth of January last past, amounts to sixteen thousand pounds, and some odd money."

"Odd money, sir?"

"Yes, odd money!"

"Allow me to suggest that you name the exact amount."

"Oh, very well; the odd money amounts to six hundred and thirty-seven pounds eight shillings. Will that do?"

"I don't know."

"Oh, you don't know?"

"How can I know? I have only your word for such being the amount of your receipts. Of course, it will be for Lord Francis to verify the fact."

"Only my word, sir! Then you doubt it?"

"I certainly do."

"Then, sir, I can tell you——"

"Stop, sir! If I have any more insolence from you, I shall be at the pains of kicking you out of the library, and then reporting to Lord Francis, that in lieu of coming here to balance your accounts, you came to pick a quarrel. I give you the option of quietly proceeding from this moment, or of courting the alternative I have mentioned."

"As to kicking me, Mr. Courtley," said Oxley, turning white with passion, "you cannot afford it, sir; and so we will go on. If I am wrong in the account I state, that is my look out. I will now account for the amount I have mentioned to you. If you look down the page of this book, you will see it accounted for."

Courtley did look down the page of a book, which professed to give a list of disbursements to the amount of sixteen thousand six hundred and thirty-seven pounds eight shillings; but upon carefully adding the column of figures up, Courtley found a serious error, and turning to Oxley, he said quite calmly—

"There is something wrong here, even in the sum, before we proceed to say anything about vouchers."

"Oh, indeed!"

"Yes, Mr. Oxley. The total is one thousand pounds short of what you make it."

"Ha! ha! I know that," said Oxley, as he suddenly closed the book with a vehemence that made a noise that echoed through the library.

"You know it, sir?"

"Oh, yes, I know it; and what then?"

"What then, sir?"

"Dear me, Mr. Courtley, I am very sorry that all you can do is to echo my words—very sorry, indeed; and so all I can do is to repeat them, and I, too, say as I have already said—'What then?'"

"Mr. Oxley, this is a mere farce," said Morris Courtley, as he rose and looked sternly at the steward, who for a moment or two quailed before the honest indignant look of the young man. "This is a mere farce, sir. God only knows what your motive may be in thus conducting yourself; but be it what it may, my duty is clearly and plainly before me."

"Indeed, sir?"

"Yes. It is to report to Lord Francis Bloxdale what has occurred at this interview. Be assured that I shall tell all, aggravating nothing, but keeping back nothing."

"We shall see that."

"We shall, sir. Good morning."

Oxley found some difficulty now, with all his insolence and arrogance, in holding his way against the calm dignity of Morris Courtley, but he had not yet winged the shaft that he meant should reach the heart of the young and accomplished secretary.

After one hasty glance around him, as if a shadow of suspicion that they might not be alone had crossed his mind, although he had no grounds whatever for such an idea, Oxley fixed his eyes upon Morris Courtley, and spoke in a low, deliberate voice—

"Mr. Courtley, I do not depend upon the friendly feeling of any man in this world, but I do depend upon the feelings of interest—self-interest, which all men have; and, therefore, I depend upon you, sir."

"Upon me?"

"Yes. Pray hear me out. It is true—strictly true, that I am deficient in my accounts. If I had time I might be able to put all to rights; but I have not, it appears; for in the exercise of your office, and the profound character of your great virtue, you will go to the young Lord Bloxdale, and blurt out the whole truth about the thousand pounds deficiency.'

Courtley slightly inclined his head in token of assent to this proposition, and looked fixedly at Mr. Oxley.

"Yes, I quite understand that that is your determination, Mr. Courtley, unless I show you reasons to alter it."

"Show me reasons to alter it, Mr. Oxley?"

"Oh, yes; all men have their little secrets, my good sir."

Courtley shrunk back as he would from the touch of a reptile as Oxley stretched his ugly head and form over the table that was between them.

"Yes, my good young friend, all men have their little secrets. I have mine. It is here"—Oxley dealt the account-book a blow with his open hand—"It is connected with these accounts. Well, you have yours."

"I?"

"Oh, yes, Mr. Courtley; but where is the harm. You can do me a favour, and I can do you one. Why should we set about wrangling and contending together, when we may be of such immense mutual benefit to each other?—I say, immense benefit. I can, and will do much for you—all that you desire; and you may, if you please, save an explanation just now that, I candidly admit, would have the effect of damaging my plans at present."

"Damaging your plans, sir?"

Poor Courtley spoke in a low tone, and his colour went and came like the sun of an April day. Oxley saw the triumph he had obtained temporarily over the fears of the young secretary—those fears that were not for himself, but which pointed all to Lady Fanny. The terrible thought came over Courtley that her secret—Lady Fanny's secret, was known to the fiend in human shape, Oxley—and from that moment he began clearly to comprehend the scene that had just taken place.

The coy, nonchalant impertinence of Oxley—the cool, seeming indifference with which he had taken the discovery of the defalcation in his accounts, and the odious manner in which he had tried to intimate that they might make common cause together in the conservation of each other's secrets, all came across the brain of the secretary with lightning-like rapidity, and he looked with loathing upon the grinning, sneaking, animal-like face before him.

With a deep sigh, Courtley sunk back into the chair from which he had so recently risen, and glared at Oxley with some such feeling as one might look at some monster, from whose fangs the problem of extraction seemed preternaturally difficult.

Oxley looked upon his triumph as certain.

"Ha—ha!" he said, for it was not a laugh. "Ha—ha! Mr. Courtley, you see, I am quite an old fox. Oh, quite. You did not know me, now, did you—candidly speaking, you did not know me? But come, there is not the slightest occasion for you to look so down as you do. I will be your friend."

"My friend?"

"Yes, and why not? You can be mine. I am an old man compared to you, although none so old in point of actual years. I have my objects, and you have yours. We will make common cause. Ha! ha!"

"Common cause?"

"Why, yes; hang it all, it comes to this: I have made the most of my situation, and I admit to you, as I feel I may do, that the accounts are not as they ought to be; and you will keep my secret because I know that you love Lady Fanny! Ha! ha!"

"Love—Lady—Fanny! Oh, a dream! A dream!"

Courtley covered his face with both his hands, and rocked to and fro in the chair in agony of spirit.

"Yes, you do," added Oxley, rubbing his hands together, and quite enjoying his triumph over the secretary, "yes, you do, and you know it, and she knows it, too; and what is more, she reciprocates the feeling, as the song says. Ha! ha! and she comes here and meets you, and she meets you in the picture-gallery; and, in fact, you and Lady Fanny—I admire your taste—quite understand each other. But she is a lady of title —the heiress to immense wealth, and the descendant of a noble family, while you are the poor dependant, Morris Courtley; and if the earl only thought for a moment that a daughter of his could stoop so low, it would make him idiotic as he is mad—mad—quite mad; and the countess would kill Lady Fanny, I do think, and Lord Francis would, in his quiet way, show you the door, Mr. Morris Courtley—that is to say, if I tell them. Ha! ha!"

Courtley still rocked to and fro.

"But I won't," added Oxley; "don't you be afraid. As long as you credit my accounts, and just say to Lord Francis that all's right, you understand why, I am mum as a stockfish about your little affair, you see, and what's more, I'll give you a helping hand when I can. I don't care what you do in the affair, not I. You may marry her, or you may seduce her, if you like.—Ha! ha! I daresay she——"

Courtley sprang from his seat with a short, sharp cry, and flung himself upon the steward. To grasp him by the throat, to shake him too and fro till his jaw dropped, and he was half dead with fear, and half choked besides—to drag him to the door of the library, and then with one kick, to send him sprawling some twenty feet along the hall, were all the actions of Courtley's that were comprised in the next half-minute of time, and then the library door was closed again, and Courtley staggered to the seat by the old fireside, and fell into it more dead than alive.

The servants in the hall, which was close at hand, heard the fall of Oxley, and his cries of "Murder!" when he recovered speech sufficient to give utterance to that sound, and in a body they rushed towards him to see what was the matter.

His cravat hanging loosely round his neck —his coat torn, and blood upon his face, while his eyes seemed to be starting from their sockets, the steward presented a terrific spectacle.

"Murder!" he shouted, "help! murder!"

They raised him from the ground: he fought at them with insane rage, and then he fell fainting, and lay perfectly insensible.

In the meantime Morris Courtley had so far recovered as to feel all the perils of his position. He clasped his hands and murmured out the name of Fanny, in an agony of grief; for he felt that it was upon her gentle head that the storm which he might, if he chose defy, would break.

"My love, my life!" he cried. "Oh, how shall I shield you from the villany of this man, whom I have now defied and angered past all conciliation? Fanny! Fanny!—my own, my beautiful, our love will be to you a curse and a desolation!"

"Morris," said a low, soft voice. "Oh, Morris!"

THE QUARREL IN THE LIBRARY ABOUT THE ACCOUNTS BETWEEN MORRIS COURTLEY
AND OXLEY.

CHAPTER XVIII.

RELATES WHAT PREDICTION THE WITCH FAVOURED MR. OXLEY WITH.

COURTLEY sprang to his feet as though from the impulse of a shock of electricity. One of the tall painted windows of the library, that looked into the flower-garden, was gently opened, and Lady Fanny, trembling and agitated, appeared at the entrance, and protruded her little hands and her beautiful head, with its myriads of waving curls with which it was adorned, through the window. At that moment she appeared to Morris Courtley far more beautiful than he had ever seen her look. Perhaps in consequence of the haste she had made, and the information she had received, the blood mantled to her cheeks with greater speed than was its usual wont when nothing disturbed her gentle spirit.

She had a heightened colour, and her voice was tremulous as she spoke.

"Oh, Morris, I saw that you were here alone, and thought that I might not have a better opportunity of saying that which I have to say."

"Alone—alone!" he sighed. "Shun me, Fanny—oh, shun me, dear one. You know not—No—no! When you go, the sunshine has gone likewise. I must speak to you."

"If you help me, Morris, I can come into the library."

Distracted by the dangers that surrounded him and her, and yet so delighted even at the touch of her little hand, that he could not resist the beautiful seduction, Morris Courtley tremblingly assisted her into the library, and placed her in the old chair by the fireside. He then crept to the immense oak door, and shot a bolt that kept it fast from all intrusion, and quietly, then, he came back to where the dear one was seated, and knelt at her feet, and looked up into the fair child-like face with such an aspect of delight, mingled with the very agony of grief, that Fanny's tears began to crowd on her eyelids, and she trembled to feel assured, that although she had come to give an alarm to Morris that something had happened inimical to their love he had that to tell her which might be of ten times the moment.

"Morris!—Morris! you are ill!"

"No, love—oh, no!"

"But you tremble, Morris; and you are so pale!"

"Dearest and best! you too are sad!"

He took her hands in his and held them to his lips; and then she smiled upon him, as she said—

"How foolish I am, Morris. But my mother has commanded that I leave Bloxdale this day week."

"Leave Bloxdale?"

"Yes. She says that it is time I saw a little of the world, and she is about to send me to London, to a Lady Rockington, who, she says is the leader of the fashion. Oh, Morris, what care I for fashion?"

"Lady Rockington?"

"Yes, Morris. Do you know her?"

"The lady was here some months since upon a visit to your mother; but I do not wonder that you saw little of her. She is a mass of false pride, vanity, and sensuality. Is it to such keeping that your mother would consign you? Oh, no—no!"

"Then I won't go, Morris. Why should I go, if you disapprove of it? Have not I, wilful as I am, said a hundred times that I would only do just what you like, my Morris?"

"Oh, Fanny—Fanny! there is another danger that, before a week has elapsed, will, I fear, alter the whole aspect of affairs here."

"Another danger?"

"Yes; our secret—the innocent secret of our love—for surely it is an innocent secret, when the love is innocent and humble—is known to one who will use it to our ruin."

"Oh, Morris, who?—who is it?"

"Oxley!"

"Then, indeed, we are lost."

Lady Fanny burst into tears; and, now, Morris Courtley felt that it was for him to play another part than to weep, and he strove to comfort the young creature in whose bosom he had lit the flame of an affection which was to be undying.

"Fanny—Fanny!" he said, "it is true that we love, but ours is not a love for which we should weep. It is a pure affection, which will, and which no doubt has, won the approval of Heaven. Never, by thought, word, or deed, has aught unworthy of either of us mingled with the tender sentiment of our affection. We may be accused of affection, but nothing more. The word leaves no blush upon our cheeks."

"Oh, no—no, Morris!"

"Then, do not weep."

"But, my poor Morris!"

"Yes; I—I am poor Morris."

"Oh, I did not mean that. I meant, that others would not think as I think—I meant, that others, who did not know you as I know you, would say that, because you are not noble, not wealthy, you should not aspire—they will call it aspire—to one such as I am. But I, Morris—I feel, that in your love I am only truly distinguished, for the affection of an honest heart is an incident of our existence, greater and nobler than all the accidents of birth or wealth. Is it not so, my Morris?"

"It is—it is, my dearest—it is! But the world will not think with us. Ah, no—no! It will accuse me of the base wish to drag you down to my level, in order that the vanity of one who has nothing but his heart to offer might be gratified by so noble a connection. But—but, Fanny, you will be told that my motives were unworthy. All the eloquence of those who will seem to bear all the reason upon their side, will be brought to bear upon you, to convince you of the evils of a misalliance."

"I shall heed them not, Morris."

"But you will suffer so much in the struggle that is to come, that if my death—"

"Morris—Morris! why do you speak thus to me? If you will die, I will die likewise! We will be united then in the grave, if we may not be upon this earth! Oh, Morris, what dreadful thoughts you fill my poor brain with!"

"I did not mean to do so."

A violent knocking at the door of the library at this moment attracted their attention, and Morris started to his feet; for he had hitherto preserved the kneeling posture by Fanny.

"What is that?" she cried—"oh, what is that?"

"The door."

"Let me fly, Morris—oh, let me fly!"

"Yes; some one comes. If you are found here, it will be the most flat confirmation of all that Oxley dares to say."

"Stop, Morris—stop!"

"Oh, no—no! The window which has enabled you to come here, will aid your escape."

The knocking at the door continued.

"Yes, I am going. But, Morris, you dreaded a confirmation of all that Oxley could say. Now, he can only say that I love you, and that you love me, and we must ourselves confess that much. We must not prevaricate with our own hearts, Morris. We must confess all. There needs no arrangement—no concealment. We will admit, and we will justify our love."

"Oh, sweet saint! when shall I ever be worthy of you?"

"You are worthy."

The knocking was more violent, and a voice cried—

"Courtley—Courtley! Are you here?"

It was the voice of young Lord Francis.

Poor Fanny turned now as pale as death itself, and she trembled so when she heard the voice of her brother, that she was scarcely able, even with the assistance of Morris Courtley, to get out at the low window from the library to the garden, and yet it was but a step. Courtley folded her for one moment in his arms, and kissed the pale cheek, and then she glided from him, and he sprung to the door.

"Courtley—Courtley! Are you here?" cried Lord Francis again.

Morris Courtley withdrew the bolt, and the door yielded. Young Lord Francis entered the library.

"Why, Morris," he said, "why did you make the door fast? Were you asleep that you did not hear me?"

"I am not very well," said Courtley, avoiding the question, for his repugnance to even a concerted lie was so great, that he would do anything rather than utter one.

"I am sorry, indeed, to hear that, Courtley."

Morris felt from the tone of Lord Francis that, as yet, he knew nothing :and, although he felt that that was a state of ignorance that would not last, under the circumstances, very long, it was yet a relief for the present. Lord Francis flung himself into a seat, and in a tone, the friendly confidence of which cut Courtley to the heart, he said—

"Oh, my friend, what can I say to the countess? Another scene with her only just now."

"Yes—I—that is, indeed," said Courtley.

"And all about Fanny this time."

"Fanny!" gasped Courtley. "Lady—Fanny!"

"Yes, all about her, poor girl; for you know, Courtley, that, after all, she is but a girl. One might almost say a child."

"Yes," said Courtley faintly, but he knew not what he said. If Lord Francis had asserted that Fanny was an elephant, Courtley just then, in the state of mind he was in, would have said yes.

"Just so," added Lord Francis. "Now, would you believe it, Courtley, my mother has taken it into her head that Fanny should take a plunge into fashionable life in London; and she has hit upon one of the most abominable of women to be the chaperon of the poor young thing—a Lady Rockington."

"Ah!" said Courtley.

"But I must prevent it. I plainly told my mother that it should not be, and that it would be sacrificing the girl. Why, who shall say but that, with her kind, unsuspicious, susceptible nature—for she is quite an infant in the ways of the world, and a little kindness goes a long way with her—but she might be actually picked up by some needy adventurer?"

"Some needy adventurer?" said Courtley.

"Exactly so ; and there would be a pretty piece of business! Well, I and the countess are at war upon that point. She says Fanny shall go this day week, and I say she shall not."

"She shall not!" said Morris.

"Certainly not. But, oh! Courtley, how weary I am of this constant contention at home, and how detestable it is to all concerned, is it not? I am quite sick at heart."

"And so am I," said Courtley.

"My dear friend, I well know your generous sympathy with me, and your deep and disinterested interest in all that concerns the family. If I could only induce my father to rouse himself up to make a firm stand, much might be done."

"Oh, yes."

"A child like that! Why, Heaven only knows what ideas that Rockington woman might put into her head—she who now is as innocent as a sucking dove, poor little thing."

"Quite."

"Ah, Courtly, if I could only bring about a match between her some of these days and a young friend of mine, Lord Meadowbout! He is the son of the Duke of Naesby; and as fine, frank, and open-hearted a young fellow as ever I met with. We were inseparable at Venice."

"Very," said Courtley.

"But my peculiar horror is, that some smooth-tongued fellow of low origin, and not worth a farthing, and whose grandfather nobody knows, should get hold of her, and pour the insidious poison of his flattery into her ears. I do think I could kill him, if such were to take place ; and they tell me that that odious Lady Rockington has always what she calls a *protege* of the male sex whom she desires to get well married ; and that is the sort of woman my mother would send Fanny to."

"The very sort," said Courtley.

"Eh?"

"I—I—said the—the——"

"Why, Courtley, you are ill."

"Oh, no—no! A thousand pounds, if it be my destruction to tell you, I will. Mr. Oxley is deficient in his accounts, according to his own story, in the sum of one thousand pounds. What more may be discovered upon a careful revision of his statements I cannot say ; but that is the first discovery."

"The rascal!"

Morris Courtley held up both his hands, and in a tremulous voice he said—

"Thank God I have done my duty!"

"Why, what is the matter with you, Courtley? You don't seem at all yourself to-day. I am certain you are ill."

"No—no—I—that is, I only——"

Courtley rose and staggered, and Lord Francis rose at the same moment to assist him, for he thought he would fall, when something went crash under the foot of the young noble.

"Why, what is this?" he said. "An ivory fan! Why, whose is it? I declare it is the very one I brought from Naples, and gave to Fanny. Has she been here, Courtley?"

The door of the library was opened at this moment, and a footman said, respectfully—

"Mr. Oxley, my lord, presents his dutiful respects, and begs to know if, at your lordship's convenience, you could favour him with a private interview?"

CHAPTER XIX.

THE WITCH OF SOUTHAMPTON COMMON PROMISES GREAT THINGS TO OXLEY.

WHEN Mr. Oxley was in the wood, lying to the left of the common of Southampton, he had scarcely expected to be terrified by any supernatural appearances.

The power of prophecy which the reputed witch had, had never been associated with any tales of that character; but when the singular being whom, it will be recollected, he met upon his route appeared before him, the guilty steward shook in every limb with the idea that it was from a darker intelligence than he had been aware of that she derived her knowledge.

Oxley felt at that moment as if he would have given anything to have found himself in safety at Bloxdale again; and yet his curiosity to know what the old hag would say to him was so great, that it prevented him from turning away, as no doubt he might have done, and regaining his route homewards.

The mysterious figure with the lurid light, that cast a strange, metallic-like lustre upon the branches of the old trees, went on before him, and the steward followed with fear and trembling.

Sometimes the elfin-looking figure would trot on after the fashion of any ordinary mortal; but at others it would take a fancy to going upon its hands with its heels stuck up in the air, and now and then it would execute a somersault, and utter a strange scream, as if quite delighted in the office of guide to Mr. Oxley.

What astounded the steward, too, was that in all these evolutions of the twisting sprite the light did not go out, and his fears forced him to associate a supernatural character to the appearance.

Once or twice he thought he would speak to the strange being; but as often as he tried to do so, his fears overcame him, and he did not feel able to utter a sound.

The route that Oxley's odd conductor took was into the thickest part of the wood, and no doubt such a route in the summer time, as well as being one of singular beauty, would have been all but impassible.

They passed a little streamlet, then frozen over, and into which Mr. Oxley went up to his knees, owing to the thinness of the ice in that sheltered situation; but the sprite appeared to skim over it without the slightest indentation of its glossy surface.

It is quite surprising how any stern and ordinary reality puts to flight any imaginative fears. The immersion of Mr. Oxley's feet in the little partially-frozen stream made him quite a different man for a few minutes, and he cursed and swore as if there were no such things as witches and elfins in the world; and in his solemn moods, he firmly believed in both.

Upon this ebullition of wrath on the part of Oxley, the imp seemed to be so delighted that he made the most ridiculous antics that can be imagined, and certainly very much endangered the safety of the light.

Oxley cooled down then a little and blundered on; upon which the elfin, suddenly darting into a narrow pathway that seemed quite impervious to his feet, disappeared.

Oxley paused.

"Where the deuce am I now?" he said.

"Ha—ha!" laughed a voice close to him.

Oxley gave a start, and fell into a bramble-bush, as he cried out—

"Keep off—keep off, now!! I don't want to be plagued here. I have come to seek Mother what's-her-name, the witch."

"Nerminia!" said a voice.

"Eh?"

"It is Nerminia you come to seek. Advance!"

"Well, that may be her name; but as to advancing, I don't know about that, for I can't see an inch before me. Which way am I to go? I am a respectable man, and, of course, mean to pay for the information I ask. But I am half dead with cold, and scratched terribly with the brambles. Where is the—the—what do you call him with the light?"

"Behold!"

What Mr. Oxley was to behold, seemed to be a blue light among the bushes, which trembled and sputtered for a few moments and then expired; but, he understood, or fancied he understood, that it was intended as a guide to his progress, so he proceeded as well as he could in the direction it pointed out, and found himself in a few moments free of the entanglements of the underwood of the mimic forest, and upon a clear space of about thirty feet square, a portion of which was filled up by the witch's hovel.

Through the solitary window of that miserable abode there shone a strong reddish-looking light.

"I'm sorry I came," said Oxley to himself; "but as I am here, I should like to know what she has to say to me."

A loud scream at this moment burst upon the night air, and Oxley fell to the ground with fright. His nervous system was not in a very good state before that sudden alarm, but now he was, to use his own expression, all of a shake.

It is highly probable that the precise object of the loud scream was to produce some such an effect upon the nerves of the seeker into the secrets of futurity.

After a few moments, now, a voice called out—

"Who approaches?"

"It is I," said Oxley. "Don't you know me?"

"I know," said the voice, "that it was one whom fortune delights to favour, and now I know the name of the minion. It is Oxley."

"Yes, I am Mr. Oxley. I said I would come and see you, and here I am, your friend; but I really thought I should never get here."

"You were sure to get here."

"I don't know that."

"Yes, you were quite sure to get here. It was your destiny to come here to-night, and not the whole world could have kept you away. Enter! The door is open. Enter!"

The door of the hut was opened, and within the whole atmosphere seemed to be full of the strange red light that had streamed through the window and guided him to the spot. The moment Mr. Oxley, though, crossed the threshold, the door shut with a loud report, and the red light, the source of which he had not had time to discover, disappeared, leaving the interior of the cottage in a state of the most intense darkness.

"Where is the light?" said Oxley.

"Gone a wandering," said a voice.

"A light gone wandering? What do you mean by that?"

"It was only borrowed, and its time was up. It has gone back again to its master."

"Oh, well, I don't pretend to understand all that sort of thing, of course; but I come here to ask some questions, just out of curiosity, you know, nothing more; but I would rather have a light here."

"There is light enough to discover what you come here for, and what you want to know. You do not come for mere curiosity."

"Indeed?"

"No, you do not. If you did the spirits of the unseen world would answer you nothing. You come in faith, and that is what they ever require as a condition of their revelations being heard by mortal ears."

"Oh, well—be it so."

"Convince us that you have not that faith, and you may as well depart at once, for you will know nothing here."

"Well—well, I do come in faith, then. I suppose I must be tolerably explicit as to what I want to know?"

"Not so. Your soul has been read."

"My soul read? I don't understand what you mean by that."

"I mean that your motives are known."

"Well, if you can convince me of that, it will go to strengthen the faith that you say is necessary for me to have."

"Hiss!" cried something, and in a moment, from some vessel upon the floor, a bright green light sprung up like a tall column of flame for a moment, and then disappeared as quickly as it came.

"Down! down!" said the voice. "Down, dread spirit!"

"What was that?" said Oxley, in a voice of alarm.

"Amelli!"

"What? Who?"

"A spirit. Be not alarmed—it has gone again. It will come no more to-night. But what does it matter?—there will be one more potent than he was or ever will be. Oxley, you are engaged in a transaction that will make you or ruin you in this world for all time to come that may yet make up your mortal pilgrimage."

"Well, it may be so."

"But," added the voice, "another grasps at the jingle of worldly title, while to your eyes the pleasant music of countless hoards of gold will be a more delightful acceptation. Vanity will be delighted with the empty sound of a name, while your enlarged experience will prefer the solid value of wealth. Is it so?"

"Why, in a manner of speaking," said Oxley, in a low tone, "I may say that it is."

"Where is Peter?" said a strange voice.

"Eh?"

"Answer," said the voice which Oxley had recognised, in the first instance, as that of the hag. "Answer him at once. One of the spirits asks the question of you, and they are an impatient race."

"I don't know then," said Oxley.

Hiss! came an odd sound again, and a blue flame sprung up right to the ceiling of the hut, even as the green one had done only a few minutes before, and the hag, whom he, Oxley, could just see crouching on the floor, cried out—

"No, no! Down—oh, down!"

The flame disappeared.

"What is the meaning of this?" said Oxley, shaking with apprehension, although he tried to give his voice a firm expression and tone.

"I hardly know," was the reply. "But the spirits are more impatient to-night than I have ever known them to be. They will not bide their time. But I do not say that they come in anger; if they did, I should advise you to go at once."

"Oh," said Oxley, "you are sure—that is to say, you think that there is no danger at present?"

"There is none at all."

"Very good. I will pay you anything in reason, now, if you will say whether I shall be successful in what I am trying to do in the affair which you have spoken of, and which you seem to know all about as well as I do."

"I will consult the spirits. But first of all, I will ask you if I am right in what I shall say to them."

"I will answer you."

"In the first place, you are the steward of the Bloxdale property, and you have overdrawn your accounts."

"Well, go on."

"Then, you have married a Mrs. Lerew."

"I have."

"And she has a son named Peter."

"Go on."

"You have discovered that previous to the marriage of the Earl of Bloxdale to the countess, he knew something of this Mrs. Lerew, and that she did all in her power to entangle him in the meshes of an intrigue with her, in order that she might have an after-hold upon his purse."

"Yes, I——"

Something came swinging through the air, and fell heavily at the farther end of the hut."

"What's that?" said Oxley.

The witch laughed.

"There is a spirit at hand," she said, "who does not approve of the way in which I am telling the story, that is all. But that is of no consequence. The spirit is a foolish one, and may hurt itself much more than it can possibly hurt me. Is what I have said true?"

"All," said Oxley.

"Well, this woman, Lerew, failed in her intention, for the earl had an aversion to her; and some time after that she married the man Lerew, who was but a low professional man of London. He died, leaving her with Peter, who was apprenticed to a Jew attorney named Jacobs. Peter is out of his apprenticeship just now and has all the cunning of his employer engrafted upon all the dexterity of an originally bad disposition."

"Well, Peter is a kind of——"

"You need say no more. I will tell you all. The object that you and Peter and Mrs. Lerew have in view is rather a pretty little plot. It is just this:"

"Don't speak loud," said Oxley.

"Oh, there are none but the subtle spirits of another world to listen to us in this place. You have nothing to fear from any mortal ears."

"Well, you are a wonderful woman. Pray go on."

"I will. Your object, then, is to try to substantiate, by fraud and good management, the pretended fact that the Earl of Bloxdale was positively married to Mrs. Lerew before his marriage with the present countess, and that, consequently, Peter is his son, and heir to the estates."

"Well, I—that is——"

"Do not deny it. You and Mrs. Lerew either wish to press the claim to absolute expulsion, and so place you all in Bloxdale as owners of the vast property—your marriage with Mrs. Lerew being kept a profound secret—or to extract from the Bloxdale family an enormous sum to waive the claims altogether, and not litigate it at all."

"Well—hem! that is——"

"The truth. You know it."

"I suppose, then, under the circumstances, there is no use in disputing it?"

"None in the least. Your errand here, then, is to ascertain if the project will be a success or a failure?"

Bang! went something in the hut, like the discharge of a gun, and a bright red flame shot up to the ceiling, while a strange croaking voice cried—

"When L. and P. and O.,
On Bloxdale fair cast eyes,
The ancient lineage pass away
Like vapour in the skies.

"Let me go, I can bear no more!"

The flame disappeared.

"What does that mean?" said Oxley, in a tremulous voice.

"It is favourable," said the witch. "Will you consult another?"

"No—that is, yes, I will."

"Silence, then. Do not, as you value your life, utter a word."

Another loud report ensued, and a violet coloured flame of great beauty lit up the dingy hovel, converting it for a few brief moments into a very fairy palace of beauty.

Then a voice, different from the other, and deep and hollow in its tone, shouted out, while Oxley held his very breath for fear and dread, lest he should lose any of the tones—

"He who humbly waited,
Waited on shall be;
He who bowed to others,
Will see others bend the knee."

"Enough—enough."

The flame disappeared, and the witch said—

"Oxley cast gold upon the floor at your feet. I can tell you that the prophetic greetings of the spirits are in the highest degree favourable. You will be completely successful."

"I rejoice to hear it," said Oxley. "I shall now pursue the affair with some degree of spirit. I have cast ten guineas on the floor, and if I can do you any favour, you have only to send to the castle, and it shall be my great pleasure to do it."

"You had better go, now," said the witch; "the sprits are getting restive again. I can hear them."

A strange hissing noise rather alarmed Oxley, and he hastily left the hut. How he got through the wood, and over the Itchen, and finally home to Bloxdale Hall, he hardly knew himself, he was in such an agitated frame of mind; but he did, without encountering any danger by the way, reach the mansion.

Throwing himself into a chair, he cried out in a tone of exultation—

"I shall succeed—I shall succeed! All will be as I wish! Glorious—glorious!"

CHAPTER XX.

MR. OXLEY COMMUNICATES TO THE COUNTESS COURTLEY'S LOVE FOR LADY FANNY.

WHEN Mr. Oxley, after the sudden and unexpected attack that the secretary had made upon him, mused sufficiently to ask himself what he should do, his rage prompted him, as Courtley fully expected it would, to a speedy carrying out of his threat to declare to all concerned the love of the secretary for Lady Fanny Bloxdale.

Oxley mused in his mind for a little time as to whether he should let the countess or Lord Francis know first.

After considering the matter a little, he determined upon informing the countess of the fact, for he thought it highly probable that if he, in the first instance, addressed himself to Lord Francis, that young nobleman might lay upon him the interdict of secrecy to all others regarding the affair, and try to hush it up, as he was so attached to both his sister and to Courtley.

" No—no, I will be beforehand with him there," said Oxley. " I will tell the countess, and then it will be too late for Lord Francis to try to arrange a matter that, after the first flush of vexation, will probably appear to him each moment less and less guilty. I will inflame the mind of the countess with the idea that the whole affair is a plot concocted by Francis, Fanny, and Courtley, and we shall see what her ladyship's ire will effect. Let the consequences to all parties be what they may, they must be favourable to me and my plans. The more dissension there is here, the better for me. I will seek her now at once."

It was while Morris Courtley and Lady Fanny were having the agitated interview that they had had in the library that Oxley, with all the evidences of the recent conflict with the secretary about him, sought the apartments of the countess, to tell her all he knew, and a little more.

The waiting woman of the countess, who, it will be recollected, was quite in the confidence of Mr. Oxley, or, perhaps, we might say, that he for the present was in her confidence, was rather astonished to see the state of agitation in which so very great a man as Mr. Oxley was in; and the idea that something uncommonly serious regarding the accounts had occurred struck her at once.

" Oh, Mr. Oxley! what is it—oh, what is it?"

" Pray, don't be alarmed. I must see the countess."

" Yes, but——"

" For Heaven's sake—that is—hem! for the sake of the other place as well—let me beg that you will ask me nothing just now; but say to the countess that I wish to see her upon a matter of the very greatest importance, concerning which I will do myself the honour and the favour of consulting you, Miss Wicks, as soon as I have possessed her ladyship of the facts."

Upon this Miss Wicks made the desired communication to her mistress, and in such a fashion, too, as to excite the countess's curiosity very much.

" Admit Mr. Oxley."

The countess, to tell the truth, was neither in a very amiable nor very self-satisfied mood, for she had been deeply considering the peculiar circumstances in which she was placed, and just a little trembling at their possible result.

When Oxley made his appearance, then, is the countess's boudoir, he saw that there wan a cloud upon her ladyship's brow, rather, as his step-son, Peter, would have said.

" Well, sir."

" Madam, I—that is, I deeply regret that I feel myself bound by the duty I owe to your ladyship to be the bearer of intelligence that—that I much fear——"

" Pray speak your message, Mr. Oxley, at once. I am rather occupied, and would be glad to know quickly whether this matter of which you have to speak be or be not one that calls for any special attention from me."

" Your ladyship will be induced to admit that it does. I have to state that your daughter, Lady Fanny, and Mr. Courtley, the secretary, are—I don't know what to call it, but in my humble sphere, I should say engaged—or keeping company—or courting or—or——"

" Or what, sir?"

" Intriguing!"

The countess advanced two steps towards Oxley, with such an expression of face that he was alarmed, and had serious thoughts of escaping from the room, now that he had done all the mischief he possibly could; but as she paused, he, too, paused, and then, when she sank into a chair with a sigh, Oxley could hardly refrain from a smile of congratulation to himself at the idea that he had so far succeeded in bending the haughty spirit of that imperious woman.

" Mr. Oxley."

" Madam."—Oxley bowed very low.

" Be careful, sir, what you say."

" I am—I will, my lady."

" Are you, then, quite—sure that—that—"

" Quite, my lady. Your ladyship will permit me only to make one condition in this matter, and that is, that I may not be asked to give up the name of my informant; but as that can have no bearing upon the fact, it is of trivial importance. I beg to state that I could not help, when I heard of such being the case, remonstrating upon the impropriety of such a proceeding with——"

" With whom, sir?—Not my daughter?"

" Oh, no, my lady; that would have been a freedom I could not, for one moment, have dreamt of. I spoke of the poor young man— the secretary—the—I don't know what to call him: the poor, wretched dependant, who lives here more upon charity, and by flattering the weaknesses of the earl, and by inflaming the mind of Lord Francis against one whom he ought to respect and obey——"

" Silence!"

Oxley bowed. He did not want to finish his speech; he knew that the couneess, in her heart, finished it for him. She rose and paced the room with evident agitation; and then, suddenly pausing opposite to the steward, she said sharply—

"The proof?"

"The state that I am in, my lady, and the blood that is upon my face, are proofs sufficient of the sort of reception I got from Morris Courtley, when I reported to him mildly what an outrage it was upon the noble family whose bread he eats, that he should, with those devilish arts that to some men are nature, seek the seduction of a mere child, such as Lady Fanny."

"Peace! I did not ask you for that."

"I humbly beg pardon, my lady."

Oxley knew perfectly well that when the countess had asked for the proof, it meant the proof of his allegation regarding the good understanding that there was between the secretary and Lady Fanny, and not for the proof of what he affected to have suffered in the cause of virtue; but he was determined that, whether or not the countess got her information, he would tell his story.

"Mr. Oxley," she said, "this statement of yours, which I do not offend you by supposing for one moment you do not fully and implicitly believe in yourself, is so monstrous, that I may well ask for some further proof of its truth."

"Certainly, my lady. I don't think that Lady Fanny, although, no doubt, well schooled by the secretary, would be able to look you in the face and deny the fact."

The face of the countess turned ghastly pale and she held by the back of a chair, as she added—

"And—and—how far—that is, Mr. Oxley, you do not—you cannot suppose that——"

"Madam?"

"Oh, no—no, she is too pure for that! It cannot be. You do not come here, sir, to tell me that this beggar—this hireling, has dishonoured a daughter of such a house as this?"

"Certainly not, my lady."

"Oh, certainly not? That is something."

"My belief is, my lady, that Morris Courtley, the beggar, for he is nothing more—his young brother is a sheep boy — the mere hireling—for he is nothing more—he came here in rags, and by his soft and glossing tongue practised upon the weakness of the earl."

"Speak to the point, Mr. Oxley, I can think all else that you would say in your evident ill will to Courtley, whom I too hate!"

Oxley shrunk back: he found that he had gone too far, since he had let the countess see that he had come there from ill will to Courtley, and not from a hidden regard to the house of a noble family.

"My lady," he said, after a pause, "my impression is, that Morris Courtley is ambitious; and that some day you will have to deplore the fact that he has invested himself with rights that it will be quite impossible to resist."

"Rights, sir?"

"Yes; he will, if this serious mischief be not nipped in the bud, inveigle Lady Fanny into a private marraige, probably, and then defy you."

"The villain!"

"Oh, madam, I fear that in allowing that man in the house you have all been warming the serpent that will sting you."

"And she, too, with so much apparent innocence—so much seeming gentleness, and child-like purity——"

"My honoured lady, there is the mischief. It is over such natures as Lady Fanny's that such men have power. Those of sterner material would laugh the hollow hypocrisy to scorn. Oh, my lady, if I could only feel that by this timely warning I had averted from this noble house the ruin, the disgrace, from such an alliance, I should feel that I was rewarded; notwithstanding Courtley has said that, if I dared to tell you—and he took occasion to use an expression towards you that I cannot repeat—he would so falsify my accounts as to make me appear a defaulter, and get me dismissed from the hall, with all the disgrace and contumely that can be heaped upon my head."

"Indeed! did he?"

"Yes, my lady; but I am content to suffer, if I have the satisfaction of knowing that I have done my duty."

"You will not suffer."

"But, my lady——"

"Silence, Mr. Oxley; I will protect your interests. The Countess of Bloxdale, although at war with her own children, is not so utterly powerless but that she can stretch her protecting hand over you."

"But, my lady, he pretends that I have taken a thousand pounds—oh, oh! I, who, to the last farthing—oh, oh!"

"If there be any question of accounts, Mr. Oxley, I will take upon myself to settle that. Be satisfied with my word in that matter. Refer them all to me."

"I will, my lady; and I have now only sincerely to apologise to the noblest and the best of mistresses for appearing before her in such a guise as this, and for being the bearer of such intelligence." •

The countess gravely inclined her head, and Mr. Oxley, with a look of profound devotion, left the room.

"Ha! ha!" he said to himself, as, with slow and stealthy steps he crossed the picture-gallery. "Ha! ha! my friend, Courtley, I think now that I have laid a mine for you, which will blow you and all your fine sentimental flirtation with Lady Fanny to the winds. Oh, I am even with you now. And yet I have the young lord to speak to. I have to set him upon you; and I will do it! Revenge is in my grasp; and if things go on well with Peter, why—I—I shall tread this place with a different feeling to what I do now, some day. Ha! ha!"

The countess, when she was alone, sat for half-an-hour, and never uttered a word; but the expression of her countenance was truly awful. She then summoned Miss Wicks.

THE MEETING OF MR. OXLEY'S FASHIONABLE RELATIVE AND LORD FRANCIS IN THE GARDEN.

CHAPTER XXI.

LADY FANNY MAKES AN UNEXPECTED DETERMINATION.

THE precise state of affairs now at Blox-dale Park requires a little consideration and explanation, inasmuch as within the quarter of an hour succeeding Oxley's interview with the countess, some three or four people of our *dramatis personæ* were engaged in an attempt, the one to get the start of the other in a matter of no small importance.

Thus then, it fell out.

Morris Courtley had managed to let Lady Fanny, in the brief interview that had taken place between them in the library, know that it was from Oxley they had to fear an immediate communication to Lord Francis of the fact of their mutual love.

Oxley had, as soon as he was released from his interview with the countess, sent, as will be recollected, a footman to Lord Francis, craving the honour of an interview with him.

Miss Wicks was watching to catch Oxley, in order to get from him the secret of the news he had brought to the countess, although she had a shrewd suspicion of what it was, and Ann was watching Miss Wicks.

Leaving, then, poor Courtley completely maddened by the complexity of his position, Lord Francis had proceeded to meet Oxley, whom he had ordered should be shown into a room upon the ground floor that was called the cloak-room, although it was then fitted up as a kind of study or counting-house, and was an apartment in which tenants and others who came to the hall upon business connected with the property were usually seen.

Now, the footman who had taken Oxley's message to Lord Francis had found out, long since, that Ann, Lady Fanny's waiting-maid, was a pretty, engaging, kind-hearted young girl, and he was an honest lad enough; he had thought, that if she would only look upon him with an eye of favour, what a delightful thing it would be.

Of late, this young lad of a footman had fancied that he always secured a smile and a kind look from Ann if he brought her word what Oxley was about, if it had any reference especially to the secretary; and, indeed, the footman might almost be said to be in a kind of half-confidence with Ann, regarding the little love affair between Courtley and her young mistress.

Now Samuel, as the footman was named, when he took back the order to Oxley to wait for Lord Francis in the room we have mentioned, heard him, as the door closed upon him, clasp his hands together, and exclaim—

"I have him now. Lord Francis shall know all. Ha!—ha! I have him now quite safe!"

These expressions induced Samuel to think that there was some mischief brewing, and so he ran off to find Ann, and luckily did so in the picture-gallery, as she was looking for Miss Wicks, to see what that worthy was about.

"Oh, my dear Ann—my sweet Ann!"

"Hoity-toity, Mr. Samuel, what do you mean by that?"

"I do mean it, Ann. Green peas in March isn't half so nice as you."

"Go along with you!"

"No; but now, I say, Mr. Oxley is going to say something to young master, and I heard him say that he had him now, and I do think he meant Mr. Courtley."

"Mr. Courtley?"

"Yes; there seems, my sweet Ann, to be something a-going on, indeed there does. Oh, Ann, I likes Yorkshire pudding done very brown, under roast beef, but you is—oh!"

Ann had flitted away like an apparition, and darting into her young mistress's room, she said—

"Oh, Fanny—I mean my lady, all the fat is in—oh dear, no, I mean, there's such a kettle of—bless me, what am I saying?—but Mr. Oxley is going to tell your brother something, Samuel tells me, and it's about Mr. Courtley."

Fanny actually screamed.

"Oh, don't—oh don't!"

"Lost—lost!" cried Fanny.

"Oh, Miss Fanny, we will find it again. What have you lost?"

"All—all!"

"You don't say so?"

"Oh, Morris—Morris, you are now destroyed. Oxley will tell my brother; and then—and then—"

"What then, Fanny—what then? Lor bless me! we are all made and put into the world to love and multiply one another, don't the scriptures tell us? In course they do. Why, what if he does tell him, Miss Fanny? He can only say that he loves you, and you love him, and—Oh, can't he, though!"

"What do you mean?"

"I have just thought of it. Oxley is such a wretch, he will say to him one true thing that is no harm at all, and a hundred untrue things that are harm, and that will look like true things, just by being in good company with a truth for a little while—that's what he will do."

"Oh, yes—yes, he will! Morris warned me of that man; and he knows him well."

"He is a bad one."

"He is, indeed. Why, this is, indeed, a wretched day! Oh, if I were only dead now!"

"Dead! Miss Lady Fanny?"

"Yes, that would be happiness, because that would be peace; and peace is all that I can hope for—the peace of the grave! Oh, my poor Morris! you will now, just because you love me, be turned from this house, as though you had committed a crime! That bad man, Oxley, will give such a false colour to the story he will tell, that the anger of my brother will be raised, and all will be lost before any one can persuade him to listen to the truth!"

"Oh, Miss Fanny—oh——"

"You doubly alarm me, Ann! What do you mean now?"

"I have just had such a thought. You know, now, your brother cannot be kept longer in ignorance of the—the——"

"I know what you mean. Our fatal love!"

"It isn't a fatal love yet, Miss Fanny. You ain't married yet, you know."

"No—no!"

"Well, then, as it seems—oh, I'm so out of breath, for I want to say it all at once and I can't—as it seems that your brother must now know all about it, why, oh, dear, isn't it better—yes, by a thousand times, of course—oh, my heart does go bump, bump, so!—that he should know only the real truth instead of bushels of farrididdles?"

"Of what, Ann?"

"Plumpers, my dear lady—oh, I mean lies, up in great heaps. Isn't it better for me to go and lay hold of him, and say, 'They do love each other; and scripture says, Multiplication is——'"

Fanny sprang to her feet.

"Ann, I understand you. It *is* a million times better that my brother, since he must know the fact, should know the truth. He shall know that Morris Courtley loves me; and he shall know that that love has been so pure, so innocent, so holy, that it is without stain, and without reproach. He shall know that, never by deed, word, or look, has Morris Courtley overstepped that sacred devotion which — My bonnet, Ann — my bonnet! I will tell my brother all. Oh, that it should ever come to this! My mantle! quick—quick—quick! Oh, that I should be hurrying to disclose a secret that I have trembled night and day for months at the idea of ever coming to his ears! Quick, Ann—quick! I must see Francis before that man poisons his ears with falsehoods."

"That's right, Fanny—oh, that's right! Here's the drawn one, with the pink lining, and then if you turn a little pale, it won't be seen so much. Here's your mantle. Oh, don't shake so; I can't get your arm into it."

"Yes—yes! I will throw myself upon my brother's mercy—upon his love for me—upon his justice to Morris! He shall know all—the truth! I will tell him how poor Morris struggled with the first dawn of his passion, but how it crept silently but surely over his heart, as daylight will silently and surely succeed to the dawn of a new day—I will tell how guiltless is the love that—that——"

Fanny burst into a passion of hysterical weeping.

"There, now,' said Ann, "you have done it now."

"What—oh, what?"

"Why, of course you ain't able to go now."

"I am—I am!"

"No you ain't."

"Yes, Ann, I tell you. The strong will enables me to overcome even these tears. I am ready to go now at once."

"No you ain't."

"How dare you say that, Ann?"

"Because you will do nothing but go crying all down the staircase, and going into hysterics, so that you will alarm the whole house, that you will."

"No, Ann, I am better now. Those tears have been to me a relief. I am able to go at once. Where is my brother?"

"In the library; and I will go and stop him, and tell him you want to speak to him."

"Do so—oh, do so."

"But I know you will not be able to speak to him; but when you see him, you will go right off into a faint, or a swound, or crying, or something of that sort; and though you oughtn't, and though it is almost, as we may say, a matter of life and death to Mr. Courtley, of course you will not be able to speak."

"Ann, you are very wicked. I am very angry with you. Go and stop my brother at once."

'Yes," said Ann, as, followed by Fanny, she ran down the staircase from the picture-gallery. "I'll find him; and, what's more, if I hadn't said what I have, I know quite well that Miss Fanny would have gone on crying, and be fit for nothing at all; but now that I have told her she can't speak, won't she?—that's the natural amiability of the female sex, I rather think."

Ann's contradictions to Fanny, and her prophecies that she would break down in her enterprise, had had all the effect she had wished, and had recovered the young girl from the state into which she had been falling more rapidly than all the sympathy in the world, assisted by all the *sal volatile*, could possibly have accomplished.

Half angry—half maddened at the fact that Oxley should dare to make such a communication to her brother, poor Fanny followed Ann, who had the good fortune just to see Lord Francis upon the point of emerging from the library-door, as she got half way to the hall.

"My lord—my lord! Master Francis!"

He looked up.

"Oh, Ann, is that you?"

"Yes—oh, dear, yes. I want to speak to you—no I don't. Here's Lady Fanny."

"Brother—brother!"

"Why, Fanny, what is the matter?"

"Nothing—oh, nothing! I—Oh, Francis—Francis!"

"There you goes again," said Ann. "I know'd it."

"No—I am not crying now."

She clung to her brother's arm, and made a great effort to control her tears.

"Courage!" said Ann. "Courage!"

"But what is it all about?" said Lord Francis.

"Brother, I must—speak—with you."

"So you shall, dear. I have some business to transact with Oxley, just now, and as soon as I have done with him I will come to you."

"No, no, no!"

"No?"

"It must be now, brother. You must not—you shall not, see the villain, Oxley, brother. Oh, Frank — Frank, I know that you do love me. Do you not?"

"With all my heart, my dear Fan."

She sobbed, and rested her head upon his bosom.

"There she goes again!" said Ann.

"No—no! I am well—quite well. Brother—brother, will you listen to me?"

"Truly yes, Fanny."

"And now—now, in preference to that man, Oxley?"

"If you wish it I will. I made no appointment with Mr. Oxley, and he can wait my convenience. Come now, Fan, what on earth does all this mean? Why, you and Courtley are enough to make one believe that something is really the matter, and that there is some terrible secret in the family."

Fanny shuddered.

"Come, brother—come. Walk with me."

"Where would you go to?"

"I am cold. Let us walk in the conservatory. There we shall find an artificial summer around us, all the more delightful from its marked contrast to the inclemency of the out-of-door world. Oh, brother—brother, I lean now upon your affection for me, and I feel that if that were withdrawn I must fall into the grave."

"You really alarm me, Fanny."

"No—no. I did not mean to do that—I did not think to do that. But I will, indeed, I will, tell you all. I will be most ingenuous—I will conceal nothing."

All the time that Fanny was speaking to Lord Francis in this rather, it must be confessed, incoherent style, she was leading him to the great conservatory, as it was called, of the mansion, which was some fifty feet in length, and about half that amount of feet in breadth, and which, during the whole of the winter, was kept at a pleasant temperature of summer heat.

It was, in truth, as Lady Fanny said, a delightful thing, to pace down the broad pathway in that conservatory, and contrast its genial warmth, and its rich and varied floral treasures with the cold sterility of everything without at that season of the year. Even as she entered the place a feeling of self-possession such as she had not before felt, came to her aid, and she felt that she should be able to say all that she wished to say to her brother.

Lord Francis was quite lost in wonder, as well he might, at all this extraordinary conduct upon the part of his sister, Fanny; and although he could not possibly, up to that time, have any idea of the real truth, yet, somehow, the evident distress and con-

fusion of Morris Courtley was coupled in his own mind, he knew not why or wherefore, with the present agitation of his sister.

Lord Francis was soon to have a solution of that mystery.

"Come, now, Fanny," he said, "shall I guess what it is that so much distresses you?"

"Oh, yes—yes."

"You really dread to go to London; and you think, from long use in so thinking, that our mother can and will enforce compliance with her orders upon that matter."

"Oh, no—no!"

"No?"

"That is not what I have come here to speak to you about, brother. Oh, God, why am I not dead?"

"Because Heaven has something better to do than to create such fair and delicate beings as you are, my dear Fan, merely for the purpose of then destroying. Neither you nor I will talk of dying, if you please, for many a long day. You have something to tell me now. Is it some girl's grief that the affection of one near and dear to you as I am can assuage?"

CHAPTER XXII.

MR. OXLEY IS RATHER THROWN OUT IN HIS CALCULATIONS.

LADY FANNY gladly accepted the seat in the conservatory to which her brother led her. She tried to smile, too, when he plucked a rose, and placed it in her hand. Oh, what a faint and sickly smile that was!

It was like the gleam of sunshine we sometimes get upon a winter's day in England.

"Now, Fan," he said, "since I am to play the part of father-confessor, let me hear exactly what you have to tell."

"Brother—Frank—I always used to call you Frank."

"And do so still, Fan. I love the old familiar sound of that name. When we call each other Frank and Fan, the tones seem to carry us back to childhood again, when we gambolled for long summer days together about this old mansion, and were very thoughtless, and so very happy."

"Oh, yes—yes; and now—we are full of thought and many cares, dear Frank. But mine are the worst of all."

"As you think?" smiled Lord Francis.

"Nay, as I know."

"Well, we will hear. Come, now—the confession."

She trembled like an unfledged dove, and held him by the arm, as she said—

"Brother, Mr. Oxley—who is not my friend nor your friend, nor the friend of Morris Courtley—was about to tell you what I am now about to tell you."

"Ah?"

"Oh, brother—brother!—oh, Frank, you will not judge me harshly? You will, if you must condemn, at least pity while you do so?"

"Then, Fanny, I am to understand, at the outset, that the confidence that I am about to be indulged with is an enforced one, on account of the fact that I was about to get at what it refers to from Oxley?"

"Yes. I dare not dissemble with you."

"Dissemble? You dissemble, Fan? You cannot. It is not in your nature. Well, I accept even this equivocal compliment of a confidence that comes at the last moment just to stop the fact it refers to coming from another."

"That other, Frank, would have falsified all he told. That other would have lent to his statement the false light of his own vindictive passions, brother; and that is why I felt that I ought to tell you the simple truth."

"Go on."

"Brother, I—love!"

"Your father—me—your birds—your pet dog—flowers—music: Of course you do. Well?"

"Brother, Morris Courtley——"

A glow of colour spread itself slowly over the face of Lord Francis. The truth was dawning upon his mind

"Go on."

"Morris Courtley loves me!"

The colour fled from Lord Francis' face, and he turned very pale, indeed.

"Go on."

"And, brother, I—I—love him!"

Fanny let her head droop upon her breast, and wept. She had told all. The confession had been wrung by circumstances from her. That confession which, twenty-four hours since—twenty-four, do we say? we may say the odd four—that confession which, only four hours since, she would no more have dreamt of uttering than she now dreamt of retracting it.

The silence that ensued was terrible to both brother and sister; yet it was not all silence, for at short intervals it was broken by the sobs of Fanny, who dared not look up to meet the gaze of her brother—that gaze that she knew was bent upon her. She felt that it was.

Was it in sorrow or in anger?

He spoke at last. It was quite a merciful thing of him to break the stillness of the place.

"Fanny—Fanny?"

"Yes."

She did just manage to say yes.

"My poor Fanny!"

"Oh, Frank, Frank, you are not angry—you——"

"Hush! I am not angry with you, you poor innocent thing. You are the victim."

"The victim?"

"Yes, the victim of a man of knowledge —of learning—of tact and deep reflection. It is upon the head of Morris Courtley that the sin of the transaction lies."

"The—the sin?"

"Yes, the deep sin—the black ingratitude —the devilish wickedness that could induce one who has been so treated as he has been here, to play the part of a thief!"

"No—no!"

"Yes, of a thief; and steal the most peerless treasure of our house. Oh, who will have any faith in human nature now? I tell you, girl, that Courtley's conduct is base— base and full of wickedness. He knew—he saw that you were but a beautiful child—he knew well the difference of station placed an insurmountable barrier between you—he must have felt that for your misery only could he have spoken to you of love. Love? It is hate!"

"Brother—brother!"

"Yes, I say it is hate to seek the gratification of a passion or a vanity, call it which you will, at the expense of the object pretended to be loved."

The voice of Lord Francis was high and cracked; and now there was a fixed glow of excitement upon his cheeks as he spoke.

Fanny rose.

"Brother," she said, "I told you at the commencement of this interview that I was about to make to you an enforced declaration, for that Oxley, our mother's steward, was upon the point of informing you, with what embellishments his nature might induce him to add to the tale, of what I now have told you. How he acquired his information I know not, and care not. Let it suffice, that he has used it as a means of attempting to awe Morris Courtley into an acquiescence in the robbery of you and all of us. Morris would not—Morris could not stoop to such a compromise."

"Indeed!"

"No! He defied the villain, and he chastised him for the insolence of making such an offer.

"Go on. Let me know all."

"Maddened, then, at his reception from Morris Courtley, Oxley avowed his intention of disclosing the secret. I have been, I hope, beforehand with him?"

"You have, sister. But the conduct of Morris Courtley is in nowise improved thereby. Tell me. I—Oh, Fanny, Fanny! there wanted but this blow!"

"Brother—Frank!"

"No—no. Trust me. I do not know—"

"What—oh, what?"

He shook with emotion as he said—

"When did he tell you that he—loved you, and what has he proposed?"

"He told me that he loved me, brother, long after I knew that he did so, and knew, too, that I loved him. He proposed that he should leave Bloxdale—he proposed that I should forget him; and that I should strive to be happy as the bride of one in my own station. He did not say that he would forget me, but he said that he would take his sorrows far from me, and that he would pray for my happiness; and he spoke of you and of my father, and said that—that——"

" Go on !"

" That it would be base of him to so act towards you as to take me to his arms ; and so that he would go."

" Why went he not ?"

" Oh, brother, I would not let him."

" Fanny.—Fanny !"

" It is true—it is all true, brother ; and—and Morris Courtley will go to-day from Bloxdale. You can tell him that he is wicked—that he is base, if you have the heart to do so, and he will not reply to you except by a sigh. He will go away—far away, and you and I and all of us will never see him more. But Oxley will not have succeeded in poisoning your mind, or in, for one moment, persuading you that Morris Courtley ever behaved to me but as a noble gentleman. Oh, brother, he loves me—he worships me ; and—and if you, brother——"

" No more—no more !"

" Nay, if you, brother, had been Morris Courtley, the poor secretary, and had seen me, and heard me singing to the birds and the sweet flowers, and felt that I was the guileless girl I think and hope I am, and I had been the daughter of a king, you might have loved me, brother—dear Frank, you might, you know, have loved me."

" No—no ! not unworthily."

" Ah, no ! Neither has Morris."

" Fanny—Fanny !"

" And you would have struggled with that love, and told yourself it was not right that you so lowly born, although a gentleman in all the gentility of nature, should look so high."

" I would—I would have pictured to myself the fact, that the husband drags down to his level the wife."

" And so did Morris. Oh, how he struggled with his love, till one day——"

" That day should never have come."

" Ah ! but you would have, if you had been Morris Courtley, when the maddened steed fled with me, and he caught it at the peril of his life, and saved me, you would, if you had then been he, have told me in the present moment of your joy, that you loved me."

" But if I had been Courtley I should have gone—gone far away."

" But I should not have let you."

" Oh, I should have trembled at the precipice to which I was dragging you. My days would have passed in terror—my nights in grief !"

" Alas ! so has his ! But it is over now, and he will go—yes, he will go—for ever !"

Fanny tottered to the conservatory door ; but her brother ran after her, and placed his arms around her.

" Fan !—my own Fan ! I will, I do forgive him all !"

She turned and gave him one look of unutterable gratitude, and then fainted in his arms.

Lord Francis was much afflicted at this interview that he had had with his sister, and he was now inexpressibly alarmed at her condition. He dreaded to call for assistance from the servants of the house ; and yet, at the same time, he could not quite make up his mind that he was justified in not doing so.

Luckily, he thought of opening one of the windows of the conservatory, used for the purpose of ventilation in the heat of summer. The rush of chill, frosty air that came into the building revived Fanny, and she opened her eyes, and looked in her brother's face vacantly.

" My dear Fan," he said, " are you better ?"

" Oh, God !"

" Come—come, let me assist you to the house ; or shall I fetch Ann to you ?"

" Brother—brother !"

" Yes, Fan, I am your brother."

Amid a flood of tears she spoke, evidently, for the moment, quite oblivious of the scene that had passed.

" Brother ! oh, do not despise me—do not curse me—do not say that you will not love me ; but, brother—Frank, love Morris Courtley !"

Tears gushed to the eyes of Lord Francis ; but without another word, he lifted his sister in his arms, and carried her to her own rooms, and left her in the care of Ann, who looked as pale as poor Fanny, as she took charge of her.

———

CHAPTER XXIII.

THE COUNTESS TRIES TO AROUSE THE EARL TO A SENSE OF HIS SITUATION.

THAT something dreadful had taken place, as a result of the interview between the brother and sister, poor Ann, when she saw the insensible form of Fanny, and the pale and agitated countenance of Lord Francis, could not but believe ; and she shook so that she was quite incapable, for a few moments, of asking the questions that were struggling for utterance.

Poor Lady Fanny ! She was all unfit to struggle with the events that now appeared to be thickening around her. Her gentle and affectionate nature should have had nothing to think of—to dream of, but of loving well, and of being beloved. The storms of fate might have done better, surely, than seek to expend their fury upon so frail a being.

When Ann did find words in which to express herself, it was with a perfect army of questions that she besieged poor Fanny.

" Oh, what is it ? What did he say ? What has happened ?"

" Ann—Ann !"

" Yes, my lady—yes, I mean Fanny. Oh, how pale you are !"

" Pale—and—and—dying."

" Gracious Heavens !"

Lady Fanny fell into the arms of Ann, and the saddened heart, for a brief space, knew no more of the world and its sorrows than if the grave had closed over it for ever.

We must now leave Lady Fanny, with all her griefs, to find such consolation as she may from a better-consideration of her position, while we follow the more artful, and more stormy proceedings of others of our characters, who are working so much woe for themselves as well as for her.

As Lord Francis descended the staircase from the picture-gallery, a thought struck him, and he paused.

"Oxley may yet be waiting," he said. "I will see the rascal, and hear his version of the story, before I say one word to Courtley. Yes, I will hear the complexion that that false knave will put upon the tale, before I say one word to Morris. Oh, why should it be that through those whom I love best in all the world I am most to be wounded? My father, my mother, my sister, and Courtley, whom I held to my heart with such a fancy that if all the world proved false he at least would be true."

The young nobleman paused in the hall for a few moments, for a feeling of irresolution had come over him, as to whether or not he should seek the steward; for he felt that he was scarcely in a frame of mind to successfully do mortal battle with such a man as Oxley.

"Shall I meet him or shall I not?" was the anxious question that Lord Francis asked of himself. "In my present state of mind, may not such a villain imflame me to some act that I should bitterly repent of? It is possible."

The door of the apartment in which Oxley had been so long waiting for Lord Francis opened a little, and the face of the steward, hideous in its natural ugliness, and with the reflection of the gross and bad passions that found a home in his heart, peered out into the hall.

"Oh, my lord."

"Oxley?"

"Your most humble servant, my lord. I had the honour of sending to say that I hoped your lordship would favour me with an interview."

"Well, sir."

"I—I presume that your lordship was graciously coming to me, as I was ordered to wait here—"

"I was."

The cunning of Oxley was getting the better of the prudence of Lord Francis.

"I humbly, then, and most respectfully wait your lordship's most gracious leisure."

The words that Oxley used were such as would carry the idea that he was treating the young nobleman to rather a large dose of irony; but the manner of the steward was so carefully subdued that not the smallest item of such a feeling was exhibited.

But from the rather hyperbolical character of the expressions that he used towards Lord Francis, it would have been impossible to quarrel with the tone in which he spoke to him.

"Now, sir, I attend to you," said Lord Francis, as he walked into the room, and took up his position with his back to the light. He did not wish that villain to see how deeply he was affected.

Oxley carefully closed the door.

"My lord, pray be seated."

"No, Mr. Oxley. The communication you have to make to me is, I dare say, very brief; I will hear it at once as I am."

"Oh, my lord!"

"Well, sir?"

"A glance at me will, perhaps, show your lordship that I am not exactly in my usual condition."

"How so?"

"I have been subjected to the personal violence that blunt, plain honesty not unfrequently receives at the hands of those who only wear a mask, and who were maddened at the idea that any hand is raised to tear it from their faces."

"Go on."

"Your lordship, then, perceives that I have been ill-used—fearfully insulted. That is sufficiently evident, I presume?"

"I will take your word for it, Mr. Oxley; but if that is what you intend to let me know, I decline to interfere, as I am not in the commission of the peace. You should apply to some magistrate."

"I had hoped——"

"You were wrong then. Good morning."

"Oh, my lord, stay. That which I have to say to you is so important that you would linger here to listen to it could you but guess its import, though all your ancestral house was in a blaze, and a breath of yours would extinguish the conflagration. I have that to tell you which will so move you."

"Indeed!"

"Oh, yes, my lord, I—I—excuse this inundation of feeling, if I may call it such; but I have been so long—so very long in the service of your noble father—so long——"

"That you got tired of that service," said Lord Francis.

"Tired? Oh—oh!"

"Yes, tired, Mr. Oxley; and left it for the easier service of my noble mother."

"Oh, my lord, this from you?"

"From me, Mr. Oxley? You are my mother's steward, sir, it appears; and the only fault that any one can find with the appointment is, that she who has bestowed it has not the power to do so; and that bot she and you are dealing with affairs and with funds out of either of your control."

"My lord, I beg humbly to say that that is not the subject upon which I presumed to speak to your lordship. It is of the Lady Fanny."

"My sister?"

"Yes, my lord."

"Then you may well call it presumption, Mr. Oxley."

"I know it to be such; but with your gracious permission I will proceed."

"At your own peril, sir. I give no permission."

"At my own peril, then, my lord, I proceed. The truth is naturally wrapped up in such small, impenetrable ovaries that those only who cling to it are protected."

"Well spoken, sir; but at times falsehood will so demean itself, that at a casual glance one would be led to believe that it was the fair and the beautiful spirit of truth itself, although no kin to it."

"How very true, my lord. Well, I now take the great liberty of stating that it was Morris Courtley who struck me—me, an old man, old enough to be his father. It was he who left these marks of violence upon my face."

"But Mr. Morris Courtley is not my sister," said Lord Francis coldly. "I thought it was of her you were about to speak?"

"In good time, my lord; there is no hurry."

"Nay, but there is, Mr. Oxley. Do you fancy, sir, that I will remain here to listen to your ravings—to your roundabout stories? No, sir, if you have aught to tell, tell it. If you have any information to give me that it befits my honour I should hear, give it. But, beware!"

"Beware of what, my lord?"

"Beware that you lie not."

"Oh, my lord!"

"Well—well, go on. I would fain think you honest, Mr. Oxley. Those gray hairs would ill accord with knavery; and yet is there something tugging at my heart which tells me to distrust you."

Oxley affected to shed tears at this very unkind speech from his young lord and master; and then he said—

"My lord, I have had a very difficult part to play in this house, and Heaven only knows how I have wished for your arrival, in order that affairs might assume a different aspect. It cannot now any longer be a secret from you that your noble father is not very capable of attending to affairs that, let the station of a nobleman be what it may, it is necessary at times he should attend to."

Lord Francis slightly inclined his head in token of acquiescence in this view of the case.

"Well, then, my lord, your noble mother became—excuse me for the expression, but I am so plain and blunt—quite a woman of business."

"Go on."

"And, finally, you come, and depute Mr. Courtley to examine my accounts, all of which he finds correct. Correct!"

Lord Francis did not, by the movement of a muscle, betray that Morris had told him of the thousand pounds defalcation.

"But," resumed Oxley, "but he said that if I did not wink at certain proceedings of his, he would report to you that I was deficient in my cash accounts; and as it was

your noble mother who had had the money, and as—as——"

"Go on, sir why do you pause?"

Oxley ventured upon a bold lie at once, so he added—

"And as the countess had ordered me not to enter certain sums in the books which I had paid to her, I thought myself at least justified against any ill turn upon the part of Mr. Courtley."

"Then there is a deficiency?"

"Why, a—that is, I—oh, yes, apparently—apparently."

"You said just now that the accounts were correct?"

"Yes, my lord, I meant really correct—really correct, although to the eye they looked a little wrong — strictly correct, but apparently wrong. Appearances, my lord, are very deceitful in this world."

"They are, indeed."

"Well, then, Mr. Courtley threatened me that if I did not wink at certain proceedings of yours, he would tell you that I was wrong in my accounts; and when I refused the offer, he struck me."

"Then you say that Mr. Courtley, finding an error in your accounts, offered to conceal it upon certain conditions?"

"He did."

"Why, you said just now that the accounts were correct, but that Mr. Courtley threatened you with a report that they were not."

"Oh, no; pardon me, my lord, for contradicting you. It is the countess, your lordship's noble mother, who will vouch for the correctness of my accounts."

"Not a doubt of it."

"Hem! You are so—so—I feel it to be my duty to tell your lordship what it was that Morris Courtley wanted me to keep secret from you."

"Well, sir, and how long have you known it?"

"Known it, my lord?"

"Yes. How long has the secret been in your keeping?"

"Oh, my lord, as a suspicion, it has been in my heart for some time; but the honour of noble families is too precious a commodity to be trifled with."

"I am glad to hear you say that, sir."

"I think it, my lord; and so, until I had proof positive, I could not, I dared not speak.

"Proof positive of what?"

"*Morris Courtley loves Lady Fanny, and Lady Fanny reciprocates the passion of the secretary!*"

"Is that all?"

"All?—all?"

"Is that all, I say?"

Oxley staggered back till he was stopped by the wall, and glared at Lord Francis as though he would devour him with his eyes.

"Oh, my lord, is it not enough?—is it not enough that a beggar, a mere creature of your lordship's bounty should aspire to an alliance with your noble house? All? It

THE INVALID EARL OF BLOXDALE ATTENDED BY HIS SERVANT.

is, indeed, all—that is, I hope it is all ; but it remains for your lordship to find out if it be really all."

"Have you done ?"

"I—have !"

"Then my time and yours, Mr. Oxley, has been alike wasted, for I knew it before. Good morning, sir."

With a slow and stately step Lord Francis left the room, and Oxley staggered to a chair, upon which he sank, feeling very like a man might be supposed to feel who had newly awakened from some very perplexing dream.

It was some minutes before he could speak, and then it was only in choking accents that he managed to say—

"He knew it before !"

Of all the strange conclusions to the interview that he had sought with the young noble, the one that had occurred was, to the imagination of Oxley, the most strange. A chilling fear came over him that, after all, Lord Francis was so infatuated with Courtley, that instead of being the foe of an attachment subsisting between the secretary and his sister, he would be their friend in that state of things. This was an idea that at one fell swoop upset a large portion of the steward's schemes.

"Oh, fool, fool, that I have been!" he cried. "I have but done Courtley good by all this! At a time when I thought to deal my enemy a deadly blow, I fail—I do him a service, by only bringing about an open declaration of a state of things that I thought would destroy him!"

Mr. Oxley fairly groaned, and let his head droop upon his breast, as he now repeated the last words of Lord Francis—

"He knew it before!"

The question then arose of who had told the young lord? Had the secretary really had the hardihood to declare his own passion? or had Lady Fanny herself told it to her brother? or had the calm and silent observation of Lord Francis himself been sufficient to read the secret of the two hearts? For a time Oxley was puzzled.

"I have it," he said, at length. "It is a result of his own discovering. There could be no mistake about the fright that Courtley was in when I held out a threat to him of such a disclosure. He is not the informant of Lord Francis. Oh, no—no!"

Mr. Oxley rose, and rubbed his hands together, and tried to think that things were not quite so bad as they had looked.

"Then, again," he said, "Lady Fanny has not told him. Oh, no—no! First of all it is so contrary to her nature to be able to do so, that she could never bring herself to utter the words; and, besides, if she did, it could only be with the prompting and the concurrence of Courtley himself. No, she has not told him. He has seen it—he has seen it in their eyes, and he will not let me know what he thinks, that is all—that is all."

This view of the matter was much more charming to Mr. Oxley.

"Oh, that is all," he said. "I feel now, each moment, only more and more convinced that that was all. Lord Francis was not taken by surprise, and so there was no exhibition of his amazement; but I have confirmed him in what he suspected, and he must now take some notice of it. Ha! ha! Mr. Courtley, I have you now. Oh, yes, I shall have my revenge. But I will not be satisfied with your expulsion even from this house—I will not be satisfied with your disgrace—I will hunt you still. You have made me your deadly enemy, and so I will pursue you to the death—yes, to the death."

Mr. Oxley, with this resolve—which in his case was no idle one, for a man of more desperate and deadly habits than he was could not by any possibility exist—left the apartment, determined to pry about as much as possible, so as to ascertain what was going on, and through his agent, the waiting-woman of the countess, too, to get what information she could procure for him of the secret events in the family.

"If Oxley had known how heart-smitten, in good truth, Lord Francis was by the fact which concurrent testimony now proved to him, he would have had no cause to be at all disappointed at the effect of the communication.

———

CHAPTER XXIV.

LORD FRANCIS WRITES A NOTE TO MORRIS COURTLEY.

THAT Lord Francis Bloxdale found himself now in one of the most painful positions that it was possible for any one to be in with such feelings and opinions as his, does not admit of a doubt.

By travel — by extensive reading, and by a naturally noble and liberal spirit, the young nobleman had got rid, in a great measure, of the foibles and opinions which generally beset those of his rank in life.

Lord Francis had learnt to know that his position was rather an accidental one than in any degree contingent upon a difference in reality between him and other men; but then, at the same time he could not conceal from himself the fact that the social position he and his sister occupied was one that was not to be lightly trifled with.

It was true enough that Morris Courtley was a young man of education, of good manners, of unimpeachable propriety of conduct; but the marriage of the only daughter of the Earl of Bloxdale with him would be a very grievous *mesalliance*, for all that, and it would be an awkward thing for her to stoop to a level with the commonalty, after being on the height that she had occupied as the daughter of one of the oldest peerages in the kingdom.

While he felt all that, there was still a struggle in the young man's mind between the more rational view of the case, which told him that, after all, the ladyship of his sister was but a mere form, and that her happiness was the principal thing to look to.

After a time, he asked himself what he should do, supposing he were to fall desperately in love with some young and gentle creature in the same line of life that Morris Courtley was in? "Marry her at once," was the reply that he made to himself; but, then, he could raise her to his level, whereas by his sister marrying Courtley, she sunk to the condition of her husband. That was a very essential difference.

From that course of reasoning, then, there came another idea, and that was the point of view from which he considered, and, perhaps, with justice, too, that the conduct of Courtley was very blamable indeed."

"It was Morris Courtley's business," he said, "with his education, his extensive reading, his fine, keen intellect, and great knowledge, to feel that the passion he might not be able to help entertaining for my sister, was one which was in itself a wrong both to her and to her family, and he ought to have concealed it, at any sacrifice to himself. There Courtley is wrong!"

Alas! Lord Francis little knew how the young secretary had struggled to do that very thing—how he had prayed for strength of heart and purpose to conceal the love that had filled up his whole thoughts; and how, at last it was, that love had triumphed as it will ever triumph, and not Courtley that had fallen.

And now Lord Francis left that it devolved upon him to separate their attached hearts—that it was his duty to preserve his sister in the sphere in which she had been born, and that he must discard the man whom he had hoped to make a friend for life.

This was a stern and terrible duty, but it was one that he settled in his own mind must be done. All he could promise himself was, that he would do it as gently as possible.

In such circumstances, if Lord Francis had had his father to consult with, or if he could with any degree of rationality have talked the matter over with his mother, he would have been relieved from a weight of care; but such was not possible. Thus he was completely isolated now, for, in addition to all other separations, his sister and Courtley were now at arms-length, as it were, from him.

"I am quite alone," said Lord Francis, as he paced the library. "I am quite alone now. Fate seems to have not been content until barriers were raised up between me and all that I loved. Firstly, the state of my father's mind precludes any other connection with him than sympathy with his weakness. Then the infamous conduct of my mother estranges her from me, and now this sad and fatal secret of her love separates me from my sister, and digs an impassable gulf between me and Courtley. Well—well, I must do my best."

After considerable thought, Lord Francis determined to have an interview with Courtley expressly upon the subject, the aim and object of which interview should be to request him quietly to leave Bloxdale, and to offer him such means as would enable him to push his fortune elsewhere.

With this view the young nobleman sat down at the table usually occupied by the secretary, and wrote the following note for Courtley:—

"Lord F. Bloxdale will meet Mr. Courtley in the library at eight this evening, upon a matter of importance."

The note, brief and cold as it was, Lord Francis sealed and left lying upon the table, addressed to Courtley, so that before the hour mentioned in it, he would be sure to get it; and from the tone of it, Lord Francis wished him to guess the subject of the conversation that was to take place between them.

It was now the wish of Lord Francis to avoid encountering either his sister or Courtley before that hour in the evening that he had named as the one at which he was to meet the secretary; so he sallied out from the mansion, and, notwithstanding the inclemency of the weather, he took a long stroll into the woods, that at one point were so close to it.

While all this was going on, Lady Bloxdale was not quite idle. The news that had been brought to her, by Oxley, had had the effect of violently agitating her, and the idea, after some consideration, that took possession of her was, that Lord Francis was in the plot to bestow his sister's hand upon the secretary.

Maddened at such a thought, and believing that if such an event took place in the family all the power that she had contrived to wrest from the feeble grasp of the earl would at once pass from her before such a coalition as Fanny, the secretary, and her son; she rushed to the chamber of the earl, with the hope that he had yet intellect sufficient to make common cause with her against this desecration of the nobility of the family.

It was now that the countess found, that by subduing, as she had done, the fading flame of the earl's intellect, she had been keeping down the only power which could in such a strait aid her, and she shuddered to think that possibly she had been too successful in crushing the mind she now would fain have made active and powerful in a cause that she felt was of higher moment than the handling of the rich revenues of the Bloxdale property.

Imperiously ordering the earl's valet from the room, she approached the wreck of what had once been a man of, at all events, average intellect, and looked him in the face.

The vacant and half alarmed look that she saw there made her heart sink within her; but still she would not abandon her enterprise without a struggle.

She took his hand, and in a kinder tone of voice than she had used in speaking to him for many a long day, she said—

"Are you better to-day?"

"Eh?"

"I say how do you feel to-day? Well, and able to talk to me, and to understand what I say?"

"Oh, dear!"

"Come—come. Rouse yourself. It is necessary that you should do so, for the honour of your family is at stake, I tell you. Do you know who you are?"

"I—oh—I—exactly."

"You are the Earl of Bloxdale, are you not?"

"Oh, dear no. You are."

"I?—nonsense! Come—come, I am quite convinced that one half of this is mere acting. You cannot be so—so—" idiotic she was going to say; but a slight flush of shame crimsoned her face as she recollected how often she had used that word, idiot, to him, when asserting her own superiority to his fading powers of mind. Verily, there were some slight symptoms of a retribution overtaking her imperious ladyship, even in this world, for her conduct to the earl.

The poor crushed nobleman looked at her vacantly, and with a faint "Oh, dear!" he turned his eyes away.

"I have gone too far with him," thought the countess. "I did not think I had so totally subdued him. Listen to me now. Do you hear me?"

"I know I am."

"You know you are what?"

"Oh, anything—oh, dear, anything you like. I only—that is—no."

"I want you to exert yourself to save a great disgrace from falling upon your family. Do you comprehend that?"

"It has fallen!"

"Has fallen? She is not married to him?"

"Eh? Eh? Oh, dear! There she goes again."

"What was I saying? My lord—my lord! if you put on this folly to drive me mad, it will succeed at this present time. What do you allude to when you talk of the disgrace having fallen upon the family already?"

"Excuse me, my lady, I—oh, dear! I was trying to think."

"Try again."

"Yes, if I may presume, I was only thinking that—that—nothing."

"He will not, or he cannot think," said the countess to herself. "My lord, I do not know if this strange manner which you persist in be real, or in part or, indeed, wholly assumed; but I will tell you that which, if it do not nerve you to some sort of energy, will convince me that you are, indeed, dead to all intellectual exertion."

"Dead!" said the old earl.

"Your daughter Fanny——"

"Heaven bless my darling!"

"Ah, that is the chord, then," thought the countess, "which will, after all, be responsive to my touch. You daughter Fanny—our child, Fanny; will be destroyed!"

"No!" shouted the earl, springing to his feet; "oh God, no!"

"Good," said the countess, as she laid her hand upon his arm. "Be seated, and I will tell you all."

"Woman, tell me no more. Already you have destroyed too much—already you have destroyed me. Oh, spare my daughter—my innocent child, my own dear, smiling Fan! Oh, spare her!"

"You are mad. It is not I."

"Not—not—you?"

"No. I would preserve her."

"You—would—preserve!—Oh, no! you are a destroyer, not a preserver. Oh, no, no! The leopard cannot cast his skin, and so you may know him!"

"This is the very height of folly, my lord. I, as your wife, come to consult with you about the interest of our daughter, and you meet me with a parcel of insane reproaches. Be calm, my lord—be calm."

"I—I am. Oh, I am!"

"There now—there now—that is better. Well, you must know, then, that Mr. Morris Courtley—"

"A most worthy youth. He shall not go—no—no—my boy Frank said as much as that—no—no!"

"For the love of Heaven do not interrupt me. I say, he is a villain, is this secretary, and has won the affection of our child, Fanny. I tell you, my lord, that if you have one spark of pride in your ancient name and lineage—if you would save it from an alliance with base-born beggars, you will rouse yourself in this matter. This Morris Courtley, whom we have fed and cherished, and made so much of, has at last turned upon us, as he was sure to do, and would rob us of our child."

The old earl wrung his hands.

"Do you comprehend all that? Tell me that you comprehend it, for to do so is to act in it. You cannot understand such a state of things, and not take some steps to alter them. The one proposition involves the other, my lord.—Why do you not answer me?"

"My son! My boy, Frank! My boy!"

"What of him? What would you say to him?"

"He is young. His mind is—is firm yet. He has not been here, or he, too, might be such. I do not know what all this is, but there seems something at my brain that is hot and cold by turns. What did you say about my darling Fan, or said you aught of her at all?"

"I did."

"Then send her to her fond old father's arms, and let him feel that there is one whom he can still love—one heart that still overflows with gentleness and pity for the poor old man. God bless her! God bless her! And my boy, Frank, too—of course, my boy, I will sign the authority; but don't—hush! my dear boy—don't let your mother know!"

"It is all in vain," said the countess, as she rose and paced the room, and her very lips trembled. "I must act alone. I have gone too far. And yet, no: who shall say that it is my doing?"

"Too hard a hand has bent the bow," said a voice at the door of the apartment, "and it has broken!"

The countess started, and saw Lord Francis standing on the threshold of the room.

"Francis—I—that is, you here?"

"Yes, mother."

"Then, my son, I, as your mother, tell you that your conduct is most unworthy—most—unworthy—and I—most unworthy—I leave you—you and your own heart, to its bitter—bitter reflection—my bitter—"

She shook like the last leaf upon an autumn tree as she left the room, and Lord Francis looked after her with a sigh, as he said—

"It has begun. The never dying worm of remorse has begun its dreadful work at her heart.—Oh, God, when and where will all this end? Father!"

"God bless my child!"

The old earl fell heavily to the floor from his chair.

CHAPTER XXV.

MR. OXLEY HOLDS A COUNCIL OF WAR WITH MRS. LEREW AND PETER.

WE left Mr. Oxley in no very amiable frame of mind after the very unsatisfactory interview he had had with Lord Francis Bloxdale. We now return to the steward and his subsequent proceedings, from which it will be seen, that while he would have destroyed the secretary in the opinion of those whose opinion was to him of the highest importance, he had yet a plot in hand of, to him, much greater importance.

- From what the reader has already heard and seen, incidentally rather than in a clear and precise form, it will be tolerably well understood that Mr. Oxley, Mrs. Lerew, and her amiable and accomplished son-in-law, were together engaged in an undertaking that threatened serious calamities to the Bloxdale family, so far as appeared upon the surface of the affair.

It is proper, now, that we should place our readers fairly and clearly in possession of the grounds upon which the false steward thought he might interfere with the status of the Bloxdale family.

A very few sentences will suffice to do that much.

The Earl of Bloxdale, as may be supposed from the complete state of prostration into which he had fallen under the torturing influence of his lady, had always been a man of weak and unsteady intellect.

That weakness, and want of stability of mind and purpose had laid him, in the earlier periods of his life, particularly open to the designs of those who were willing to take the trouble to impose upon him for their own selfish ends and purposes.

At no less a distance of time than twenty years before the incidents we are now relating took place, the woman, Lerew, resided in the neighbourhood of Bloxdale. In fact, she was the daughter of a small shopkeeper, named Green, at Southampton, and Maria Green, as she was then called, was very well known to possess rather a bold, overbearing, and adventurous disposition. The Earl of Bloxdale had, at that time, just came, by the death of his father, to the family estates at Bloxdale ; and, in a storm off the Southampton Water, at the village of Lyndhurst, on the New Forest side of the water, encountered Maria Green in a blacksmith's shop, whither he had ridden for shelter, and she had run for the same purpose.

The bold and insolent manners of the young woman had at first had some effect upon the earl, and he was imprudent enough to meet her several times in the neighbourhood, and to write to her a few letters. Disgusted with her vulgarity, and wondering at himself for ever for a moment looking at such a coarse specimen of the sex, which ought to be all gentleness and feminin grace, the earl repudiated all acquaintance with her, and married the daughter of e respectable house, who was now the mother of his children.

From that time forth, Maria Green and the Earl of Bloxdale had never met, and what had become of Miss Green, as she called herself, for twenty-two years, no one very well knew, and she reappeared at her native place under the name of Lerew, without any one for a moment recognising her.

There she resided for some time, till she boldly called upon Oxley and asked the rent of the cottage on the Bloxdale property, in which she resided immediately afterwards. The steward was charmed with the masculine charms of the gigantic Mrs. Lerew, and the result of this interview was, that after an inspection of the letters of the earl, which she showed to him, and after a conversation with Mr. Peter Lerew, whom she introduced as her son, just out of his apprenticeship to a Jew solicitor in London, Mr. Oxley privately married the lady at Winchester, and placed her in the cottage with the understanding that she was still to go by the name of Lerew, and that they were to aid each other in the prosecution of one of the most infamous plots that three people ever put their heads together to concoct.

The plot was this :—

The Jew attorney, whose name was Lilos, had heard from Peter that his mother had certain letters from the Earl of Bloxdale, and had prevailed upon that lady to show them to him, upon which he had ordered that a threat of their publication should be held out, if the earl would not come down with a handsome sum of money to stay such a proceeding.

This was agreed to without any qualms of conscience on the part of the lady ; but a subsequent event modified the plan, and made it much more fascinating in its possible result, although much more dangerous if it should fail.

That new plan was to assert that the earl had, twenty-two years ago, privately married Maria Green, and that Peter was the delightful issue of the marriage, and that the lady had been quiet so long from an idea that the marriage was not a legal one, but had found out recently that it was perfectly so, and, therefore, that she would, to use the language of Peter, " Go in for her rights like a brick."

Things were in this state when Tom Musgrove, a young gent upon town, in a moment of abstraction put Mr. Lilos's name to a cheque. Now this Tom Musgrove's real name was Thomas Musgrove Williams, and he was the only son of a poor curate who resided at Newport, in the Isle of Wight, where, for eighty pounds per annum, he performed the duties of two church dignitaries, who between them shared for doing nothing, no less a sum than one thousand four hundred pounds per annum, besides other little advantages too numerous to mention.

The forged cheque was only for twenty pounds, and Mr. Lilos did not prosecute.

That *looked* kind on the part of Mr. Lilos, but it was only cunning. He knew that a prosecution took the life of Tom Musgrove, as he was called; but he knew that his silence kept poor Parson Williams and every shilling he could scrape together under his thumb.

Thus the plot reveals itself.

There then was Oxley, his wife, Mrs. Lerew, Peter, Tom Musgrove, and Mr. Lilos, all engaged in the affair to prove the Earl of Bloxdale had married Maria Green; and poor Parson Williams was to be worked upon through his fears for the life of his scapegrace son to aid in the nefarious affair.

Having thus explained the relative position of the parties thus far, and let the reader know what they were trying to do, it only remains for us to show how they tried to do it.

We now proceed to follow Mr. Oxley in a visit to the cottage of Mrs. Lerew, after he had spoken, as we have recorded, to Lord Francis, and got so unexpected a reply from him.

Before the events of that day the feeling of Oxley towards those whom he was working against at Bloxdale was rather one of triumph, and, perhaps, of a little seeming pity at the idea that they should seem to be such mere puppets in his hands, who could be crushed or not at his pleasure.

The kind of reception, however, that he had got from Lord Francis for his news that he had so cunningly given to him, combined with the punishment he had received at the hands of the secretary, had roused into activity every malignant passion in the heart of Oxley, and he now fought for revenge as well as for interest.

We do not mean to say that such was the case; but, certainly, if at any time there had been in the mind of the false steward the least shadow of reluctance to make such a return to the family whose bread he had eaten for so long, as to endeavour to oust them from name and home, it was set at rest now; and, henceforth, he can only be looked upon as a man fixed in his resolve to do all the mischief in his power to those at Bloxdale, as though his had been an inexorable fate.

With these thoughts and feelings then, he hastily put on a great coat, to shelter him from the intense cold of the air outside, and betook himself to Mrs. Lerew's cottage.

To such a woman as she was it did not take a second look to assure her that something rather unusual had taken place at the mansion, and she welcomed her husband with a torrent of questions.

"What has happened? Tell me at once. I know there is something. What is it? Speak, John Oxley, speak."

A horrible imprecation was the reply of Oxley; and then flinging himself into a chair, he added—

"Give me some of the old wine that I brought here, and be quick over it. I am dying of rage and thirst."

The wine was brought to him by Mrs. Lerew, and all the questions that her imagination conjured up were asked, and she was terribly anxious to know what had taken place to reduce Oxley to such a condition.

"Now," she said, after he had taken a full draught. "Now tell me all at once, do, and don't keep me in suspense."

"Listen, then. I will have somebody's life."

"Whose?"

"Morris Courtley's."

Mrs. Lerew shrugged her shoulders—it was a habit she had acquired during some continental rambles, that had been rather more discursive than creditable—and she said—

"As you please. I have not the shadow of an objection to such a thing, I assure you."

"If you had, it would make no difference. Where is Peter?"

"No difference do you say, Mr. Oxley?'

"Not a whit!"

"Then I tell you, sir, it would make a difference. Pray, sir, when has it been that I have allowed you to hold such language as this to me, you ill-conditioned cur? When, I say?"

"Curses on you and everybody else!"

Mrs. Lerew laid hold of Oxley by the cravat, and shook him to and fro till he was within an ace of strangulation, exclaiming as she did so—

"I'll teach you to come here with your ill tempers, you wretch! Is it for this that I condescend to meet you, and to give you the chance of being what you may be? Oh, I will shake the life out of you!"

"Murder—murder!"

"You may call murder as much as you please. Peter—Peter! Bring me the carving-knife directly!"

"No—no!" cried Oxley in a voice of mortal terror. "No—no! I was vexed, and you ought to bear with me. We cannot all command our tempers at all times, Maria, you know. Think no more of it."

"Peter—Peter!"

"What's the row?" said the delightful Peter, coming in from the garden with a cigar in his mouth, and a tumbler of some steaming liquid in his hand. "What's the row, now?"

"She will be the death of me!" said Oxley.

"Sarve you right."

"Oh dear—oh! this is a dreadful day. Everything goes wrong. Maria—Maria, I came to you for sympathy—I came to you to tell you all that happened at the hall; and to ask your advice, I may say your direction; and this is the treatment I meet with. Oh—oh!"

"Then behave yourself better, Oxley. Now mark me: I know you. You are one of those who will be a tyrant or a slave, according as others let you. There are thousands like you, John Oxley. But I am not that kind of woman to give way to you. It won't do. Be civil and respectful to me, and attend to what I tell you to do, and all will be well; but don't try to show off any of your temper here. It won't do."

"I'm sure, Maria, I——"

"Be quiet, then."

"But I didn't mean——'

"Very well, then, hold your tongue, and put your cravat in order—a nice state it is in, to be sure, and a mighty respectable man you look now."

"Well, Maria, that is very likely, considering that somebody has had hold of my cravat, and been knocking my head to and fro, as if it had no sort of feeling of what was done to it."

"What a jolly row!" said Peter. "I say, step-dad, you don't know the old 'un yet. I do."

"Peter!"

"Oh, you needn't try it on upon me, respected maternal relative, 'cos if you do, I'm off; so don't attempt it. Why can't you let the man be, eh?"

"What! is this possible? My own son turned against me? Oh, I am a wretched woman!—a very, very—oh—oh!"

"Gammon!" said Peter, in the most unfilial way in the world, as he handed the brandy-and-water to Oxley—"gammon!"

"Oh, you wretch!—you hound!"

"Hilloa! Come—come! Hilloa! Pull up, or else you'll be running against something, and have a regular split."

"Oh, dear—oh, dear! I—feel——'

Quite abstractedly Mrs. Lerew snatched the glass of brandy-and-water from Oxley, and finished it off at a draught in the most business-like way that can be imagined.

"Well," said Peter, "I think you will do after that. Come, now, don't be having any rows. If we go falling out among each other, there had better be an end of the whole affair. Old Lilos is coming down here to-day, and a pretty sight it would be for him to see you and step-daddy here having a regular set-to. I tell you, it won't do. You'd better give up the whole affair at once than come this sort of caper. Only say so, and I'm off."

Mrs. Lerew wept, as she said in a snuffling tone—

"I'm sure I don't want to quarrel—I'm quite a sucking dove; but that man would aggravate a saint."

"Oh, dear!" groaned Oxley, "I——"

"So you would!" shouted Mrs. Lerew, with the air of a tigress.

"Easy!—easy!" said Peter. "Grease the axle, and don't try the springs too much. Easy, old 'un—easy! I'm off!"

"Oh, my son—you cherub!"

"What?"

"Oh, lor!" said Oxley. "She calls him a cherub!"

"And if I do?" screamed Mrs. Lerew—"and if I do?"

"There you go again," said Peter. "Moderate your delightful voice, if you please, most exquisite paternal relative."

"Oh—oh!" sobbed Mrs. Lerew, suddenly dropping into the lachrymal vein. "Oh—oh! have I lived to see the—the day that—that my own son—my beautiful boy, who wins all hearts, and who has only to show himself to make every—every one admire him, go against me? Oh—oh!"

"Go it!" said Peter.

"Why am I not dead?—dead?—dead?"

"'Cos your time hasn't come, old gal," said Peter.

Oxley rose and buttoned his great-coat right up to his throat. Then putting on his hat, and giving it a blow upon the crown that sent it nearly on to his nose, he said—

"Maria, I am sorry, very sorry to see that you and I don't agree. Perhaps, under such circumstances it will be far better not to run the risk of attempting to carry out an enterprise that requires the most perfect agreement in all particulars, and the most strenuous mental exertions. I think, and I speak now from my heart, I think that I had better abandon the idea of attempting to prove your title to be Countess of Bloxdale; that is my candid opinion."

"John!" said Mrs. Lerew.

"I hear you, madam."

"You are an idiot! You don't know what I have to contend against; and when you see me a little flurried, and ill, you make no allowances, as you ought to do. Think no more of the past, and let us understand each other for the future."

"Ah!" said Peter, "that will do. Confound it! between you both, you will chouse me out of my patrimony. Ain't I to be Lord Peter till the old man kicks the bucket? and then, ain't I to be the Earl of Bloxdale?"

"To be sure you are, you fascinating creature," said his mother.

"So I thought."

"And you shall," she added, folding Peter in a voluminous embrace, "you shall, too. Come, Mr. Oxley, for this once I forgive you."

"Oh, thank you."

"But,"—and here Mrs. Lerew put on a look of most angelic and injured innocence—"but never again wring the heart of a poor, weak, fond, confiding woman!"

"Oh—oh!"

"Never again, I say, John. Do you hear me, sir?"

"Yes—yes."

"Very well; now let us forget all this, and proceed to business. What has happened at the mansion? for that something has, I feel well assured."

Oxley could have said much upon the subject of the forgiveness that was so kindly tendered to him; but his opinion of the gentle lady who called him her husband was such that he thought it was better to leave it unsaid; so he, too, let the past sink into oblivion, and told all that had occurred that day at Bloxdale.

Oxley was listened to with attention, both by Mrs. Lerew and by Peter; and then the latter said—

"Well, it seems to me that things are coming to a crisis. I wish old Lilos had come, for I am tired of being here, and doing nothing."

"Hush!" said his mother.

"What for?"

"There is some one at the door. Hark, there is a footstep on the gravel path outside. Go, Peter, and see who it is. Go, my cherub, at once."

CHAPTER XXVI.

COURTLEY FINDS LORD FRANCIS'S LETTER, AND SEEKS LADY FANNY.

THE person who was on the gravel path outside the cottage of Mrs. Lerew was the Tom Musgrove of whose antecedents the reader knows quite enough to enable him not to feel strange in that young gentleman's company. But it will be necessary now to leave the party at the cottage, in order to return to the mansion, to take notice of what is passing there.

Little did Lord Francis Bloxdale suspect that, in addition to the griefs that he knew of, there were others brewing against him and his that he had not the remotest conception could exist.

If that young nobleman had but known that Oxley had a much more gigantic plot to elaborate than consisted in the deflection of his accounts, or in the gratification of his enmity against the secretary, the circumstances that already filled his mind would have sunk into insignificance.

The knowledge, however, was soon to come.

Courtley, too, was in a state of mind that bordered upon distraction. There was nothing that any one could possibly have said or suggested to him concerning the impropriety and the apparent ingratitude of his conduct to the Bloxdale family, in establishing an understanding with Lady Fanny, considering the difference in their positions in life, that his own imagination did not paint to him in much more vivid colours.

His sufferings were intense, and yet his love seemed to grow along with his remorse, and never had he so adored the fair girl, who loved him, too, with one of the purest and holiest passions that could fill the heart of any human being.

It was very well that there should be times when poor Morris Courtley should tell himself that he had no right to fall in love with an earl's daughter; but when did love, in its natural and holy beauty and excellence ever acknowledge such artificial distinctions of

rank? Whenever did the feeling of affection that filled up two such young and gentle hearts as theirs wait upon the good will of such circumstances? Never! never!

It was towards the dusk of the evening, that early twilight which at that wintry season preceded by some hours the time when Lord Francis had said in his note that he would meet Morris Courtley in the library—that the poor, mind-beleagured secretary crept to the chair in which he had been wont to sit and beguile so many hours with sweet thoughts of his love.

The wood fire blazed and crackled upon the hearth, shedding its many tinted light upon the walls of the large saloon, and making the shadow of the secretary look, at times, instinct with giant life, as it danced upon the roof of the old library.

By accident, Courtley, after he had there sat for awhile, placed his hand upon Lord Francis's note, addressed to himself.

The thought—and oh! what a delightful one it was while it lasted—that the note was from Lady Fanny, came over him; but a second glance at the writing convinced him of his error.

"No, no," he said. "It is not from her.'

Poor Courtley trembled as he opened the little note; and when he had read the few lines that it contained, he let it drop from his hands to the floor, as he said faintly—

"It is all over now!"

The tone of the note was quite sufficient to let Courtley know that the subject of the communication that was to be made to him at eight o'clock by his young and noble patron was concerning the Lady Fanny; and well might the poor, dependant secretary say with a sigh, "All is over now!"

This rather afflicted, though, than surprised Courtley. The hatred of Oxley was one that he had felt quite sure would be carried out to the utmost; and now he did not doubt but that Lord Francis was fully possessed of all that Oxley knew, along with all the false calumny that an enemy could impart to the transaction.

"Yes, all is over," he said, as he sunk back in the old chair, "all is over now. He will come, and either with passion he will upbraid me with my ingratitude, or he will, with mild regret, shrink from me as one in whom he has been mistaken, and beg of me to quit his sight for ever."

Such maddening thoughts were not of the complexion that would enable Courtley to sit for long in that old chair, and he rose and paced the library to and fro with anxious strides.

"Oh, what can I say to him when he does come? What excuse? What justification can I attempt? None—none. All is over!"

There came a tap at the library door.

"No, no," cried Courtley, "it is not eight yet. Oh, God, no! Let me have some time to think!"

"Lor, Mr. Courtley!" said Ann, as she peeped into the room. "Is that you, sir?"

LADY FANNY AND MORRIS COURTLEY IN THE LIBRARY AT BLONDALE.

"Yes—oh, yes. Tell me of your mistress—speak to me of her, or I shall go mad! Is she well—happy?"

"Oh—oh—oh!"

Ann dropped into the chair by the fireside, and flinging her apron over her head and face, she sobbed so bitterly that it was full five minutes before Courtley, notwithstanding all his perseverance, could get an intelligible word from her.

"Ann, Ann!" he said, "you have come to tell me something, and you will not tell it to me now that you are here. I will guess it."

"No, no, you cannot."

"Fanny is dead!"

"Dead?"

"Yes, that is it; but you see how calm I am. Her fair and delicate spirit only waits for me upon that eternal shore which I, too, shall soon reach!"

He opened a drawer of the table at which he stood, and from beneath some papers he took a little canvas bag, from which he produced a pair of small, finely mounted pistols.

Ann uttered a scream.

"Oh, Mr. Courtley, what would you do?"

"Die, and rejoin Fanny. Did you not tell me she was no more?"

"Oh, no—no!"

"No?—I thought—oh, was it only a thought, a dream?—I thought you came with so much grief to say that she was dead."

Ann shook her head.

"Listen to me, Mr. Courtley. She has told Lord Francis all."

"All?"

"Oh, dear, yes. It wasn't much; but since then she has hardly spoken a word, and only a little while ago she looked so pale, and so sad, and yet she did not cry, but she placed her arm round my neck, and said, in such a tone of voice that it would have melted a heart of stone, 'Ann, when I am no more, tell Morris that to the last I loved him!'"

"Oh, God!"

"And then she laid herself down on her bed, and she has not spoken since, only when I wanted to call for assistance, she shook her head; and I don't know what to do.—Oh, Mr. Courtley, I have come to you, for I dare not speak to any one else about her. Tell me, oh, tell me what I ought to do!"

Courtley's lips moved, but he spoke not.

"Why don't you tell me, Mr. Courtley? Oh—oh! He, too, is going off in the same way.—Help! help!"

"Hush! hush! Ann, what — what did Lord Francis say to her?"

"Alas, I know not!"

"I will go to her! Though all the world should try to stay my progress I will go to her! I love her with all my heart—God knows that. I will go to her! Do not try to stop me, Ann! I tell you I must see her. She will die, and then I shall die with the sin of self-destruction on my soul, and so we may never meet again. I will go to her!"

"Oh, Mr. Courtley, don't—you must not!"

"Do not seek to stay me!"

"But—oh, gracious! if any one were to see you!"

Courtley rushed to the door of the library, but Ann clung to him, and still implored him to remain where he was.

"You know not what evil tongues might make of this visit," she said. "We are all watched, no doubt, now.—Oh, I was so foolish, so mad to come here; but, in truth, I was terrified."

"Let me go, then."

"No—no! Some other time you shall come and see her, but not now, for you look so strange and wild."

"What can you dread? If I were mad, why then, indeed—as they say that madmen, to prove how opposite it is to sanity, attack most fiercely those that were once loved in healthier moments—I might harm Fanny; but I am not mad. See, now, I am calmer—much calmer than you are. Come—come. There is no harm in my seeing her, and there may be much good."

"Oh, if I could only think that!"

"You may think so."

"But, Mr. Courtley, some one may see you on your route."

"No, the mansion is wrapped in gloom. Already the twilight of a brief winter's day is thickening around all things. I will follow you, Ann. Oh, I will be so very cautious. But I am to see Lord Francis to-night to talk of this affair, and it is necessary that I should see Fanny before I meet with him. Do you understand me, Ann?"

"Oh, yes, I do—I do."

"Then precede me to the chamber. Tell her that I come. Oh, go at once, and with slow footsteps I will follow you."

Ann no longer resisted him, but, sobbing as she went, she crept up the grand staircase to the picture-gallery, and so went through the gloom and increasing darkness on—on to the chamber of that poor heart-stricken one. Courtley followed her, looking more like a ghost than a living, breathing man, and he felt as if his very existence now hung upon a thread that the smallest violence would snap asunder.

In this way they both reached the door of Fanny's chamber, and in their progress thither they met no one. Ann whispered in an agitated manner to Courtley—

"Wait—wait!"

"I will," he said.

Ann then glided into the room, and Courtley, with his hands clasped, leant against the side of the door-frame, and tried to pray for her whom he loved so well; but he could not command his thought from earth to Heaven, for he heard the sound of grief within the chamber, and then there was a voice that said—

"Oh, come—come!"

He touched the door and it yielded to him, and then he rather staggered than walked into the apartment.

It was a room of rare beauty, that sleeping chamber of Lady Fanny. All that art could do to make it seem the fit abode of so much youth, and beauty, and innocence, had been done; and the rich traces of decoration were located upon all sides with reckless profusion. Silk hangings, rare vases, flowers, pictures, and the thousand and one elegancies that wealth can crowd within four walls, were to be found there in abundance.

The room was lit by one wax light, placed in a branch candlestick attached to the toilette.

Upon the bed, with its silken coverlet half thrown over her, lay poor Lady Fanny. Ann was kneeling by the bedside and sobbing. Oh, how pale and sad was the sweet face that met the gaze of Courtley—that face that he so loved! The pang that shot through his heart at that moment went nigh to killing him.

"Fanny—Fanny! my love—my life—my own darling!"

He clasped her in his arms, and raised her to her feet, and it was then, that opening her sweet eyes she looked into his face and knew with whom she was, and a flood of tears came to the relief of the overburthened heart, and she clung to him and sobbed bitterly.

"That is well," he said. "My Fanny—my Fan—my darling — God's blessing be upon you! What is this? Oh, darling, dearest and best, my foolish fears would have it that you were ill—that you were going to leave your own Morris. Fan!—my Fan!—oh, calm yourself."

"No—no! Let me weep."

"Let her," said Ann. "It is a blessed change."

And so it was, for the paroxysm of tears carried the agony of the young heart with it; and then the innocent young creature cast a glance around her, and for the first time she seemed to be aware of where she was, and of the impropriety of the scene. She withdrew herself from the arms of her lover, and covering her face with her hands, she said—

"Oh, Morris, how is this?—how is this?"

"He would come," said Ann; "he would."

"It is my fault, if fault there be," said Morris. "I heard that you were ill—I feared that you were dying, and if all the world had stood in my way, I must have come to you. Fanny—forgive me!"

"But how, Morris?"

"Nay, what matters it? To the peace of heart and purpose there is no impurity. But I will leave you darling—you are better?"

"Yes, Morris, I am better. We shall—be compelled to part."

"We shall."

"Oh, no—no, Morris! Why do you say so?"

"Did not you say so, dear?"

"Yes, but—but, you should not, Morris. I will not let you go. I will tell them all that I love you. What to me is wealth, state, dignity, lineage, all the world, if I am not with you?"

"Oh, that I had a throne to offer you!"

"And do you think, you bad, cruel, Morris, that I could love you better if you had? Oh, no—no! My brother knows all. The day will come when he, too, may love, and then he will pity us."

"What said he, darling?"

Fanny shook her head.

"I hardly know; but it was more in sorrow than in anger that he spoke, and that was worse, you know."

"It was."

"But you will not go away, Morris? You must tell him that you love me, and I will tell him that I love you."

"Alas! alas!"

"Why do you cry alas?"

"You are noble, and he will tell me that it is wrong and a great sin in me to dare to love one so far above me in rank."

"Noble! Oh, my Morris, you it is who are noble. Mine is the nobility of accident, yours of nature. I will tell him that. I will tell him that you are nobler than all of us—that you have thoughts and feelings that bestow upon you such a patent of nobility that no king could give you. You shall not go, my Morris! Oh, tell me that you will not leave me for ever?"

"What shall I do—what shall I say?"

"That you love me!"

"Do you doubt that?"

"Oh, no! But in the saying that, you say all that you need ever say; for in that is comprehended all else. You cannot go from me if you love me, Morris."

"I cannot!"

"Then you promise me that you will not? You will speak to my brother as a man should speak to a man—you will bid him make the case his own in imagination, and you will ask him what he would do?"

"I will—I will!"

"My Morris—my own Morris!"

"Hush!" said Ann. "Oh, hush!"

"What is it?"

"Somebody at the door."

Lady Fanny clung to Courtley; and her face, to which the colour had in some measure returned, became as pale as death itself.

"Is it my mother?" she said.

"Oh, Heaven! I hope not," said Ann. "What shall we do—oh, what shall we do? Mr. Courtley, Mr. Courtley, why did you come here? Oh, wretched girl that I am, what will now become of me?"

Rather a smart rap came at the chamber-door which Ann had had the good prudence to close and fasten after the entrance of Morris Courtley.

"You must hide," said Ann.

"Where?"

"Oh, I am lost—lost!" sobbed Lady Fanny.

"The window?" said Courtley.

"It is a hundred feet from the ground!" said Ann.

Tap—tap! came at the door again.

"Better death by any means," said Courtley, "than that even a breath of scandal should assail you, Fanny. Farewell!"

"No—no! Oh, God, no! Hide him, Ann, in the wardrobe. Quick! Oh, quick! Hide him, or he will kill himself!"

"Will that be secure?" said Courtley. "I don't care for myself, but for you!"

"Yes—yes! Go at once," said Ann, as she opened the tall door of a wardrobe that was fitted into a recess of the room, and pushed Courtley in among a number of dresses that hung upon pegs at full length within it.

CHAPTER XXVII.

MISS WICKS THINKS AND HOPES THAT SHE HAS MADE A LITTLE DISCOVERY.

IT was Miss Wicks who came to the door of Lady Fanny's room, as Morris Courtley made good his retreat into the wardrobe. Of the unfriendly feeling of the waiting-woman of the countess, both Fanny and Ann had had too many proofs to doubt the existence of such an animus for a moment.

Poor Lady Fanny surely had never endured such agony as now possessed her; and Ann was nearly as heart-stricken as her young mistress; for though the visit of Courtley to that room was one of the most harmless and innocent visits in the world, they could not but feel that they were all liable to the most terrible misconstruction on account of it.

Had there been any guilt in the case, or any premeditated guilt, there would have been abundance of self-possession. It is a popular mistake to suppose that it is guilt that trembles and turns pale. Innocence, when wrongfully suspected, betrays ten times the emotion.

Lady Fanny was quite unable to speak; but Ann, when she saw that Courtley was concealed, had just judgment and presence of mind enough left to feel that it would be better to admit Miss Wicks to the room, and let her see that there was nothing to see than keep her at the door, arousing her suspicions until they should grow into something weighty and dangerous.

"Did you want my young lady, Miss Wicks?" said Ann, with as quiet and calm a look as possible.

It would have required a person much less versed in the dissimulation of human nature than the great Miss Wicks was, to avoid observing the state of suppressed agitation with which the question was put to her; and she replied, as she looked scrutinizingly in the face of Ann—

"Dear me, Ann, you don't look well."

"Thank you, Miss Wicks. Did you want my lady?"

"Yes; the countess wishes to see her. But I was told to tell her herself, so if she is here I will just step in."

"Step—in—I—that is——"

"Why, what is the matter?"

"Oh, there is nothing the matter—there can be nothing the matter. What should there be the matter?"

"There should be nothing the matter, of course," said Miss Wicks, and with a stately step she marched past poor Ann, who was too bewildered to stop her, and if she had stopped her, it is doubtful if that course would have done any good under the circumstances, so it was as well as it was; and, possibly, if poor Lady Fanny had been able to control her feelings a little, and to put on an air of indifference to the great Wicks, she might have succeeded in baffling that lady's curiosity. But, alas! she could not. All the agitation that was at her inmost heart looked out from her sweet face, and was but too apparent.

"Goodness gracious me!" exclaimed Miss Wicks, with quite a toss of her head. "You must be ill, Lady Fanny."

"Ill?" gasped Fanny.

"Dear me, yes. You look so very much agitated."

"Agitated?"

"To be sure you do. Really, Ann, it seems to me that you don't take care of your young lady as you ought to do. But,"—here Miss Wicks lowered her voice to an odd snuffling whisper, that sounded so decidedly evangelical, that it was provocative at once of suspicions of its sincerity—"but, I am sure that if I can be of any service in any way whatever, it will give me the sincerest pleasure; and with my experience, I dare say that if any little matter is a trouble and a perplexity to Lady Fanny, I might be able to be of the greatest assistance. Hem!"

Miss Wicks fully meant to imply by this speech, that if Lady Fanny liked to trust her, she was an individual who would not stop at trifles, and that she had her price, which, when paid, would command her best services and zeal in behalf of the purchaser.

It is very doubtful, though, if Miss Wicks would not for a higher offer have sold her kind employer, if Lady Fanny had for a moment listened to the insidious proposal, which she did not, for her pure spirit at once revolted against it with a shudder.

What Miss Wicks had said, or rather insinuated, more by her tone than by her words, was so really insulting and hurtful to the feelings of Lady Fanny, that indignation gave her courage, and she said—

"Miss Wicks, this is my apartment, and you are not in my service. If you bring a message from my mother, deliver it at once and go."

"Oh, dear, yes. Of course I will. Your mother desires that you will come to her chamber at once, as she has something very particular to say to you."

"Say that I will come."

"But she expects you with me."

"I will come shortly."

"Very well, Lady Fanny; as the countess would be angry with me if I came to her without you, I will wait, if you please."

"What, Miss Wicks! does the fact that you are my mother's waiting-woman give you boldness enough to induce you to say that you will wait in my room whether I will or not?"

"Oh, no, Lady Fanny, I will wait outside the door."

"No—no."

"Yes," said Ann, who thought that if Lady Fanny was at once to accompany Miss Wicks, the coast would be clear for the escape of Courtley from the wardrobe; "oh, yes, my lady, would it not be better for you to go at once?"

Lady Fanny hesitated; and then a dull crash came from something that was evidently knocked down in the wardrobe. It happened, that upon one of the shelves were some empty essence bottles that Ann had placed there out of the way, and Courtley, in slightly shifting his position, threw them down, and they in breaking produced the sound that came quite plainly upon the ears of Miss Wicks.

"Oh, dear!" said Miss Wicks, "what is that?"

"No—nothing," gasped Ann.

Lady Fanny looked cold and rigid as she clasped her hands, but she said not a word.

"The cat, perhaps," said Miss Wicks.

"Yes—oh, yes, the cat!" said Ann, who was glad to catch at any straw that might float her and her young mistress out of the terrible dilemma that they were in. "I mentioned to you that we could not get the cat out of the room."

"Well, I think you did," said Miss Wicks, with quite a horrid look, "I do think you did mention that; and, after all, I think I had better go to the countess and say that as soon as you have got rid of the cat that you will come to her, Lady Fanny?"

"Oh, God!" said Lady Fanny, as she clasped her hands over her face.

"Are you human?" said Ann.

"Hey-day! What is all this? Well—well, it's no business of mine; I would be a friend if I were allowed to be one; but, as it is, of course, as I say, it's no business of mine. Take care of the cat. I never did know a cat to be so clumsy before in all my life."

There was a slight rattle at the lock of the room door, as Miss Wicks reached it to go out; but that might have been occasioned by her dress catching in it, so neither Ann nor Fanny paid any attention to it, and Miss Wicks left the room and closed the door after her.

"Oh, heaven!" said Lady Fanny, "what shall I do? Oh, what shall I do? Tell me what to do!"

"Hush—hush!"

"No, I must speak or go mad."

"Then go mad, my lady, do; but don't say a word, I beg of you, for that odious Miss Wicks is outside the door, I'd lay any wager to anybody of all my perquisites for twenty years."

"But, Ann—Ann!"

"Don't—oh, don't!"

"Kill me, Ann! I have not the courage to kill myself—I am such a poor, weak coward. Oh, Ann, do find some means to kill me!"

"Fiddle-de-dee!" said Ann.

Lady Fanny now thought that Ann, under the pressure of the perplexing circumstances in which they were placed, had gone mad; and that one of the singular effects of the aberration of intellect under which she laboured was a desire to pull up the carpet of the room, for Ann knelt down close to the door, and dragged up a portion of the thick carpet that was close to the lower part of it. When that portion of carpet, though, was pulled up, it showed that there was rather a considerable space between the door and the floor; and adroitly producing a long thin piece of whalebone from out of some mysterious portion of her costume, Ann put it under the door, and gently moved it along, so that if any one had been standing on the outside it must have encountered their feet.

The whalebone went easily to and fro without opposition.

"She is gone," said Ann, as she replaced the carpet—"she is gone, and now is the time for Mr. Courtley to go."

"Oh, Ann, are you sure?"

"Quite, my lady—quite."

"Then let him go. Morris—dear Morris!"

"Here," said Morris, opening the wardrobe and letting down another avalanche of essence jars and glasses, that the closet door only had stopt from falling.

"Murder!" said Ann. "What are you doing?"

"I really don't know," said Courtley.

"Morris—Morris!" exclaimed Fanny, we are lost!"

"Lost?"

"Nonsense!" said Ann, "you are found, you mean, Mr. Courtley, and you will be found out, too, if you don't go away at once. Oh, dear—oh, dear! one might as well be murdered outright as put into such dreadful tortures as this, and yet all the while be as innocent as angels and doves. Go, sir—oh, go!"

"Yes, Morris!" cried Fanny, clinging to him, so as effectually to prevent him from going. "Go at once."

"But dear, dear Fanny——"

"Oh—oh!" said Ann, "isn't this too bad! Oh, Miss Fanny, do let him go."

"But he won't go."

"I will—I will! I heard something about a cat."

"It was you," said Ann. "A Thomas cat. Now do, Lady Fanny, let go his coat, for Miss Wicks may come back at any moment.

"And nothing has been decided upon," said Fanny. "We have come to no conclusion, Morris, as to what we ought to do."

"We will meet again, dearest and best," said Courtley, as he held her for a moment in his arms, "and let what will come, I will take care that you be completely justified. Now, Ann, I am ready to go."

"Farewell, Morris."

"Dearest, farewell."

"Oh, stuff," said Ann. "Do come, now, at once. Oh!"

Ann uttered a shriek, and Morris staggered back as he saw her with her hand upon the handle of the door, and her face pale as death, and her very lips quivering with emotion; he was thunderstruck to see the young girl in such a state, and as for poor Fanny, she shook so that it was quite a terrible sight to see her.

"In the name of Heaven, girl," said Courtley, "why do you stand there horrifying us in that way? Let me leave the chamber!"

"No, no—you can't—you can't!"

"Can't? Why—wherefore can I not?"

"Miss Wicks! Oh! oh! she has taken the key out of this side of the door and put it into that side, and locked us all in. Oh! oh! we are, indeed, lost now! Oh, Lady Fanny, forgive your poor Ann. It is all my fault—my fault, indeed, and I wish I was dead, I do—I do—I do! Oh! oh! if I were only dead—very dead, indeed!"

Ann would have uttered another scream in her agony of spirit, but Courtley stopped it by placing his hand over her mouth until she was in danger of suffocation, and that it is to be presumed changed, as well it might, the current of her thoughts.

"Fanny," said Courtly, as he advanced to her, and took both her trembling hands in his, "what is the meaning of all this? I heard but very imperfectly what took place while I was in the wardrobe."

Lady Fanny tried to speak, but the effort was too much for her, and she could only cling to Courtley, and letting her head droop upon his bosom, sobbed convulsively.

Morris felt distracted, and turning to Ann, he cried aloud in a tone of anger—

"Wretched girl, tell me at once what that abominable Miss Wicks said to cause all this confusion."

"I am a wretched girl," said Ann. "I know it—I know it. But Miss Wicks knows you are here, and she has gone to tell the countess, and Lord Francis, and the earl, and Mr. Oxley, and all the house; and you are locked in by her, and we are all locked in and unable to escape."

"I see it all," said Courtley. "My dear Fanny, be comforted. All may yet be well. Farewell!—They shall not find me here."

"But how can you fly, Morris? Whither? The door is so thick and strong, you cannot break it open."

"The window."

"Certain death!"

"And what of that? I shall save you from worse, my Fanny ; and I have a hope—I have yet a dear hope."

"Oh, of what?"

"That I may fall so as, at least, to be able to crawl to some other spot to die than under the window, so that I may not be found. I may, perhaps, be able to reach the plantation. Farewell! It is my duty to do so, and I will save you, Fanny. May God bless you!"

"No," said Fanny, clinging to him, and screaming hoarsely. "God would not, could not bless me if I let you go to death in such a way. Help me, Ann—help me! He shall not go!"

She clung to him with a force that he dared not, lest he should hurt her, exert force enough to resist; and Ann, too, who was horrified at the idea that he would fling himself from the window, and so meet with certain death upon the stones in one of the court-yards that was below, likewise seized him by the feet as she preserved her kneeling posture; and there they all were, a most miserable group.

The sound of footsteps came rapidly along the corridor, and Lady Fanny felt as if her heart were freezing within her.

CHAPTER XXVIII.

MR. OXLEY ENJOYS, FOR THE TIME BEING, A VERY GREAT TRIUMPH, INDEED.

WE must now leave Morris Courtley and Lady Fanny and Ann for a short time, while we take a glance at the very vindictive and diabolical proceedings of Miss Wicks, contingent upon the discovery that she presumed she had made of the presence of Morris in the chamber of Fanny.

Miss Wicks based her evidence that he was there upon three conditions.

The first was, that before she was admitted to the room, she felt certain she had heard the voice of the secretary ; the second was the noise in the wardrobe ; and the third was the evident confusion of both Ann and her young mistress.

Now, the experience of Miss Wicks in this wicked world was such that she could not very well understand how there could be concealment and confusion without guilt ; and it is but fair to her to say, that from that moment she set it down in her own vitiated mind for a fact that there was a positive intrigue between the secretary and Lady Fanny.

All this, it will be seen, arose from the want of presence of mind of the parties in Lady Fanny's room ; for, under the circumstances, it would have been far better that Miss Wicks should have found Morris Courtley quietly seated there than that he should have hidden in the wardrobe from her.

The manœuvre of taking the key out of

the lock of the door upon the inside, and replacing it on the outside, and giving it the turn that fastened the door, was quick in Miss Wicks's case, and was one of those pieces of practical, malignant cleverness, that none but an old intriguer could possibly have carried out with the dexterity that she did.

Having thus her prisoners secure, the next thing was to make as much as possible of that fact.

Miss Wicks was a little bewildered now between the many excellent opportunities she had of making a thorough noise in the house. She might run to the countess and tell her—she might seek Lord Francis and tell him—she might leave the remainder of the affair to the nice management of Mr. Oxley. Ah, that was it! That was the course to adopt!

"Yes," said Miss Wicks, with a toss of the head, "Oxley will manage it. I will let him know; and if they manage to get out of that room, in the meantime, through its massive mahogany door, or if Mr. Court-ley likes to break his neck by a fall from the window, why, I will forgive him."

How light of foot, and how agile was the stately Miss Wicks when there was any mischief to be done! She was down the grand staircase, and in the room of Oxley, in so short a period of time, that one would have wondered how she became possessed of such sylphilitic powers.

Oxley was alone, and in deep thought.

Miss Wicks laid her long, skinny hand upon his shoulder, before he was even aware of her presence, and then he started to his feet, crying out as he did so—

"The devil! Who is that?—No—no—What do you want?"

"Oxley?" said Miss Wicks.

"Oh, my dear Wicks, it—it is you, is it? How kind—how very kind is the little sur-prise: I was deep in thought."

"About what?"

"Our future mutual interest, of course."

"Oh, very well; but Morris Courtley is in Lady Fanny's chamber at this present moment, and if you think you can take any advantage of the fact, it is at your disposal."

"Advantage of the fact!" cried Oxley. "It is everything. But—but you mean that he was there?"

"And is there still."

"How do you know that, my dear Wicks? He may have taken the alarm and left."

"No, the door is locked and the key on the outside. I thought that as he was there it was better to let him be until I had spoken to you upon the subject."

Oxley fairly embraced Miss Wicks, as he cried—

"You are the most charming and clever of human beings, Wicks, I declare you are. And so you locked them in? Ha! ha! Alone, too—alone! Ha! ha!"

"No."

"No—no? I thought you said that——"

"That he was there with Lady Fanny, but not alone. That odious minx, Ann, is with them; but that, you know, Mr. Oxley, really makes no difference in the world."

"Oh, no—none in reality; only it would have been so much better if they had only been alone, you know, my dear Wicks, so very much better. But do you go and tell the countess and I will tell Lord Francis. Yet stay: I think I will tell the countess and you had better tell the young lord."

"Why so?"

"Why, you see, he—he—that is, we are not upon very good terms just now, that is all, and he might just get into a passion, while if you tell him he cannot very well do so. You will find him in his own room, my charming Wicks. I saw him pass across the hall only a little while ago. There is no time to be lost. Go to him at once, and I will go to the countess. Where is she?"

"In her boudoir."

"Good; I will find her. Oh, my dear Wicks, you don't know how much pleased I am with your cleverness in this little matter; but you are certainly one of the most ad-mirable of women."

"Oh, it's nothing," said Miss Wicks. "I shall have the banns put up at St. Mary's Church, at Southampton, Oxley."

"Ye—e—s. Oh, yes. I will do it."

"Very well; but I will not have any more delays, mind that."

"Delays, my charming Miss Wicks? Oh, what a delightful day that will be when I call you mine!"

"Very well. I will now go to Lord Francis."

For the sake of keeping up the delusion in the mind of the virtuous Wicks, that he in-tended to marry her, Mr. Oxley kissed the faded cheek of the elderly waiting-woman, and then she hurried off to the study of Lord Francis, to tell him where Morris Courtley, his pet secretary, might be found.

Perhaps, of all persons within Bloxdale House, Miss Wicks felt the most independant of what Lord Francis might say or think regarding the little communication she had to make to him. She felt so perfectly secure in the patronage and the protection of the countess, that she cared little for what pas-sion Lord Francis might think proper to display upon the occassion; so it was with quite an easy, stately look, that Wicks took her way to the young lord's study.

Now poor Lord Francis surely had enough to vex him already, without this terrible communication. He sat with that feel-ing of solitude that had been lately growing upon him, brooding over the painful situation in which he was placed, when there came a tap at the door of his room.

"Come in."

Miss Wicks appeared upon the threshold, and executed rather a disdainful curtsey, for as she was in the service of the countess, she considered Lord Francis in the light of an enemy; and she would have disdained to seek him, but that she came ready armed to inflict such a blow upon his heart.

"Well?" said Lord Francis.

"Mr. Morris Courtley, the secretary."

"What of him, woman?"

"He is now in your sister's bed-chamber!"

Lord Francis rose from his chair, and then sunk back again with a deep groan. Miss Wicks executed another stately curtsey, and then deliberately left the apartment, as if she had made one of the most ordinary of all ordinary announcements to the young noble.

A mist appeared to be gathering about the eyes of Lord Francis, and he fancied that he was about to faint. He made a violent effort, both of mind and body, and shook off the delusion that would soon have had power of itself to produce some disastrous effect upon his system; and springing again to his feet, he cried in a voice of terrible apprehension—

"If this be true, then is Courtley, indeed, a villain, and my poor sister has fallen—fallen never to rise again! Oh, God, no! it is not possible, and she so pure—so innocent —so child like in her very thoughts. Oh, no—no—no! And yet, are not these the very qualities upon which such as Courtley may be frequently work upon. Oh, Heaven, spare my reason from this rude shock! But if he be, indeed, a villain, it is from the very purity, and goodness, and unsuspicious nature of Fanny that she has fallen!"

Lord Francis made a rush to a corner of the room, where, amid a miscellaneous assemblage of all sorts of arms and curiosities he had brought from the continent, he made a snatch at a Damascus sabre. The bright blade came from its sheath at a touch, and, thus armed, the young nobleman rushed from his room, and made his way up the grand staircase to the door of his sister's chamber, within which there might be, for him, such a sight of horror.

It was the hasty footsteps of Lord Francis that had been heard by Morris, and Lady Fanny, and Ann.

But we must now follow Oxley to the boudoir of the Countess of Bloxdale, where he thought that with the news he brought, he should, at all events, get a more gracious reception than from the young lord, whom he dreaded to encounter with such a story upon his lips, notwithstanding he had sufficient faith in Miss Wicks to believe its truth.

Precisely as Miss Wicks tapped at the door of Lord Francis' study, did Mr. Oxley make a similar application to the door of the countess's boudoir; and the ready "Come in" emboldened him to turn the handle of the lock.

So low was the bow that Oxley perpetrated, that while he was still, as regarded his feet, on the threshold of the door, his bald head and sleek-looking ugly face were quite within the room.

"Mr. Oxley?" said the countess, in a tone of surprise.

"Yes, my lady. Your very humble servant."

"Come in, sir."

"You are very good and kind, my lady, and nothing but the humble duty that I owe to your ladyship could possibly induce me to intrude in this way."

"It is no intrusion, Mr. Oxley, as, no doubt, you have something of importance to communicate to me."

"I have, my lady."

"What is it?"

"Oh, my lady, I fear, that is, I may say— I know that—that Mr. Morris Courtley, the secretary—the low-born secretary—he was without a shoe to his foot, metaphorically speaking, when he came here—the special protegé of my Lord Francis, of whom he thinks so much——"

"Pray, Mr. Oxley, be more explicit."

"He is now in Lady Fanny's chamber, my lady—her bed-chamber. Ah! He is there with Lady Fanny—alone, I believe. Alone!'

Mr. Oxley thought the effect would be better to suppress the little fact that Ann made one of the party.

The Countess of Bloxdale drew a long breath, and her colour went and came perceptibly, for her ladyship, as the company had left the house, had not thought it worth while to paint that day.

She turned a searching glance at Mr. Oxley as she said—

"Are you sure of this?"

"If your ladyship would condescend to walk to the chamber, you might satisfy the doubt."

"Good God!"

"Amen, my lady—Amen! I am very much gratified that your ladyship can take such a fact with so much true Christian resignation."

"Resignation!" shouted the countess, as she sprang towards Oxley, and all but trod upon his toes. "How dare you talk to me of resignation?"

"My lady, I——"

"Silence, sir! Follow me at once. I will satisfy myself of the truth of this dreadful statement. Follow me, Mr. Oxley. Oh, sir, you tremble, do you? Tell me, is this some base lie of your own, which will not stand the test of investigation, or can it be truth? Oh, you need not look at me in such a fashion, sir. I am suspicious of you."

"Suspicious of me?"

"Yes, Mr. Oxley, of you. How dare you suppose it would gratify me to hear that my daughter had disgraced herself—disgraced me—disgraced her family?"

"My lady, I really——"

"You really what, sir?"

"I really did not think that my zeal in

ANN IN ASSIDUOUS ATTENDANCE ON FANNY BLOXDALE.

your ladyship's service would have met with such a reward as it has."

The countess was silent for a few moments, and then she said, in something of a softened tone of voice—

"If I could but think it all zeal !"

"Oh, my lady," replied Oxley, squeezing a tear out of the corner of his left eye, " I did think that, after what I had suffered in your ladyship's service, I should, at least, have the satisfaction of being believed. I did think that after being nearly murdered by your ladyship's great enemy, the secretary —after being told to my face by Lord Francis Bloxdale that my accounts were wrong—after incurring, as a just steward is sure to do, the hatred of the whole household, that, at least, I should be believed when I made a statement to your grace——"

" Hush !"

" Yes, my lady – oh, yes."

" Some one comes. Oh, is it you, Wicks ?"

" At your ladyship's service," said Wicks

" Where is Lord Francis ?"

"I don't know, my lady."

"Come with me and Mr. Oxley, Wicks.

We are going to the chamber of my daughter, just to see how she is, as Mr. Oxley is afraid she is a little indisposed. Come, Mr. Oxley, we will go at once."

A glance of intelligence passed between Wicks and Oxley. Wicks slightly nodded her head, and then he knew that she had seen Lord Francis, and told him all that was desirable for him to know.

CHAPTER XXIX.

THE COUNTESS AND LORD FRANCIS MEET WITH A LITTLE SURPRISE.

LORD FRANCIS BLOXDALE stood faint and panting by the door of his sister's chamber. The speed at which he had flown rather than run up the great staircase, had exhausted him; and he paused a little before he would present himself to Fanny.

In that pause, too, the fine and gentle portion of his nature began to exert its sway over him; and the Damascus sabre that, in the first heat and flush of his wild anger he had stnached up, trembled in his grasp.

"Poor—poor Fanny!" he said.

The sword shook still more; and, finally, he placed it in a corner by the door, and turned away his gaze from it, saying—

"No—no! Fanny—my sister—my long-loved, fondly cherished sister! I will not yet believe this frightful scandal with which your name is mixed! I do not!—I will not believe it!"

With a deep-drawn sigh of great relief that he was able to say so much to himself, Lord Francis turned from the door; and it is possible that the doubt of whether Courtley was in his sister's chamber or not was so dear to him, that he would not have sought to dispel it by an actual examination of the room, had not the sound of footsteps along the corridor induced him to pause.

Another moment, and he saw his mother.

Lord Francis turned pale and flushed by turns, as he felt that now, if she was seeking the chamber of Fanny, an eclaircissement must take place, and he could not leave the spot.

He was about to advance and say something to the countess, when he saw that she was not alone; and then there came into view the sanctimonious Wicks, and at a few paces distant, rubbing his hands one over the other, and with a sickly smile upon his face, came Oxley, the false-hearted steward.

"They all know it!" gasped Lord Francis. "They all know it! That woman has told the countess!"

With a vague idea that the truth, if it were as Wicks had repeated to him, would be too terrible for his nerves, he thought that he would make an effort to put a stop, even to the investigation; and he stood in something of the attitude of a sentinel at the door of his sister's chamber.

The countess did not observe her son until she was quite close to him, and then she started as she exclaimed—

"Francis! You here?"

"Yes, mother. I am here, as you see."

"Stand aside."

"Nay, mother, what is all this about? This is Fanny's chamber, and—and I wish—that is, I——"

"Peace, Francis! I must enter this chamber. I only must enter it. The honour of Fanny—the honour of our family is—is——"

"Hush, mother!"

The countess for once in her life looked a little affected and subdued, as she said—

"It is too late for secresy. Both these know it."

As she spoke, she waved her hand towards Oxley and Miss Wicks. The steward made a very low bow, and Miss Wicks screwed up her mouth into an uncommonly small size, and with her arms firmly crossed upon her bosom, slightly shook her head, as though some general reflections upon the wickedness of society at large, and the special delinquencies of Lady Fanny were in her thoughts, but which she did not think proper to give utterance to.

"And you, mother," said Lord Francis, "you—have——"

"Have what, Francis?"

"Blazoned this vile calumny among the servants. You have spoken of your daughter and my sister as—as——"

"No!"

"Thank God! You do not believe it?"

The countess evaded the question by saying—

"The news was brought to me by Mr. Oxley."

"Ah! and to me by Miss Wicks."

"Miss Wicks! How is this? Why did you not come to me, Wicks? Surely it was your business and your duty so to do."

"If you please, my lady," said Wicks, with all the assurance in the world, "I wanted to spare your feelings; and I am sorry that Mr. Oxley has thought proper to tell you anything about it. It was he who informed me in the first instance—and as we are going to be married next week—oh, I don't see why it should be made such a secret of, Oxley—I say, as we are going to be married next week, I did not think that I ought to disobey my intended husband; so when he ordered me to inform Lord Francis and not your ladyship, I did so."

"Indeed!"

"Oh, gracious!" cried Oxley, "that is all wrong. Miss Wicks, you surely recollect that—that——"

"No, I don't."

Oxley uttered a malediction between his teeth; and the countess, after looking at them for a few moments in silence, said—

"Francis, as we are here, and both upon such an errand as this, let us at least satisfy ourselves that it is not the truth."

"Dismiss your servants, mother."

"No, Francis. Since they now believe in the fact that Mr. Courtley is in the apartment, let them either be convinced that they are wrong, or be confirmed in it. If they are now deceived, they will believe it, despite all evidence to the contrary."

Lord Francis felt that his mother, for once in a way, was quite in the right; so he only bowed his head, and said—

"Be it so."

"My lady?" said Wicks.

"Well?"

"Of your knowledge, my lady, there is but this one door to the room?"

"But this one."

"Try the key, then, my lady; and if it be locked, why, then, the investigation will convince you that your humble servant has said no more than the truth."

The countess did try the key. The door was locked, and when she turned the key the lock shot back with an audible sound that there could be no mistake about it.

Oxley, screened by the tall, gaunt form of Wicks, rubbed his hands together with satisfaction. The countess looked ghastly pale, as she tapped at the door of Fanny's chamber.

"Come in," said a voice.

They all started. The voice was cheerful and unembarrassed; and in another moment the door was opened, and Ann stood upon the threshold with a look of calm curiosity upon her face.

"Ann," said Lord Francis—"Ann!"

"Yes, my lord?"

The countess made a rush past the girl; and then Lord Francis, fearing that, in some ebullition of rage, his mother might do some mischief to Fanny, hastily followed her. Oxley peeped under the arm of Miss Wicks, who stood as tall as possible upon the threshold of the door, while poor Ann, with her hands clasped, looked from one to the other, as though she would say, "What is the meaning of all this? Are you all mad?"

Lady Fanny sat upon a little ottoman, and was very quietly knitting some little ornament, such as might lie upon a toilette-table, and be more or less useful as the case might be. She looked up in her imperious mother's face in silence.

"Fanny?"

"Yes, mother," said Lady Fanny. "What has happened? You look ill, mother. Oh, what is the matter?"

Fanny herself was as pale as death.

The countess cast a hasty glance round the room, and then she drew a long breath of relief, for no Morris Courtley was to be seen, nor, in good truth, was there, if we except the wardrobe, any available hiding place in that apartment.

Fanny's gaze now fell upon her brother, and she said, faintly—

"You here, too, Francis?"

"Yes, Fanny; I am here likewise. Are you alone here?"

"Oh, no. Ann——"

"But only Ann?"

"Only Ann, brother."

"Enough," said Lord Francis, as he gently placed his arm round his sister's neck and kissed her first on one cheek, and then upon the other. "God bless and protect you for ever and ever, my poor Fan."

Fanny burst into tears at this. She could have withstood reproaches—she could have fought up against treacherous and vindictive rage; but this noble reliance upon her, evinced by her brother, completely overcame her, and she clung to him, sobbing and shrieking, and in such a paroxysm of feeling, that both he and the countess were alarmed.

"See, mother, see," said Lord Francis, "into what a state this sudden and strange visit has thrown her. Oh, is it not monstrous that two such vile natures as those that tremble upon the threshold of this room should have had the power and the art to cause all this misery!"

"Fanny—Fanny!" said the countess. "I implore you to answer me."

"She cannot be catechised now, mother."

"Nay, but, Francis——"

"Oh, my poor mistress!" said Ann. "Indeed, indeed, my lady, she is far from well of late, and these sudden passions often will kill her!"

"Stop a little!" said Miss Wicks, slowly marching into the room like some grenadier on duty. "If your ladyship pleases, I would humbly suggest that there will be no good in asking any question of Lady Fanny."

"Leave this room!" cried Lord Francis. "Fiend, in the shape of woman, I command you to leave this room!"

"Perhaps, my Lord Francis, you would like to strike me?"

"Do not tempt me!"

"Oh, indeed! Well, my lady, it was to your ladyship I spoke, and not to this young gentleman, who is so proud of his sister and Mr. Courtley. This is not, my ladyship, a very large room, and I don't think there are many hiding-places in it. Under the sofa, I can see, is vacant, and Lady Fanny is sitting upon a real ottoman, I do think, and not a man with a chintz cover on his back."

As she spoke, Miss Wicks gave a kick to the ottoman to convince herself of the fact.

"Don't do that," said Ann, as she dealt Miss Wicks a poke in the region of the ribs which made her jump again.

"Oh, you hussy; I will have your life!" cried Miss Wicks.

"Well, mother," said Lord Francis with an ironical bow, as he still held the hand of his sister in his, "all this is very decorous and pleasant, is it not?"

"Wicks!" cried the countess. "Wicks, I say!"

"My lady?"

"Leave the room."

"And if Mr. Oxley lingers another minute by yonder door," said Lord Francis, "I will do myself the pleasure of flinging him out at one of the corridor windows."

"Oh," said Oxley, and he would have effected a precipitate retreat, had not Miss Wicks called out—

"Stop, John Oxley—stop! The countess was good enough to say that you and I should be convinced one way or the other about this affair, and her ladyship, I am quite certain, will not go from her word."

"Convinced about what?" said Ann.

"Oh, you don't know? Well, then, I will tell you, discreet Ann. It is thought—it is slightly suspected that the secretary is in this chamber."

"The secretary?"

"Oh, yes; Mr. Morris Courtley—the favourite of Lord Francis, and no less the favourite of his young and accomplished sister."

"Silence, woman!" cried Lord Francis. "Lady Fanny has already said that she was alone with her maid. Her simple word outweighs your oath."

"Then look in the wardrobe screamed Miss Wicks, clapping her hands together. "Look in the wardrobe, I say! Ha—ha! I locked the door! There is but one door! The window cannot be made available for flight, but at the chance of death; and if Morris Courtley has left by that means, his mangled body lies in the court-yard! Look in the wardrobe, my lady!"

"Why, good gracious!" said Ann, "when you were here, Wicks, a little while ago, you said you thought the cat was there."

"Yes! Oh, yes, the cat! Only the cat! I don't expect, my dear Ann, to find anybody there but the cat! Oh, dear, nothing but the cat! He, he, he!"

Miss Wicks giggled quite hysterically, she was in such a rage.

"Oh, Miss Wicks," said Ann, "you will make yourself ill. At your time of life you should not give way to such excitements. Indeed, you should not."

"At my time of life, you hussey!"

"Silence!" said Lady Bloxdale. "I will look in the wardrobe. It is better, now that we are here, that we leave nothing undone."

Lady Bloxdale looked at Fanny as she spoke; and in a faint voice Fanny said—

"Yes, ma! Look in the wardrobe!"

"Thank God!" said Francis. "Thank God! Oh, my Fan, if I could only see you smile again as you used to do years ago when we were both so happy and so——" innocent he was going to say, but he thought the word might wound her feelings at that time, so he left it unuttered, although he did not, in his own mind, append to it any feeling but that of ordinary import.

"Then I will look into the wardrobe," said the countess again.

"Do so, ma," said Fanny.

Miss Wicks shook a little, and Oxley's lips turned pale as he licked them with a parish tongue, in the dread that, after all, he might have made some terrible

mistake. It would seem, too, that Wicks had a hideous doubt now of the presumed fact, for she muttered half aloud—

"I am certain of it—oh, so very certain! Oh, yes—yes! He is there! He must be there! He could not escape! Oh, that is impossible!"

Oxley touched her arm, which he could just do by reaching as far as possible from where he stood.

"Wicks—Wicks!"

"What is it?"

"Oh, dear, are you sure? Are you really sure?"

"Wait and see."

Lady Bloxdale reached the wardrobe; and Ann stepped up to it likewise, saying—

"Allow me to assist your ladyship."

"No. I will open it myself."

The wardrobe was one of great height. The lower part of it was clear, for the purpose of hanging dresses at full length in it; and above the hooks upon which they hung there was a shelf, upon which the unfortunate essence pots and scent bottles that Courtley had knocked down had been placed by Ann. That shelf only rested upon a couple of brackets, so that a blow from underneath, such as it had accidentally got from Morris Courtley's head, would, of course, tip it up, and throw down whatever was upon it.

There were long panelled doors in front of the wardrobe, which shut it all in, and in the panels of which were mirrors.

Lady Bloxdale with a crash—for she was rather a powerful woman—had the two long doors open in a moment.

A little black kitten stepped very leisurely out of the lower part of the wardrobe, and stood looking with an air of astonishment at the persons assembled in the room.

For a few moments not a soul uttered a word. They were all too much astonished to speak, and the little cat got alarmed at the ominous silence, and drew back into the wardrobe.

It was Lord Francis who then, in a voice that rang through the apartment, cried out—

"Behold, mother! behold how this huge mountain of calumny and suspicion has been delivered, not of a mouse, but of a small cat! Oh, baseness unutterable! that the honour of my sister and of your daughter, mother, should be thus whispered away by the foul breath of such wretches as that trembling pair!"

"A cat!" gasped Miss Wicks.

"A—a—cat!" faltered Oxley.

"Why, of course, the cat," said Ann. "Didn't I tell you, Wicks, that it was the cat? Dear me, how your mind must be running on the men to mistake a harmless little cat for one!"

"Oh—oh—oh!" said Miss Wicks.

"How dare you!" exclaimed the Countess of Bloxdale, advancing to her waiting-maid. "How dare you, upon such a foundation as this, raise such a turmoil? Shameless woman, I say, how dare you!"

"My lady, I thought—I——"

"You leave my service, Wicks."

"Oh, my lady, oh, no—no!"

Miss Wicks fell upon her knees, and Oxley who saw that the eyes of Lord Francis were upon him with a meditative look, made a rush from the door of the room and went down the grand staircase at such a pace that, encountering a footman in the hall, he not only knocked him over, but away he went himself quite up to the hall door.

"Murder — murder!" he cried; "it was Wicks told me—I didn't tell Wicks! How could I? I didn't know anything about it myself. It was all Wicks' doings—it was, indeed—I declare it was all Wicks."

CHAPTER XXX.

LADY FANNY MAKES A CONFESSION TO HER BROTHER.

IT was possible enough that had Mr. Oxley remained another half minute at the door of Lady Fanny's room, Lord Francis might have carried out the threat he had enunciated against him of throwing him out at the window; but by his rapid flight the steward saved himself from that occurrence, at all events.

Miss Wicks had, as we have recorded, dropped upon her knees; for the idea of leaving her excellent place, was about the most unpalatable one that she could possibly entertain,

"Oh, my lady," she cried, "I thought, indeed, I did think that some one was in the wardrobe."

The little cat came out now and walked on the extreme tips of its toes round Miss Wicks.

"Indeed, I did, my lady; and I hope that as I did and said all for the best and for the good of the family, my lady, you will look over it, as it seems, my lady, to be a mistake rather. Oh—oh, I would rather die, my lady, than leave your service, indeed I would, my lady, and in such a dreadful hurry, too. Oh, don't—don't!"

"I am in no hurry, Miss Wicks," said the countess. "I give you the proper notice that you require. In one month you leave my service."

"But, my lady——"

"Order this woman from the room, mother," said Lord Francis.

"Go," said the countess, "go at once."

"In a month, my lady?" said Wicks, as she rose to her feet. "Did you say a month, my lady?"

"I did. Now leave the room."

Wicks left the apartment, pretending to cry dreadfully as she did so, and she made such a howling as she went along the corridor, that it was quite alarming to hear her; but when she got some distance off, she faced about, and shook her fist in the direction of Lady Fanny's room, and said—

"Oh, I'll be revenged of all of you yet! He was there! I know it was a man, and not that odious black cat that Fanny makes such a fuss with; I know Courtley was there, though how they got rid of him, unless they ate him, I don't know. Oh, where on earth could they have hidden him I can't imagine. But I will find out—oh, yes, I will find out, and be even with you yet, Miss Fanny!"

When Wicks had left Fanny's room, Lord Francis turned to his mother, and in a voice of much feeling, he said—

"Mother, what a happy circumstance this would be if it were one that had the effect of reconciling you to your children.

"Oh, yes—yes," said Fanny.

"What is the meaning of this?" said the countess. "When my children are obedient to me, I am ready to be reconciled to them."

"But, mother, you will, at least, admit that this principle of blind obedience to your mandates may be carried to excess."

"I admit no such thing. Fanny, you go to London next week."

"No, mother," said Lord Francis. "The woman to whom you would consign the care of Fanny is——"

"One of the most distinguished leaders of fashion," interfered the countess.

"Not a doubt of it; but not one of the most distinguished leaders of morals, mother."

"Oh, any one may be calumniated."

"Doubtless; but while any one is in this unenviable position, it is not fit or proper that my sister should take up her abode with them."

"She shall go: I have said it; and you go to the continent again, Francis, as soon as possible. Upon these terms, and these only, I am satisfied to forgive the past, and all may go on again as before."

"No, mother," said Lord Francis. "Hear me, once for all, and do not, I beg of you, mistake the firmness of my tone for any intentional disrespect to you; but, I say, calmly and decidedly, all shall not go on as before. Fanny shall not go to London to the care of the abandoned woman you have selected for her, and concerning whose reputation I, as a man, know more than any lady can know, or ought to know. I will not go abroad. Oxley shall leave Bloxdale in disgrace; and I leave you to keep your word regarding the discharge of your infamous waiting-woman."

"Oh, yes," said the countess, smilingly, "and Morris Courtley shall remain, and be the chosen friend of Lord Francis, and the chosen lover of Lady Fanny."

"No, mother."

"Oh! but I say yes, son. I know your meaning well."

"You mistake me, mother. Morris Courtley shall likewise leave Bloxdale."

Fanny shuddered.

"This evening I am about to tell him, that it is good for the peace of this family for him to leave, and that it is dishonourable to himself to stay; upon such showing Morris Courtley will quit Bloxdale for ever."

" We shall see," said the countess, and she abruptly left the room.

Poor Fanny, with both her hands clasped and resting in her lap, looked so pale and wan, that Lord Francis felt that he required all his moral courage to sustain him in the course which he had determined to adopt with regard to Morris Courtley.

"Fanny," he said, "I rejoice that this unjust suspicion against you, which is as odious as it is unjust, should have been dissipated."

"Yes, brother."

"Those who propagated the slander will find that the base action recoils upon themselves. You are innocent; and I rejoice, for his sake, that Morris Courtley is likewise so."

"Oh, brother—brother!"

"Calm yourself, Fanny."

"Oh, save me."

"Save you? Yes, I will save you. You allude to the project of our mother for carrying you to London; but have I not said that you shall not go? You need be under no apprehension. There is not a servant in the whole household, with the exception of the infamous Oxley, and his coadjutor Wicks, who will stir without my orders."

Fanny sobbed bitterly.

"Come—come, be cheerful. Ann, you must attend to her, and make much of her after this sad scene."

"Yes," said Ann, "of course I will. I always do."

"I know you do, Ann."

"Oh, what's that?" cried Ann, as something fell upon the floor at the door of the room with rather a clatter.

"I cannot tell," said Lord Francis. "What can it be?"

Ann ran to the door, and came back in a moment with the Damascus sabre with which Lord Francis had armed himself upon the first impulse of his passion upon being informed that Courtley was in his sister's room. Ann held it up before his face.

"What is this?" she said.

Lord Francis looked down with a flush of colour, and Fanny, as she observed the bright blade of the weapon, trembled violently.

"Ann—Ann! where got you that?"

"At the door."

"And who placed it there?"

"I did," said Lord Francis. "Upon the impulse of a moment, I brought it from my room; but the fact that I placed it where Ann found it, is a proof that—that—I repented."

"Oh, brother—brother! and did you think to kill me?"

"You? Oh, God, no!"

"Yes, me. You might have aimed it at Morris Courtley's life; but, I tell you, brother, that by so doing, you would have killed me—yes, killed you own sister. I will not be stayed in what is struggling for utterance at my heart. The truth is better than the most plausible falsehood. I tell you, brother, that——"

"Oh, no—no!" cried Ann; "you don't know what you say."

"I do—I do! *Courtley was here!*"

Lord Francis staggered back as though he had been shot, and Fanny, clasping her hands over her face, rocked to and fro in a paroxysm of tears.

"He was here—he was here! There, brother, now you know it. He was here!"

"Oh, God!" said Lord Francis.

Ann stepped to the door, and closed it, and then she went to the farther end of the room, and sat down to cry by herself.

Lord Francis now looked thoroughly bewildered. Ann had flung the sword at his feet, and there it lay, a glittering barrier, as it were, between him and his sister. He shuddered as he looked at it, and then he said, in a low tone—

"Fanny, this is a delusion. You are mad."

"No—no! He was here—he was here! I declare it to you, brother, and to you only, for I cannot—I will not look into your face, and feel that there is falsehood, either actual or implied, from me to you."

"But, consider. Do you mean to tell me that Oxley—that—Miss Wicks were both right?"

"No!" screamed Ann.

"Yes," said Lady Fanny.

"Which am I to believe?" said Lord Francis.

"Both," said Ann, as she now advanced, with her eyes red and swollen by weeping. "Believe both, Francis. But Fanny don't know what she says yes to. She only means yes to the fact that Mr. Courtley was here: I mean no to the presumed calumny that that wicked Oxley, and that wickeder, if possible, Miss Wicks, would put upon it."

"Oh, yes, Ann!" cried Fanny; "that is true. You understand, brother, he was here, but as innocently as you are."

"Innocently?"

"Do you doubt me, brother?"

"I—I—no—no, I dare not. Next to such a doubt as that, will come a doubt of Heaven!"

"Ah, dear brother! now, indeed, I can speak to you, and I will tell you all. Morris Courtley did come here; but it was at my request. He came to tell me that it was fitting and proper for my honour, and for my prospects in life, that he should leave me for ever."

"Go on—go on."

"It was to accuse himself of the imprudence—the weakness, of giving way to a love, that—that—Oh, brother, I cannot explain to you what I mean; but I tell you, that the presence of Morris Courtley here was, upon his part, to urge me to let him leave me, and was, altogether, as innocent an act as any that an angel might look upon!"

"But—but—how did he leave? Wicks said she locked him in? How did he leave here?"

Fanny pointed to the window.

"The window! Then he is dead!"

Fanny sobbed as she looked in her brother's face.

"You do not mean to tell me that he leaped from that window!" cried Lord Francis. "Good God! it is certain death—a terrible death, too. The height is prodigious! There is nothing to break the fall. The stones of the courtyard below would receive him!"

"They would—they would!"

"Listen to me," said Ann.

"Oh, speak, one or other of you! Tell me all that has happened, or you will drive me quite distracted."

"Tell him—oh, tell him, Ann," sobbed Fanny. "I cannot—I have not strength. Tell him all."

"I will. Mr. Morris Courtley came here, Master Francis — excuse me for calling you Master Francis."

"Tut—tut. Call me what you will."

"He came here, then, in perfect innocence and honour. There was no evil intent. Oh, you do not know him, Francis! But he loves Lady Fanny so well, that he would not, by a thought, injure her. He came here, then, as you hear she says, to bid her farewell, and then that odious Wicks——"

"Yes—yes. Oh, be brief."

"She came, and found that he was here, and locked the door. Poor Mr. Courtley hid in the wardrobe, and the little cat——"

"Never mind the cat. Speak of Courtley. You choke me!"

"The door was locked. There was no other door. Mr. Courtley would suffer a thousand deaths rather than one breath of suspicion of the purity and innocence of Fanny should be uttered. There was only the window."

"Oh, God! and—and he went out——"

"He—did!"

Lord Francis fell into a chair with a deep groan.

"He faints — he faints!" cried Fanny. "Help—oh, help!"

CHAPTER XXXI.

CHANGES THE SCENE TO MRS. LEREW'S COTTAGE.

WE now again follow Oxley to that cottage in which resided Mrs. Lerew and her son, Peter, between whom and Oxley so choice a specimen of mendacity, in the shape of a plot to ruin the future prospects of the great family of Bloxdale, was hatching.

After all that had taken place at the hall, Mr. Oxley began to think that some decisive step was necessary in the conduction to anything like a successful issue of that little machination, which promised, if it should chance to be successful, such agreeable results to all concerned.

Mrs. Lerew had not the remotest objection in the world to the time coming when, whether rightfully or wrongfully, she might be styled "My lady;" and as for Peter himself, he thought that the sooner he tasted some of the sweets of the lordly state, if there be any sweets at all in such a condition, the better it would be for him.

Revenge, cupidity, and fear, alike hurried on Oxley to the completion of their designs.

The villanous steward felt that his standing at Bloxdale was so very insecure, that the slightest thing would suffice to deprive him of even the privilege of living in the mansion, and that if such a catastrophe as that should occur, he would, of course, be in a much worse situation than before, as regarded carrying out the first steps of the diabolical plot.

There was an addition to the party at the cottage since the last visit of Mr. Oxley, and that addition consisted in the person of young Musgrove, the personage who has been mentioned in a previous part of this history as through whose means the clergyman was to be induced to lend his aid in the carrying out of the villanous attack upon the legitimacy of Lady Fanny Bloxdale, and her brother, Lord Francis.

Dissipation and vice had all but done their unholy work upon both mind and body of this lost young man.

"So, John Oxley," said Mrs. Lerew, "a fine time of it we have had here, to be sure. A nice man you are for a——"

"Small tea party," put in Peter.

"You be quiet, Peter, will you? You be quiet, I say, you wretch, and let me speak to him. Are we, or are we not, to remain here in this little horrible hole of a cottage, John Oxley?"

"Oh, my dear," said Oxley, "I hope and trust it won't be for long. I can only say that it really quite grieves me, it does, indeed, that you should be here one moment longer than you wish."

"Oh, you fool! that is not what I mean. We are to be traced out, I suppose, since some one has been here to make inquiries?"

Oxley turned very pale.

"Some one here?" he gasped, "and to make inquiries, too?"

"Yes, to be sure. Who was it, Peter?"

"Don't know," said Peter. "Don't know the animal by name; but if I had to give a description to any one, so that they might serve him with a writ, I should say—'Tall, rather good eyes, dark hair, and slight colour, and about as sturdy a fellow as you would wish not to see in your way, if he said 'Stop! and you wanted to go on.'"

"His dress?" said Oxley. "His dress?"

"Green shooting-coat, and buckskin leggings."

"A gun?"

"Yes, about as nice looking a gun upon his arm as ever I saw. Come, step-father Oxley, do you know him?"

"Roots—Roots! For a thousand pounds, it was Roots!"

"And who the devil is Roots?"

"A poacher—a thief—a villain!"

"Poacher, thief, or villain — call him what you will, there was the Bloxdale crest upon his buttons."

"You don't mean that?"

"It is true."

"What did he say?"

"Why, just that Lord Francis Bloxdale had given him general orders to look about for suspicious characters; so, as he saw some one was living here, he called to see who we were."

"He dies for it!" cried Oxley—"he dies for it! The wretch! Why, I got that man out of the establishment at Bloxdale myself, and it is truly monstrous that Lord Francis should take him on again. But I thought he would. Confound him, I had a notion that he would. I—I could—Oh!—oh!"

"Swear!" said Peter. "Swear away, step-father; you don't know what a deal of good it will do you."

"Go to the—Hem!"

"Go it; that's the way to do it—ha! ha! Go it, step-father Oxley. That's the way to get over the affair, I can tell you. Never mind me—go it."

"Silence!" said Oxley. "Shut the door."

A loud snore came from something upon a couch in the room that looked like a bundle of old clothes.

"What's that?" cried Oxley.

"Oh, that is our friend, Musgrove," replied Peter. "He's a little fatigued with lifting a heavy weight, and he has gone off to sleep, you see."

"A heavy weight! What need has he to lift a heavy weight? What was it?"

"A glass, and a spoon, and some brandy-and-water!"

"Pshaw! you are always at your silly jests. But, attend to me, now; and you, my dear, allow me to say that the plot thickens."

"Oh!" said Peter.

Mrs. Lerew looked inquiringly at Oxley.

"It will be necessary that we at once make some sort of demonstration in this matter. I can inform you that Lady Fanny with her baby face, and her tears, and fine lady airs—I can tell you that she is so infatuated with this secretary, that my firm belief is, that she will finally induce her weak brother to not only look over the fact of their flirtation, or love, or intrigue, or call it what you will, but he will aid them, and in all likelihood a private marrige will be the result."

"I won't permit it!" said Mrs. Lerew.

"Bravo!" cried Peter. "Bravo, old 'un!"

"Peter, how dare you?"

"Come, come, old girl." Peter did not certainly abound in filial reverence! "Come, come, old girl, don't put yourself out of the way, but listen to the old fox."

Mrs. Lerew smothered her rage, if rage that could be called which was, in truth, mingled with a great amount of admiration at the cleverness of the scion of her family and Oxley proceeded—

"If," he said, as he brought his hand heavily upon the table, "if Morris Courtley marries Lady Fanny, with the consent of Lord Francis, I would not give that for our chance."

Oxley gave his fingers rather an alarming snap close to the nose of Mrs. Lerew.

"I would not, I say, give that for our chance. Such a coalition as Fanny, Courtley, and Lord Francis, will be able to accomplish anything. They will hold the old earl completely in leading-strings—they will restore at once the solicitors of the family, who know all the affairs so well—they will be one too many for the countess, until she finds herself fairly beaten and joins them; and then where are we?"

"You are a fool!" said Mrs. Lerew.

"Bravo!" said Peter. "This is as good as the House of Commons, only that I do confess the Irish members and the religious representatives use a little worse language."

"Maria," said Oxley, "will you explain what you mean by using that expression towards me?"

"It don't require any explanation," replied Mrs. Lerew. "I am going to take a walk in the garden."

"In—the—garden?"

"Yes. You may come if you like. Peter, no doubt, will mix himself a glass of something to drink, and enjoy his cigar here till we come back."

"Oh, that's it, is it?" said Peter. "Secrets, are there, that I am not to know of? Well, it's no use me saying no to that, for if you choose to have a private conference, of course you can. Where there is a will to do so there is a way; so be off with you—or stop! I'll go."

"No," said Mrs. Lerew, as she pointed to the slumbering figure upon the couch. "No."

"Oh, you needn't be afraid of him. He is asleep."

"Over-caution in this case," said Mrs. Lerew, "is a virtue. Come, John Oxley. Follow me."

They left the room; and Peter, as he looked after them, shook his head, saying—

"Now, I wonder what my sweet mother has got in her head that she don't like to trust me with? By Jove! what a look she can put on when she likes. It's rather a teaser. She has thought of some caper, now, I'll be bound, that will make a splash at the hall, if old Foxey only has courage to carry it out. Well, so as they put me in possession

LADY FANNY CONFESSING HER LOVE FOR MORRIS COURTLEY TO HER BROTHER.

of my patrimony, I don't care how they manage it between them. It will be a rare go, after all, if I, Peter Lerew, sit in the House of Lords as Earl of Bloxdale. Oh, my eye!"

Peter was so absorbed in a contemplation of the rare go, that he sat for some time in silence; and there we will leave him, to follow his worthy step-father, and his equally worthy mother.

Although the dull and drear winter time, that little cottage garden, with its trim walks, and evergreens, looked bright and pleasant enough; and Oxley and Mrs. Lerew were able to converse, and to stroll gently along the garden path, not much disturbed by the cold air that at times whistled a tune in the branches of the leafless trees high overhead.

There was a strange look upon the face of Mrs. Lerew, and she kept silent for a time, until Oxley said, in a low tone of voice—

"You have thought further of it?"

She started, as she said—

"I have—I have. Did you suggest it, or did I?"

"You did."

"Well, that don't matter; murder is murder, let it be suggested by whom it may."

"Hush! do not say that again."

"What, again?"

"That word. It is just as well to bear it in mind. We think it, and that is just enough for us, you know."

"I said nothing. What do you suppose I said?"

"Murder!"

"Oh, no—and yet it was in my mind, John Oxley, and the lips will shape themselves at times to the words that the thoughts are full of. We will not utter it, though, if we can be sufficiently wakeful and guarded upon ourselves not to do so."

"It is better not. Have you thought further of it?"

"I have, and my opinion is, that there will be no peace for us—no safety for our project while Morris Courtley lives. You say, too, that in his keeping are papers that would be of use?"

"Immense use."

"Why, that then, is another reason; but Oxley—Oxley, I say, attend to me. What a good thing it would be if there were no Morris Courtley, would it not?"

"It would. But you have something else to say."

"Not more than we thought of before, I tell you. How dull you are. Did not the gipsy woman—the fortune teller from beyond the seas, say anything encouraging to you?"

"Oh, yes, much; but—but I don't know whether to believe her or not. There are times when I am f surprised at myself for giving credence or a moment to such matters."

"And yet, it is very strange that some of these people do unmistakably foretell the future. Well—well, did you see a red flame in the hut?"

"Oh, yes."

"Well, then, John Oxley, red is the colour of blood. Come—come, what a shivering coward you are. I say that it would be a fine thing if Courtley were no more, and it would be a fine thing, too, if Lord Francis were no more."

"Yes, but——"

"Well, well?"

"I could not—I—think—oh, I feel in a cold perspiration already at the thought."

"What, at the thought of fixing the deed upon another? Why, where is your caution, man? Where is your sense? I tell you, John Oxley, that I have thought of this affair in every shape and way, and I feel convinced that the next thing to the commission of a deed of blood with safety to the perpetrator is to find some other shoulders upon which to place the onus of the deed. What so natural, now, as that Lord Francis should, influenced with passion at the discovery of an intrigue, for it can be magnified into one — between his sister and the secretary, kill him."

"Ah! I begin to see now."

"You begin to see? Bah! how dull you are. Do you think, John, that when I advise that you should get rid of Courtley, I wish that it should be any risk to yourself? Oh, no. I wish that another should have that to contend against, and that other ought to be Lord Francis."

"In plain language, then, you really think that Courtley might be—be put out of the way, and the deed fastened so circumstantially upon Lord Francis, that he would be jeopardized?"

"Well, I do."

"Oh, if that could be done! I hate them both!"

"Of course you do, John Oxley—of course you do. There is but one difficulty, I should think, in the doing it, and that is the want of will upon your part."

"Oh, no—no! I have no want of will."

"The want of courage, then."

"No—no, not exactly that; but I cannot as yet see my way. I have the will to do the deed, and I have the courage to do it, but I cannot quite see how it can be done with any absolute safety."

"We will think over all that. Is it now, once and for all, agreed that it is to be done?"

"I—that is—it is."

"'Tis well. John Oxley, I now know you better than I did, and I now do truly think that we shall succeed."

"Would it not be as well that Peter should—should——"

"No—no!"

"Well, but he might help."

"No! Oh, God—no! I think that——"

Mrs. Lerew shuddered from head to foot at the idea of making her son, Peter, an accomplice in the projected murder. Was it possible that, after all, there lay in some odd corner of the bad heart of that vicious woman, some spark of human feeling that made her shrink from implicating her own son in such a deed? It seemed as if such were the case. Perhaps she was much more tender of Peter's conscience, than that rather discursive young gentleman would himself have been.

"I really," said Oxley, "don't see any objection to Peter's having something to do in the matter, as he is to reap the principal benefit."

"But I do."

"Really, though, I think——"

"John Oxley, I care not what you think, or what you say. Let Peter suspect what he pleases of this affair, I will not have him told of it, or implicated as a principal in it. That is my determination in the matter."

"Oh, well, if that be your determination, I can say no more about that fact, and suppose it must be as you wish."

"It shall be as I wish."

"Well—well, we quite understand that, then. And now, if you have concocted any plan of operation in this matter, that you think will be such as will enable it to be carried out easily and well, let me know it, I beg of you."

"I have been thinking, but I must think still further yet about it. Tell me clearly how affairs stand at the mansion."

Upon this Oxley gave, to his decidedly worse half, a tolerably clear account of all that had transpired at Bloxdale since his last visit to the cottage, and the lady gathered, fresh hopes therefrom, for, as she told him she thought that the misunderstanding between Lord Francis and the secretary seemed to be decidedly on the increase.

"It looks like it," said Oxley; "and yet I am afraid all will be made up between them."

"Let it be in the grave, then."

"Hilloa!" cried Peter at this moment. "Hilloa there, all of you! There's Tom Musgrove woke up at last, and I can't make him understand at all where he is.'

"We are coming," said Mrs. Lerew; "we are coming, Peter. You must clear his faculties with what has confused them namely—brandy-and-water."

CHAPTER XXXII.

EXPLAINS THE MYSTERIOUS DISAPPEARANCE OF COURTLEY.

WE gladly enough turn our backs upon Mrs. Lerew, and the dreadful machinations which found a home in her vitiated brain, to proceed to Fanny's boudoir again.

It will be recollected that we left Lord Francis Bloxdale there; and he had just, as he thought, received the rather tragical tidings, that Morris Courtley, to save the reputation of Lady Fanny, had left the apartment by the window, not at the risk, but the certainty of death.

Poor Lord Francis was so completely overcome by the idea, that he sat gazing at Lady Fanny with a stolid look of despair. She did not in that frenzy of his spirits understand what kind of error he had fallen into—for, after all, as will be shortly explained, an error it was; but Ann saw it, and resolved to do what she could for the young lover while it lasted.

"Oh, sir!" she said. "Oh, my Lord Francis! would you rather see poor Mr. Courtley dead than even the husband of Fanny?"

"Oh, God, no—no!"

"Only think, sir, that he is a gentleman by his great learning and his manners, and I'm sure he has behaved as honourably as any born gentleman could do here. Oh, my lord, if you could only have seen how he looks at Lady Fanny, and speaks to her as if he had more respect for her here, where no one was to see them, than as if they were in the sight of all the world."

"Oh, peace—peace!"

"And, after all, what did he come for, but just to say that he felt he ought not to stand in the way of Fanny making some great marriage, and perhaps becoming a duchess, or even a queen?—for he thought—God bless him!—that there was nobody in all the world like her."

Fanny sobbed, and Lord Francis clasped his hands in silent agony.

"And you, too, he loved," continued Ann. "Oh, how much he admired, and respected, and loved you; and yet here you come with this."

Ann fetched the sabre, and held it before the eyes of Lord Francis.

"And yet this is what you come with to do murder—for it is murder. Oh, sir, did you never love any one? Do you expect ever to love any one, that you should think death the proper punishment?"

"Fanny! Fanny!" cried Lord Francis, as he sunk upon his knees before his sister, and held both her hands in his. "Fanny, can you, after this, ever look into my face again?"

"Oh, Francis! Francis! you know how dear you are to me."

"And—and he who is gone?"

"Oh, brother, I have before this spoken of him."

"Fanny, if I had known—if I could have thought——"

"What? Oh, what?"

"That the love he bore to you was such as it is—if for one moment I could have thought that he would go to death for you—"

"He would—he would."

"He has! Alas, he has!"

Fanny uttered a scream, and Lord Francis sprang to his feet.

"Oh, brother—brother!" she cried, "tell me, or I shall go mad! Tell me that you are not his murderer!"

"So help me Heaven, I am not!"

She sat motionless, with the exception of a tremulous movement of the lips, and she lifted her hands, and passed them over her face as she said in a low, plaintive voice—

"Where? Where and how was it? Morris dead! dead! Oh, where and how was it?"

"He is not dead," cried Ann. "It is all a mistake, and you are just, without meaning to do it, frightening each other out of your wits only. I tell you he is not dead."

"Not dead?" cried Fanny.

"Not killed by his fall from that window on to the paved court-yard below?" cried Lord Francis.

"Ah, no—no!" cried Fanny, clapping her hands together with child-like joy. "Ah, no—no! Was that what you thought, brother?"

"It was."

"Oh, no! My Morris is not dead, then; and I shall not go mad!"

"Why, what on earth is the meaning of all this?" added Lord Francis. "Did you not both tell me that to save the reputation of Lady Fanny he had, at all risks to himself, gone out at that window?"

"Oh, yes," said Ann, quite demurely, "I saw him go!"

"And so did I," said Fanny; "but——"

"Let me explain," interrupted Ann. "I'm afraid there has been a little mistake. He did go out of the window to save even the shadow of a crime from falling upon Fanny, and I found the little cat, and put her in the wardrobe instead of him; but instead of falling headlong on to the stones of the court-yard——"

"What else could he do?"

"He managed, as he is rather tall, to climb up to the roof by the help of a water-spout that is close to the window; and I daresay he is all safe by this time."

Lord Francis walked hastily to the window, and flinging it open, he looked out. All was clear on the flag-stones of the court-yard below; and when he looked up, he saw how any man, of ordinary skill and ingenuity, could easily have clambered up to the roof above the window, and he no longer doubted but that that was the mode by which Morris Courtley had made his escape.

"Fanny!" he said as he returned to his sister, "was this right—was this ingenuous—was it like you to deceive me in this way?"

"She did not," said Ann. "First you deceived yourself, and then I had the honour of finishing you off."

Ann curtsied very low as she spoke, and there was such a mischievous twinkle about her eyes, that Lord Francis could not be angry for the life of him, although he saw clearly how he had been completely mystified in the whole transaction.

"Fanny," he said, "you and I will speak of this at some other time. This is not a fit opportunity."

"Yes, brother, it is—it is! Oh, no—no! Let me implore you now to leave me. I have one request to make of you. Oh, no—not a request: it is a question to ask you."

Lord Francis made a step or two towards the door as though he did not intend to listen to what his sister had to say to him; but his better and kinder feelings predominated, and he turned to her, and with a tone of kindness he said—

"What would you say to me, my poor Fan?"

With a shriek of joy she flung herself into his arms, and sobbed upon his breast.

Ann was too much affected to look at them, and she put her head out at the window to cry, and her tears fell upon the cold stones of the court-yard below, upon the spot where, if Morris Courtley had fallen, his mangled body would have lain.

Ah! how much better it was that the stones should be sprinkled by those tears than stained with the blood of the brave and gallant Morris Courtley!

"Now—now, my Fan," said Lord Francis, "speak to me freely. What would you say to me? I will listen to you."

"Yes, dear Francis, my own brother! you—you will not seek——"

"Seek what?"

"To injure him?"

"Fanny, I swear to you that I will not raise my hand with a hostile feeling against Morris Courtley. Feeling, as I do, that he is wrong, I feel yet, that human nature may be taxed to do things that lie beyond its power; and such has been poor Courtley's situation. I think—nay, I feel convinced that he loves you, and that is not a feeling that he could wholly triumph over; but with my aid, gently and kindly given, he can do much; for, Fanny, you and Courtley move in such different orbits, that he can never call you his."

Fanny wept.

"It would imbitter his existence, if not yours, in the time that is to come, for him to feel that he had dragged you down from your high estate to his level, and that is a feeling that you would not wish him to suffer from. Now, Fan, believe me, that those who would place an impassable barrier between you and Courtley, would do you both a favour of no mean extent."

"Oh, no—no!"

"But I say yes, sister; and it must be my duty, if possible, to place that barrier; for I shall do it with a gentler hand—doing it, as I shall, with honour and good will to both—than those who are moved only by hate and by jealousy. Be calm—be calm!"

"Courtley, brother, said all that."

"He spoke as I do?"

"He did—he did. He feels as you do. But he will die, and then the barrier you speak of will not be long between us, although for a moment it may look impossible, for I shall die likewise."

"Sister—sister!"

"Brother, you do not love!"

Lord Francis was silent for a few moments, and then he said in a sad tone—

"Ann, attend to her. Ann!"

Ann drew away from the window, and took Fanny by the arm; and Lord Francis then kissed his sister gently on the cheek, after which he left the room in silence.

"Brother—brother!" cried Fanny.

"He is gone," said Ann.

"To kill him?"

"Oh, no—no. Now, Fanny, you are unjust to your brother. Has he not promised you that he will not raise his hand with a hostile feeling against Mr. Courtley? and do you doubt that he will keep his word? I do not, for when ever did he break it?"

"Alas—alas! All is lost!"

"No—no. Don't the play tell us that

The course of true love never yet ran smooth?'

and so, why should yours, my dear mistress. Oh, have patience, and who knows what will yet, in time to come, happen?"

"No—no. If my brother had been harsh, and had threatened — if he had tried by violence to separate us, I could have risen superior to it all, and I could have then, in my love for Courtley, have felt that I possessed a talisman to defend me from all the world; but it is his kindness that will kill us both!"

"What! His kindness?"

"Yes, girl—his kindness. Do you not know that it is much more difficult to resist kindness than harshness? Ah, Ann, we may struggle onwards, and fight our way aganist the harshest and stormest wind that winter ever sent to spread desolation upon the earth; but the soft summer air, laden with fair odours, creeps about us like some gentle, loving heart, and with a smile, and imperceptible sigh, we submit to the kindly influence."

"Nay, Lady Fanny, you should rather think that this kindness of your brother will increase, until it reaches a point at which his opposition to your love will cease."

"You strive to comfort me, my poor Ann, and it is kind and good of you to do so; but I fear you do not think what you say."

"Indeed, I do."

"Really, now, and from your heart, do you think that—that there is a hope that my brother may forget, or cast from him entirely, the pride of that birth which is, or which seems to be, the only thing that stands between him and his love for Courtley?"

"I do think so. He will seek Mr. Court. ley, no doubt, this evening, and then he wil be further inclined to think as we wish him."

"Oh, no—no, Morris will agree with him I know that, even for his heart's best interests, he will not falsify his feeling of that which is right."

"It is from that knowledge, dear Fanny,' said Ann, as she wound her arms round the neck of her young mistress in all the old and fond companionship of that intimate childhood that had gone past. "It is from that, my knowledge, that I build my hopes. What can Lord Francis think of the man who prefers wealth to his best happiness? Oh, Fanny, he will see that if he and if you are nobler by accident, Morris Courtley is nobler by nature."

Fanny was comforted.

And while the two young beings were thus conversing of worth, concerning which they really knew so little, poor Lord Francis was a prey to the bitterest contending feelings."

Loving his sister as he did with all the tenderness of nature which as yet had not found the being whom he could love with a different feeling, he passionately at one moment accused himself of being the stumbling-block in the way of her happiness, and the next assured himself how much it was his duty to save her from a marriage so far below her in rank.

At times he would try to please himself with the idea that with the virtue and the talents of Courtley, surely he might go forth into the world and raise himself to a level with Lady Fanny, and then come to claim her hand as his brightest reward; but such dreams did not last long, for even Lord Francis, young as he was, had seen enough of the world to know that it was neither virtue nor talent that raised people to high stations, but the very opposite qualities.

Servile stupidity—mendacity—vice of the most degrading character—rascality so profound that in its exercise it all but reached the height of a science; such he knew were the modes by which people in England, and in all other countries that he had visited, or read of, attained to rank and power.

There were, therefore, no hopes for Courtley.

"I will see him and speak to him," said Lord Francis. "I will at once come to some understanding with him, and he will leave Bloxdale."

CHAPTER XXXIII.

THE BROTHER AND THE SELF-CONDEMNED ONE.

In the library all was profound darkness, save the occasional faint flashes of some tiny flame, as it shot up from the mass of well-burnt embers of the fire-wood that smouldered upon the ample hearth.

Occasionally that flame sent strange shadows upon the old walls — shadows that looked gigantic and full of an uncouth and fearful vitality. Among the shadows was the gigantic one of a colossal head resting upon an arm as thick as the iron stem of some huge oak.

That head and arm was partially projected upon the ceiling of the old chapel, and as now and then some little forked flame would shoot up from the decaying embers, it would dance to and fro, would that strange looking shadow, as though it were mocking the substance that had brought it into existence.

That substance was Morris Courtley.

The poor, belated, heart-stricken secretary sat upon the great chair by the old hearth—that same chair in which he had so often placed Fanny, while he would sit or kneel at her feet, and by the flickering fire-light in that vast chamber look up into those eyes which to him were as glimpses of Heaven itself.

How lonely he was now!

The account that had been given of the mode in which he, Morris Courtley, had left the chamber of Lady Fanny, was quite a correct one : he had found that it was quite possible to scramble up to the leads that were above the window, and from thence he had made his way through another casemen into the castle again, and soon sought the library.

And there he sat,

'Chewing the cud of sweet and bitter fancies,' at one moment smiling faintly, but yet with great joy at the thought that he had the happiness to be beloved by such a being as Lady Fanny Bloxdale, and at another sighing and shuddering as there came over his mind the very trouble that clouded the course of that true love.

And what could he imagine would now be the end of it all? What in the chapter of coming events could he see but woe—woe unutterable to him and to her whom he so fondly loved—his own ignominious expulsion from Bloxdale, and her disgrace with those whom she loved and to whom she was bound by the dear ties of consanguinity, while her slowly-breaking heart would testify to the endurance of her love?

Oh, what a prospect did the world now present to Courtley! How truly

"Stale, flat, and unprofitable,"

appeared to him it and all its uses. Without Fanny it was to him as :

"An unweeded garden,
Things rank and gross in nature possessed it merely."

What was he to do? Whither was he to go? What occupation would be sufficient to drive from his thoughts the ever gentle presence of her excellence and her beauty? Where would he find the Lethe which would swallow up the recollection of the happy moments he had passed in her company?—months that had rolled past them both in the long lapse of time, gone never to return!

And as he looked into the dying embers of the fire, he began, as people are so apt to do when they think of friends departed and of enjoyments gone past—to reflect how much more he might have made of those happy moments than he had made of them.

"Oh, how little I looked at her when she was here to look at," he said, with a sigh.

"How little I said in comparison with what I might have said. How soon I sometimes let her go when I might have prevailed upon her to stay yet a little longer."

Like some faint and weary traveller in the desert dying but for a draught of water, who thinks with agony upon the many pure springs, with all their sparkling contents, that he has during his mental pilgrimage passed by unheeded, craving not to taste a drop of the pure nectar; so did Morris Courtley think of opportunities lost and time wasted when he might have spoken to Fanny and looked in that sweet face which was all the world to him.

Well, who among us is there that has not felt some such regrets? If there be any one who can say "I have not," let him preserve, if it be possible, such a happy state, for when he least thinks it, it may slip past him to return no more.

"Yes, oh, yes!" said Morris Courtley, "I love her surely as never was human being loved before—as we will once more be loved again. And yet I must go from her. Oh, Heaven! why did I ever set foot in this place to be enthralled by so much excellence, and then to lose it for ever and for ever?"

The fire shot up a little flame that was of more than common brightness, and at the moment, too, that it did so, Morris Courtly thought that he heard a low sound, as of a faltering footstep near to the door of the library.

He sprang to his feet.

Could it be Fanny? Could it, indeed, be his lover? Ah, no! The foot fell heavier upon the old oak flooring than her tiny slipper possibly could. She did not come to him.

Some one, though, in the darkness had sought the library, and was advancing with slow and steady steps towards the fire-place.

Morris Courtley strained his eyes to penetrate the darkness, and see who it was. He placed his hand up in the way of a shade, and strove to look under it, and so to concentrate his gaze; but all he could see was a tall dusky-looking figure slowly approaching him. A feeling of superstitious dread—it was the first that had ever found a home in his breast—came slowly over him, and he remained sitting upon the old chair, into which he had sunk again upon the conviction that it was not Fanny who sought that place and him.

"Who is it? Who is it?" he asked himself.

The figure came on, on, till it got quite within the sphere of the little flame that had sprung up from the fire, as if on purpose to reveal its approach, and then Morris Courtley saw that it was Lord Francis who had come to seek him.

A faint feeling came over the secretary, as the brother of her whom he loved so well appeared before him, for he felt that in that love he had, to all outward showing and appearance, committed a great piece of treachery; and that he had come into that house like a thief, trusted with access to its brightest ornament, which he had all but stolen.

We do not say that Morris Courtley ought to have felt in that way, but we merely record the fact that he did. In our opinion he took by far too serious a view of the question.

"Morris Courtley," said Lord Francis.

"I am here," replied Morris.

"'Tis well. Are we alone?"

"We are, my lord. You come to kill me: do it!"

"No, Courtley, I do not come to kill you. I know not what part of my conduct should make you think that of me. I have, in the first place, to ask a question of you."

Courtley felt almost choking, for Lord Francis spoke in a kind, though deeply affected tone of voice. It was with difficulty that the secretary could manage to say—

"I will answer."

"It is a question that I have already asked my sister, and she has answered it. I will not say what that answer has been, but I now come to ask the question of you."

"The same question?"

"The same, Mr. Courtley."

"If Fanny—if Lady Fanny has already answered you, my lord, you know the truth."

"I yet desire your answer, Courtley. Were you, or were you not in my sister's chamber, hidden, at the time that certain persons in the house, who are no friends of yours, came to tell me that you were? That is the question I wish you to answer me."

"I was there!"

"You venture to say that, not knowing what reply my sister has made to me? You know not but you may be falsifying her."

"Oh, my lord! do not say I know not. It is as impossible for her to say to you that which is not true, as it is for the sun to shine upon the face of nature, and not impart to it a new beauty. When you told me that she had answered the question, I well knew that she could have spoken but as I have. There was no fear of falsifying her!"

Lord Francis was silent for several minutes, and when he spoke again his voice faltered as he said—

"Morris Courtley, it would be an insult to you to doubt the purity of your interview with my sister. An interview based upon so great a love for truth can have in it nothing that is degrading."

Courtley merely bowed his head rather proudly.

"I do not accuse you of anything," added Lord Francis, "but of the imprudence of allowing your affections to become entangled. I believe that beyond that fact, there is nothing that the most rigid moralist could find fault with."

"Angels, my lord, are, let us hope, all as pure in thought and in deed as she is," said Courtley.

"And you respected that purity?"

"On my soul's dearest hopes I did."

"Courtley, I believe you. From my heart I believe you."

"My lord, I thank you. It is something to be believed in this sad world, even when we speak the truth."

"It is so, Courtley; and believing you as I do, I the more wonder why you should have concealed yourself in Fanny's chamber."

"It was a sudden impulse, my Lord—it was a giving way to the suspicions of the world—it was from the feeling, at the moment, that not only must the innocent continue innocent, but that they must not seem to do aught that, in the eyes of those whose coarse perceptions cannot enter into the spirit of their better nature, shall seem like guilt."

"I comprehend you."

"With you, my lord, it was a mistake; but to Lady Bloxdale's waiting-woman, and to Mr. Oxley, it was a mercenary act."

"You exculpate yourself well, Mr. Courtley. But what took you there?"

"To bid your sister a farewell. A last farewell."

"Indeed."

"It was so. If there be blame, let it fall upon my head only. Oh, my lord, love and cherish your sister, for she is one to be loved and cherished as an angel upon earth. Be to her kind and gentle. Say of me what you please, so that it will lessen one regret of hers, and—and——"

Courtley came to a pause. His feelings, at the idea of parting for ever from Fanny were such, that his voice failed him.

"Mr. Courtley," said Lord Francis, "in speaking to you, I fancy that I speak to a man who, if he be not from actual experience deeply versed in the affairs of this great world, has read and thought much, even as I have myself. I come now to appeal to your judgment."

"I will listen to you, my lord, as I would to none else."

Lord Francis spoke now in rather a cracked tone of voice; for at the bottom of his heart lurked a conviction of the utter fallacy of all that he was saying, and so his tones were more like a man who was trying to convince himself of something, than one who was laying down fixed principles to another.

"Morris Courtley, you are a man whose conduct—whose manners, and whose mind I think highly of; but my sister is the daughter of an earl, and much as I respect you—much as she may love you, it is quite impossible that she can ever make a *misalliance*. I feel that if such were to take place, it might be the prolific source of misery to you both. The husband may raise the wife to his own level, be his origin what it may, provided he finds in her the materials with which to make a lady; but the wife possesses no such social privilege as regards the husband."

Courtley slightly bowed.

"And so, Morris Courtley, it is with a sad conviction of the deep and imperious necessity of such a course that I now say to you, we must part, and this house must no longer be your home."

"That is all true," said Courtley.

"You agree with me, then?"

"I do."

"You really do? You do not think that all this distinction of nature is but the false and feeble folly of a vicious state of society —you do not meet me by the arguments that it is intellect, education, and conduct that confer upon a man the true nobility of nature?"

"I do not."

"And yet, Courtley, you might do so."

"I know I might, my lord, but I will not. I would not run the risk of causing one tear to flow from the eye of Fanny to purchase my own happiness in this world. It is possible that before God, in a brighter and happier sphere than this, we may appear hand-in-hand, and there be suffered to love each other; but I say that here, with all the feelings and the habits of society to contend against, and dreading all that you can dread in such a case, you can say nothing that I will not do."

"But not from your heart, Courtley?"

"Oh, my lord, let it suffice that I will do as you wish me, and do not probe too deeply the poor, lacerated heart that would fain wrap up its wounds from mortal sight. I am here at your disposal. Tell me now to rise and depart, and I will go, for I feel that I have done wrong. I ought to have been stronger to fight against this fatal passion— I ought to have been stoical enough to look upon excellence and not appreciate it—to gaze upon beauty, and not to feel its influence upon my soul; but I could not, and so I am contented to suffer, provided that the suffering be all mine."

"You would have the suffering all yours?"

"I would—I would!"

"Do you think that possible?"

Courtley was silent.

"No, Courtley," said Lord Francis, sadly. "There is no wrong done in this world— there is no error of judgment committed, which does not fall in its consequences, near or remote, upon other heads as well as upon that of the wrong doer. Mark me, Courtley, I do not say this to oppress you—I do not say it for the purpose of reproaching you, for I think that you feel much more deeply than I can suggest to you."

"I do so."

"'Tis well; I only then communicate it as a truth. You know, and I know, that Fanny must suffer."

"Heaven aid her!"

"Amen to that wish. But the past, however it may seem to be forgotten, will ever leave its traces behind it."

"That is true."

"You feel the truth?"

"I do in my inmost soul. Hear me, Lord Francis Bloxdale: I admit that, most unwit-tingly, and out of the weakness of my nature, I have done wrong in loving your sister— I admit that in telling her in a weak, and yet, oh! how happy a moment, that I so loved her, I have done doubly wrong. I will, so far as mortal man may do so, repair that first error, and that last one."

"Courtley, I know you will."

"I have said it, and I will keep my word. I only ask of you to tell me what you would have me do, and I will do it."

Lord Francis rose and paced the ancient chapel to and fro twice, and then he started suddenly, as he cried out—

"What was that?"

"What?" said Courtley.

"I thought I heard a noise up above there."

"It is not possible, my lord; we are alone here."

"It was, then, some accidental noise caused by a current of cold air, doubtless, or some of the old books shifting in their places, as they became damper or drier, as the air dictates to them."

"They often move with a dull, strange sound," said Courtley, "as though the spirits of their departed writers were shifting them upon the shelves, and fingering the leaves they have made instinct with their thoughts."

Lord Francis Bloxdale stepped up to the fireplace again, and in a deep and earnest voice, he said—

"Courtley, I will not deny that I love you, but you must leave this place. Do you comprehend me?"

"I do. When?"

"To-night."

"I—will go. The time?"

"At one in the morning, when all here are wrapt in repose, I will meet you, and see you to the old gate in the park-wall, and then bid you farewell, and place in your hands such a remembrance of my love, as will show you that we part as friends."

Courtley bowed his head, and only sighed.

"Is it agreed, Courtley?"

"It is."

"And now let me ask of you to give me your word of honour—for when once I have that I know that I am safe—that you will not seek another meeting with my sister before you leave Bloxdale."

"I promise."

"Enough. I am satisfied."

Courtley sighed again deeply.

"At the old gate with the sculptured stag upon the wall above it," said Lord Francis, "at one of the clock we will meet. You will be punctual. Tempest shall not stay me, nor sleep overtake me, for I will not rest until I bid you farewell."

"I shall be there, my lord."

———

OXLEY WATCHING FOR AN OPPORTUNITY TO ENTER THE COTTAGE OF MRS. LERKW.

CHAPTER XXXIV.

LADY FANNY SEEKS AN INTERVIEW WITH HER FATHER.

WHILE the fair and gentle spirit of Morris Courtley was thus shrinking before what it conceived to be the well-merited reproaches of Lord Francis, and promising almost everything that could be dictated to it, poor Fanny was enduring an agony of suspense and mental disquietude that it would be impossible to describe.

After the scene which she had had with her brother, and after the conversation that had been the result of that scene, to the effect that, however much Francis regarded Courtley as an individual he never could be brought to consent to receiving him as one of the noble family from which he sprung, a feeling of despair had come over the heart of the young girl.

She had, almost unknown to herself, up to that period cherished the idea, that, sooner or later, in her brother she would find one who would rather aid her in her affection than blame it; but the struggle that had taken place in his feelings, even when he supposed that Courtley was near, was of such a nature, that she now might have said to have completely abandoned that fond and, for the present fallacious hope

"Oh, Ann, Ann!" she said, "advise me what to do, or I shall go distracted! Why was I created, if I am only to suffer all the pangs that now beset me?"

"My dear Fanny," said Ann, as she twined her arms around her young mistress with the familiarity of old times, "do you not know and feel how wicked it is to say such things?"

"What things? Oh, what did I say?"

"Ah, now, I thank Heaven, you darling, that you spoke without your heart being in your words; so I will not repeat them to you. And now I will advise you."

"Oh, yes, Ann, do so—do so."

"But I don't think that you will do what I advise you to do at all."

"What makes you think that, Ann?"

"Because people very seldom do what they are advised to do, you know; but if I were you, now, mind if I were you—but as it is impossible I can be you, perhaps it is wrong of me to say so—but if I were you——"

"Oh, Ann, is this kind to keep me in so much suspense?"

"Well, then, I won't; but if I were you I would run away."

"Run—away?"

"Yes; but not alone."

"With you, Ann?"

"Lord love you, no! What on earth would be the use of running away with me? I am not a handsome young man."

"Ah, I understand you You would say that—that—if you were me, you would leave Bloxdale with Morris Courtley?"

"I would."

"There is one objection, Ann, that I do think would be insurmountable."

"And what may that be?"

"He would not go with me."

"Not go with you?"

"No, Ann. Morris Courtley loves me—I know that he loves me; but it is not with a selfish love. It is with a self-denying and a holy affection, that looks more—oh, much more to my good and to my happiness than to his own; and so I know that he would not take me from Bloxdale, in a clandestine manner, any more than he would say anything to me that I ought not to hear. No—no, Ann, I know poor Morris better than you do."

"Well, but," said Ann, squeezing out a tear or two, "young lovers do run away sometimes from castles, you know, and this is a castle, and you and Mr. Courtley are young lovers."

"But there is no need that we should commit so imprudent an act, for all that, Ann; and I know that Morris would never ask as much of me."

"Well, then, I don't know what to advise."

"I have thought, my good Ann. They say that at times my father has a gleam of intelligence, and that his benighted mind is lighted up, as of old, with all the vigour of a cool and calm understanding. He loves me, and if I go to him, and interest him in my story, he may yet be able to direct his child."

"But would you tell him?"

"Oh, yes, all—all! What I have said to my brother, surely I may say to my father."

"Oh, Fanny! the poor earl cannot advise you. The old can so very seldom, even when they are in their right senses, advise the young in affairs of the heart, that now that your father is in such a state of mind as we all know he is, how can we expect him?"

"It is my duty."

"Alas—alas! I cannot help thinking that that is a worse plan than the running away one."

"Yes," said Fanny, as she rose, "I will go at once to my father. Who knows but that I may, by speaking calmly to him, and detailing all that has happened, so far interest him, as to light up the nearly expiring flame of intellect in his brain again? He will stand between me and all the world; and in his affection for me, he will be able to tell me what I ought to do."

However inconsistent this determination, upon the part of poor Fanny, might be in such a crisis of her fortunes, it was certainly a natural enough one for a young girl to take. It was only wild on account of the condition of the old earl.

At the age of Fanny Bloxdale, the mind naturally looks for support from other judgments. The intellect has not yet acquired the habit of self-reliance.

Oh! if this fair young girl had but had a mother, upon whose breast she could have rested, and to whose heart she could have whispered all her hopes and all her fears, how much misery might have been spared to her! But, alas! the mother of Fanny Bloxdale was but a mother in name, and not one in affection.

The insane desire to rule in that large establishment—the wild, ungovernable love of command, had so far taken possession of the intellect of Lady Bloxdale, that her proper feelings had, at all events for the time, become completely submerged in the torrent of angry passions awakened by her son's resistance to her ill-assumed authority.

Hence, then, poor Fanny partially seemed to say that she thought her mother more mad than her poor father, since she repaired to him with her sorrows in preference to her.

Ann did not longer attempt to urge her own advice upon Fanny; for she began to think that it was just possible enough Morris Courtley would be a greater obstacle to the carrying out of the idea of an elopement than Fanny herself.

Flitting, then, like a spirit along the picture-gallery, and so by every door, and along another old corridor, not so large as that one that had been passed in the picture-gallery, she suddenly encountered a figure walking rapidly along.

Upon observing her, the figure bowed with reverence, and then she saw that it was her father's valet.

"Where is the earl?" she said.

"In his chamber, my lady."

"He is up?"

"Oh, yes; and I think he is much better to-night than he has been for a long time past."

Fanny felt so choked with joyful emotion at this speech, that she could make no reply to it, although she tried to make a gracious one; and she passed on in silence. The valet overtook her, and said respectfully, as he bowed again to her—

"Shall I announce you, Lady Fanny, to the earl?"

"No, I thank you. It does not matter."

In a few minutes she reached the door of the outer of the suite of rooms in which her father passed so much of his time, and in which it may be almost said he was kept a prisoner by his imperious lady. The courage of poor Fanny almost failed her at this juncture, and she was compelled to pause for several moments before she could turn the handle of the door.

It was only then the dread that she was an object possibly of curious observation by the valet that inspired her with courage sufficient to open the door, and to enter the room.

The Earl of Bloxdale sat in an old arm-chair, reading by the light of a lamp that was provided with a green shade, that cast a grateful colour to the eye upon the pages of the book, but left the rest of the room in comparative gloom.

Lady Fanny had time to look at the wreck of what had once been a man of tolerable intellect, as he there sat, for some moments before she spoke to him. It was then in a very low and tenderly affectionate tone of voice that she said—

"Father!"

At the sound, the Earl of Bloxdale looked up hastily.

"Who said that?" he cried. "Who spoke?"

"Father, your own dear Fan it was that spoke."

She tottered forward and fell upon her knees at his feet; and resting her head upon her hands she wept convulsively.

Poor old Lord Bloxdale seemed for a moment or two to be thoroughly confounded, and he made some odd movements with his hands over the head of Fanny, as if he were engaged in some kind of conjuration.

"Father—father!" she sobbed, "speak to me!"

"My child—my darling!"

"Oh, you do know me?"

"Know you? Who has said that I should not know my own darling Fan? Know you, my child? When will your fond doting father cease to know you?"

"And you are better, father?"

"Yes—oh, yes, much better. She—she is not coming?"

"Who, father?"

"Your mother, child. Oh, only keep your mother from me, and I think that I may yet —Hush! What is that? She is coming!'

"No—no. See, I will lock the door, and we shall be quite alone. Oh, father, why is, it that you have this dread of my mother?'

"I know not. But there are times when I think that it is some spell that is cast upon me. But what is it that my little Fan wants of her fond father?"

"Oh, father, you are, indeed, better.'

"Yes, much. Is it a new doll?"

"A doll?"

"Yes, my poppet; or is it a little pony? Oh, in what can I please my little darling?"

' Oh, father, I am too old for a doll."

"Old? Oh, no—no — no! I get old — at least, I fancy I do, but not you, my cherub."

"Father, indeed, I am too old for the toys of childhood. It is with a story of the sufferings of mature years and mature thoughts that I come to you."

"And so welcome are you!"

"Yes, father, I told my heart that I should be so welcome, and that was what induced me to come. I know that Francis loves me—I know that Ann loves me—I know that—that——"

"Morris Courtley loves you!"

"Father!"

"Well, my dear, and all the house loves you, surely. I do not think it possible that any can help loving you."

"Morris Courtley loves me!" she said, as if she felt a serene joy in the very repetition of the words. "Morris Courtley loves me!"

"To be sure—to be sure, my Fan; and I will do something for the boy yet—that I will."

"The boy, father? What boy?"

"Why, Morris, to be sure; a fine lad—a fine lad!"

"Oh, father, you forget how time passes; and you speak of us and think of us all as if we were all a parcel of children."

"Children? You are my dear child?"

"Yes, father; and yet not a child."

"Ha! ha! Oh, yes. Come, you shall read with me. I was reading when you came, Fan."

"What were you reading, father?"

She glanced at the book, and her heart sunk within her as she saw that it was an old story book that she had cherished years since; and that the fading intellect of the earl was engaged in the perusal of the history of " Little Red Riding Hood!"

Poor Fanny felt that her mission there was hopeless, and she sobbed bitterly in her father's arms.

CHAPTER XXXV.

MR. OXLEY PONDERS OVER THE ADVICE OF MRS. LEREW.

HAVING then, so far as we have been able, presented to the reader the thoughts and feelings of the inhabitants of Bloxdale, in whom, it is to be presumed, he has a kindly interest, let us now look upon the darker picture presented by the wicked ruminations of John Oxley.

What had passed in the chamber of Lady Fanny had convinced him that his stay at the castle might be reckoned by hours, and that, like Miss Wicks, his reign was over. Feeling that Lord Francis would assuredly seek an interview with Morris Courtley, for he was not deceived by the idea that the secretary was dead by any fall from the window, he availed himself of his knowledge of the secret passage to the upper portion of the library, to watch what took place there.

In the armoury at Bloxdale there was, behind a suit of plate mail that had, by accidently falling from the rusty chain that had held it for half a century to the wall, disclosed the fact, a small moveable panel in the wall.

It had so happened that Oxley was in the armoury when the fall of the suit of mail had taken place, so that the secret of the opening in the wall remained with him. By dint of considerable exertion he got the suit of armour into its place again, and then, at some more suitable opportunity, he determined upon exploring the passage.

To a man of shifts and contrivances like Oxley, the possession of a secret connected with the house in which he resided, offered to be of importance, and he was not long before he sought the opening in the wall again, with a determination thoroughly to explore it.

It was not without some misgivings though, that Oxley took down the suit of armour again, and opened the panel. Such men are cowards by nature, and the dread that the secret passage might lead him to some danger, was strong upon Oxley.

With cautious footsteps, and the aid of a hand-lamp, he slowly advanced, until he found that the secret passage conducted him to the old chapel, which had been converted into a library.

This was a discovery which, at the time he made it, had not promised to be of much importance; but latterly it had played a much more important part in the history of the proceedings at Bloxdale Castle.

It was by the aid of that secret passage that Oxley had contrived to introduce his step-son, Peter, to the library, so that he found out the grand secret of the attachment subsisting between Fanny and Morris Courtley; and it was by the aid of that secret passage that he had himself become cognizant of some of poor Courtley's secret thoughts.

Oxley, then, thought that the interview which was certain to take place between Lord Francis and the secretary could not fail to be one of great interest, and he hurried to the armoury, in order to be cognizant of it.

From that secure retreat, then, the steward had overheard by far the greater part of what had taken place between the secretary and Lord Francis, and he wholly and distinctly heard the appointment made for one o'clock in the morning, by the park wall.

When the conference was over, Oxley retired to his own room, and there he sat in the dark, for he blew out his light, in order that if the gentle and immaculate Miss Wicks should come there to seek him, she might, seeing no light, fancy that he was not there.

There, then, in the dark, although he trembled at it, and by no means liked it, sat Oxley to think.

Oh, what a procession of frightful images passed through his brain at that time, and how every scheme, full of violence and hatred to all that was good and great, coursed each other through his imagination!

Above all, though, came the advice of Mrs. Lerew, that it would be better to dispose of Lord Francis, and better still to place the onus of the deed upon the shoulders of the secretary.

" Why," muttered Oxley to himself, in the faintest of faint whispers—" why, they play into my hands. It seems as if fate had sent these two men, bound hand and foot, into my power; and yet what an awful thing it is to kill!"

Oxley had not the courage to pronounce the other word that came to his lips in lieu of kill. Murder! was that other word, but even in the silence, and surely the security of his own chamber, he shrank from its pronunciation to himself.

The hour of midnight was rapidly approaching—at least, he thought it was, and the night wind could be heard careering round the old building, as though seeking for some entrance at which the spirit of old winter could make its way, and render all within that lordly abode as desolate as all was without.

A drifting snow, too, was falling, and as in the cold air every particle that effected a lodgment there remained, the whole aspect of nature without was assuming the unbroken beauty of the falling snow. The wind rattled at the window-frame of Oxley's room.

" No—no !" he cried. " What is that ?"

The frame rattled again, and then he knew it was but the wind that he had heard so often, but which his fears at that moment, when he was meditating a dark and terrible crime, had transformed into something alarming.

" It is only the night wind," he said. " Oh, that is all—that is all ! Only the night wind. What have I to fear ? Let me think—let me think !"

His thoughts all tended in one direction, and that was towards murder ! He found himself calculating all the chances of success—glancing at the possibilities of failure, and its consequences. The latter seemed few and far between, in proportion to the former.

"They meet at one o'clock," he muttered. "A dismal hour at this period of the year; and they meet at one of the most unfrequented portions of the whole estate—at the door in the park wall. Why, it is so far off the house, too, that the most piercing shrieks could not be heard, especially if the snow should fall. Ay, the snow will be the thing."

Again the wind careered past the window.

"The difficulty would be," said Oxley, "to get the young lord there first. No—no—why so? Courtley will leave him, and go his way; and then—then he, Lord Francis, will be alone—yes, alone. Is that the better way?"

It showed that Oxley had made his mind up to a very great extent, when he got so far as to consider such particulars.

"Yet, no," he said, suddenly. "What's so easy as to detain Courtley a little—only a little? Well, well, I must think—I must think of all this. The time may come, when the remotest circumstances may be of the greatest possible importance to me."

A tap came to the door of his room, and he started; but replied not to it. The room door was not locked.

The tap was repeated, and then the voice of Miss Wicks came upon his ears, pronouncing his name.

"Oxley! John Oxley!"

He did not answer, although for about a moment a vague thought came across his mind of trying to make her an accomplice in the crime that he was meditating. Another moment's consideration, though, upon that head, told him that it was too dangerous so to do.

"No—no," he thought, "if I fail at all it will be by trusting some one who I should not have trusted. I will not tell her."

"John Oxley," said Miss Wicks, again.

As he did not answer, she tried the door—finding it open, she stepped a pace or two into the room. Oxley, quite noiselessly, slid under the table, close to which he had been sitting.

"Not here," said Miss Wicks. "Where can he be? He is not in the castle. Another of the mysterious absences, concerning which nobody can give me any sort of information. He does, at times, leave the castle for hours together, and no one knows where he goes to. I must find out all this in good time, and I must see him soon, too."

Miss Wicks left the room, closing the door behind her.

"Oh," thought Oxley, as he emerged from beneath the table, "that is it, is it? You have begun to speculate about my visits to the cottage. Humph! If I am not particularly careful, there will be a collision between the two women, Lerew and Wicks.

I must see to that. But now again to the business in hand."

Oxley buried his face in his hands, while he thought deeply now, not of whether or not he should murder Lord Francis Bloxdale, for he was past that consideration, but as to the best and the safest mode of doing the deed of blood.

After about an hour he rose, and shook like a man in an ague.

"I have settled it," he said; "but I must have brandy! Brandy! My very heart is cold now!"

We need not carry the reader through the tortuous reflections of such a man as Oxley; we place pro and con before him the means which induced the murderer in though to prefer one line of conduct to another. What he did do will be sufficiently shown in the story.

Let it just now suffice, that Oxley had resolved upon the murder of Lord Francis, and upon doing his utmost, likewise, to place the onus of the deed upon the innocent Courtley.

The evening was rapidly wearing away now, and Oxley had much to do. In the first place, he relit his light, and then he rang his bell, for so important a man as the steward was waited upon by the under-servants.

A tall, raw-looking lad, who had been recently taken as a footman in the establishment, answered him.

"Stephen," said Oxley, "you will ask the cook to make me some gruel, and bring it to me, if you please, in about an hour. I am not very well, and am going to bed at once. If I should be asked for, just say that I am gone to bed very much indisposed."

"I wool," said the footman.

"That will do. What sort of a night is it?"

"Snewing a bit."

"Ah! I thought it was."

Oxley actually did go to bed; and the gruel was duly brought to him, when he desired that he might be left without interruption for the remainder of the night.

The moment he felt that the footman had gone, and that there was no likelihood of his return upon any officious errand, Oxley rose again, and dressed himself completely for the night's work that he had to do, but in such a manner that he could easily rid himself of his apparel, as it was part of his scheme to be able to do so at a moment's notice.

It had now just struck eleven o'clock, so that he had two hours yet before him in which to mature his plans.

At Bloxdale, on the ground-floor, there was an immense apartment, eighty feet in length, which went by the name of the Grand Hall. This was the most ancient part of the whole building.

There can be no doubt but that this great hall was, at one time, the principal apartment, and in which, in feudal times, some great baron had been in the habit of holding grand carousals, surrounded by his men-at-arms and his retainers.

At one end still remained the enormous chimney-piece, and the deep fire-place which would have held half a tree in a state of combustion. At the other end of this great hall there was a spacious gallery; and the roof throughout was so crossed and recrossed with immense oaken rafters, that it was quite a sight to see.

The walls, too, were all of oak, and the flooring was of the same. Upon the former hung many rude trophies of the chase, and of the battle-field; and over the chimney-piece there were always some half-dozen fowling-pieces, charged, in case of one being wanted on an emergency, to let fly at a pigeon hawk, or any other bird of prey that might approach the mansion in sight of any of the servants or visitors.

Since the building of that hall, though, the mansion of Bloxdale had had so much added to it that it had been neglected, only being left existing rather as a rude specimen of old times than for any use that was made of it.

Indeed, it was principally a thoroughfare between the two wings of the house, although, after nightfall, the servants generally had a superstitious dread of crossing its vast expanse. There was an idle legend among them of some ghost, with clanking chains, who, at certain times, had the peculiarity of making the great hall its place of parade; although what it could want there, except just to frighten a few rustics, it is hard to say—ghosts, however, so far as we can hear, generally do very foolish things.

The story, however, with all the additions and exaggerations that the lover of the marvellous and the supernatural was sure to make to the original story, effectually pervaded the hall after nine or ten o'clock at night, and, therefore, Oxley knew well that there he would be safe enough if he chose to make it his place of hiding, in order to see if Morris Courtley and the young lord really went forth at one o'clock, as had been arranged between them.

He did not doubt that either party would keep his word; but still, in the chapter of accidents of a few hours, something might happen to induce a change of intention by mutual consent.

How still the house was!

Oxley opened the door of his room, and projected his great, ugly, sensual features out into the hall beyond, and listened. There was not a sound to be heard in Bloxdale. No doubt all those who had easy consciences upon which to sleep, had retired to rest. Could he so have slept?—Ah, no! How strange a thing it was, that it never struck Oxley he was gaining nothing by all his viciousness and all his wickedness but a disturbed imagination.

It is the peculiarity of wickedness, though, that it never does see the pit that it is digging for itself to fall into.

"All still—all still," said Oxley. "Ah, even that unquiet spirit, Wicks, has gone to rest by this time. It is a long and weary evening, at this time of the year, from sunset until now. I will to the great hall."

He trod very lightly over the new hall which had been built, and which was paved with marble flags, and he opened the old gothic door that led into the great hall we have described.

The cold air was whistling around it, and Oxley shuddered as he crossed its threshold, and in the vast expanse of its area, felt as though he had stepped quite out into the open night.

He found the hall lighter than he expected, which was to be attributed to the quantity of snow that lay outside, to the depth of several inches, and which, having fallen since sunset, had not been trodden upon, or in any way disturbed, so that it reflected the faint light of the night sky; for, after all, night is but a relative term, and there is no such thing in the open air as entire darkness.

Some reflected beams from other planets, came through clouds—some faint radiance yet from the sun, although it should be at our antipodes, still interferes with the reign of utter darkness; and the mere fact that at night objects are visible, although faintly, for each is sufficient to convince us that there is some light in the air which the eye can take cognizance of is of sufficient importance to convince us that light must exist in the darkest night.

To get utter darkness, we must shut up a given space by something more material and dense than atmospheric air.

And so it was, upon that winter night, at nearly twelve o'clock, Oxley could see a little about him, and in a confused way even could trace the architecture of the old hall, and see the waving banners that hung from some of the old cross beams of the roof.

With a stealthy step he approached the chimney-piece, and felt for the fowling-pieces that hung there. His hand fell upon the lock of one of them, and he lifted it carefully down.

A slight inspection with the ramrod and with his finger upon the priming, sufficed to convince Oxley that the gun was loaded. "It will do," he said. "It will do."

This gun he then placed upon the floor close to one of the doors leading from the great hall, so that he could possess himself of it in the dark without the danger of throwing it down; and then he went upon a much more troublesome and difficult errand.

That errand conducted him to the first floor of the house, and to a suite of rooms leading from the picture-gallery, in one of which Morris Courtley had slept, but never again was he to sleep there.

Oxley found the room with ease, and when

there, he had the courage to light a match, for it was darker than in the great hall.

While the match lasted he looked about him, and found a coat of Courtley's, which he wrapped up and placed under his arm, and hastened with it to his own apartment.

"Now," he said, "I have but to wait my time. What is to foil me? What is to stay me now? Blood—blood! I will have blood as the sweetest revenge of all. I hate them both — the young lord and the secretary. They shall both die, and then my hour has come. Yes, they shall both die!"

CHAPTER XXXVI.

MORRIS COURTLEY WRITES A LETTER TO FANNY, AND FANNY WRITES A LETTER TO COURTLEY.

WHILE John Oxley was thus adopting such means of compassing his dreadful intentions, others were up in Bloxdale.

Lady Fanny, little suspecting, though, that Courtley was about so soon to leave her, had not retired to rest. She lay upon a couch, and Ann watched over her, and entreated her from time to time to go to bed.

Courtley, too, sat in the library in the dark, communing with his own sad thoughts. These thoughts wandered to the future, such as the thoughts of some poor belated voyager, who is cast upon an unknown shore, which he finds full of dangers, wanders to the boundless and unknown ocean that lies before his gaze.

At times, though, Morris Courtley thought of a little cottage home that he had in the New Forest, where a young brother resided who yet tenderly loved him. There were other old and dearly loved forms in that cottage home, for it was there that he had passed his early days.

"Ah!" he said. "It is not there that I shall find peace. It will be only in intense occupation that I can henceforth live; I must mingle with the great world. Solitude and the charms of nature all around me would but turn my thoughts more to prey upon themselves, and it is my duty to resist each glance of positive despair. Who knows but I may yet win a name that even Lord Francis will not think too despicable an one to be united to his own?"

This was the dream that kept life in poor Morris—this was his hope—this the star that shone brightly for him in the future. He thought that he might go forth at this juncture from Bloxdale, and come back again while yet youth and love belonged to him and to Fanny, with a repute that would make him an acceptable alliance.

Alas! how little he knew of the world when such thoughts crossed his imagination. He did not dream that it is insolence, mendacity, dishonesty, and all that is despicable and vile that succeeds, and gets to the high places of the world, while genius is trodden down, and is but too glad to earn its daily bread for those whom it despises.

No—no, there was no hope for Courtley in the world!

But yet it was to him a delightful delusion to think that there was such a hope. It gave him the strength that he wanted at that dreary time, and without which he must have sunk completely.

"Yes," he said, "time will come when I shall visit the stately halls of Bloxdale, and say to the proud representatives of that ancient race, 'I come to tell you all, that I love the fairest being that ever wore your name, and that I demand her.'"

This was, indeed, a blissful hope; but what a despairing thing it was to go without saying as much to Fanny! But had he not promised that he would not seek her? Yes, and that promise was sacred. It was not lightly given, and it would not be lightly kept.

After some further thought it struck poor Morris that he might write to Fanny; and fearing in so doing he might be playing, as it were, with the spirit of his promise, he pleased himself by saying that he would give the letter to Lord Francis, and trust to his honour and his feeling to deliver it.

It was a great solace to Courtley now to carry out this idea. He lit a couple of wax lights, and sat in the profound stillness of the apartment writing this letter:—

"The Library at Bloxdale. Eleven at night.

"MY OWN FANNY,—I have made a promise to your brother, and I have made one to you, and I have made one to myself. The promise to your brother is, that, as I am not noble, I will leave Bloxdale to-night.

"The promise to you, dear one, is, that while this life remains to me, I will love you.

"The promise to myself is, that I shall yet be able to raise such means as will enable me to come back and say that I can confer reputation upon her whom I so dearly love, and who stooped from her high estate to love me when I was but the poor secretary.

"Ah, my Fanny! this is a pleasant dreamy thought. It is the principle which upholds me in the fight against the adverse circumstances that have made, for the time being, our love an affliction. Do you, too, put on that corslet of the affection, sterner than burnished steel; and do you, too, feel that in the thought that we shall meet again, you are armed against all the trammels and all the trials that the world can have in store for you.

"And, my Fan, I have a hope that you will live in calm peace until I come back again. Your brother loves you, and he will protect you. Cling to him, Fanny, as to your guardian angel. He can powerfully support you, while I can give you nothing but my prayers.

"Do not mourn my departure. It is for

the best, dear, dear Fanny. But, oh, believe, present or not, I am still ever and ever,

"Your own,

"MORRIS COURTLEY."

It would be wrong to say that this letter did not cost poor Courtley some pangs to write; but he did write it, and carefully folded it and addressed it to her who was the bright star of his affection.

Having, then, secured this letter in his bosom, and having made the few preparations that he needed for his departure—London being his destination—Courtley extinguished the lights again, and sat in the old library waiting for one o'clock.

What a sad vigil that was for him!

And now, although it may appear at the first glance rather strange as a coincidence, yet if we come to consider the unity of feeling that there was between Courtley and Fanny, it was nowise strange, we have to state, that at the very time he was there writing to her, she was finding a great relief for her overstrained feelings in writing to him.

After a feverish sleep upon the sofa upon which she had thrown herself, she awoke to weep, and to accuse her brother of wickedness in what he had said of Courtley, and to bemoan the situation of mind in which she had found her father.

It was then that Ann said to her—

"Oh, Fanny, if I were you, I would just write to Mr. Courtley, and tell him all that Francis has said, and all that you have done in going to your father, and I am sure then that he will yet think of something that will put things to rights again; for nothing in the world will convince me but that the time will come when your brother will be the person to take your hand and place it in that of Mr. Courtley."

"Ah, no—no, I have not such a thought, I would that I had, Ann; but yet, I will write to Morris. It will be almost like speaking to him, will it not, Ann?"

"It will, indeed."

"Then it is a happy thought."

Ann was quite delighted to see the increased animation of her young mistress, and she hastened to place her pretty writing materials before her, that such a state of things might be continued; and, so it was that Fanny wrote the following letter to Courtley.

"Bloxdale.   Eleven at night.

"MY MORRIS,—I can hear the rough winter's wind surging past my window, and the snow is falling thickly, yet I am up and thinking of you, and only of you, dear Morris. I have told you that I love you; why, then, should I hesitate to write it? for if you are not true to me, it is as well that you should break my heart utterly as not.

"You must not go from Bloxdale, Morris. My brother loves you well, and when he has had time to familiarise himself to the idea of your loving me, I think and hope his objection will vanish. He has my happiness, I know, most at heart.

"And now, Morris, above all, do not quarrel with Francis. I don't know why I write this, but it came to my mind at this very moment, although upon further thought I do not think it at all probable—I rather think, that what I wish to say was, do not agree with him over much.

"I mean, dear Morris, that you should not, in your quiet way, say—'Yes, my lord, you are right; I will leave Bloxdale'—because it is not at all right you should do so.

"I have been crying, Ann says, and the eyes you were pleased to think the brightest in the world are but dim now with tears. Morris, I can write no more; but I know that you love me, and I would not barter that consoling thought for all the world;

"And so, my dear Morris, I am, as you know well,

"Your ever-constant loving

FANNY."

The young girl looked up with a sigh and a smile.

"Ann," she said, "I don't think—"

"What, Fanny?"

"That I ought to send this letter. I declare, I have put down just what I think."

"And is not that just what you ought to put down, dear mistress?"

"Well, I don't know."

"Oh, yes—yes, you do know. It is the very thing. You will let poor Mr. Courtley have the letter, will you not?"

"I—cannot say; and yet——"

"It will make him so happy."

"Do you really think it will, Ann?"

"I am quite certain of it, for if ever any one loved truly and tenderly, he does. It is impossible to doubt Mr. Courtley. Oh, only think of his respectful and gentle conduct to you—of how he never by a word or a look did anything that could offend in the slightest. Why, I do think that poor fellow, when he was in this room here, was in quite a fright, for fear you should think he was too bold."

"He shall have the letter, Ann!"

*   *   *   *   *

Lord Francis Bloxdale, too, waited for one o'clock.

After arranging, as he thought, everything with Morris Courtley, he retired to his own room, and placed in a small pocket-book notes to the amount of a thousand pounds which he intended to hand to Courtley when they should part upon that night, or rather early morning.

Nothing could be clearer than that, beyond the mere fact of the great disparity of rank between his sister and Courtley, no one could have had more freely and completely the entire approbation of Lord Francis than the secretary; but the young lord, as regarded

MR. OXLEY, MRS. LEREW, AND PETER IN CONSULTATION AT THE COTTAGE.

his social position, had been brought up in a particular class of ideas, and he could not shake them off.

The princely present that he intended to make Courtley was quite a sufficient indication of his high opinion of him. Then, again, the manner in which Courtley had consented to go without arguing the affair at all, had raised him considerably in the estimation of Lord Francis.

With all this, though, there was in the mind of the young nobleman an uneasy impression that he was not doing what was right, and that he was, after all, only stultifying his reason, and acting upon a prejudice instead of a principle.

Such a state of mind was particularly distressing to such a person as Lord Francis, and the more he strove to shake it off the more it clung to him. Truth is not so easily got rid of.

As twelve o'clock approached, a strange, nervous feeling took possession of Lord Francis; and as though he, too, were going a journey, he began to arrange his papers and effects, and to destroy some matters that he did not wish should meet any eye but his own. More than once he asked himself why he did this; but he could give himself no satisfactory answer, except as far as he considered that at times a man takes a fancy to make, as it were, a dart among his private papers, and to put them to rights a little.

One of the habits of Lord Francis was to keep a diary, in a condensed form, of all the events of importance that occurred to him. He had found the advantage of such a mode, for in some cases a wilful perversion of facts and acts upon the part of people made such memoranda of importance, and in other cases a real lapse of memory was rectified by them.

In the hour, then, that he still had before him, Lord Francis set about writing in his diary, in a condensed form, the events of the day, and ended the page by the following memorandum—

"I am to meet Courtley in an hour. It is now twelve. I take with me a thousand pounds to give him, and my present wish is, that he may prosper and be happy. God bless him. He has a noble soul, if we at Bloxdale have a noble name."

Such, then, was the position of affairs on that night, and such, for the last few hours, were the arrangements and the various occupations of the principal persons concerned in the scenes that were about to take place to give Bloxdale a far and wide celebrity before the coming dawn.

CHAPTER XXXVII.

TWELVE O'CLOCK, AND THE SNOW FALLING FAST.

WE have now, up to midnight upon that awfully eventful night, brought the proceedings of our various characters; and it remains to us to state with clearness and precision the various events which took place after that hour, and before the sun of a winter's day again dawned upon Bloxdale Park.

We might well hesitate to record the wickedness of such a man as Oxley, only that the record even of wickedness is, like all things in this world, not without its good. If such details only have the effect of putting upon their guard the pure spirits of the world, and teaching them what they may have to fear, surely some good end is to be accomplished; for such is the constitution of modern society, that it is necessary to have some knowledge of what evil looks like in its ordinary as well as in its extraordinary aspect to be able to avoid it well.

No doubt John Oxley, in the recesses of his own heart, had a hatred against Morris Courtley and against the young Lord Francis, which of itself would have been quite sufficient to make him wish them dead, although it might not have been sufficient to induce him to run the personal risks of killing them.

When, however, we find, that in addition to this personal hatred, all his interests seemed to pull in that one direction of their deaths, we can scarcely wonder that a man who never had any other guiding principle in life than his personal interests, and the gratification of his personal feelings, should readily fall into the train of circumstances that would be likely to cause their destruction.

Then he, Oxley, was virtually no longer the steward of Bloxdale—no more of the money of the weak earl, his master, although master only in name, would pass through his hands; and he might truly have said— "Oxley's occupation 's gone!"

There could not be a doubt but that now Lord Francis would, so far as regarded him, Oxley, and the dear, delightful Miss Wicks, make a clear house of it.

By-the-by, talking of Miss Wicks, it would have been a very pleasant thing for Oxley to have been enabled to crush her in the general destruction that he hoped would alight upon his other enemies.

During the course of his intriguing career in Bloxdale, and while the process of transferring his allegiance from the earl to Lady Bloxdale was going on, Wicks was a very useful object and assistant to Oxley; and as that rather distinguished personage had been looking out for a husband any time for the last thirty years, she thought that the portly and well-to-do steward might answer the purpose very well, indeed.

Oxley soon found that the only way of bending Miss Wicks effectually to his interests, was to flatter her with the idea of becoming his wife; so he set about it with for her, fatal success, as will be seen eventually.

Miss Wicks, of course, had not the slightest idea that John Oxley, at his time of life, was such a gay Lothario as he really was, and the very existence of a Mrs. Oxley in the person of Mrs. Lerew never crossed her imagination.

Now, however, that affairs were assuming an attitude of great importance, Miss Wicks was becoming a very troublesome personage, and Oxley knew not what to do with her. It is the fate of all persons who associate together for bad purposes, that, sooner or later, they should wish each other anywhere but in a place agreeable to human nature, after the troubles and the turmoils of this life are over.

Miss Wicks had not begun to wish Oxley in such an abode, for she had not found him out; but he most devoutly wished her there, and would gladly have aided her progress.

We will now proceed to state what actually did take place upon the night when such dreadful deeds as may very well make the heart sick with terror, took place at the old mansion of Bloxdale Park.

Morris Courtley sat in the old library until it wanted but a quarter to one. He knew that five minutes of rapid walking would easily take him to the place of appointment where he was to meet with Lord Bloxdale, so he calculated upon being, as he wished to be, a little before his time at the appointed spot.

It was, indeed, a pang with which Morris Courtley rose to leave the place he loved so well—the place which to him was sacred as being the abode of her who was so dear to his heart—the only place in which he had ever felt what it was to love—the home, for it was a home to him, was crowded by a thousand fond and tender recollections.

In the soft night air of the library—that air that was transferred almost to a spring-like gentleness by the fires of the house—he could fancy that the tones of Fanny's voice lingered.

Oh, it was a hard struggle to leave that hearth by which he had sat so often, and which was hallowed by the presence, upon so many occasions, of Fanny Bloxdale!

At the door of the old monastic-looking library, Courtley paused, and something like a sob rose to his lips as he cast his eyes round it in the gloom of that winter's night.

Every object there was so familiar to him—their relative positions were so well known to him, and the place altogether was so like some old friend, the peculiarities of whose mind he knew completely, that he wanted no light to enable him to feel quite at home in the place.

"Farewell!" he said. "A long, perhaps an eternal farewell to this place. It may be that I shall visit it again—it is possible that kind fortune may permit me so to do; but there are many chances against that supposition. And yet if I fall in the attempt to earn for myself a name that will waft me on the halo of its popularity with honour back to Bloxdale, my shadow, if that be a possibility, shall visit this place, and here with calm delight review some of the incidents of its mortal condition."

Morris Courtley crossed the threshold of the room, and the door swung lazily shut.

The old library of Bloxdale was now for him only a place to dream of in the time to come.

In the hall—that is to say, the more modern hall of the mansion, and not the great hall where John Oxley kept watch for his victim—there burnt a light all the long winter night. There it was, in the hand of a statue, and casting a dim and wavy radiance upon the ornamental statuary, the portraits, and the suits of armour that hung there, and gave the place an aspect of such rich antiquity.

The footsteps of poor Morris were slow and unsteady as he stepped onwards, and twice he turned completely round with the vague idea that he heard some voice call upon him.

This was nothing but imagination.

All was profoundly still in Bloxdale. It seemed as if he, the poor wan and half-fainting lover, who was going out into the night air to bid adieu at such a time to all he loved, were the only living breathing thing that durst not sleep in the old house.

But he knew there must be another who was a watcher of the progress of that night. He knew that the young lord who fancied him not an equal mate for his sister, because he was but a man, would soon be on his footstep to see that he really left the palatial abode.

Across the hall, and through a pair of folding-doors at one extremity of it—then down a narrow passage, vaulted and built of stone, and of the length of twenty of Morris Courtley's steps, he went, and then a low gothic door opposed him passage.

That door led to the great hall—that ancient portion of the house to which we have already drawn attention, and where Oxley held his watch for the coming of those who were as much superior to him as angels to fiends.

The low gothic door was always troublesome to open, but Morris Courtley knew the trick of the lock, and it soon swung back upon its heavy hinges, and the young secretary entered the great hall.

How cold the air was in that place! With what a shudder he moved, slowly, and scarcely casting a glance around him, for he had never held any secret meeting with the Lady Fanny there. Ah, no—it was in the old solemn library, where, from associations with the ancient usage of the place, she might think that Heaven looked down upon her, that she loved to sit by the feet of him whom she loved, and revel in the rich eloquence that flowed from his lips.

Or it was in the garden, when the soft sweet flowers were nodding all around to the evening air, and while the trembling notes of many a wild bird filled the soul with tender thoughts, that she used to meet Morris Courtley, and lean upon his arm, while they strayed amid the fragrance of a scene that belonged all to nature.

There were no such associations with the great hall, and so the secretary passed through its dreary length without a sigh.

The steward saw him.

From the deep recess of the old fire-place the glaring eyes of the man who meditated so fearful a deed saw one of his victims pass on, and he muttered to himself—

"It is Courtley—I know him by his height. The young lord is not nigh so tall; but he will come soon."

Courtley paused only for a moment upon the threshold of the great hall, and, because the place was one that belonged to the old house, he said in a deep, solemn voice—

"Farewell!"

Oxley almost scrambled up the chimney from fright to hear the voice, for at the moment he could not but think that Morris Courtley had seen him, and was saying something to let him know that such was the fact. A few words that poor Courtley added, however, soon aroused Oxley to a consciousness of the fact that it was the hall and not he that was addressed.

"Farewell!" added Courtley, again. "I shall perhaps never look upon your gloomy extent again. Farewell!"

A door through which the secretary passed slammed shut, and he was gone from the dim observation of Oxley.

The state of suspense in which the steward was now, was so great for the appearance of Lord Francis, that after waiting in the chimney about five minutes he began to think that he must have gone by some other way, and he emerged, fancying that the turret-clock of Bloxdale must have struck one, and he had not heard it.

How that could be, considering that he had been listening for the sound with great impatience, he hardly knew; but his impatience made him rather a bad hand, just then, at calculating time.

"It must have struck," he muttered, "and I shall miss him. Oh, yes, it must be one o'clock."

With these words Oxley made his way to the door through which the secretary had entered the great hall, and was in the very act of placing his hand upon the lock when it was rather sharply opened.

Oxley had only got time to shrink up as close to the wall as he could, behind the door, when Lord Francis stepped through the opening into the great hall.

The young lord was wrapped up in a large cloak, and had a travelling cap upon his head. In his hand he grasped the pocket-book in which he had placed the money that he intended to give to Morris Courtley before he let him go.

Lord Francis was evidently in a state of great agitation. The war of real feeling and of sorrow against the prejudice of his education was even then going on within his bosom.

At one moment he was inclined to fold Morris Courtley in his arms when he should see him, and to cry out to him—"Morris—Morris, you shall be my friend, and the husband of my sister, for God has made you one of the nobility of nature, and ours is only the nobility of art;" and then again the idea of what the world would say at a match taking place between his sister and one of so lowly a station as Courtley came with a chilling effect on his mind, and he trembled to do what his better nature prompted him.

"I fear I am late," he said, as he hurried through the great hall without waiting to look about him.

Bang! went the door at the other end of it, and Oxley was alone in the large gloomy place.

"Oh—oh!" he gasped. "I thought I was lost when he came. I am all in a profuse perspiration, though it is so cold—so—so—cold. I—my teeth chatter too, and I feel so ill."

Oxley had now a reasonable enough dread that excitement had done its best, and that a reaction of his system was about to take place, that might deprive him of all power of action.

The villain was not unprepared, though, for the rigours of that cold and sterile night. A small flask of brandy that he had with him, was his panacea for such evils.

"Yes—yes," he said, "the brandy, I should not be able to live now if it were not for the brandy."

Somewhere about a quarter of a pint of the insidious spirit was in the flask, and when John Oxley put it to his lips he did not take it away again while a drain remained.

"That will do," he said, with a gasp. "That will do. Ah! I feel—a—little—better now. Oh, yes!"

One! struck the turret clock of Bloxdale.

Oxley dropped the flask to the marble floor of the old hall, and the crack with which it went convinced him that it was broken, notwithstanding its leathern covering.

"Curses on it," he said. "It is gone, and I must not leave it here. Yet, what matter? It is of no consequence. An empty dram bottle? What can it signify if found? Nothing—nothing! I have, perhaps, no time to lose."

Oxley did not think it likely that the young lord and the secretary would part from each other without some little conversation, but yet, as he could not tell how brief that might be, he felt that he ought to be up and stirring, and upon their track.

To feel along the floor, now, till he came to the gun that he had laid upon the floor, was his next task; and soon finding it, he clutched it with a nervous grasp, and left the hall.

The route to the little gate in the park wall, where the secretary and the young lord were to meet, was as well known to Oxley as to either of them; and at any time, either by night or by day, in winter or in summer, he would have found no sort of difficulty in going the nearest possible way to that spot.

It is worth while now, as it is a spot which is frequently alluded to in the course of this narrative, that we should say a few words about its position.

The door, then, in the park wall was made of rinded oak, like the wall itself, and immediately beyond it there was a small meadow, across which a footpath led to a copse of great beauty in the summer time; and in the centre of which there was a little kind of grotto, or summer-house, and a fountain at the door of it.

That place had been a favourite retreat of Lord Francis Bloxdale when quite a boy, and many an idle hour had he whiled away reclining upon the soft green sward, and watching the splash of the waters of the little fountain as they fell into the basin below.

The meadow, then, was between the park wall and the copse, and was shut in upon three of its sides—one side by the park wall, and two others by the trees of the copse, so that it was only open at one side, and that was to the south.

A better spot than that for Courtley to take leave of Lord Francis could not be, for there was a diagonal path across the meadow in the north-westerly direction that led to a stile which, when once crossed, conducted by a lane of about a mile in extent right away in the direction of Southampton, which would take the secretary clear of the Bloxdale dominions by a shorter route than he could elsewhere have found.

With a slow and stately step Morris Courtley arrived at the door in the park wall; and opening it by the aid of a key that he had to it, and which he intended to give up to Lord Francis before he took leave of him, he passed out into the meadow.

The wind was whistling among the trees of the copse, and flakes of snow were sailing about and occasionally finding a place to alight upon; but it could not be said just then that there was anything in the shape of a snow-storm going on. Morris Courtley only walked about six paces from the door in the park-wall, and then he paused and looked around him. He felt nothing of the inclemency of that night; his thoughts were by far too intently occupied by other considerations of a far greater magnitude. As he had increased his distance from the house, a tremulousness came over his heart that was truly dreadful, for it appeared to him as if miles and miles of hills were being piled up between him and Fanny.

"Oh, Fanny—Fanny!" he cried, "shall I, indeed, never look into your eyes again? Oh, God! is it possible that I should be endowed with the capacity to love such a being as I love her, and then that it should be my fate to be torn from her thus?"

Poor Morris did not mean to burst forth into such a paroxysm of grief, but he could not help it, and now he clasped his hands, and covered his face with them, and wept.

Yes, the strong spirit was subdued again; and at the thought of the loss of all he loved, he gave way to tears that the greatest pain would not have wrung from him.

How long this excess of grief upon the part of Morris would have lasted, it is hard to say; but a voice, pronouncing his name, suddenly resisted it, and he started round.

"Morris Courtley," said the voice.

"Who speaks? Who—who?"

"Morris, do you not know me? May I say, it is your friend, Lord Francis Bloxdale who speaks to you? Are you ill, Morris?"

CHAPTER XXXVIII.

THE EVENTS OF THE NIGHT OF MURDER CONTINUE TO COMPLICATE.

UPON this, Morris Courtley stepped up to the young lord, and in a voice which was struggling with emotion, and which struck quite to the heart of Lord Francis, he said—

"I am not ill in body, my lord; but I am here to bid you and Bloxdale farewell, according to my promise."

Lord Francis was silent for some moments, and then he said in a low tone—

"Morris Courtley, when first you came to this house, which we may now but dimly see between the trees, denuded as they are of their sweet summer blossom, you were young and friendless; and I recollect you told me that your fortune consisted but of your knowledge, and of that rectitude of heart and purpose which is above all price."

"I did say so."

"It has been proved, Morris Courtley, by all who know you here, and who have the candour to own and to speak the truth, that in saying so much, you did not enlarge upon the truth, but rather kept your merits backward, and said the less of yourself than you might with a liberal enlargement of your qualities have said."

"My lord, I can make no reply to your kind appreciation of me. I can only ask, in return for all I have tried to do to fill worthily the place I held in yonder house, that you would do me one favour."

"Name it, Courtley. It is all but done."

"I dread to ask you."

"Nay, do not dread to ask anything of me. My desire is to do you all the service that is in my power. It is my great grief that I am forced to part with you."

"I promised, my Lord Francis, that I would not see your sister, that is to say, that I would not seek her again before leaving Bloxdale this night."

"You did so promise, and I will be bound, Morris, that you kept your word."

"I did."

"I could have sworn as much."

"Yes, my lord, I did keep my word; but to beguile the tediousness of the weary hours till now, and in some faint degree to give my heart that was so full a little ease, I penned a letter to her."

"You wrote to her?"

"I did, my lord."

"Oh, Courtley, was it within the spirit of your promise to me so to do?—It may be within the letter of that promise; but was it, I ask you, within the spirit of it?"

"If I had sent the letter, no—but as it is here, and as the favour I had to ask was that you would place it in her hands, I hope you will acquit me of breaking my word, either in the spirit or the language of that promise."

"Morris—Morris, I do—I do! Give me the letter. Fanny shall have it. The letter that such as you give to the brother to hand to the sister is too holy even for suspicion."

"Blessings on you for those words, Francis —pardon me, I mean my lord."

"Nay, call me Francis."

"I cannot now. That old familiar name would stick in my throat now. Have you not, my lord, by thus taking leave of me, with such regrets as I know well you feel in doing so—have you not practically taught me, never to forget you are a lord?"

"I have—I have! Oh, Morris Courtley, would that you were noble, or that we were all humble tillers of the soil, with no old state or rank to gall our better nature and hang like a chain of rusty metal round our hearts. Why, Morris, then we might all be friends, and all be happy."

"Ay," sighed Morris, "all friendly and all happy; but the world, with its false usages and cruel feelings, says no."

"They are, Morris, false usages and cruel feelings. You rightly name them, my friend. But yet do I find myself so hedged in by them, that I dare not move, as you see, but in obedience to their dictates. Oh, Courtley, it is hard to say farewell to you, but it must be said!"

"Say it, my lord, and I will go."

"Not yet—not yet!"

"Nay, say it now while you are thinking gently of me; and if I should in the great world, that now lies drearily before me, make the means that I could now covet for her dear sake whom I love so truly, would you welcome the wanderer back again?"

"With all my heart."

"Would you take me by the hand and call me brother?"

"With my whole soul I would."

"Well, then, now say farewell to me, and we shall part like brothers that are to be."

"Morris, before you go, here is a little remembrance of me."

"It is welcome."

"Take it, Morris; and may you and the world agree well together. Why do you hesitate?"

"This is a pocket-book. My heart misgives me. Is there—oh, tell me truly—is there money here?"

"There is."

"I cannot take it."

"This is a foolish scruple, Morris. Take it, I implore you. Do not go forth from me thus. It is unwise to go to fight for fame and fortune in the world without the most ordinary weapons to commence with. The bravest soldier that ever stepped takes his sword and his armour into battle with him."

"No—no, I cannot! I cannot, now! Under any other circumstances, perhaps, I could, but not now. I had a fear of this, my lord; for well do I know your generous nature; but—but it would look like being paid to leave *her!*"

"Courtley, this is folly."

"Perhaps it is; but I cannot help it. No! Poor and friendless will I leave Bloxdale as I came to it. Farewell! Deliver my letter to her. I know you will, for you have said as much. And now, farewell!"

"Oh, Morris, will you cut me to the heart thus?"

"Let it not cut you to the heart, my dear friend. Believe me, that I love Fanny, and that your image lies very close to hers in my heart of hearts. Once more, farewell!"

"No, Morris, no! This cannot—this must not be! You will not leave me thus, I feel assured! Stay yet a moment! The snow is falling quickly. Stay, Morris, stay! Take my cloak, I implore you! Oh, God, he is gone!"

Morris Courtley waved his hand to the young lord, and then, with only his ordinary apparel upon him, which was so ill calculated to withstand the winter's blast, he sped across the meadow we have mentioned towards the lane that would lead him in the direction of Southampton.

And now for a few moments Lord Francis Bloxdale stood still and sad upon the spot where Courtley had left him, and the snow was falling fast around him. Suddenly, then, with a bound, he sprang forward in the direction that the fugitive had taken, and called out in a loud voice that rang clearly and distinctly in the night air—

"Courtley—Morris Courtley, I say! The picture of superstition and of false pride has fallen from my eyes! Come back! oh, come back, I say, and with my full consent, with my blessing—and, I doubt not, with that of Heaven—you shall be my sister's husband! Courtley, come back; the struggle between pride and nature is over, and I feel that I can think and act like a man! Courtley— Morris Courtley, I say, come back to Bloxdale, and be, indeed, to me a brother! Courtley, I say!"

There was no reply.

The young lord ran half way across the meadow.

"Morris, it is Fanny calls you!"

"Hilloa!" cried a voice. "Who says that?"

"I, Morris—I say it! Come back!"

Like a black toad, hideously large, or like some snake so coiled up that you lost the identity of its lengthy shape, there came a something from the door of the park wall along the snow. On—on after the young lord it came.

That black object was John Oxley!

"Come back to me!" cried Lord Francis, as he ascended a little knoll that rose some six feet above the surrounding surface of the meadow. "Come back, Morris Courtley!"

"No—no!" replied a faint voice in the distance.

The black-looking figure rose up, and stood calmly in the snow-light. The gun was levelled—there was one sharp ringing report—a shriek—and then Lord Francis Bloxdale, with a couple of bullets in his heart, fell backwards, and rolled over and over, grasping the snow with both hands, and shrieking as he writhed in the deep agony of death!

With one convulsive spasm, then, he turned upon his back, and the spirit of the murdered man fled straightway to the foot of the great God who has said—"Thou shalt do no murder," and who saw through the mists of that night of gloom and terror the deed done.

Oxley flung the gun across his arm, and then ran up to the spot where the body lay. He felt that only one half of his unholy work was done.

He laid the gun by the side of the body—he stripped off the coat of Courtley's that he had taken from his room, and tearing one of the cuffs from it, he placed the fragment of cloth in the hands of the corpse, and held the dead limp fingers down on it for a moment. The coat he flung over a fence close at hand, and then he fled to the door in the park wall, and darted through it, and so on through the passage, the old hall, and to his own chamber, where he bolted himself in, and fell upon the floor in a swoon.

* * * * *

"Was that a shot?" cried Morris Courtley, as he jumped from the top of the stile at the end of the meadow back again into it, and ran in the direction that he had left the young Lord Francis.

After traversing about half the distance, Morris Courtley stopped, and placed his hand up to his eyes, trying to retain sufficient light to see what was in the meadow; but all was still.

"My lord," he cried, "why did you call me back again? Did you say that Fanny called me?"

No answer.

"This is strange," said Courtley, as he ran on through the snow-drift, that each moment began to assume a more and more definite character, and then he suddenly stumbled over something.

That something was the dead body of Lord Francis Bloxdale.

"Good Heavens! what is this?" exclaimed Courtley. "A corpse! No—no—not his lordship. I heard a gun fired—Oh, God—Hush! It is too terrible a supposition!"

The snow fell thick and fast, and Courtley fought with it with his hands, so that it should not fall upon the face of the corpse, and so aid the darkness in concealing its identity. The winds howled through the trees in the copse most dismally.

"What can it mean?" said Courtley. "Oh, for light enough to look upon this face! It is warm, too—quite warm. What is this dark stream upon the snow? Blood—blood! Is there murder done here? Oh, my poor brain! will it throb to madness? This is the end of all. Why, I had not left him the space of a minute, and lo! he is murdered!"

Morris Courtley sprang to his feet, and looked around him.

The snow came down in such a drift now, that it was impossible to distinguish even the boughs of the trees in the hedge-row close at hand; and after another moment or two of hesitation, Courtley, with a shrieking shout that reached Bloxdale Hall, and awakened most who slept beneath its roof, cried out—

"Help! Murder!"

Startled and amazed at the wild vehemence of his own voice, then the secretary cowed down, trembling like an autumn leaf, while the blinding snow still fell, covering up both him and the corpse in its beautiful mantle of white.

Again, then, he drew a long breath, and again went forth the shout of—

"Murder—murder!"

Oxley, in his chamber, awoke from his swoon, and heard the shout. With an answering shout, he rose and reeled to his door, and held it fast, crying—

"No—no! I did not do it—God, no!—Help! I did not do it! The corpse—the meadow—the gun! Ah—ah—I—did—not——"

He fell back again, and struck his head against the edge of a chair, so that he fell insensible from the blow.

Windows were flung open in Bloxdale—lights flared in the galleries—the watch-dogs bayed loudly; and above all the alarm and all the din, again came the terrific voice crying—

"Help! Help! Murder!"

CHAPTER XXXIX.

THE DISMAL NIGHT AT BLOXDALE.

IN ten minutes—they seemed to poor Morris Courtley to be ten hours, the whole of the inhabitants of Bloxdale were armed, and with such weapons as they could in their haste lay hold of, rushed to the hall in wild confusion.

Many of the servants carried lights, which they had hastily lit upon the spur of the occasion; and from the lamp in the hall, many were procuring a light to torches and candles that they brought with them.

Amid all the glare of frightened faces there, there came one that looked more pale and ghastly than them all. Lady Bloxdale, followed by the trembling Wicks, appeared half way down the grand staircase, and looked at the throng below.

"What is all this?" she said.

"Murder!" cried thirty voices at once.

The effect was terrific. In another moment a light figure, clad in white flimsy robes, flitted past Lady Bloxdale, and appeared in the hall. The little white feet, without shoe or stocking, trod upon the cold marble floor, and Lady Fanny, for it was she, cried out in a frantic voice—

"Who says murder?"

"We all heard it," cried a dozen voices.

"Oh, God! she will die with cold," shrieked Ann, from above.

"Silence!" said Lady Bloxdale. "Who can explain this frightful alarm? Let one speak."

They were all silent now, for the fact was that none could explain it. They could all only say that there was a frightful alarm, but as to explaining aught concerning it, that was quite out of the question.

"Speak! Oh, God, will no one speak?" cried Fanny. "Where is my brother? Where is Mr. Courtley?"

At this everybody looked round, as though these words of the Lady Fanny's were sufficient to act as a sort of exorcism to produce both the persons she named upon the spot. In another moment, though, all eyes were directed to the grand staircase down which, carrying a light, there came a tall figure in a dressing-gown. Following this tall figure, was the earl's valet, looking very much frightened, for it was the Earl of Bloxdale himself who then, looking calm and collected, and rather stern, descended the grand staircase.

When the countess, who was by this time upon the bottom step of all, saw him thus descending, she hastily called out—

"To your room, my lord—to your room. This is no place for you. To your room, my lord, I say."

The earl still slowly and calmly advanced.

"Take your master back to his own room," cried the countess, then, to the trembling valet.

"I—I can't, my lady."

"Silence!" said the earl, in a calm and rather deep tone of voice. "Madam, this is very unseemly for you to be here in such a dress in the midst of the household. I beg that you will retire, and allow me to inquire into the cause or causes of this disturbance."

"My lord?"

"Do you hear me, madam?"

"I—that is——"

"Oh, father—father!" shrieked Fanny, "it is murder!"

"You here too, Fanny?"

"Yes, father, I heard the dreadful cry."

"Go to your room, my dear, I beg of you. No possible harm can come to you. It is my duty to see to this affair."

"But father, you seem—that is, you don't seem——"

"What, my dear?"

"Nothing—I only am so glad to see you better."

"Better? I am quite well. Get stable-lanterns, for the wind and snow will extinguish any other light, and search round the house for the meaning of the cries we have heard. Let half a dozen men go in one direction, and the same number in another. Go armed, for we don't know what characters may be about the grounds at this season. Allow me again to suggest that you retire, Fanny. Your mother, I see, does not feel inclined to do so, but that forms no rule for you."

The tone and manner in which the Earl of Bloxdale delivered this speech astonished the servants, Lady Fanny, and the countess. Never, in his best days, had he been more completely self-possessed and confident in his own power.

The voice was full and firm—the expression of his countenance was altogether different from what it had been of late; and in the glance of his eye the Countess of Bloxdale trembled to think she saw the signal of the downfall of her power.

What had produced this miracle, no one could conceive.

Was it possible that the cry of "murder!" from Morris Courtley had struck upon some slumbering chord in the intellect of the old earl, which, when once awakened, had made the whole mental machine work bravely again?

Was it that nature, in some mysterious manner, had roused up the father to intellect and action at the moment that the son fell beneath the base arm of the assassin?

There are, indeed, mysteries in nature which we cannot fathom, and this might well be one of them. Hamlet was right when he said—

"There are more things in Heaven and on earth
    Than are dreamt of in our philosophy."

But if Lady Fanny was surprised, and almost doubted the credence of her own senses with regard to this wonderful recovery of her father to mental health and aptitude, she was no less delighted to see such a result. She sprang towards him, and clinging to his arm, she cried in tones of joy—

"Father, dear father, you are yourself again. Now you will be able to protect your child."

"Protect you?"

"Yes, father, you will, indeed you will."

"Who dares for one moment make it necessary that the daughter of the Earl of Bloxdale should need more protection than the name she bears carries with it?"

Fanny could not help it for the life of her. She did not mean to do it, but she did glance towards her mother as though she would have said—"It is from the countess I require protection."

The countess took the hint, and advancing with a look of rage, she screamed rather than said—

THE EARL OF BLOXDALE.

"To your chamber, girl! To your chamber, I say! This is no place for you. How dare you remain here a moment contrary to my orders?"

Fanny clung to her father.

"Madam," said the earl, "this insolence is unbecoming a lady, and still more unbecoming in my wife, in the presence of her domestics. I command you to retire to your room on pain of my displeasure."

"Your displeasure?"

"Yes, madam, my displeasure. Retire at once, I order you."

The countess staggered back"and leant upon a marble column that was in the hall.

"Who removed the bust from that column?" said the earl.

"I did," said the countess. "It shall not be there. It is the bust of your brother, my lord, and he is no friend of mine. I had it removed."

The earl turned to a couple of the footmen who were close at hand, and said in a calm voice,—

"Return the bust to its place. You act under my orders."

"They dare not!" screamed the countess.

"Madam," said the earl with a bow, "they dare not disobey the orders of their master. This insolence does not become you. I shall be under the necessity of sending you to your friends in Scotland for a time, until you learn to treat with proper respect your husband and your master."

"My master?"

"Yes, madam, your master; and by Heaven you shall find him such."

The countess staggered back against Miss Wicks, who, finding her toes trodden upon so unceremoniously, treated her to such a push that she nearly fell down in the hall. Now this must be considered to be quite a provident interposition in favour of the Countess of Bloxdale, for just what she wanted was somebody upon whom she could vent her accumulated rage, with which her bosom was bursting. The push in the back that Wicks gave her did the business in a moment.

With a yell something like what one might suppose would be the warwhoop of an enraged Indian, the Countess of Bloxdale turned upon Wicks.

In a moment two thoroughly bewildering boxes on the ears, one on the right side of Miss Wicks's head and the other on the left, decided the battle, so far as regarded which was to be the conqueror, for Wicks positively reeled again. The box with the right hand would have knocked her over, but the box with the left hand came quickly enough to hold her up again.

"You wretch!" cried the countess, and then she seized Wicks by a mysterious sort of head-dress she wore, and heaven only knows what she intended to do with her, but the head-dress and a wig, which composed the entire head-dress of Miss Wicks, came off in the enraged countess's hand, leaving the object of her vengeance perfectly bald.

Miss Wicks fell into a corner fainting, and the countess ascended the grand staircase, carrying the wig in her hand after something of the fashion of a savage with the scalp of his enemy.

It was quite a capital retreat that; for the countess, by going off in that way, saved herself from any further collision with the earl, at the same time that she had the appearance of leaving the field of battle covered with the spoils of victory.

This little episode would have amused the servants more than it did, but that at that moment Roots, the poacher, as Oxley called him, but the gamekeeper as the Earl and Lord Francis Bloxdale would have him to be, ran into the hall.

"There is a cry of murder," he said, "in the copse. Where is my gun? Who has seen my gun?"

"It hangs in the great hall, Roots," said one of the men-servants.

"No."

"Oh yes, it does; I saw it there only a few hours ago."

'No, I say. I have been there to look for it, and it is gone, I tell you. Who has it?"

No one replied, so Roots turned to the earl, and bowing respectfully, said—

"My lord, shall I take some of the men, and look over the grounds?"

"Yes, Roots, do. After all, I daresay it is nothing particular."

"Perhaps one of my lady's traps caught somebody," said a servant in a hesitating tone of voice.

"One of what?" said the earl.

"My lady's man-traps, please you, my lord. She saw Mr. Courtley once in the little flower-garden, looking for rose-buds in one of the beds; so she had a great steel trap brought from Southampton, and set them with the hopes of catching him, my lord."

"Remove it, and destroy it."

"Yes, my lord. My lady has given me a month's notice to go, because I said as it wasn't right."

"You stay. Roots!"

"Yes, my lord?"

"You get some of the most active of the men together, and we will go to the copse."

"You go, my lord?"

"Oh, yes. Get me a cloak, Hill."

The valet bowed, and ran off to execute the order.

"We cannot find anything, my lord," said one of the party that had already, in pursuance of the orders of the earl, gone out to look round the house, for the fact was they had confined their search to the lawn and garden, and had not gone past the park wall at all.

"Where did you look?" said Roots.

"Oh, all about."

"In the copse?"

"Why, no."

"Well, it was thereway that the sound came from; and if you will come with me, my lord, we will soon find out what it means."

"Certainly," said the earl. "Fanny, my dear, do go to your room."

"Yes, father. Kiss me."

"There, my darling—there. God bless you."

"And you, too, father."

"Amen!"

With tears of grateful feeling in her eyes at the happy thought of her father's recovery from the state of mental alienation that he had been in, Fanny retired to her own room.

In the course, now, of five minutes more, the earl, Roots, and about eight or nine of the most courageous of the men-servants, sallied out of the hall to go to the copse. Three or four of them had stable-lanterns with them, which defied the snow, which was now, in good truth, falling in a perfect storm, while far off the roar of the sea came upon their ears with a booming sound that might have been mistaken for thunder by uninitiated ears.

The great hall was reached, and the men

with the lanterns held up their lights so as to cast as broad a radiance as they could upon the ancient place. The snow could be seen coming past the windows in large flakes.

"Help—oh, help!" cried a voice.

They all started and looked in the direction from whence it came, and then they saw something that looked like some gigantic figure of snow dart past one of the windows, and then another, and then another, until it reached one that could be opened from the outside.

"Help—oh, help!" cried the voice again.

"Why, that is Morris Courtley's voice," cried Roots, as he sprang towards the window at which the figure had stopped, and hastily flung it wide open. It was a French window, that is to say, it opened like folding doors, though why such windows are called French we don't know, as they are common enough in old English mansions. The moment it was opened, such a dashing storm of snow poured into the great hall that the floor began to be piled up with it.

In the middle of this, in tottered the gaunt figure, all covered with the white frosty particles, and in a wailing voice it cried again—

"Help—oh, help!"

They all saw now what it was that made the figure look so big. It carried something—a somebody else upon its shoulder. This was poor Morris Courtley with the dead body of Lord Francis Bloxdale.

Despairing of making any one hear him through the snow-drift, and feeling all but certain that it was Lord Francis who lay in his blood upon the meadow, Courtley had made a great effort, and raised the body in his arms and staggered with it towards the hall, calling but feebly for help as he came along, for the first wild excitement had passed away, and his words seemed to stick in his throat as he strove to give them utterance.

Courtley fell to the floor of the great hall with a deep sigh, and the dead body rolled from him.

"Lights this way!" cried Roots. "Lights, I say! Good God, what is this?"

"Murder!" shouted Courtley, lifting up his arms, and in that last effort using up all the strength that he had left, for he then lay by the side of the body some time without movement or speech, and they thought he had fainted; but such was not the case

"Lights this way!" again shouted Roots, as he flung himself on his knees by the side of the dead body of Lord Francis Bloxdale—perhaps he had a horrid presentiment of the truth at that moment; but it was not left long to conjecture.

Those who had the stable-lanterns hurried forward, and cast the full glare of them upon the face of the dead. Roots, with his broad, large hand, at one sweep dashed the snow from that face, and then they saw who it was that lay in death before them.

After the first start of surprise and horror, and the first few hasty exclamations, the men drew aside, and the Earl of Bloxdale stepped slowly forward.

"What is this?" he said. "Well, Roots, my good fellow, what is it?"

With one hand Roots covered his own eyes, and with the other he covered the face of the dead.

"Here has been some foul deed, apparently," added the earl. "Who is it?"

"God help the father!" said Roots, as he lifted his hand off the dead face. The earl looked melancholy. He stooped lower and lower, till his eyes were within a few inches of the face of the dead, and then, with a shriek, he fell over the dead body in a swoon.

"It is over!" said Courtley. "God, it is over! Father and son both! One gun will do for them! One gun—one gun!"

CHAPTER XL.

THE SCENE OF CONFUSION AND GRIEF STILL CONTINUES AT BLOXDALE.

SIMULTANEOUSLY with the fall of the earl the whole of the servants in the great hall recognised the features of the dead, and they looked at each other terror-stricken. Some one then called out—

"A surgeon! Go for a surgeon!"

"A surgeon?" said Roots. "Not all the surgeons the world ever saw or ever will see will be able to put the breath of life into this cold clay again. He is gone! Yet, stop. The earl may not be passed help. Take a horse and ride to Southampton some one or two of you, and get the doctor, and the nearest magistrate, too, for there will be work for him. Oh, Mr. Courtley, how is this?"

"Yes," said Courtley, passing his hand over his brow, as though his faculties were in a mist. "Yes; how is this?"

Roots lifted the earl from the body of his son, and the servants brought a great old arm-chair, into which Roots placed him, and then from the kitchen they brought vinegar and dashed it upon the old man's face, so that in a little time he opened his eyes, and looked dimly around him at the throng of persons in the great hall, which comprehended every living soul in Bloxdale at that time, except four.

Those four were the Countess of Bloxdale, Lady Fanny, Miss Wicks, and Mr. Oxley, the steward.

They were the only parties absent from that dreadful scene; and the reader can easily, from what has passed, account for their not being just then present.

"Are you better, my lord?" said Roots.

The earl looked at him with an incredulous look, as he said faintly—

"What is it all about?"

"Oh, dear, he don't recollect," said Roots. "Oh, Mr. Courtley, do come and speak to him, I can't. You are a scholar and a gentleman, and know what to say on such occasions as this; but we poor rough fellows make a regular bungle of such affairs."

Courtley staggered up to the earl, and twice or thrice he tried to speak, but could not. The old nobleman looked at him as he so stood before him, and then placing his finger upon his vest, he said—

"Courtley, is this blood?"

"Yes," gasped Courtley, "the—the blood of——"

"No—no!" cried Roots, "don't tell him!"

"Ah!" cried the earl, as he sprang to his feet, and held his head in both his hands with a frantic aspect. "Ah, I know it all again now! It is the blood of my son! my murdered son! Oh, unheard-of villain! what had he done to you that you should kill him?"

"To me?" cried Courtley.

"Ay, to you There is his blood upon you! Deny it not! Why, there is a guilty look even now upon your face! You were with him! Who else—who else, I ask? Murderer!"

Courtley staggered back at this unexpected accusation, until he reached the wall, against which he leant, and then he said—

"May God forgive you as I do, my lord, for this unjust accusation. I am guiltless of the death of your son. If my own life sacrificed a hundred times would have saved him, I would freely have rendered it."

"Francis—Francis, my son! my son!" cried the earl. "Oh, who has done this deed? Were there no lightnings in Heaven to strike the wretch to the earth who lifted his hand against you, my son—my son?"

"Be a man, sir," said Roots.

"A man? Why, am I not a man? And so it is that I 'suffer! I curse him! that smiling fiend! No, no! Did he smile?"

"I, my lord?" said Courtley. "You dream."

'Don't mind him," whispered Roots. "Don't mind him, Mr. Courtley; he don't know what he says. Did you find the body?"

"I did."

"At such an hour, too?"

Courtley thought for a moment, and then he felt fully how much it was required of him that he should give an explanation of his seeming connection with the dreadful deed of blood. The strong conviction of that necessity strengthened him to speak, and stepping first to the side of the corpse, he lifted up his hand, and said in a solemn voice, struggling with deep affliction—

"Hear me, all here present!"

They all turned an attentive gaze at him. The earl had sunk upon his knees by the side of the dead body of his son, and he only paid no attention to Morris Courtley, and did not, in fact, seem to know that he was speaking at all.

"Hear me, I implore you all," added Courtley, "and I beg that you will treasure up what I say, for it may be wanted to be repeated and well remembered at another time."

"You hear him, all of you?" said Roots. They listened intently.

"This night," added Morris Courtley, "I had an appointment with Lord Francis Bloxdale, to meet him at one o'clock by the little door in the park wall leading towards the copse meadow."

The servants looked at each other with surprise, and some with incredulity. The idea of an appointment upon such a night at one o'clock in the open air appeared too out of the way for them to fully entertain belief of.

Courtley saw their looks.

"You doubt this," he said, "or, rather, I should say, you do not understand how it can be; but there were reasons which, at a proper time and in a proper place, I will explain and make known, which will render the making of the appointment no longer a strange thing. Let it now suffice that I tell how I came to find the body."

"Ah, Mr. Courtley, that's it," said Roots.

"We met at the appointed time—we held some conversation, and then we parted. I went over the meadow to the lane, and he, as I thought, returned to Bloxdale; but before I could get over the stile I heard some one calling to me, and I paused to listen. Again I heard my name pronounced, and then I heard a shot."

"A gun shot?" said Roots.

"Yes, a gun shot. It came tolerably sharp and clear to my ears, and yet for the moment I was puzzled to know the direction of it."

"That was the snow," said Roots.

"Yes, doubtless; but full of an unknown fear I ran back, and stumbled over the body as it lay in the snow. There was not light enough for me to know that it was the dead body of Lord Francis Bloxdale; but as I had left him so recently upon the spot a terrible suspicion that it might be such came across my mind—that suspicion grew into a certainty, and I shouted as loudly as I could for help."

"We heard you," said Roots.

"I shouted murder!"

"We heard that, too," cried the servants.

"I know not whether my voice reached the hall—the snow was falling quickly, so I raised the body in my arms and brought it here. I know no more, but that my heart is so full of grief that I wish I instead of him lay there in death, and he still lived to bless and cheer those who will now mourn him for ever."

"That's all plain enough," said Roots. The servants were silent.

"But the question is, who did the deed?" added Roots. "You see, that is the question."

The galloping of horses was heard without, and then the hasty sound of footsteps, and then the door of the great hall was flung open and a party of men entered, accompanied by a tall elderly gentleman in black.

"What is the matter?" said the tall elderly gentleman. "A mounted man from here met me as I was going to my own home, from attending the last moments of Sir John Marley, so I came here with him at once. He spoke of murder."

"Why, that is Mr. Roachford, the magistrate," said one of the servants.

Roots stepped forward.

"Mr. Rochford," he said, "there has been a murder. Lord Francis Bloxdale is no more."

"My son, sir," said the earl, rising, and trembling in every limb—"my son is murdered. There is his body, sir. You are, Mr. Roachford, a magistrate of the county, I believe are in the commission of the peace, and as lord lieutenant, could take jurisdiction in this case; but—but, I—am the father!"

A copious flood of tears came to the relief of the earl, and he sobbed aloud for some minutes. No one dared to interrupt the current of that grief, and it was well not to do so, for it was a relief to the overcharged heart: and but for the welcome tears, there is no knowing what might have happened to the bereaved father before the dim light of another winter's day shone upon his brow.

When the earl had a little recovered, Mr. Roachford stepped up to him, and taking his arm, slowly walked him to and fro in the great hall for about five minutes, talking to him earnestly as he did so; and then the earl turning to the servants, said—

"The will of Heaven be done! Henceforth, I think—I hope that you will all see me calm—very calm and resigned to this sad stroke of fate. The grief will remain, but it will not be upon the surface."

"Let me beg of you to retire to your own room, my lord. You may trust me to do all that is necessary in this sad affair."

The earl suffered himself to be led from the great hall by some of the servants, and then the magistrate gave orders that the body should be carefully laid upon a table in the place. A sheet was hastily fetched and covered over it, and then it looked more ghastly than before, for as the sheet hung in folds over the head and heels, it was awfully suggestive of the sight that was beneath it.

"I shall hold at once," said the magistrate "a preliminary inquiry upon this matter. Not in this room, however, for we shall all be perished with cold here. Perhaps the steward can show us somewhere else. Where is the respectable Mr. Oxley?"

Creeping forward from the door of the hall, with his face as white as paper, and his hands clasped together to prevent their trembling from being so evident as otherwise it would be, came the respectable Mr. Oxley.

"I am here, sir," he said.

"This a sad affair, Mr. Oxley."

"Oh, sir, it is. It—it will kill me.'

"Oh, no—no; you must not give way in this way. Even the earl is getting resigned."

"Yes, sir; but who did it—oh! who did it? Oh, sir, may the dreadful wretch who did it, hang—hang!'

"Amen," said Roots.

Oxley started, and then panted as though he had hardly any breath left him.

"The shock of hearing that this happened," he said, "so unnerved me, that I fell out of bed, and you see, sir, that I have given myself quite a bruise on the side of my head."

"A serious bruise, indeed," said the magistrate.

"Yes, sir, and it aches. If you will step this way, I will show you into the back parlour, sir. There is a fire there, we keep it in all night with turf, if you please, sir; and I will send you all—(turning to the servants)—some of the elder wine, that you can warm in the kitchen, for I am sure you must be all cold."

"We don't want it," said Roots.

"We don't want it," said all the others.

"Oh, very well," said Oxley; "it was your comfort I looked to, that was all; but if you prefer retiring again to rest, except such of you as can give Mr. Roachford any evidence upon this dreadful affair, go, and God bless you."

"Ah," said the magistrate, "I am afraid that in Mr. Oxley you have a very indulgent overlooker, all of you. This is, indeed, a sad affair, and must be investigated clearly The real criminal must be brought to justice."

"Oh, yes," said Oxley. "Do you think, sir, that the—the real criminal, now, ever does escape?"

"Never."

"I—that is, I hope not."

"You may be sure not, Mr. Oxley. Sooner or later, the real offender, especially in cases of murder, is sure to be found out. There is, I do believe, a special providence to fix the guilt at last upon him. I am not a man given to superstition, but I really think that."

Oxley felt sick at heart.

CHAPTER XLI.

TREATS OF THE AFFLICTON AT THE CASTLE AND AT THE COTTAGE.

IN the midst of all the grief, loud as well as still, at the old ancestral abode of the Earls of Bloxdale, it must not be forgotten that Morris Courtley, too, had near and dear friends who were ever ready to sympathise with his griefs—to rejoice when he rejoiced, and who looked upon him both with admiration and love.

Deep in the New Forest, which the reader, by a glance at the map, will be enabled to see cannot be very far from Bloxdale, commanding the situation of that princely building in the immediate vicinity of Southampton, was one of those old cottage farms, or homesteads, that have stood the brunt of some centuries of wind and weather.

The old place had at one time—that is to say, in the early part of the reign of the first Charles — been a verderer's cottage, and had had appertaining to it only the little slip of land—about a quarter of an acre—which those official personages were entitled to.

The then verderer was one Michael Courtley, the ancestor of the secretary, whose position at Bloxdale is now so very painful and precarious.

It so happened that when the troublous times commenced in England, and when the people thought proper to teach to kings a rather practical lesson, by casting at the feet of Europe the head of Charles the First, various gentlemen of the roundhead profession cast their eyes upon the post that Michael Courtley held in the forest.

The result of this was, that the old verderer was ousted, and became, as old verderers and old gamekeepers generally do, a poacher.

During his depredations in the New Forest for a subsistence for his family, this Michael Courtley one day heard a horse galloping at mad speed among the trees, and presently through a glade of the forest there came a cavalier covered with blood and foam, and bent low down in the saddle to avoid a collision with the low branches of some of the trees, and his horse flew on at maddened speed.

Pursuing him were three well-armed men, whose costume at once proclaimed them to be some of the officials of the new state of things.

The cavalier's horse fell not far from where old Michael Courtley was hidden, and he saw the rider wave his arm once, as if bidding adieu to the sweet sky or the green trees, and then he lay quite still.

The pursuers were upon his track hard and fast.

Now Michael Courtley knew quite well that these base underlings of the communion, that was then in full power to hunt for royalists, did not hesitate for a moment in killing, for the sake of plunder, any one whom they might hunt down in such a fashion; and although, in his heart, Michael blamed the cavalier for not turning round and giving the whole three of them a sound drubbing, yet he could not remain where he was and see them butcher him as they would do.

With a bound over a fallen tree, and a rush of some few yards, old Michael was by the side of the fallen man and horse. The only arms of the old man consisted of a staff—a kind of quarterstaff, then much in vogue, and his knife, which hung at his girdle.

"Forward—forward!" he heard the pursuers cry. "Down with the malignant! Smite him even with the sword of Gideon!"

"Sir Cavalier," cried Michael, "rise, and stand by me, and we will fight these fellows. Rise, sir, and stand front to them."

Alas! the cavalier was past reply, and by the glance that the old man gave to his blood-dashed face, he thought that death had already put an end to his share in the combat.

By an instinct then of self-preservation, as well as with a feeling of indignation at the death of the cavalier, the old man determined to do his best against the advancing foes. Luckily, his eye fell upon the holsters to the saddle of the prostrate horse, and from each of them there peeped the stock of a richly ornamented pistol.

"The knaves!" cried Michael, as he seized the weapons. "I have them now, I trust."

"Down with the fiend! Down with Satan!" cried the three horsemen, as they dashed up to the spot.

Bang! went one of the cavalier's pistols, as old Michael knelt behind the horse and man, and one of the saddles of the roundheads was in another moment empty.

"Fire—fire!" cried the others.

A couple of carbines were discharged at Michael, but only one of the bullets just grazed his shoulder, and he did not find that out till after the affray.

With a cool and deliberate aim, the old verderer fired the other pistol, and down went a second of his foes. The third took one glance around him at the state of affairs, and then fairly turned tail, and galloped off at full speed.

"The devil go with you!" said old Michael. "It is well for you that you have made off, for it would have gone hard with me if I had not finished you with my quarterstaff."

The old verderer was thus left master of the field; and his first care was to remove the cap and plume of the cavalier, and to take a good look at him. He placed his rough hand upon his heart, and then he placed his ear to it, and he thought that there was a faint fluttering there, which gave him the hope that the cavalier, after all, although badly hurt, was not dead.

Overwhelmed with joy at this discovery, Michael Courtley, with infinite labour, succeeded in carrying the inanimate form of the cavalier to his little hut; and then his son, and his son's wife, and his grandchild, tended him and nursed him into life again; although, from the result of many wounds that he had, it was eight weary weeks before, pale and thin, he could crawl to the door of the hut, and sit with a ghastly smile looking at the sunlight, as it played in beauty among the fruit trees.

During all that time neither Michael nor any of his family had said to the cavalier—"Who are you?"

They did not think they had any right to ask such a question. They had taken him in, and fed and protected him, and they waited his own good leisure to tell them who and what he was.

Youth, a good constitution, and the pure and sweet air of the forest glades soon did wonders for the cavalier; and when once he began to mend, his recovery was very rapid indeed.

One fine morning, when Michael Courtley and his family rose, they found that the cavalier was gone!

Now this looked a little ungrateful upon his part; but it took a good year or two before old Michael could convince himself that he should hear nothing further of him; and then the old man stood up in the midst of his family, and said solemnly—

"I make it a request to you all, that you will never again, in my presence or hearing make mention of the man whom we res' cued from death, and who then left us without so much as a ' God bless you!'"

From that hour till the first of June immediately following the restoration of Charles the Second, not a word was mentioned in the verderer's hut of the cavalier. No less than nine years had elapsed since his residence at the little home in the New Forest.

That first of June, however, broke the spell.

At about sunset there appeared in the forest a brilliant assemblage of about twenty horsemen, with a retinue of servants in rich liveries, and to the surprise of old Michael, our cavalier, attired in purple velvet and silver embroidery, galloped up to the cottage, and flinging himself from his horse, he said—

"Hilloa! Michael, is my old bed well-aired? Are there any crape-covered knaves in the forest, think you?"

"The Lord be good to us!" said Michael, "it is the ungrateful wretch himself."

"No, Michael," said the cavalier, "it is not the ungrateful wretch; but the fact is, I was powerless to do you any good when I was here before, and if I had begun to speak at all, I should have had to tell you too much, and so have burthened you with a far heavier secret than you already had upon my account. Now that the king has his own again, the Duke of Buckingham can say and do a great deal."

"The Duke of Buckingham!" exclaimed old Michael—"you don't mean to say that—that you are—really——"

The duke laughed.

"Ask yonder crew of varlets," he said, "who look forward to fattening at my expense for the term of their natural lives, and they will soon tell you that what I say is the truth."

"My lord—your grace—I—I——"

"Tush, man! put on your cap, and let me have a rasher of cured venison, such as I used to have, and then tell me what I shall do for you."

"Nothing."

"Nothing! Is that possible?"

"Oh, grandfather," cried one of the lads who were present at the scene. "Let the duke give us our old cottage again, that mother often weeps for."

"Ah, yes," said the old man, "our old dear home again."

"It is yours," said the duke, "and forty acres around it of wood and glen, which I have begged of the king for you, and there is wherewithal to stock the snug farm that I know well you will make of the old place. God bless you all, and whatever you may hear of Buckingham, do not fancy that he forgot, or thought of forgetting his old friends of the New Forest."

Leaving an embroidered purse, in which were two hundred pounds, a large sum in those days, Buckingham mounted his gallant steed, and rode off again with his goodly company.

From that time the fortune of the Courtley family was on the rise, and the forty-acre farm and homestead in the New Forest was a very model of careful management; but one person, and that was the grandfather of the secretary at Bloxdale, was a blight upon the fair prospects of the family. The gaming-table and the tavern shared his regards between them, and Courtley's father only inherited the shadow of his real patrimony.

A lawsuit with a neighbour ruined the Courtleys completely. The father of the secretary died broken-hearted, and his widow removed to the same hut, for cottage it hardly was, which had sheltered the princely Buckingham in bygone times, and there resided with her three children upon a small annuity that was given her as the price of her and her children's renunciation of all further claim upon their land and ancient home.

Of these three children Morris was the eldest. Then there was a girl, a gentle, but sickly creature, and the third was a boy who promised to possess all the noble and manly qualities of his brother Morris, along with a much stronger and more robust frame.

Under the hands of Morris and his brother, the cottage-home had risen from its old remains like a butterfly from its grub estate, and a prettier little dwelling, all covered with roses, clematis, woodbines, and jessamines, could not have been found than that of the widow Courtley, which lay

"Deep in a forest dell,"

and by the door of which sparkled and leapt one of the little streams that are common in that part of Hampshire, and which seek the sea with many a tortuous, serpentine course around trees and flowers.

The notice that the great family at Bloxdale had taken of Morris was the joy of his mother's heart, for she knew that it was purely upon his merits that Morris was at the castle and so much thought of, and that, therefore, his position was likely to be an enduring one.

It too often happens that those who have that species of power that wealth gives to its possessors in an artificial state of society, take under their auspices some one or more of those who are not so smiled upon by fortune as they are; and the poor dupe of the sunshine of the moment is not unfrequently done irreparable injury to by such a deference.

Elevated to the post of favourite for no cause or merit—deposed again for no fault, such persons commit havoc among those who do not find them out.

Such was not the case with Morris Courtley and the Bloxdale family. For his own merits he obtained his hold upon their esteem and their affection, and they esteemed him and loved him because they knew that he was superior to others, and had noble and great qualities.

No wonder that the widow's heart sung with joy at the thought that her son, Morris, was then upon the highway to fortune and repute.

Alas! what a change was about to take place. How the roses were to fade in that pretty house!—how the old house was to lose its air of antiquated comfort—how all the world was to appear changed to the children at the little cottage in the wood!

It is now the sunset of that brief winter's day which had followed the fearful events that had taken place at Bloxdale, when the sky over the new turret suddenly darkens prematurely, and a dull gleam of misty light is streaking the west.

"Mother," said Ned, the young brother of Morris Courtley. "Oh, mother, how cold it is to be sure, is it not?"

"It is, Ned, but the soft and sweet summer will soon come, and then we shall scarcely recollect the snow and the frost."

"Oh, yes, it will so; I do like the summer to come, for then, you see, I can go and see Morris, and wander about the orchard and the pretty gardens of Bloxdale."

"Oh, yes, Ned, that indeed you can, for they love Morris so well up at the great house at Bloxdale, that any one akin to him is as welcome as the first violet that peeps out upon the world from a hedge row. But Morris does not come now so often as he used to do."

"No," sighed Ned, "I was thinking of that, mother. He does not. It's very cruel of Morris that——"

"Oh, no—no, you must not say that, my dear; only I think that when nearly a whole month passes and we hear nothing of him that—that——"

"That what, mother?"

"Oh, my dear Ned, what is that?"

"Only the snow coming with a dash against the window. There is a drift. Oh, how it does come down now!—what flakes! Why, mother, they do say, that in old times, when there was a fierce wind from the northwest, that the New Forest was so filled with snow, you could hardly have guessed it to be other than just a little bit of scrubby land, with stunted bushes on it; and then they say that Rufus the Red King, as he was called, who was killed down yonder by the old tree, rides through the storm and shouts out—"

"Hilloa!" cried a voice at this moment outside the cottage door, "Hilloa!"

Ned sprang to his feet, and his mother, with a scream, dropped the work she had been in vain trying to fix her attention to amid the dreary darkness occasioned by the rapidly approaching sunset, and the snow-drift that filled the air.

A young and beautiful girl—the sister of Morris Courtley—came rushing from an inner room, exclaiming—

"Oh, mother—mother, what was that? How cruel of you, Ned, to frighten me about King Rufus, and then to make a noise and make me—believe that—that——"

"But I didn't—I——"

"Hilloa!" cried the voice again.

The little party in the cottage became profoundly still with fright, and yet they hardly knew what they should be terrified at, after all, for there was nothing very much out of the way in some person who had lost his path in the forest calling for aid at the cottage—such an event was, at all events, of sufficiently frequent occurrence to rob it of any alarm; and now that the snow lay thickly upon the ground, and that the ancient paths, and roads, and well-known land-marks were all obliterated, this occurrence ceased to be anything but what might have been expected.

Yet the Courtleys trembled and looked at each other in dismay. The old hound, who up to that moment had remained passive upon the hearth, rose dubiously to his feet and uttered a plaintive howl, and then dropped into a crouching posture again.

"Lion is frightened," said Ned.

The dog shook himself as if to arrange in his large loose skin the old bones that were soon to be laid in the grave, for he was past all work, from age, and then whined.

"It was somebody," said Alice, faintly.

"In the forest," said the mother.

"Yes, oh yes; I thought it was Ned trying to frighten me about Rufus, as he used to do in the summer."

"Yes," said Ned, "but I should not have done it if you hadn't gone out in the moonlight to see Simon Larpent, the young glover from Lyndhurst, I can tell you, Miss Alice."

"I didn't see him."

"No, because you know that——"

"Silence, children, silence," said Mrs. Courtley; "for the love of Heaven let this humble abode be one of peace and love. There are but few of us now in the world, and if we wrangle with each other I don't know what will become of us."

"Oh," said Ned, as he stepped up to his sister and flung his arms round her and kissed her, "little Ally knows well enough that I love her, and if I was angry with the young glover, or with that dainty-looking fellow from Southampton who came to survey the wood, but did nothing but survey Alice, it was only because I did not think either of them worthy of her."

THE QUARREL BETWEEN LADY BLOXDALE AND FRANCIS.

"Hilloa!" cried the voice from without again.

The snow now dashed against the casement of the little cottage with a force that seemed to be sufficient to beat it in—the wind howled through the branches of the old trees around, and the darkness each moment became more and more intense.

"Some one has lost his way," said Ned, " in the snowdrift. I will go out and see."

"Oh, no—no," said his mother.

"No," said Alice. " No, dear Ned, you know that—that——"

"That what, dear?"

"That it is sure to be William Rufus, with the arrow in his heart."

CHAPTER XLII.

THE PEACE OF THE LITTLE COTTAGE IN THE NEW FOREST IS FOR EVER FLED.

THERE was an arch simplicity about the manner in which Alice said these words with which we have concluded our last chapter, that let Ned know at once that she was paying him a little in his own coin about William Rufus; so, snatching his cap from where it hung, he turned to the door, saying—

"Oh, yes, Alice, it's all very well now while you are by the side of mother, and the old hound is with you, though he has but two teeth left, and the fire is burning and crackling in the old grate; but if you were by the haunted spring now, or——"

Bang! came something at the door of the hut.

Alice screamed, and the old dog rose and strode to the door—Ned laid his hand upon the fowling-piece that hung over the chimney-piece, but his mother cried out to him—

"No, no, Ned. Look at Lion."

"Lion, mother?"

"Yes, it is a friend. It is some one whom he knows—only look at him, Ned. There is no danger."

The old hound had placed his nose at the crevice at the bottom of the door, and then he uttered a whine of gratification, and with wonted gaiety rolled over upon his back, despite his age and infirmities, and strove to show a playful and pleased aspect by short barks and strange noises.

"It is some friend of Lion's, that's quite clear," said Ned. " I will open the door at once."

Mrs. Courtley seemed still fearful that even the sagacity of Lion had been at fault, and that it was possible the person at the door of the cottage might not be a friend; but yet she did not actually interfere to prevent Ned from opening the door.

The dashing shower of snow that tore into the cottage the moment the door was opened had the effect of rendering it quite impossible to see any one; but Lion made a bound through the open doorway upon the visitor, and was evidently upon the best of terms with him.

It was then, as the snowdrift cleared away a little, and as the log fire which was stirred by Mrs. Courtley gave out a more cheerful light that a tall figure, covered with snow, stepped into the cottage, saying—

"Don't you know me?"

"Why, it's Roots," cried Ned. "It's our friend Roots, after all, mother. Don't you know him?"

"Shut the door, lad," said Roots, as he sank into an old arm-chair that was near to the fire. "Shut the door, Ned. Down, Lion, down. I see you. Well—well, poor dog—I didn't mean to say down to you; but —but I—there—there!"

The old hound rested its head upon the knee of the gamekeeper, and whined his satisfaction at the notice taken of him. Roots patted the dog, and when Mrs. Courtley spoke to him he made no answer, and when Ned touched him upon the arm he did not speak, and even to the gentle, sweet voice of Alice, he deigned no reply; but leaning forward in the chair, he leant his face upon that of the hound, and they could hear him weeping.

Yes, that great, rough, strong man sobbed like a child for a few moments, and then, when they were all terrified into silence, and were each regarding him with looks of the most painful inquiry, he sprang to his feet crying—

"There, that's over! Once and for all, that's over. And now I am a man again, and can do my duty like a man. I have felt it coming all the day, and thank God it is over. These are the first tears I have shed since I thought myself a man. Down, Lion, now, that's a brave dog. I have work to do, and cannot attend to you now."

The old hound shrank on to the hearth, and lay profoundly still.

"Oh, Roots," cried Ned, "what do you mean? How strange you speak. What has happened?"

"Ah, lad, that's it. Something has happened. You have it there, Ned—that's it. What has happened, that is the question."

"My son!—my son!" cried Mrs. Courtley.

"Oh, no. It's not about brother Morris, is it? Oh, Roots, you don't mean to say that anything has happened to Morris?"

"I do.'

Alice looked pale and faint. The mother tottered to a seat; and there, with a tremulous motion of her knees, as though she were rocking some vexed child to sleep, she sat in silence, waiting for the communication which she feared would crush her spirit in this world. Ned stepped up to Roots, and while the tears sparkled in his eyes, he laid his hand upon the rough man, and said as firmly as he could—

"Morris is dead?"

"No."

"Hurt—ill—wounded?"

"No."

Mrs. Courtley uttered a cry of joy, and

clasping her hands over her face, she sobbed out—

"Oh, how cruel to come and raise such frightful alarm—oh, how wicked to come here and make me think my darling was no more!"

"Hold a bit, Mrs. Courtley," said Roots, raising his head, and speaking in a strange, unnatural voice. "Don't blame me yet till you know all—then you can do so; but I have news to tell you. I love Morris—I love you all, and I think you know it. Among all at Bloxdale, gentle and simple, kind and honest, there was not one who would venture here upon the errand that brings me, so here I am. Somebody must tell you, and it had better come from me than from some chance visitor, or from report, that always tells the wrong thing the wrong way."

This was such an unusually long speech for Roots to make that the Courtley family were quite astonished at it, and looked at him eagerly for an explanation. Roots then drew a long breath before he said—

"Young Lord Francis is dead."

"Lord Francis?" exclaimed Mrs. Courtley. "The friend of my Morris—the hope and joy of his family?"

"Ah, dead as a buck with a half ounce bullet from a grooved bore in his heart. Dead—dead!"

"Dead!" gasped Ned. "Dead! But how—how?"

"Murdered, of course. Now you know it all—all. Oh, no, you don t. You don't know half of it. Listen to me. It will drive me mad to think what I have to say, so I must out with it at once. Lord Francis Bloxdale was murdered last night, and they say Courtley did it. That's all."

Mrs. Courtley fell from her chair in a swoon, Ned staggered back, but he could get no further for the wall of the cottage, and Alice knelt shrieking by the prostrate form of her mother.

The old hound lifted its head and howled dismally.

"Yes," added Roots, "that's all about it. Now you know it, and it's off my mind. Lord Francis Bloxdale is murdered, foully and brutally murdered, within a stone's throw of the old hall, and they say that Morris Courtley did it. They know he did—no they don't. They will hang him for the deed—no, I'm—hem! excuse me, Mrs. Courtley, but I don't think they will be able to do that. There's no more to tell, though, so you can now all of you set to work and make yourselves just as miserable as you like—but I won't—oh, no!"

"He did not do it!" cried Ned, doubling his fists, and looking at Roots almost threateningly.

"Go it," said Roots, "go it. Oh, I feel quite comfortable now that I have told you all about it—I—that is—poor, poor Morris!"

Roots turned and walked out into the snow again, but Ned called to him—

"Oh, come back—come back. We want a friend now. Roots, where are you? It is cruel to leave us now."

The gamekeeper staggered back again into the cottage, and seizing Ned round the waist he lifted him up in the air, as he cried—

"No, Ned; your brother Morris did not do it. He could not do it, boy. It's against nature, and nothing, you know, can ever happen that's against nature."

"Thank you, Roots."

"And I thank you, likewise," said Alice, as she stepped towards Roots with her hand extended.

"Don't thank me," cried Roots, as he kissed Alice, and then muttered something about quite forgetting that she was not the little child she used to be. "There, go and look to your mother."

"Is it morning yet?" sighed Mrs. Courtley.

"Morning, mother?" said Alice. "Oh, what are you thinking of? It is scarcely night yet."

"Do not tell me that, my child. Oh, I have had such a dream about Morris and Bloxdale."

"Mother, it is no dream. Look up."

Mrs. Courtley did look up, and at the sight of Roots and Ned, and the fire on the hearth, and the old hound, and the snow, she felt that it was, indeed, no dream, and she wrung her hands and sobbed aloud.

"Ah, that's the way to do it," said Roots. "Go it, Mrs. Courtley, that will do a deal of good, won't it? You don't see me making a fool of myself, do you? Why, Oxley sent me off about my business—no he didn't, but he sent me away from Bloxdale and my business was to be there; but young Lord Francis when he heard all about it took me on again; and now there he lies in the old hall stiff, and dead, a bleeding corpse, I tell you all, and Morris they say did it. Yes, that's the best of it—to say that Morris did it. By this right hand, if an angel met me and said that Morris did it, I would say, you—no—no, I would say, you are a little mistaken, that's what I would."

"My cup of bitterness is full," sobbed Mrs. Courtley.

"No, it ain't," cried Roots. "Be a man! No, I don't mean that; but look alive, and keep your powder dry! D—m it, I don't mean that either; but recollect that Morris is in danger, and that it isn't tears and lamentation that will save him."

"That's true," cried Ned—"that's true!"

"Of course it is, boy."

"Mother, do you hear that? We are not to stay here hesitating; but knowing, as we all know, that Morris is innocent of the deed, we are to go and say so to everybody, and we are to save him!"

"Oh, brother Morris—brother Morris!" sobbed Alice, "where are you now?"

Mrs. Courtley looked like a ghost; but she put on an appearance of quiet calmness, as she said—

"We will go to him—we will go to

Morris. Where is my cloak, Alice? there quick—quick! We will go to him. Come, my children, with me. Your brother calls us. My Morris—my first born—my son—my son!"

Mrs. Courtley would have gone out into the night air from the cottage, but Roots detained her, and carried her half fainting back to a settee in the corner of the room.

"Close the door, Ned," he said. "I must now tell you all I know about it, and how it all happened, you see. Mind you, there is nothing now to hear but good news—you have heard all the bad. They accuse Morris, that is the worst that can be said. Of course, they don't accuse him for nothing. It is, because there are circumstances that make it appear as if he might have done it; but the more they enquire, you know, the more they will find out they are wrong. Now listen to me, and I will tell you all I have heard about it."

They did listen to Roots, and he told the story pretty exactly from first to last. It is impossible to describe the agony with which Mrs. Courtley, and Ned, and Alice, heard the particulars of the death of Lord Francis Bloxdale, and how it was that Morris came to be apparently mixed up in the perpetration of the deed. When Roots had finished his narration they looked at each other with such despairing faces, that he cried out—

"Come—come, cheer up, all of you. Between this and to-morrow morning you must think of what can be done in this matter. I don't like lawyers as a general thing; but I suppose for all that we shall have to have one. What do you say to that, Mrs. Courtley? Come, cheer up a little."

"Yes, I thank you."

It was quite evident that poor Mrs. Courtley spoke quite vacantly, and was so subdued and broken down by the shock of this accusation against her son that she was incapable of thinking rightly upon the subject at all. That wretched family sat looking at each other and at Roots with feelings of despair.

The old hound howled dismally, and the snow beat against the casement, and the wind roared and moaned through the forest.

CHAPTER XLIII.

THE INVESTIGATION AT BLOXDALE FURTHER INVOLVES COURTLEY IN SUSPICION.

In the midst of all the horror and all the excitement at Bloxdale, the long, dreary, winter night—that night which would be remembered by all who were in that old mansion as the saddest and the most terrible they had ever known—passed away.

Over the snow-drifts—over the old trees glistening with the hoar-frost, and loaded with the white particles—over the great roof-top of Bloxdale, and upon the field, the snow in which was yet faintly tinged with blood, came the dull morning light.

What a chilling look it had, that heavy leaden-looking colour in the east—that light without joy—that rising sun without any of the cheering sights and sounds which should have made it sweet and picturesque.

The hedge-sparrows were too cold to twitter forth their morning song—the herds, with misty breath, looked forth in sadness upon the sterility of nature—the pretty bubbling streamlet, that in the summer-time was wont to run leaping and dashing merrily through the garden at Bloxdale, where Lady Fanny loved to stroll and think of Morris Courtley, was still.

Above, around, and all over the bleak landscape there was an air of desolation. It did not look like repose—it was more like death.

Up to that time, which was a period of four hours after the discovery of the dead body, and after its identity with Lord Francis Bloxdale had been fairly and fully established, there were yet three persons in the old mansion who remained in ignorance of the fact of the murder.

The three persons consisted of Lady Bloxdale who, in her indignation, had retired to her own apartments before the awful discovery had become known to the household.

Lady Fanny, who, at the command of her father had left them full of joy at the great change that had taken place in the character and the mental disposition of her father.

Ann, the young girl who waited upon Lady Fanny, and who found herself quite engaged in attending upon her young mistress.

These three persons, then, remained in ignorance of all that it was most terrible to know. That something was amiss—that there had been cries for help from somewhere in the neighbourhood of the mansion—that when they heard what was the matter, there would be somebody to pity, and perchance to relieve, were self-evident propositions to Lady Fanny and Ann; but Fanny little suspected how nearly the whole affair would touch her heart.

As regarded Lady Bloxdale, she considered that the whole affair arose from some squabble between the gamekeepers and poachers, and she was much more interested in what was likely to be the result of the strange change that had evidently come over the mind of the earl than in anything else.

It appears, at first sight of the fact, odd that for such a space of time as four hours these three people, residing in the house, could be ignorant of the afflicting truth that was patent to every one else beneath its roof; but when we come to consider the extent of the Bloxdale establishment, when we reflect that the mansion was of enormous size, and that anything inducing any amount of disturbance might take place in one part of it, and scarcely be heard in another, we may understand how this state of things could happen.

Then, again, who would willingly undertake the job of being the bearer of such news?

There are people who have no objection in life to be the bearers of news that attacks our pockets or our pride; but there are few who are fiendlike enough to feel any gratification in directly assaulting the affections.

Therefore was it that for these four hours, the great world rolled onwards, and Lady Fanny knew not what she had to suffer.

This was a state of things, though, that could not possibly be allowed to last, and it now remained for Miss Wicks to put an end to it. That exalted fiend, smarting with rage at the treatment she had experienced at the hands of her mistress, sought to deal at her heart, if she had such an article, the heaviest blow that surely could be dealt at the heart of a mother.

Miss Wicks determined to have the gratification of telling Lady Bloxdale that she had no son.

It was when the passion of the countess had subsided into sullen calculation, when she sat thinking by the bright fire she had lighted in her drawing-room, and reposing upon a heap of cushions that were piled around her, that Wicks made an appearance before her ladyship.

Now the countess felt that she had acted imprudently towards Wicks; for although the waiting-woman was under orders to leave the house, yet, upon mature reflection, the countess had thought it would be a difficult thing to find another so suitable to her in all respects, and had adopted such a tone to her as had induced her, Wicks, to conclude that if she said nothing of the notice to quit which had followed up the scene in Lady Fanny's chamber, the countess would preserve an equally discreet silence upon the subject.

It was, therefore, with a feeling that she had gone a little too far with her unscrupulous attendant that the countess now saw Wicks enter her apartment, and she was rather curious to know what sort of humour the waiting-woman was in.

Wicks, feeling that she was so armed against the peace of the countess, really looked quite amiable as she approached, and said—

"Did you ring, my lady?"

The tone in which these words were uttered was quite sufficient to let the countess know that Wicks, as it were, surrendered at discretion, and did not intend to carry on the contest; so, with an ungenerous feeling of triumph, the countess at once put on an air of authority that she would have not thought of had Wicks shown a sense of injury.

"No, Wicks, I did not ring."

"Oh, I beg your ladyship's pardon, I thought you did."

"You may stay, though."

"Thank you, madam."

The countess turned her head hastily, and looked at Wicks. Such humility upon her part was so rare a thing that she began to think there was more in it than met the eye.

"Where is the earl, Wicks?"

"In his study, my lady. Mr. Roachford, I think, is with him."

"Mr. Roachford the magistrate?"

"Yes, my lady."

"Oh, about the disturbance that has taken place. Well, surely it was not worth while to send for Mr. Roachford upon such an occasion."

"So I think, my lady."

"Well—well, Wicks, you observed the earl when he was in the hall? By-the-by, Wicks, I cannot say that I approve of your conduct in all respects; but you may have that white satin dress and the velvet shawl, and you may clear my wardrobe of the gloves and slippers."

"Thank you, my lady."

"And, Wicks, what do you think of the earl's manner? Was it not—rather as—as if he had—that is——"

"Got back his senses, my lady?"

"Why, yes, in some sort."

"That is just my opinion, my lady. The earl has got back his senses again, and is no longer the imbecile he has been for so long."

"It is very strange."

"Yes, my lady, it is very strange; but I have heard of such things happening before; and after all, perhaps, it will be for the best for him to be master now in his own house. I think, my lady, he means to carry things with what we may call a high hand."

"Master—a high hand? What do you mean?"

"Why just, my lady, that he intends to have everything his own way, and not to leave your ladyship the least shadow of authority in the house. I have no doubt but that every one who has kept to your ladyship, and been anxious to do your bidding will be sent out of Bloxdale, and that the earl will for the future rule like an old king; that is my idea, madam."

"Indeed! But I understand it all. My son and the secretary — they are at the bottom of all this; and Fanny, by her rashness, her criminal rashness, as I may call it, has aided them in the abominable plot. Oh, yes, that is it. They have put the old dotard up to playing this part for the moment; for, after all, it is but playing; and when I see him in private he will at once relapse into the idiot that he has been so long."

"You think, madam," said Wicks, suddenly shifting one of the lights, so that a more complete glare fell upon the face of Lady Bloxdale. "You think, madam, that Lord Francis has done the mischief?"

"I do."

"And his great friend, the secretary?"

"Of course I do."

"Aided by Lady Fanny?"

"Those were my words."

"Well, that is over, at all events."

"Over! What do you mean by over?"

"Why ended, you know, my lady—ended, and over. It can't happen again, you know, for I daresay Lady Fanny will scarcely ever look up again, and it's more than likely that the secretary will be hanged."

"Fanny not look up again?"

"No, my lady."

"The secretary hanged?"

"Hanged, my lady."

"Are you mad, Wicks, or have you been drinking?"

"Me drinking? Oh, my lady, I don't ever indulge, as your ladyship does, in *Eau de Cologne* of rather a deep colour, only being in the proper bottle, of course it can't be anything else—hem!"

"Wicks!"

"Yes, my lady?"

"I feel certain that you are playing with me. If you have anything to say, for God's sake now say it at once."

"What, don't you know, my lady?"

"What?"

"Didn't they come and tell you all this while—Oh, dear!"

"Tell me what?" cried the countess.

Wick's stooped, and placed her hands upon her knees in not the most lady-like attitude in the world; but it enabled her to look fully into the face of the countess, as she said, with a terrible deliberation of tone and manner—

"Is it possible, my lady, that all this time has elapsed and no one has come to tell you that the disturbance you heard outside the house was in consequence of Mr. Morris Courtley, the secretary, having murdered Lord Francis?"

The countess uttered a shriek, and grasped the cushions on each side of her.

"Ah!" added Wicks, "they ought to have come and told you. Murder—murder! That's what has happened. Morris Courtley has murdered Lord Francis, and all about Fanny, no doubt. The body—the bleeding dead body lies in the great hall. The great hall. Do you hear me? Do you understand that, my lady? What is the matter with you?"

Wicks was alarmed at the effect she had produced, for the arms of Lady Bloxdale were stretched out and shaking to and fro, while the expression upon her face was terrible to look at.

"My lady—my lady!"

Wicks shook her mistress by the shoulders.

With one piercing shriek, that was heard throughout the whole house, and which struck dismay to many hearts, Lady Bloxdale rose. Scream followed scream now; and at moments she shrieked, "Murder! murder! My son! my son!"

A torrent of blood gushed from her mouth; and she fell upon the floor like a log, striking her head violently as she did so against an ottoman.

Wicks was really alarmed now; and, rush-ing to the corridor, and thence to the picture-gallery, she called out—

"Help! help! My lady is dead! Help! oh, help!"

A bell somewhere in the house was violently rung, and there was the trampling of feet. But before any one could get from the lower part of the house to the picture-gallery a figure in white rushed to the spot, followed by another; and Lady Fanny—for it was she—grasped the hand of Wicks, as she said—

"Oh! what is this? Speak to me! What is the meaning of all this?"

Wicks gasped three or four times before she could speak, and then she could only say, "The countess! the countess!" and point to the direction of Lady Bloxdale's room.

"Oh, Ann," said Lady Fanny, "something has happened to my mother."

"Calm yourself, Fanny," said Ann—"calm yourself. It may not be anything of consequence, after all. Hush! oh, hush! dear Fanny! Do not scream and tremble so."

Ann held Fanny back as much as she could, and delayed going to the countess's room to the utmost of her power; but that could not produce above a moment's effect, and they together crossed the threshold of the room.

The sight that then presented itself was such as, indeed, to strike poor Fanny, who never was none of the strongest, with terror. Lying upon the floor in a pool of blood was the Countess of Bloxdale, to all appearance dead!

Fanny at that moment forgot all the harsh-ness and all the unkindness that from time to time she had experienced from her mother, and only remembered how years and years ago she had sung her to sleep in her happy infancy. With cries of anguish the young girl knelt by the side of the prostrate coun-tess, and then she called frantically to Ann to get help.

Help was near at hand. The screams of the countess for help, and the shouts of Wicks in the picture-gallery, at the head of the great staircase, had sufficiently alarmed the house. Some half-dozen people reached the coun-tess's room before Ann could run from it; and among them was Mr. Roachford, the magistrate, and a gentleman, who was a stranger to Lady Fanny.

This gentleman was a surgeon, who had been sent for from Southampton to look at the body of poor Lord Francis. It had been thought proper that the body should be seen as soon as possible by a medical man, although the fact of death having taken place was but too apparent to the most superficial observer.

It was a lucky thing for the Countess of Bloxdale that this gentleman—who was well skilled in his profession, having been for some years attached to the army when in Spain, where he had seen more practice in a month than usually falls to the lot of house-keeping professional men in these

"Piping times of peace"

in twenty years—was in the house, for he was able without trouble or excitement to adopt the best means for her recovery.

A blood-vessel had given way, as a result of the frightful excitement of the countess, and her recovery was exceedingly doubtful. In the course of the next half hour the imperious, violent Countess of Bloxdale was lying in her bed, pale and feeble, and forbidden, from fear of death, to attempt to utter a sound.

Oh! what ample time now for serious reflection had that vain and worldly woman! How very

" Stale, flat, and unprofitable"

would surely now appear to her all the power, all the dominion, and all the wealth, with its concomitant patronage, that she had struggled for and for awhile obtained. If the Countess of Bloxdale had any feeling left, now was the time when it might modestly and gently whisper soft counsel to turn and change the haughty spirit to gentleness and peace.

We shall see in the course of time, though, whether or not this good effect was produced by the circumstances which had laid the imperious, wrong-headed woman so low.

The earl had not appeared while all this was going on, nor had any one said a word to Lady Fanny of the death of her brother. The confusion in the house had resulted only from one of the three persons who were ignorant of the murder of Lord Francis having been informed of it; and even Miss Wicks, with all her diabolical wickedness, was too much terrified to try the same experiment upon the feelings of the daughter that she had tried with such tremendous effect upon those of the mother.

Wicks slunk away and shut herself up in one of the top rooms of the mansion, and there sat trembling and wondering how and where it would all end. A couple of the other women servants of the establishment staid with the countess, as Wicks could not be found; and the surgeon, seeing how very urgent Fanny was to stay with her mother, insisted upon her leaving the room.

Poor Fanny! when she got to the landing-place, leaning upon the arm of Ann, she looked up in her face, and said—

"Ann, you must find Francis and tell him of this as quickly as you can, for he still loves his mother."

Mr. Roachford was close at hand and heard this speech of poor Fanny's, and he looked curiously at her and at Ann, who replied—

"I will go to the library and ask Mr. Courtley where he is."

Mr. Roachford shook again as he heard this, for it let him know that Lady Fanny was as yet in ignorance of the awful occurrence that, when once known, could never be forgotten. Ignorance was, indeed, bliss to her in such a case, and yet it was impossible but that shortly she must know all.

After a minute's thought, the magistrate said to Ann—

"I am going to the library. Will you come with me after you have led Lady Fanny to her room?"

"Yes, sir, if you please; I dare say we shall find Mr. Courtley there, and, perhaps, Lord Francis himself. Come, Fanny, all may yet be well. Don't cry so, dear—dear Fanny. Oh, don't!"

———

CHAPTER XLIV.

MR. OXLEY SEEMS TO BE ENJOYING QUITE A TRIUMPH OVER ALL HIS ENEMIES.

MR. ROACHFORD felt hot and cold by turns as he heard Fanny weeping for her mother, and felt how much more care she had for tears than she yet knew of. He dreaded to make the communication he had to make even to Ann; but yet he felt that as it had to be made it was better to come from lips that would utter it gently than from those that might bluster it out with a terrible suddenness.

"I will meet you in the library," he said to Ann; "you will come soon, I presume?"

"Oh, yes, sir. Immediately."

Upon this Mr. Roachford hurriedly repaired to the library to wait the coming of Ann, whom he knew to be upon such kindly and friendly terms with her young mistress that she was not to be by any means looked upon in the light of an ordinary domestic.

"It is my duty," he said, "to tell Ann, in order that she, from her knowledge of Fanny, may be able in the gentlest possible manner to break the awful intelligence to her."

The magistrate paced the now deserted library with anxious steps, passing and repassing the chair which was wont to be occupied by Morris Courtley—that chair in which the secretary had sat so often, and looked into the soft and gentle eyes of Lady Fanny, and wondered if in all the world there were one to compare with her in goodness and in beauty.

And all the while the grey sombre light of the early dawn was growing into daylight. Objects in the dim old library, which had lain, as it were, in a confused mass together, began to indivdualise themselves, and to stand out from the gloomy walls clearly and distinctly—the smouldering fire-logs upon the hearth had a struggle with the daylight to preserve their lightness, and the leafless trees waved to and fro past the deep oval windows of the old place.

The door opened gently, and Mr. Roachford turned rapidly in that direction.

"Ann," he said, "I have something to tell you, that——"

The magistrate stopped short. To his confusion and dismay Lady Fanny was with Ann.

"I have come, likewise, Mr. Roachford," she said, "for I would fain see my brother and Mr. Courtley together. This is no time for them to quarrel; when such sad sickness is in this house they should hand in hand strive to assuage the grief of those whom they both love."

"Lady Fanny—I—that is—be seated."

Fanny looked about her with disappointment.

"Morris," she said, and then blushing at the familiarity of her mode of speaking of the secretary, she corrected herself, and added, "Mr. Courtley is not here I perceive."

"Not here?" said the magistrate.

"What sound is that—a carriage?"

The rattle of a carriage drawing up at the principal entrance close at hand came plainly upon their ears. Mr. Roachford knew well what it meant. He had sent for the mayor and the principal stipendiary magistrate of Southampton together, with the official personages connected with the respective courts. He had thought, upon consideration, that it was proper in so serious an affair to do so, and had kept all inquiry till they should arrive.

Courtley was in one of the lower rooms of the house a prisoner.

"What arrival is that?" said Fanny.

"Some visitors, I believe," said Mr. Roachford. "Pray oblige me by being seated, Lady Fanny. I have something to tell you.

Fanny stepped up to the magistrate, whom she knew was an old friend of her father's, and placing her little hand upon his breast, she looked him in the face.

"You have something to say to me, sir. Oh, God!"

"Lady Fanny, I pray you to be calm."

"Then it is something more terrible than I yet know. Oh, what is it? Ann, do you know? Cruel Ann, you have deceived me. Ah, now I guess! Morris—Morris! where is he? Not here—not here? Oh, no—no, nothing has happened to him?"

"My dear Lady Fanny, I pray you—"

"No—no! Nothing has happened to Morris! He is one of God's pure spirits, and is protected by that special Providence that will not permit the fall of a sparrow to pass unheeded!"

Ann trembled. She had begun to see from the manner of Mr. Roachford that he had something to tell which would be dreadful in the telling.

"Speak, sir—oh, speak!" said Fanny. "Believe me, this suspense is worse than any truth can be."

"I wish I thought so."

Fanny shook now so violently that Mr. Roachford forced her to sit down; and then he said—

"My dear young lady, you must summon all your fortitude—all your religion—and all your strength of mind, to carry you through a grievous trial. An accident has happened."

Fanny did not speak, but her lips moved to the words—"Go on," though no sound came from them.

"We do not know exactly how it was, but an accident has happened to Lord Francis."

Fanny burst into tears. It was the name of Morris Courtley she had expected to hear; and, although she loved her brother tenderly, it was a relief to hear his name mentioned instead of that of the secretary. Mr. Roachford was well pleased to see these tears. They terrified Ann, but they did not terrify him, and he was resolved that she should know all while they continued to flow.

"I said that you would require all your fortitude," he continued; "and you should reflect that, after all, this life is one of the most uncertain of possessions. The strongest and the best of men are at the mercy of a thousand accidents of daily occurrence: and so, Fanny, when I tell you that you have no longer a brother——"

Fanny sprang to her feet.

"Dead—dead! My brother Frank—dead! What is that? Oh, no—no—no—no!"

"He is, let us hope and believe, with his God," said the magistrate; "and at this moment hoping that you will not too violently vex your spirit with regrets for him."

Fanny dropped into the seat again, and fainted.

"It is over," said Mr. Roachford. "Attend to her, Ann. Alas, poor girl, this is truly dreadful! The hand of Heaven is laid heavily upon this family; but now that she knows the worst, it is a relief to me."

"Can this be all true, sir?" said Ann, confusedly.

"It is; and the murderer is Morris Courtley."

"Morris Courtley!"

"Yes, the much cherished, highly-prized secretary."

"Ah, now I know that it is all a dream!"

Ann dropped on her knees at the feet of Fanny, and rested her face upon her lap, and wept.

"A dream?" said the magistrate; "what makes you think that? Come, come, Ann, this won't do. You must rouse yourself, and get your young mistress back to her room Calm her as best you may when she recovers. I feel glad now that she knows the worst."

Ann looked up.

"Sir, she does not know the worst."

"Not the worst?"

"No, sir. Oh, no—no!"

"I have told her that her brother is murdered. There is nothing beyond that frightful fact for her to know. You are not aware of what you say. Lord Francis Bloxdale, I repeat, is murdered, and to all appearance Morris Courtley, the secretary, is guilty of the deed."

Ann held the hand of Fanny in hers, while she looked up in the face of Mr. Roachford, and said, sadly—

MORRIS COURTLEY ESCAPES FROM HIS GAOLERS TO MEET LADY FANNY.

"Secrets now may be told, that only one hour since need not have been uttered. She loves the secretary."

"Loves him?"

"It is so."

Mr. Roachford staggered back a pace or two. He now felt that if this were, indeed, so, Lady Fanry did not know the worst, for she had fainted before he had had time to add to his information of the death of Lord Francis the other terrible fact, that Courtley was suspected of the deed of blood.

"Alas — alas, poor girl, she does not, indeed know the worst."

A strange shadow crossed the chimney-piece of the old library; both Ann and the magistrate turned hastily towards the window opposite, from some obstruction at which it must have come. What was the surprise of both of them to see Morris Courtley on the outside, upon the little terrace, opening the window, as he knew well how to open it, for many a time had he found his way back to the library by that means, after meeting Fanny in the little flower garden.

The magistrate could scarcely believe his eyes, for he imagined Courtley to be a prisoner, and well guarded; and yet there he was, apparently quite at liberty, and entering instead of flying from the house which one would suppose, was so fatal to him.

The window opened, and a rush of cold air made its way into the room, and fanned the face of Lady Fanny. She opened her eyes and shuddered. Morris Courtley sprang forward, crying out her name, and with a shriek of joy she was in a moment in his arms.

Mr. Roachford was confounded. What to say or do, under the circumstances, he knew not. There was the suspected murderer in the embrace of the sister of his supposed victim. It was too terrible a thing to let continue, and with a voice of authority, and yet a tone that struggled with emotion, Mr. Roachford called out—

"Lady Fanny Bloxdale, do you remember that I told you your brother was no more?"

"Oh, God, I do—I do! And now there is but one to love me, besides my poor father. Morris—Morris! oh, why were you not at hand to save poor Frank? He is murdered—murdered! They say that he is murdered! Can it be true? Oh, tell me that it is not so."

"Fanny, dear—dear Fanny!" sobbed Morris.

"Yes," said Mr. Roachford, as he made his way to the door of the library, "it is true; and if suspicion be rightly directed, you now rest upon the bosom of the murderer!"

"No!" cried Courtley in a voice that found an echo in every corner of the old library. "No! so help me, Heaven, no!"

"You? Morris Courtley a murderer?" said Fanny. "Oh, no—no! There needs no denial to that! Who dare to say it?"

"Help! Hilloa! Help here!" cried the magistrate from the door of the library. "The murderer will escape!"

"Murderer!" said Fanny. "Murderer! What murderer is here? They do not—they cannot mean you, Courtley?"

"They do, Fanny."

"Help! Ho! Help!"

There was a rush of servants and officers of police, who had come with the mayor of Southampton to the house, and in a few moments some twelve or fourteen men were in the library.

"Secure him!" cried Mr. Roachford. "That is the suspected murderer of Lord Francis Bloxdale."

"Hold!" said Morris Courtley. "I wish not to escape. The innocent need surely, in this land of boasted freedom to high and low, fear nothing. I would not take two steps to avoid the investigation that I court for the establishment of my innocence for the wealth of worlds."

"You *have* escaped from the room in which you were placed."

"One word, sir, in explanation of that. I should have gone mad if I had not found an opportunity of seeing this young lady, and saying to her I am innocent. I have been in nearly every room in this large house in search of her. You will find your officer who was upon guard over me, I hope, not much injured. I was compelled to cast him from me, and he lay insensible, but not much hurt."

"Seize him!"

The officers made a rush towards Courtley, but Fanny placed herself before the secretary.

"No—no! He did not do it! He could not do it! I tell you all he could not do it! I loved my brother, God knows I loved him well; but let the causes of his death be what they may, Morris Courtley is innocent of them."

"You are infatuated, girl," said Mr. Roachford, "and know not what you say. Stand aside, I beg of you. This is no scene for you."

"No—no! He is innocent!"

"One moment, gentlemen," said Courtley, "only a moment. Fanny?"

"Yes, Morris, yes!"

"Your brother, whom I loved next to you and from whom I would have sacrificed my life, is dead! They accuse me of the deed! I am innocent! That was all I sought you to say! God bless you, and farewell; and now whatever you may hear, you will still tell yourself, Morris Courtley is innocent! Now, gentlemen, if you please, I am quite at your service."

CHAPTER XLV.

LADY FANNY HAS CONFIDENCE IN THE HEART OF HER LOVER.

THE arrival at Bloxdale Park of the mayor and the principal stipendiary magistrate of Southampton, with a posse of officers and official personages, rendered any further delay in the examination of the suspected murderer not at all necessary.

One of the principal apartments on the ground floor of the mansion was at once devoted to the purpose of the official inquiry into the cause of the murder of the son and heir to the title and estate of Bloxdale. It was thought by the magistracy that as there was no special objection to the first examination of the accused taking place at Bloxdale Park, it was better that it should be so for more reasons than one.

In the first place, there was no difficulty in the recognition of the corpse of poor Lord Francis, since there it lay ready to receive official investigation.

Then again, there was no delay in getting at the evidence, while it was fresh and unexaggerated, from the servants and others who knew anything of the fearful circumstance.

The magistracy well knew how, in many minds, facts grow by keeping, and how difficult it is for the intellect, and for those who have been unaccustomed to think closely to give an unembarrassed account of any transaction whatever.

This exaggeration, too, by no means

arises from a wish to falsify events; but an active imagination, if undisciplined by education, will be seen to run riot with any facts of real, or seeming importance, and will quite unnecessarily add to them in one place and take away from them in another, to make up a good story for the telling.

Hence, then, by holding the investigation at once, and so close upon the event at Bloxdale Park, the magistracy had the advantage of getting at all the evidence before the witnesses had time to recover from the first alarm, and to think over the matter, and talk of it to each other, that latter state of things being as dangerous to the integrity of evidence as any.

How Morris Courtley was seized in the library by the officers—and how poor Fanny was conveyed to her own room after the sad scene that had taken place between her and her lover, the reader may well imagine without a painful description of the feelings of either party. Suffice it to say that such was the state of the things as regarded Courtley and Lady Fanny, when the magistrates took their seats in the smallest and most modern hall at Bloxdale.

The domestics and the officers who had come from Southampton filled the lower end of the apartment, and Mr. Roachford, to whom the principal conduct of the proceedings were given by common consent, ordered the prisoner to be brought before that preliminary and temporary tribunal that had assembled.

Before this order could be obeyed a door opened in the side wall of the hall, and the Earl of Bloxdale entered.

The earl was very pale, and in his hand he carried a white handkerchief, which he held with a nervous clutch. It was considered that he was affected very deeply by what had taken place in his house, and that it was only by the greatest efforts he could calm himself down sufficiently to show any degree of composure.

There was, however, another thing equally evident, and that was, that by some extraordinary means the Earl of Bloxdale had completely recovered from that eclipse of the mind which had for so long rendered him a mere nonentity in his own house, and placed him and all at Bloxdale at the mercy of the imperious countess.

No one could fail to be surprised at this sudden change in the earl, but no one, of course, made the least remark upon it. It did certainly appear as if a benign providence had, at the very time when intellectual exertion was demanded of the Earl of Bloxdale, given him back that energy of soul which for a time had passed away from him.

It is, however, not by any means an unusual thing for some sudden shock to the senses to recover an intellect which has only become for a time dormant; and we must consider the shock that the earl had received in this matter to be the cry of "Murder!"—

and "Help!" that had come upon his ears when Morris Courtley uttered such sounds.

Upon the earl reaching the hall the magistrates rose and bowed to him, and Mr. Roachford offered him a seat, saying—

"My lord, we should not have thought it consistent with our fellings towards you to request your presence here; but if you think you can remain during the investigation, we shall be happy to be guided by your judgment."

It was an effort for the earl to speak, and when he did so, it was only in a low voice that he said—

"Half an hour ago, gentlemen, I told myself that I had not sufficient command over myself to come here upon this occasion; but I feel that it is a duty. It is a duty I owe both to the dead and to the living to possess myself, as fully as possible, of all that relates to this dreadful affair."

The magistrate bowed.

"Do not mistake my motives for coming here," added the earl. "I come merely as a spectator, however deeply I may be interested in the inquiry. Do you, gentlemen, act as though I were not with you."

"Permit me to say, my lord," said Mr. Roachford, "that that is a highly proper, and, as I think, a wise determination upon the part of your lordship. We will, then, if it please you, begin the inquiry at once?"

The earl gently inclined his head, and there he sat with the handkerchief still grasped in his hand, and his mouth slightly moving in a strange spasmodic fashion, as he strove to look calm and collected.

Our readers can appreciate the difficulty of the task the father had set himself to look calm and resigned, within four or five hours of the murder of his son.

At this juncture, Morris Courtley was brought into the hall by two officers; and if the Earl of Bloxdale was pale, the paleness of Courtley was by many degrees whiter still. It seemed as if years of suffering had passed over the soul of the young secretary since last those who now looked with a painful and terrible interest in his face saw him.

Courtley did not see the earl at first coming into the room, but when his eye fell upon him, an expression of the tenderest compassion came across his face, and he bowed respectfully.

"This way," said one of the officers, rather roughly, as he placed Courtley opposite to Mr. Roachford.

A slight flush for a moment came across the face of the secretary, and then he was white and calm again. It was the calmness of great suffering, though. The mind of Courtley could hardly be said yet to have awakened to a proper sense of all that had happened during that fearful preceding night.

There was now a death-like stillness in the hall, which Mr. Roachford even, although well accustomed to judicial examinations, found it difficult to break ; but it was his duty to do so, and he said—

"It appears there has been a murder committed. Let any one who can say aught concerning it, step forward at once."

No one moved.

Courtley then, in a low and gentle voice, spoke—

"I opine, sir, that no one here present can possibly know half so much as I do of this sad affair."

"You stand here accused, or suspected of the deed," said the magistrate, "and you will consult your own interest by keeping silent."

"I have no interest to consult," said Courtley, "but the interest of truth ; and, what I know of this matter, I am ready and willing at all times to state to you or to any one authorised to inquire."

"We will hear you presently."

One of the servants stepped forward, and showed a disposition to speak, and being sworn, he said—

"I was sitting up rather late, and had to go through the laundry to get to the servants' staircase, leading to my sleeping-room, when, as I passed a window looking into the park, I saw a tall figure stealing along towards the wall. I looked intently, and as the snow was upon the ground, I saw the figure well. It was the secretary."

"What did you thereupon?" said Mr. Roachford.

"Nothing, sir ; but went to bed. I did not think much of it, as Mr. Courtley was accustomed to wander about at all hours, especially in the summer time ; so, I thought he might have taken it into his head to do so in the winter."

"You will swear it was the secretary ?"

"Yes, sir."

"At what time was this ?"

"Nearly one."

"This witness is, no doubt, quite right," said Courtley.

"Here's a gamekeeper, your worship, named Roots," said one of the officers, "who seems to know something about it."

"Stand forward !"

Roots stood forward, and was duly sworn.

"Pray, what do you know of this affair," said Mr. Roachford.

"Just this much, sir, that it was with my gun that young Lord Francis was shot."

"With your gun ?"

"Yes, sir. I left my gun, as I had been in the habit of leaving it years and years before I was got out of my place by John Oxley—it was Mr. Courtley and Lord Francis that took me back again—I left my gun, I say, in what we call the old hall ; and when there was an alarm, and I wanted it, it was gone ; but I found it lying by the park wall, and, discharged. It only remains to be seen if the bullet fits the piece. The doctor has it, I think."

The earl groaned sadly.

At this, Roots seemed to awaken to the fact that he was speaking too plainly of the real facts of the murder, and he said—

"The father ought not to be here."

"Go on—go on," said the earl ; "don't heed me."

"When I heard that it was towards the copse-meadow, as we call the field out yonder, close to where the gun was found, that the cries of help came from, I naturally wanted my gun ; but it was gone, you see, sir, and before I could think of what to do, Mr. Courtley came into the hall with the dead body of our young master, rest his soul, in his arms."

"Is that all you know ?"

"No, sir."

"Go on, then."

Roots turned and looked at Morris Courtley, and then reaching out his great embrowned hand, he placed it upon the shoulder of the secretary, and in a voice that sounded thick and harsh with emotion, he said—

"You think it likely among you all that he did it ; now, I tell you that he no more did this deed than I did, or than you did. It can't be, and there's an end of it. You may try to turn the blackamoor white, and I don't know but by some sort of devilry it might be done ; but you can't make a heart like Morris Courtley's the heart of a murderer. I tell you I have known him since he was a boy playing about in the old glades of the New Forest, and I say he could not do it—he could not do it !"

Courtley held out his hand to Roots who shook it heartily.

"Roots, I thank you !"

"Stuff ! no thanks at all. It's the truth, and there's an end of it."

"That is quite sufficient," said Mr. Roachford ; "we do not want the opinion of every witness. We only want the facts to which he can depose."

"That's a fact, then," said Roots. "He didn't do it."

Satisfied, then, that he had said all he wanted, Roots gave place to other witnesses, who described how they heard cries, and then how Morris Courtley brought in the dead body of Lord Francis Bloxdale.

There was now a slight pause, and John Oxley crept slowly forward, and rubbing his hands together, looked the magistrates in the face, while he said—

"Your worships, may I be humbly permitted to say a few words on this deeply afflicting matter ?"

"What is it, Mr. Oxley ?"

"Just this, your worships, that from the kind—the humane, the considerate, and the pleasant manner of the young man now before you, I cannot think him capable of the act imputed to him ; for even if Lord Francis did oppose his union with Lady Fanny, and did discharge him, and tell him that he should leave Bloxdale, I don't think he could possibly lift his hand against the young lord who had loaded him with benefits. Oh, no—no! Human nature is not, and cannot be so bad as that."

"It is very kind of you, Mr. Oxley," said Mr. Roachford, "to come forward and speak in that way; but you must not judge of human nature by yourself."

"Oh, sir!"

"Have you any evidence, Mr. Oxley?"

"None, your worship, but that when I heard the noise I fell out of bed."

"We will not, then, trouble you further, Mr. Oxley. Can any one depose to the fact that Lord Francis had discharged the prisoner now before us?"

"Yes," said Courtley, "I can. It was hardly what may be called a discharge, since we were both agreed that I should leave."

"When?" said the mayor.

"It is better not to ask questions of the prisoner," said Mr. Roachford.

"I will answer all questions freely," said Courtley. "It is for the guilty to dread the truth, not the innocent. I was to leave, and, in fact, had left, at the hour of this dreadful murder. I had taken my last leave of Lord Francis before the shot was fired by the unknown hand that deprived him of life."

"Recollect, prisoner, that whatever you say is written down, and may be used against you at another time and in another place."

"Sir, if I were guilty, I might thank you for the caution; but my intent is manfully to court the fullest investigation into every fact connected with this sad affair, and, therefore, I will answer any question, and am ready to make any statement."

"That's right," said Roots; "keep cool, too, as you are now."

"I can scarcely call myself cool," said Courtley; "but I think my horror at the murder exceeds my horror at this accusation."

"That's it," cried Roots.

"Let me beg of you to be quiet," said Mr. Roachford. "I have heard the late Lord Francis speak of you as a good servant, but we cannot have the court interrupted in this way."

Roots made an awkward bow, and stepped back, and then the surgeon who had been sent for from Southampton came forward, and was duly sworn to tell the whole truth and nothing but the truth.

"Do you know Lord Francis Bloxdale by sight?" was the first question put to him.

"I do."

"Very well, sir; then pray detail to the court what you know of this affair and the cause of the death of the deceaed."

"I was sent for from Southampton, to attend at Bloxdale, as the messenger said there had been a murder. When I reached here I was shown into what they call the great hall, and I found a dead body covered over with a sheet; upon examination I found the body to be that of Lord Francis Bloxdale."

The poor earl hid his face with his hands, and rocked to and fro.

"Oh, my lord," said Mr. Roachford, "let me beg of you to leave the apartment. All that is necessary for you to know you shall know from me."

"Let me stay—oh, let me stay! I would hear all. Heed me not, but let me stay."

There was no saying nay to the earl if he really would stay, so the surgeon continued his evidence.

"I found a gun-shot wound at the back of the head of the deceased, and death must have been all but instantaneous. I extracted the bullet. It is here."

"Let me see it," cried Roots, springing forward.

Mr. Roachford nodded assent, and the surgeon placed the bullet in the hands of Roots, who called out—

"Will, have you the gun?"

"Here you are," said a gamekeeper, handing a gun to Roots, who instantly fitted the bullet to the barrel.

"I knowed it," he said. "It's one of mine. This gun did the deed, and the Lord have mercy upon him whose hands it was in at that moment, for if I had hold of him I would have none."

"You will swear that that bullet came from your gun?"

"To be sure I will—I cast it myself—here is the mould—only look how it fits it."

From amid a vast assemblage of all kinds of tools, connected with guns, that he had in a capacious pocket, Roots produced a bullet-mould; and placing the fatal piece of lead in it, he handed it to the magistrates, in order that they might satisfy themselves by ocular demonstration of the fact he had asserted, that the bullet was one of his.

This was a point in the investigation, then, concerning which there could be no possible deception; and after a pause, the stipendiary magistrate from Southampton said—

"And where were you, Mr. Roots, at the time the murder appears to have been committed, which has spread such desolation over this house?"

"Where was I?"

"Yes, where were you?"

"Oh, yes, that's all right, and a very proper question to put to me, sir, seeing that it was my gun and my bullet with which the deed was done. That's all right, sir. Well, I was asleep in the great kitchen; for I was going to sit up all night to look after Lord Francis's pheasant poults, that he was trying to keep alive all the winter; you see, they were last year's birds, and had never been very strong. Will was with me."

"I *were*," said Will, making a great effort to be terribly fine and grammatical, and, of course, absolutely failing in the attempt.

"That will do," said the magistrate. "I am bound to say that already, even if no further evidence should be offered against the prisoner at the bar, there is amply sufficient to warrant the magistrate in remanding him for further inquiry. There will be a coroner's inquest, of course, but with that we have nothing whatever to do."

CHAPTER XLVI.

THE EVIDENCE AGAINST MORRIS COURTLEY APPEARS TO BE MARVELLOUSLY COMPLETE.

At this juncture the old earl looked up, and fixed his eyes upon Morris Courtley, who met his gaze with sad composure.

"Oh, God!" said the old man, "why did you permit this man to kill my child? Morris Courtley, I beseech you to tell me now, what my boy had done to you that you should kill him? Had he not loved and cherished you?—had he not treated you ever as a brother? Oh, Morris Courtley—Morris Courtley! what did my son do to you that you should play the part of Cain, and slay him?"

"Alas—alas!" said Courtley, "this is the saddest trial of all. Is it, indeed, possible, my lord, that you can think me guilty?"

"Tell me what I am to think."

"Think, that in its own good time, Heaven, although I may be in the meantime sacrificed, will proclaim the truth. I am innocent! May Heaven, who knows the guilty head, have mercy upon it. I am innocent, as I here, in the name of the Great Maker of all things, declare!"

Courtley held up both his arms, as if by such an appeal, so solemnly couched, there might possibly be some vindication of him specially from that Heaven whose justice he had invoked.

At the moment a gleam of wintry sunshine—it was the first and last flash of the glorious orb of day that shone into Bloxdale during that time—fell upon the face of the accused, and lit it up with a wondrous grace and beauty.

The ray of light fluttered for a few moments only upon the fair and thoughtful countenance of the secretary, and then glided like a spirit away.

There was such a stillness in the hall that you might fancy you could hear the beating of any one's heart; and then the earl, after a vain attempt to speak, fainted, and fell from his chair.

Morris Courtley, upon the impulse of the moment, sprang forward to support the earl; but the two constables who had him strictly and specially in their charge laid their hands upon him, and he awakened again to the sense of being a prisoner.

The earl was removed from the hall to his own chamber; but a sad and fearful impression was left upon the minds of all who had seen the look of despair upon the face of the bereaved father.

The magistrates strove to look and to speak as though they were above all consideration but the carrying out of the duty they had in hand; and Mr. Roachford, after a short consultation with his fellow-justice, was about to make out a remand for Morris Courtley, and an order to carry him to the old jail at Southampton, when one of the servants stepped forward in an agitated manner to speak.

"What do you wish to say?" said Mr. Roachford.

"If you please, sir—that is, sir, I—oh, dear!"

"What is the matter with the man?"

"Nothing, sir; only, you see, sir, that we have all been hunting about the meadow by the copse, and so just over one of the hedges I found this, you see, sir."

"What is it?"

"A coat, if you please, gentlemen."

The man held up the coat—the very coat that John Oxley had purloined from the chamber of Morris Courtley, and taken with him when he went to do the deed of blood.

"Yes, gentlemen, a coat," added the man, with a look of horror, "and one of the cuffs is torn off, and one of the lappets is soaked with blood."

There was a shudder of horror, and then Mr. Roachford said in a low tone—

"Can any one identify this coat as belonging to the deceased young nobleman?"

The servants crowded round the garment, and they all shook their heads, till one said in a reluctant voice—

"Please, your worship, I have seen Mr. Courtley wear it."

"Seen me wear it?" said Morris Courtley. "Let me look at it. Is it a dark green?"

"It is."

"Has it several of the buttons upon the right side away?"

"Yes—yes."

"Why, then, it is a coat of mine!"

"Prisoner—prisoner," said the stipendiary magistrate, "are you mad? Beware of what you are saying. Do you consider that it is your business to confirm and substantiate any doubtful piece of evidence against you?"

"It is my business, sir, to testify to the truth; I did not commit the murder, and, therefore, it can be no intent of mine to conceal or to falsify any circumstances that may bear upon the truth as to who did commit the deed. I see that that is my coat, but how it came to be where this man, no doubt, found it, is to me a mystery."

Mr. Roachford rose, and turning to his brother-magistrates, he said in a voice of considerable emotion—

"I have some evidence to give in this case, if you will have the goodness to allow me to be sworn, if even, after making myself a witness, I shall abandon all further ideas of sitting judicially upon the matter; but what I have to depose to is too important to be trifled with. While the fact to which I am about to call attention stood alone, I thought but little of it, and, at all events, it was better to say nothing concerning it, lest

I might put the really guilty person on his guard, but now I feel that further concealment would amount to a criminal falsification of justice."

When the magistrates heard Mr. Roachford speak in this manner they felt quite certain that it was upon no light grounds, for they well knew the careful habits of thought of that gentleman. The oath was administered to him at once, and the stipendiary magistrate said—

"Mr. Roachford, we are now prepared to hear with all attention any statement you are ready to make on your oath respecting this case."

Amid the most breathless stillness, then, Mr. Roachford spoke. Poor Morris Courtley looked at him while he did so with wonder and amazement, and felt that he was more and more lost amid the complexities of a position that he saw no escape from.

"When," said Mr. Roachford, " I saw the corpse of Lord Francis Bloxdale, I paid particular attention to its appearance; I perceived that, with a natural horror at the fearful spectacle it presented, the servants had forborne to meddle with it; and after some careful examination I saw that the right hand was firmly clenched, and it struck me from the appearance of it that it held something. With some difficulty I opened the dead fingers, which were already stiffened with the cold, and I found a small piece of torn and ragged cloth."

A movement took place among all there assembled in the hall when Mr. Roachford uttered these words.

"Go on, sir," said the stipendiary magistrate.

The feelings of Mr. Roachford were too much excited to allow him to go on for a moment or two, as he considered the evidence he was now giving to be of the most fatal character to Morris Courtley that could be imagined. With a strong feeling that he was but doing his duty to society, he yet trembled at the idea that upon his testimony depended the life of a fellow creature. He looked compassionately at Courtley, who observing the look, said in a calm voice—

"Heed not me, Mr. Roachford. I feel assured that you utter words of truth. God in his own good time will explain all this."

"Amen!" said Mr. Roachford, and then putting his hand in his pocket, he produced a piece of torn cloth, and added—"This is what I found clutched in the hand of the murdered Lord Francis Bloxdale."

The stipendiary magistrate made a sign that the coat found over the hedge close to the scene of murder should be handed up to him, and it was duly placed in his hands. Mr. Roachford then held out to him, tremblingly, the piece of cloth he had taken from the hand of the corpse. After a few moments' spent in careful examination, the magistrate spoke—

"It is quite clear," he said, " that the piece of torn cloth is a portion of this coat."

Everybody drew a long breath.

"It is equally clear that it has been recently and violently torn from the wrist of the left arm."

"In the struggle," said a voice, " between the murderer and his victim!"

That voice was John Oxley's.

"Silence!" said the magistrate; " we want no one's comments on the evidence. Officers, you will take care of this coat, and of the piece of cloth produced by Mr. Roachford. Prisoner, have you any questions to put to the last witness in the case against you?"

"None whatever," said Courtley. " I have no doubt in the world but that Mr. Roachford has sworn to the truth; and as he has told all he knows, I cannot have anything to ask of him."

"Then, prisoner, it is my duty to remand you for one week, and you will be taken to Southampton jail at once."

"Stop a bit," said Will, the gamekeeper. "Roots, old boy, where is you?"

"Here!" cried Roots.

"Where did your gun hang last night in the old hall?"

"Over the chimney-piece, just within reach."

"Very good, and whoever got it took it down from there, and about that I have to say a summet."

"What is it?" said the magistrate; "speak out. We sit here only to discover, if we can, the truth, and we are only too glad to hear anything that may elucidate it"

"Whether it lucidate anythink," said Will, " or whether it don't, is about too larned a notion for me to come over; but owing to the cold, and the wind, and the snow, you see, of late, the soot has been falling down the old chimney of the great hall at never such a rate, and it kivered the hearthstone so; you see, whosoever stood there to get down Roots's gun, left the mark of his blessed feet—I mean his cussed feet, in the soot, you see!"

"A true shot that, by Jove!" cried Roots.

"Ah—yes!" cried out John Oxley. " That is well thought of. I will go at once and see if the mark of the footsteps in the soot is or is not like the——"

"No you won't," said Roots, as he caught Oxley by the back of the neck just as he was going out at the door of the room. "No you won't! Oh, dear, no!"

"Help—murder!" shouted Oxley, kicking and struggling to get free from the iron grasp of Roots.

"Silence!" said the stipendiary magistrate, rising. " What is the meaning of this most unseemly uproar? It is the duty of the proper officers to examine the footmarks made upon the hearth in the great hall. I will myself go. Mr. Mayor will you accompany me?"

The mayor signified his assent, and there was a general movement to the door of the room. Roots had left go of Oxley, but he took good care that he should not get past him; and every time that the steward tried to bolt by him, Roots was in his way, and gave him such awkward kicks, and trod so heavily upon his toes, that Oxley was nearly mad.

That the footprints in the soot on the hearth of the great hall were his own, Oxley could not for a moment doubt, and his agony to obliterate them made him look like a man who was rapidly losing his wits.

"Let me go!" he cried. "Let me go! Why is this rascal of a gamekeeper in my way? Wretch! Beast! Villain!"

"Silence!" said a voice close to Oxley's ears. "Silence!"

It was Wicks who spoke.

"Oh, dear—oh, dear!" groaned Oxley. "I only—that is——"

"Silence fool!"

"Yes, but——"

"Hush! All is well!"

"Well? I—I——"

Wicks nearly pinched a piece out of his arm, as a hint to him to say no more, and then he followed the party to the great hall. The two officers who had charge of Morris Courtley brought him with them by order of the magistrates; and, in the course of a few moments the door of the great hall was opened, and the throng of persons who were so deeply interested in what was proceeding made their way towards the ample old hearth.

"This way," said Will. "Here you has it—here's the soot and here's the footmarks—Eh? oh——"

"What's the matter?" said Roots.

"Gone, by all that's—hem! Done again!"

The hearth was scanned by eager and curious faces, but the footmarks in the soot were completely obliterated.—Some one had evidently been there, and had trampled the soot, and scraped it with the sides of their feet in all directions.

"Saved!" gasped Oxley in a whisper.

"I told you so," said Wicks, in the same tone.

"Oh, dear Wicks——"

"Hush!"

"I'm done!" cried Will. "The marks was here, but they isn't now. They was the marks of a large broad flat foot, and no more like Mr. Courtley's than my hand is like that of some nice little young lady who never did no more work with her dear little bit of a paw than a sparrow might do with hisen!"

"Officers!" said the stipendiary magistrate, after a whispered conference with Mr. Roachford and the mayor, "the prisoner stands remanded for one week from now."

Oxley laughed hysterically.

———

CHAPTER XLVII.

THE COUNTESS OF BLOXDALE BIDS THE WORLD FAREWELL

WHILE all this judicial proceeding was going on in the hall at Bloxdale, poor Lady Fanny was a prey to increasing terrors and anxieties. The state of the countess's health was such that a communication was made to her that nothing short of a miracle could prolong her life.

At that time, when her mother lay upon a bed of sickness, and when death hovered in the chamber, poor Fanny forgot all but the tender memories of some kindness that had been shown to her in childhood by the countess, and flew to her side.

Alas! Fanny had much grief yet to know. The death of her brother had been communicated to her, and that event had all but stunned her. Ann, who had told her of the dreadful fact in some of its particulars, had not had the courage to let her fairly know that Morris Courtley was, in the opinion of all who did not know him, condemned for the ─d.

But this was an information that could not be long kept from Lady Fanny. It would be too fearful and harrowing to the feelings to attempt to describe all that she felt and thought upon the occasion. We must pass over in silence the soul's agony that was hers.

Let us look at her at the hour of midnight on the night succeeding the appalling incidents at the old mansion of Bloxdale Park, and the reader must conclude that she knows all that there is to know.

It is a great thing, and a good thing, when we have any serious affliction to bear, that we have generally at the same time some great duty to perform. The one acts as a kind of counterpoise in the mind to the other; and so was it with poor Fanny in the present instance.

The evidently dying state of her mother divided with her mind the attention that otherwise would have fallen wholly, and with crushing seriousness, upon the situation of Morris Courtley, and the death of her brother.

But still, as we shall now look at Lady Fanny, we must not imagine that she has got fully awakened to all that she has to suffer.

Great mental afflictions act frequently for a time as sedatives to the mind. The imagination is bewildered, and it takes hours, and in some cases days, before the fancy can admit the truth of anything so tremendous happening to us.

With death this is specially and particularly the case.

We read and we hear of the deaths of others in whom we have no sort of interest, and with whom we have no companionship, with a calm indifference; and if we speak of the event at all, it is but to philosophise upon

THE INTERVIEW OF LORD FRANCIS BLOXDALE AND MORRIS COURTLEY IN THE LIBRARY.

the folly of grief for an event that must sooner or later occur to all.

But when some one with whom we were in the habit of daily converse, or some one specially nearer and dearer to us, suddenly quits this mortal scene, we are stunned at the fact, and can hardly believe in its possibility.

Fanny's case was worse than that. Not only was her brother, standing as he had been upon the very threshold of existence, snatched from her by death, but the person of whose humanity, and of whose good mind she had the highest possible opinion, seemed by the concurrent testimony of circumstances to be guilty of the crime.

This combination of terrible circumstances would have been about enough to have toppled the young girl's reason from its seat, but that she was stunned by the shock, and likewise much occupied by the precarious position of the countess.

Let us now take a glance into the bed-chamber of the woman who but a short time before was the imperious and the exacting mistress of Bloxdale.

What is she now?

The hour, as we have said, is midnight, and the life of the countess hangs upon a thread. The chamber is one of the largest and handsomest in the mansion—her lady-ship generally looked pretty well after her-self—the state bedstead was one in which royalty had slept, or tried to sleep—the hangings were of cloth of gold, and through-out the whole chamber there was an air of regal magnificence and state.

From the ceiling depended a massive chandelier of green crystal, which, when it was lighted, shed over the room and every-thing within it a cool and grateful colour to the eyes. The double casements shut out any noise that might otherwise disturb the slumbers of the occupant of such a chamber.

Truly it seemed a sad thing that any one with so many of the luxuries and the amenities of life around them should be subject to so very vulgar a state of things as illness and death.

The countess only the day before would have had such an opinion; but now the proud spirit was humbled, and the vain-glorious heart was all but broken.

In the room were a couple of physicians, one from Portsmouth and another from Southampton. A general practitioner from the latter place, too, was there, and they all three looked gravely professional, as men of their calling will do when they know that nature is too much for their poor aid.

Propped up by pillows in the state bed—for if she had been permitted to lie down, even for a moment, the great Lady of Bloxdale must have been choked like any very common person—was the countess, look-ing as pale as if death had already

"Set his insignia on her heek."

She seemed to be in a lethargic state, even then.

Kneeling upon some cushions by the bedside, with her sweet face buried in the clothes, was Lady Fanny. Close to her stood poor Ann, trembling and terrified. A table close at hand was covered with all the paraphernalia of the sick chamber. Bottles with labels, glasses with strange coloured liquids, were there; cups, spoons, sponges, fruit, vinegar, and all the varied necessities for supporting the sinking spirit when it is struggling to free itself from its mortal tene-ment, and to fly to the footstool of its maker.

A deep stillness reigned in the apartment. The two wax candles that were upon the table shed but a feeble light. The physicians had objected to the green chandelier being lit, as it would mislead them as to the looks of their patient.

The clock in the clock-tower of the mansion had just struck twelve, when Lady Bloxdale opened her eyes and looked dimly about her.

"She moves," said one of the physicians, as he glided towards he bed. "She moves again."

Lady Fanny, upon this, looked up, and uttered the one word—

"Mother!"

"Hush," said the physician; "no excite-ment. It would be fatal. Again I sincerely advise you to leave the room."

"No," said the countess, as she moved her head aside, and looked at Fanny, "no—not now."

"Do not speak, madam," said the physi-cian; "allow us to beg of your ladyship to be silent."

The countess looked at him for a moment or two in silence, and then she said—

"If I speak not now, when shall I speak?"

"When you are better, madam."

"That will never be; what I have to say in this world must be said now and at once. My minutes are numbered. Look there! Look there!"

She pointed to the foot of the bed, where no one was standing. Every eye was directed to the spot.

"Oh, mother," said Fanny, "what shall we look at?"

"That!—that!"

"But what is it, mother?"

"There, at the foot of the bed. Oh, do not pretend that you see it not, all of you. It is a false kindness to say that.—There it stands. It is a tall figure, with a white cloth about its head and its face and it points out into the night air."

Fanny shuddered at this evidence of the fearful state of her mother's mind, but she still could not help looking in the direction that the countess indicated with a terrible doubt as to whether there might or might not be anything there. Of course there was nothing there, but the eyes of the countess were still fixed upon vacancy.

"Oh, mother," said Fanny. "This is a delusion, indeed it is. There is nothing there, I assure you."

"Hush!" said one of the physicians, in a low tone to Fanny. "It is in vain to argue with her. To her imagination, there no doubt is a something; but say no more about it."

The countess now looked in the face of Fanny for a few moments in silence, and then in a low wailing voice she said—

"You cannot—No, no—you cannot!"

"Cannot, what, mother?"

"Forgive the past."

"Yes—oh, yes. All is forgotten, and so needs no forgiving."

"Yes—oh, yes, it does. I care not who is here now to listen to these last words of mine. Let them sink deeply into all hearts. By pride have I fallen from what might have been much happiness. It was the demon of pride that took possession of my heart, and closed it against all better influences. I am dying now, and the veil is lifted from off my eyes. I see myself as I have been, and I feel what I might have been."

"Do not speak in this way, mother," said Fanny. "Oh, do not, I implore you!"

"You had better rest, madam," said the physician.

"Alas! There is no rest for me. Where is the earl?"

"He is sent for, madam," said the medical man from Southampton; "but the earl has been very much indisposed."

"I know it—I know it! Oh, who should know it better, or so well as I know?"

There came now a slow and solemn step into the room, and the Earl of Bloxdale made his way to the bed-side of the dying woman, who, in that dread and awful moment, when her soul was fluttering upon the confines of eternity, felt all the errors of her life.

The Earl of Bloxdale folded Fanny in his arms, and kissed her tenderly. He felt that she was now all that was left him in the wide world to love.

One glance at her father's face convinced Fanny that the change so sudden and startling that had taken place in his mind, was permanent. There was no longer the vacant look of a bewildered mind. The eye no longer shrunk from a steady gaze, and the shape of the mouth was very different. The shock that the intellect of the earl had received by the cry of "Murder!" when his son, Lord Francis, breathed his last, had had the strange effect of restoring him to this state of mental vigour, which the continual tyranny of the countess, no doubt aided by some disease which had dissipated, had so far obliterated.

"Stand aside!" said the countess.

The earl moved his position.

"No—no!" she added, "not you—not you, my lord. There was some one trying to pass between me and that figure."

"What figure?"

"Oh, father—father!" sobbed Fanny, "do not ask her. She thinks—but that is only a delusion that there is some figure standing by the foot of the bed. Is it not so, mother?"

"Yes, my child, it is so; and there it is still. I cannot see its face; but it is slowly now moving to the window and pointing out into the night air. Oh, God, I must follow—I must follow!"

"No—no!" said the earl, as he laid his hand upon the countess's arm. "You dream. Let me beg of you to be at peace."

She looked up in the earl's face, and while the tears streamed from her eyes, she said—

"And can you too speak thus to me? Can you speak to me without cursing me? Oh, is that possible?"

"It is most possible. Let the past be no more referred to. It is over, and should not, by the spectre of its memory, disturb the present. Heaven has sent us affliction enough without it. Oh, my son—my son! My poor Francis!"

The earl sunk into a chair, and covering his face with his hands, he wept aloud.

Fanny did not expect this sudden outburst of feeling upon the part of her father, and it deeply affected her. She did not weep though, with any passionate and frantic grief but she sat gazing upon him as if panic-stricken.

In a few moments the countess spoke again.

"My child, Fanny, forgives me," she said, "and so does my husband. I have something yet to say. Yes—yes, Oxley—Oxley. Trust not that man. Let not his shadow again fall upon the threshold of this house. Trust him not!"

"He shall go," said the earl.

"And Wicks. I suspect her much. She is wicked. Trust not her. You ought to have better and purer spirits around you than those who have been my assistants. Do you think with me all of you?"

"We do," said the early sadly.

"Oh, not yet—God, not yet!" cried the countess. "See, the figure is even now at the window! I cannot! I dare not come yet! My son, Francis! I wait for him—for him!"

"Oh, God!" said the earl. "Does she not know, or does she forget——"

"Hush, father, hush!" sobbed Fanny.

"Yes, when my son comes, I shall then have the forgiveness of all," added the countess. "Call him! Call Lord Francis Bloxdale! It is my son—my only one that I now wish to see!"

The persons in that chamber looked at each other and shuddered; but no one liked to step forth and declare that it was the dead that she called upon. There was a fearful and a dreary silence in the room and in the house, and then a howling sound of wind coming past the window came upon their ears, and the rattle of hail upon the casement was plainly to be distinguished.

"Francis!" shrieked the countess. "Francis, my son! I call to you to give my shrinking soul your forgiveness before it flies to its creator! Francis, my son! Oh, my child—my boy, Francis! Come—come! Oh, come to me now!"

"This is dreadful!" said the earl.

Fanny stepped towards her father and clung to him, so that no one was by the bed-side of the countess but the physicians. Suddenly then raising herself in the bed, the countess held up her head in an attitude of listening.

"He comes," she said. "He comes—he is a long way off, but he comes. Oh, yes, he will come to his mother's call at such an hour as this, for there was a time that I was kind and good to him, and that is all he will remember now. He comes—he comes."

It was by a general impulse that every eye was now turned upon the door of the room, as though they expected it to open, and the dead that lay so calm and still below in the great hall to enter that apartment in answer to the call of the dying countess.

"Hush! hush!" she said. "How far he has to come through the snow, and over the bleak hills; now—now stand aside, sir. Way for my son—my Francis! Here! Here! Here!"

She pointed to the door, and then slowly moved her finger along the room, at about the speed that a person might slowly walk, until it paused at the chair by the bedside, and then clasping her hands, she said—

"How pale you are, Francis. Oh, God, how very pale. Can you forgive me, my son Francis?"

Fanny uttered a shriek, and hid her face in the bosom of her father. The earl trembled, and the physicians changed colour, and stepped to the door as though they would leave the room.

"Speak—oh, speak!" cried the countess. "Francis, speak to me. Say you forgive me. Do not look at me in that cold, lifeless manner. I am your mother. Kiss me, my son—kiss me. Oh, joy! joy!—I am forgiven! I come, I come—come—all—fading away—night—night—death!"

CHAPTER XLVIII.

LADY FANNY NERVES HERSELF TO DO JUSTICE TO THE INNOCENT.

THE Countess of Bloxdale fell back upon her pillow a corpse.

At that moment the wind came in a furious gust from without, and dashed open the casement of the room. The lights in the death chamber were in a moment extinguished, and it was only the dull red gleam from the ample fire that had been blazing on the hearth, but which had gone nearly out, that cast a sort of radiance around the room.

The earl sprang to his feet, with Fanny still clinging to him, and in a voice of alarm he cried out—

"Lights! Bring me lights! The window—the window! Oh, Heaven! what is all this?"

"Father—father! be calm," said Fanny.

"Calm! Who can be calm with such sights and sounds to appal them? My son, Francis, if you are within the confines of this room in the spirit, speak—oh, speak to me!"

"No—no!" said Fanny, "it would be too—too dreadful. Father, do not ask it."

There was a rush of feet, and the servants brought several lights into the room. The casement was swinging open, and the snow was beating into the apartment.

It did not take a moment to close the casement again and to re-light the candles that had been extinguished, and then the earl looked about him wildly, as he said—

"What is all this? Do we live in a land of dreams? Has the age of miracles and of superstition come back to us?"

Fanny looked at her father with a dread that this new shock to his nervous system might damage again the reason he had only so recently recovered. It was such a dread that in some measure divided her attention from the terrors that would otherwise have taken hold of her young imagination, and there ruled triumphant. It was a fortunate thing for Fanny that she had mind enough in the midst of her deep affliction to feel that she had duties that imperatively called upon her to perform.

The principal one of these now was to look to her father.

Taking him by the hand, she said to him in as firm a voice as she could possibly command at the moment—

"Father, come with me. This way—this way, father."

She led him to the side of the bed, and then pointing to the dead countess who there lay, she sought to distract his mind from the thoughts of the supernatural that had come over it.

"There, father," she said, "there is my mother—dead—dead! Oh, what sad funeral pall is this that has fallen upon our house?"

The earl looked in the face of the dead in silence for a few moments, and then turning to the physicians, he said—

"Gentlemen, is this so? Has this poor piece of clay parted, indeed, with its very essence? Has the soul fled to its maker?"

One of the physicians laid his hand upon the heart of the corpse, and said in a low voice—

"The countess is dead, my lord!"

The earl shuddered for a moment, and then he stretched forth his hand, and evidently had the intention to close the eyes of the corpse, but he shook so that he could not do it; and Fanny, who was scarcely less agitated than he, clung to his arm, and whispered—

"Come with me, father. Oh, come with me. Will you not be good to me, and take me away from this dreadful scene? On, remember, father, that I have only you now to love me of all my race. Take me away from this room, dear father."

How judicious of Fanny thus to call into requisition the protecting powers of the earl in her favour! He felt at once the force of the appeal, and placing his right arm round the waist of Fanny, and holding her by the left hand, he said in a low, gentle voice—

"Come, my darling—come, moderate your natural grief. You have still a father to love and cherish you."

As he thus spoke the earl led her gently from the room. His valet was waiting in the corridor, and in silence he lit his master and Fanny to a room that was not frequently used, but in which there was a cheerful fire, and which was well lighted.

"Why here, Hill?" said the earl.

"The night is so rough a one, my lord, and this is so much warmer than your own room."

"Be it so. But Fanny, you will sleep—you will go to rest?"

"Not now, father, if you do not. Will you let me sit with you?"

"Yes, dear one, if you will."

The valet closed the door of the room gently, and left them together, that afflicted father and daughter. Fanny looked at her father for a few moments in silence, and then she drew a little footstool close to his feet, and knelt upon it, and looking him in the face she tried to speak, but for some time tears choked her utterance.

"My darling," said the earl, "what would you say to me?"

"Much—oh, much, father."

"You are full of grief."

"Indeed, and in truth I am; but it is of the living as well as of the dead that I would speak. Father, I think—nay, I know that you love me."

"My darling," said the earl, and his voice faltered as he spoke, "were it not for the love of you, I do not think that I should have outlived the shocks of the last twenty-four hours."

"And I, father, if not for the love I bear to you, think that I should go mad—quite mad; and, even now, I feel strongly the hope of awaking suddenly and finding that it is all a dream."

The earl shook his head.

"Would it were so—oh, would it were so, my child! But it is too—too real—indeed, it is too real."

"Alas—alas! I tremble to think so. But now, father, at this time, when we are quite alone, and the hour is a solemn one, and death holds disputed dominion with the living in this house, I implore you to tell me all that has taken place here without reserve or abstraction from the truth. It is better—far better that we should from this time forth have nothing to conceal from each other."

"What is it you would know, my child?"

"All the—the circumstances connected with my brother's death, and the accusation of Morris—I mean, the secretary."

"I think, my child, that you do know all," said the earl; "but I will satisfy myself that you do, by telling you over again, however painful the task may be."

In that solemn hour, then, as his daughter knelt at his feet, and while the tears coursed each other down both their cheeks, the Earl of Bloxdale went through the whole narration of the death of Lord Francis by, as it was supposed, the hand of Courtley, just as it had been told to him by the magistrate.

"Now, my child," he said, "you know all. Nothing is concealed from you, and it has been a relief to me to tell you."

"Father!—father!"

"Yes, dear one?"

"Morris Courtley is innocent!"

"Innocent?"

"Yes, father. There never yet was any great affliction but that there might be found some great duty connected with it, which was the one ray of sunlight amid what else would be all gloom. The great duty that I have now is to proclaim the innocence of Courtley."

"But, Fanny——"

"Oh, father, do not be deceived. I tell you that I love him! I have told you that before this dreadful time. Father, I love him still."

"Oh, my child, beware!"

"Of what, father?—of loving him? Oh, no! Rather ought I to beware of allowing the smallest doubt of his truth and innocence to enter this heart. It is impossible, father, that he could do the dreadful deed. When the lamb arms itself for slaughter, and goes about seeking whom it may devour—when the dove swoops upon its prey with the avidity of the hawk—when angels come down from Heaven to mix up their pure natures with the follies and the passions of human nature, then may Morris Courtley go forth to murder; but not before that time of universal contradictions."

There was an intensity of soul about the manner in which Lady Fanny spoke that struck the earl with anguish. At that moment she no longer looked like the timid shrinking girl she had ever been; but from out of the fearful circumstances in which she was placed there seemed to have sprung a new nature for her—or, rather, the latent energies of her heart were at once called into action by the force of circumstances, where they otherwise would have slumbered for ever, and no one would have suspected their existence.

"Fanny," said the earl, "I know that you loved your brother."

"As my life!"

"I knew it; and so I feel that there is a heavenly sincerity now in what you say."

"There is truth, too, father. Sooner or later the plot, for it must be one, which has involved Francis in death, and which is seeking still its development in the destruction of Morris Courtley, will be revealed in all its hideous iniquity. The time will come—oh! that it might come soon, and before the innocent have suffered—when all will be known, and when the author of that dreadful deed will be dragged to justice!"

"Oh, hush, my child, hush! You are excited—you know not what you say."

"Yes—oh, yes, dear father, I do indeed; but it is better that I should feel as I do, than—than weep like a child."

Poor Fanny did weep like a child, notwithstanding, and the earl strove to comfort her, as he said—

"My darling, I am as willing as you or any one can possibly be to absolve Morris Courtley from the accusation that hangs over him; but if he did not do the deed, who did?"

"Mr. Oxley, my lord," said Hill the valet, as he gently opened the door.

Fanny uttered a sharp cry, as she said—

"He—he? Oh, yes—oh, yes!"

"Hush," said the earl—"hush! What of Mr. Oxley, Hill?"

"He says that he has something of the greatest importance to say to your lordship."

"Tell Mr. Oxley," said the earl, "that his mistress, who is no more, discharged him almost with her last breath. See that he and Wicks, the late countess's waiting-woman, leave this house within one hour from this time. Heed not what they may say—or what they may do. Heed not storms or any other consequences. Turn them both from my house. That is my orders!"

"Yes, my lord."

Hill turned to the door; but it was pushed a little open from without, and Oxley appeared, looking ghastly pale, and licking his parched lips in an odd manner that he had recently contracted. He glanced at Fanny, and then at the earl, as he said—

"My lord, I have something to say—something important, and that I feel I ought to say at once."

"Begone, sir!"

"But, my lord, I—"

"Hill, go for some of the servants, and bring here a sufficient force to remove this man from Bloxdale."

"Go to the devil!" cried Oxley. "Curses on you all! I will say what I came to say, in spite of you all! Tremble, my Lord Bloxdale, for there is yet another catastrophe hanging over your house. Your name, your title, your estates will pass away from you. Into the hands of others—ha—ha! and—Lady Fanny will inherit that —that! Ha—ha!"

Oxley snapped his fingers in the air to signify the extent of Lady Fanny's possessions.

"I came to give you some idea of what was going to happen," added Oxley, "and to offer to aid you; but if you won't be friendly, you may do the other thing, and be hanged to you all."

The earl advanced two steps, but Fanny clung to him, saying—

"No, father, no—you are a gentleman. You must not touch that man. Let him be. The servants are coming."

"He—he!" laughed Oxley, "and your fine lover, Morris Courtley, will be hanged, Miss Fanny. He—he! Hanged by the neck! A dance on nothing, instead of a quadrille in the saloons of Bloxdale!"

"No!" said Fanny.

"But I say yes—yes! Ha—ha!"

"No!" said Fanny; "because, there never yet was a murder committed but sooner or later it was found that the murderer had made some slight mistake, which like the smallest cranny in a dungeon wall, is sufficient to let in the light of truth upon him and his deeds. Oxley, you will be found out yet!"

Oxley gasped again, and staggered back without uttering a word.

"Murderer!" cried Fanny, as she pointed at him. "Man of blood! you will yet be found out!"

"No—no—I——"

Oxley stamped with his foot, and tried to say something that should be at once expressive of his rage and his fear; but the valet at that moment arrived with a couple of stout gamekeepers, who threw themselves upon him, and dragged him from the spot.

CHAPTER XLIX.

MR. OXLEY AND MISS WICKS FIND THAT IT IS AN INDIFFERENT NIGHT.

THE night was a fearful one upon which Miss Wicks and Mr. Oxley were sent forth in disgrace from Bloxdale.

The servants of the establishment had executed the orders of the earl in quite a liberal spirit—that is to say, they had, without the smallest ceremony carried them out to the letter; and both the steward and the waiting-woman found themselves in the open air, with just what apparel they happened to stand upright in at the time.

To be sure, Mr. Oxley had protested against his eviction, and had very kindly promised to go to law forthwith with every one who had any hand in it, from the earl down to the little stable-boy, who gave him a kick on the shins as he crossed the lawn; but that had not much effect.

Miss Wicks, too, sadly scolded the two footmen who went to fetch her, and declared that she did not intend to leave the hall till she had collected all her best things; and in confirmation of that threat she sat down in the hall, and there defied them.

The footmen then called Roots, who suggested at once the mode by which Miss Wicks might be taken off the premises, in comfort to himself and every one else.

"There's nothing in the world," said Roots, assuming a meditative look, "equal to a wheelbarrow in such cases."

The very thing," said an under-keeper, "there's one in the orchard that is used for wheeling rubbish away."

"Then," said Roots, "it is not making it do any sort of work that it is not accustomed to. Fetch it at once."

When Miss Wicks found that there was a serious determination to bring the wheelbarrow to carry her away, she rose, and solemnly cursed Bloxdale and everybody in it; and then stalked out of the hall like a tragedy heroine.

She met Mr. Oxley, looking very blue and very cold ,at a pathway that led to the high road to Southampton. He had been waiting for the partner of his iniquities and crimes, for she was so far the partner of the very great crime that he had committed, that although he had not thought proper to make her the confident of it, she knew from a number of concurrent circumstances that he had done the deed.

The night had advanced considerably, and the morning in another couple of hours would begin to break; but yet an utter darkness was, as yet, upon the face of nature, and the snow was coming down in a thick drift that gave every promise of lasting a liberal length of time.

Oxley would fain have gone off at once to the cottage where Mrs. Lerew lived in such easy state, but that he dreaded the lynx-eyed Wicks would find him out then; so he felt the necessity of waiting for her, and of getting rid of her in as quiet a manner as possible, consistent with his safety.

Burning with rage at the indignation she had been obliged to endure, Wicks reached the spot where Oxley had been waiting for her, and making up to him—for she could just see him by the reflected light from the snow—she accosted him in not the most gentle strains possible—

"So, Oxley!—this is the sort of market to which you have brought your pigs at last, is it, sir?"

"My dear Wicks."

"Oh, don't dear me, sir."

"But what would you have me do? Really, now, I cannot help what has happened, my charming Wicks."

"Charming fiddlestick! Hark you, John Oxley. I have a secret to tell you, and it is, that if you don't mind what you are about, you will be hanged!"

"Oh, dear, hanged did you say?"

"I did. And now, what are you going to do?"

Oxley groaned.

"What should I think of doing, my good Wicks, but of providing for your comfort and your safety in the manner most suitable to your happiness and convenience? That is the principal thought with me now."

"Is it?"

"What else can so much occupy me?"

"Consideration for your own safety, Oxley. Hark you—I know what has happened."

"You—know—what—oh——"

"You did the murder!"

"Hiss! Hush! I didn't!"

"Fool, do you think that I cannot read your heart aright? Why, even at this light I can see your guilt in your face. Who was it that like a fool left the print of his foot on the soot that lay upon the hearth-stone of the old hall? You, Oxley. Who was it that scattered the soot so that the foot-print, that would by its simple evidence have consigned you to the hangman, was no longer visible?"

"Gracious goodness, don't speak so loud! Oh, be careful what you say!"

"Careful? Why should I be careful? I have done nothing. I tell you it was I who saved you from the consequences of that little oversight connected with the foot-marks. It was I whom you have treated scandalously."

"Oh, don't say that. My dear Wicks, I am nervous rather—you know I am. Don't say I did it."

"Dare you say to me that you did not?"

Oxley was silent.

"Hark you," added Wicks, "I hate the whole lot of them at the hall, and if, while you were about it, you had cut the throats of some more of them, it would not have mattered to me a jot. I tell you, you did it! You know you did it, and you know that I know it."

"Oh, Wicks!"

"Well?"

"I don't think that there is anything which can escape your penetration. But my life is in your hands, you know, dear Wicks, and what a delightful thing it is to me to feel that I can trust you."

"Indeed! I did not know that you had trusted me."

"Don't I confess to you that I did it?"

"Yes, after I found it out myself. You have acted like a fool in this affair, as you always do. If you had only consulted me you might have had better revenge upon the whole lot of them. Not that I regret the death of Francis. He was no friend of mine, as you know well; and they may hang Courtley, too, with all my heart, and the old earl may go mad again, and Fanny may, as I sincerely hope she will, make away with herself, and so there will be an end of the whole lot of them; but we get nothing by it but revenge."

"Oh, Wicks! revenge is sweet."

"It is, but I want money likewise. How much does your pecculations in the family fairly amount to?"

"How much?"

"Yes, in round numbers."

"In round numbers, Wicks?"

"To be sure. Why do you echo my words, fool? As we are to be married now, I presume at once, it is as well that I should know the extent of your resources beforehand."

A gleam of hope shot across the heart of Oxley, that if she thought him poor she would not have him, and he replied—

"I am very sorry to say that I have not realised anything like what I ought to have done. The fact is, the countess was short of money just before all this that has ended in her death took place. I lent her a thousand pounds in cash, for which I have no acknowledgment, so that I cannot recover it."

"Really! Well, how much is left after that?"

"I don't think, my dear Wicks, that I have enough left to make you as comfortable as you ought to be."

"Perhaps not. Oh, Oxley, you should have taken better care of your opportunities; but, however, if you have not enough, it would be quite insane of me to marry you."

"It would—it would."

"And so you may as well hang."

"May as well what do you say?"

"Hang!"

"Oh, Lord have mercy upon me! You don't mean that? It's a joke?"

"I am glad you think it so. The fact is, Oxley, I am resolved to make something of you if I can. If you have not means enough to make it worth my while to marry you, I must see what I can make in denouncing you as the murderer of Lord Francis Bloxdale."

"No—oh, no! What do you mean? Wicks—Wicks, I will wed you—indeed, I will, my dear Wicks!"

"But you are poor."

"No—not so very poor. I have a few thousands yet, and we shall be so very happy, my dear Wicks, shall we not? Oh, what will become of us? Where shall we go now, Wicks?"

"To Southampton."

"Yes, and after that, don't you think we had better go and live in London? That is to say, you—no, I—dear me, I mean you can live in London, you know, Wicks. It will be so cheerful for you."

"And you?"

"Oh, I think I will travel a little, just to relieve my mind from uncomfortable emotion. But now we need not discuss all that; you know, Wicks, you can go to Southampton at once. That is the road, you know. You will soon get to the Itchin Ferry—very soon. Good night!—Ha! ha!—I ought to say 'Good morning!' rather. How dark! Where shall I find you at Southampton?'

Wicks laid her left hand upon the arm of Oxley, and touched his nose with something that she held in her right.

"Good gracious! what is that?" he said.

"Cannot you guess?"

"Oh, no—no! How cold. How severely cold."

"Oxley, it is the barrel of a pistol that touches you, I have a pair of them with me, and I know how to use them. Do you comprehend that?"

"I—I don't know."

"Well, I wish you to feel that I am quite safe as I go to Southampton alone, you comprehend, that is all. I shall go at once to the Royal Hotel, which is near the Platform : you know it. There I shall take apartments of distinction, and live like a lady—you will pay for them, Oxley; and I shall expect you to-morrow at about eleven o'clock to arrange about our marriage."

"Ye—e—es," gasped Oxley. "But what a—a——"

"A what?"

"Oh, I was only going to say, what a pity if you were to meet with any accident with the pistols."

"Don't you be afraid of that—I quite understand them. My father, or my reputed father, was a sergeant of dragoons, and the soldiers in different barracks taught me, among other things, the use of fire-arms."

"Oh, lor! Among other things!"

"Yes; so you see I know a little more than even you thought, Oxley. But why don't you come to Southampton with me?"

"Because, my dear Wicks, I hope to get an interview with one of the servants of the hall, and to bring him over to our interests, so that we may be informed of all that takes place."

"Very well, that will do. Mind you are punctual in the morning, for I don't like to be kept waiting for any one, and least of all will I wait for you."

With these words Miss Wicks, with the air of a soldier on a march, stepped out at a good pace along the lane that led to the high road to Southampton.

"Oh, goodness gracious!" gasped Oxley, "that woman will be the death of me. How can I get the better of her? A sergeant of dragoons, did she say? Why, she looks like one herself. Armed, too, with pistols that she knows the use of. To come to her at eleven to-morrow—to marry her, and I already the husband of Mrs. Lerew! Oh, dear—oh, dear! Wicks does not know how great a stake I and Lerew play for, and so she does not know how necessary it was to get two such opponents to the game as Lord Francis and Morris Courtley out of it. But she will persecute me now, and what will become of me? I must poison her—I must find some subtle means of settling with Miss Wicks. Oh, bless her! yes, I must—I must. And now for Mrs. Lerew."

It was well for Oxley that upon such a night as that he had a home so close at hand as at the cottage of Mrs. Lerew, although, after the changes that had taken place at the hall, he could hardly expect that any protegé of his would be allowed to remain for long upon the estate of Bloxdale. That, however, was not so much his present concern as how to dispose of Wicks. What made this difficulty a worse one, too, for Oxley was that he dreaded to mention it to Mrs. Lerew at all, for fear she, with her wild, jealous nature, should make more of it than was necessary,

MISS WICKS WATCHING JOHN OXLEY.

and commit some sudden and awful extravagance consequent upon the information.

Truly Oxley felt bewildered, and half maddened by the exigencies of his situation; and as he ran along the snow towards the cottage, he did not notice that he was dogged from time to time by a form which crouched low down to escape observation.

That form was Miss Wicks.

The motives with which the dear delightful Wicks had consented to go to Southampton at the request of Oxley had arisen solely from the determination to watch him.

If Oxley had, upon that occasion, been in his usual condition—if he had had all his senses about him, and had been as cool and collected as he sometimes was, he would have suspected her motives; but such was not the case, and he went direct to the cottage.

Blundering through the little rustic gate that shut in the front garden of the little dwelling, which in the summer time was such a wilderness of flowers, Oxley reached the porch, and rarg the bell that communicated with the domestic portion of the place.

Wicks crouched down by the gate and watched him.

"Who is there?" said a female voice from one of the windows.

"I," said Oxley. "It is I—open the door."

"You, John Oxley?"

"Silence. Yes. Be quick, I am almost perished with snow and cold.—Open the door."

The window was closed, and the door in a few seconds more was opened, and admitted Oxley. Miss Wicks ran across the garden and round the house, till she got to a window which had no shutter to it. All was dark within the room to which it opened; but she thought that a faint light shone into that room from another, the door leading into which was not close shut.

To break a pane of glass in the latticed window, and then to introduce her hand and unfasten it, was the work of a moment, and Wicks then was able to lean forward into the room, and to catch the sound of voices in the next apartment.

Wicks had had too enlarged an experience in listening at doors and key-holes to feel much trouble in hearing all that took place between Oxley and Mrs. Lerew upon that occasion.

Mrs. Lerew was rather alarmed to see Oxley at such an hour, and with such looks of distress about him. That the dreadful deed she had enticed him to do had been done, that infamous woman knew too well; but Oxley had not thought it prudent to leave the hall since the event, even for the purpose of receiving the congratulations of Mrs. Lerew.

"What is the matter?" she cried, as she hastily put up chain and bolt to the door of the cottage after admitting Oxley—"what is the matter? Oh, what has happened?"

"I don't know—that is, yes, of course; but it is nothing."

"Nothing that brings you here at such an hour?"

"I am discharged, that is all."

"Discharged?"

"Yes, by the earl. The countess is dead, and the earl, instigated by that little imp, Fanny, no doubt, has sent me out of the house; that is all that has happened. Not much, is it? Ha!—ha! Not much with our prospects now, is it?"

"You look wild, Oxley. All ain't well with the—the——"

"Out with it," cried Oxley—"the murder! There, you see, I am not afraid of the name."

"Hush! Listen to that."

Oxley did listen; and pacing to and fro in the room above, he heard a footstep. He turned pale and red by turns, as he heard the footstep to and fro, like a sentinel on duty.

———

CHAPTER L.

PETER MAKES QUITE AN UNEXPECTED DETER-MINATION, AND DISCONCERTS OXLEY AND HIS MOTHER.

It was with some degree of difficulty that Oxley gathered strength and courage enough to say—"Who is it?"

"Peter," replied Mrs. Lerew.

"Only Peter?"

"That is all; but I don't know what to make of him lately. When he heard of the murder of Lord Francis, he dropped into a seat as if he, too, had been struck with death. He has not said much, but since then he has never gone to bed, and all the night he has paced his room as you hear."

"He—has not said much?" gasped Oxley. "What has he said at all?"

"He asked me if I thought that the secretary really did the deed, and, of course, I said without a doubt. Hush! that is Peter."

"Who is there?" cried Peter from above; "who is there?"

"Mr. Oxley," said Mrs. Lerew.

"Good; I want to see him."

In another moment Peter, with rather an extensive meerschaum pipe in his mouth, descended to the room below, and walking up to Oxley, he said in a calm, clear voice—

"John Oxley, who killed Lord Francis Bloxdale? By Jove, I don't like it at all. It gave me a turn it did; and I have been—d—n it, yes, I have been sick ever since. Who did it?"

"Morris Courtley. He has confessed it," said Oxley.

"Confessed it?"

"Oh, yes; at his examination before Mr. Roachford he confessed it all quite clearly."

Peter drew a long breath, and took the meerschaum from his mouth, as he said—

"Well, that's a relief, any how. Father-in-law, give us your hand; I'm glad to see you. Confessed it, has he? Well, that is everything. But I tell you what it is, mother of mine, and you, father-in-law, I wouldn't step into Bloxdale—no, nor into St. James's Palace to be made king of England, over the corpse of that young chap, mind you, if it were by my coming into his property that he met his death. I don't wish to say more. Perhaps I have said a deuced deal too much already; but let it drop. Courtley has confessed, and that's quite enough."

"Why, Peter," said his mother, "I wonder at you. Any one would think that you suspected Mr. Oxley of it."

"Ha!—ha!" laughed Oxley. "He!—he! Suspect me!—me! Ha!—ha!—ha!—ha!"

"Don't laugh in that kind of way," said Peter. "It's cold enough to freeze one's blood to-night, without your laughing in that hyena-like fashion; so don't do it. I never felt so uncomfortable in all my life."

"My dear Peter," said Mrs. Lerew, "you

should think of the delightful prospect before you."

"Oh, should I? Well, perhaps this infernal piece of business about making out that I am the heir to the Bloxdale property may succeed, after all, and if it does, I know what I will do."

"What?" cried Oxley.

"I'll let Lady Fanny have such an allowance as will keep her as a lady all her life; and the old man shall find me a jolly fellow, I can tell you. I won't have him put into one of those mad-houses that drive fellows clean and clear out of their senses, when they are only a little way gone; but he shall have everything that can make him comfortable about him, mad though he is."

"My dear Peter," said Oxley, "I have to inform you that a change has come over the mind of the earl. He is not mad—he has recovered his senses, and he appears to have recovered some one's elses along with them, for never, in his best time, was he anything like what he is now for energy and decision of character. The most serious obstacle to us all will now be the earl himself."

Peter executed a long whistle, and Mrs. Lerew looked vexed.

"I did not anticipate this," she said. "It is a blow, indeed. What is to be done now, Oxley?"

"Persevere in our plans, and be at him with all his senses about him," said Oxley. "I don't see the difficulty. He will, of course, deny all that we allege to be true; but there is one thing greatly in our favour."

"What is that?"

"You can say that while the countess lived you would never have brought forward the case, out of kindness to her, and because it would have induced a criminal proceeding for bigamy against the earl; but now that she is no more, your natural affection for Peter —your maternal feelings, and all that sort of thing, prompt you to act—you comprehend me?"

"I do."

"Upon my life, father-in-law," said Peter, "you are a rum 'un to tell the truth, and no mistake."

"It is for you that I am always full of thought," said Oxley.

"Oh, dear! you don't say so?"

"I not only say it, Peter, but I think it; and I do hope that I shall meet with a grateful return for all I am doing in your favour. Heaven knows it is a thorny path that I have chosen; and if I had not been ambitious for your sake, and for the sake of your amiable mother, you both know as well as possible that I might still have continued the highly respectable and the respected steward of the Bloxdale property."

Mr. Oxley's voice grew thick and husky as he spoke, for there was a deep conviction in his own mind that, as yet, he had not profited by taking the downward path in sin and in degradation that he had chosen, instead of that fair and open course which would have made him, as he truly said, respectable and respected.

"Gammon!" said Peter.

"Oh, dear—oh, dear!" added Oxley, "I am very much afraid that I am not appreciated."

"Hold your noise!" said Mrs. Lerew. "If the affair succeeds it will be all very well; but you know as well as I do that it entirely depends upon old Musgrove, the parson. If he will, on account of his son, consent to all that we wish him, why, there will be an end of it, I do think; for it will be quite out of the question for the earl to meet such a case."

"That is true," said Oxley, "that is true, and as we are man and wife now, you know my dear Maria, why—Oh, gracious!"

Something more nearly resembling a howl than a sound from any human throat at this moment intruded itself upon the conference between Mr. Oxley and his amiable family. Peter dropped his much-cherished meerschaum pipe, which broke with the concussion - Mrs. Lerew would have turned pale, but the paint with which she so freely bedecked her cheeks, in order to get up a vivid contrast between them and the long artificial hair that she wore, was not at all sympathetic.

Oxley grasped the arms of a chair upon which he was sitting, and looked as though he thought the end of the world might, in all probability, be very near at hand, and was announced by that terrible howling cry.

There was then, before either of them could speak, a sudden smashing noise, as of glass shivering to atoms.

"By Jove, it's in the next room!" cried Peter. "I'll see to that."

"We are betrayed," said Mrs. Lerew.

"We are lost!" said Oxley.

"D—n it, no!" cried Peter; "it's no use your saying that. Where's that old gun?"

"Oh, yes, the gun!" cried Oxley, as the idea of more bloodshed flashed across his guilty soul as the only means by which he might save himslf from the consequences of his already committed crime. "The gun —yes, the gun!"

Now Oxley had brought the gun in question from the hall as a kind of safeguard to the sweet Mrs. Lerew, and he had placed it in a corner of the very room in which they now sat. If it had not been tampered with, Oxley knew that it was loaded.

Making a rush to the corner where he had left the gun, he seized it, and with alarm and rage struggling for a mastery in his heart and brain, he rushed into the adjoining room.

The window was swinging open. It was a window that opened upon hinges like a door. A number of the diamond-shaped pains of glass which composed the window lay broken upon the floor. One glance into the night air showed Oxley a dim looking figure in relief against the snow, and just turning the angle of the house, apparently to get to the front garden, from whence escape would be easy.

"My life," cried Oxley, as he levelled the gun—"my life or yours, be you whom you may!"

In another moment the sharp report of rather a heavily loaded gun awoke the echoes of the night.

Oxley was nearly thrown upon his back by the recoil of the weapon as it struck his shoulder. A scream came from some one without, and then Mrs. Lerew and Peter rushed into the room with lights.

"Hit—hit!" cried Oxley. "I hit him! Didn't you hear that? Ha! I hit him!"

"Bravo! father-in-law," said Peter, as he patted Oxley in a very animated kind of way upon the back. "Bravo!"

"Who was it?" said Mrs. Lerew.

"I don't know. How can I know? What did we say? Anything to criminate, eh?"

Mrs. Lerew gave Oxley a pinch on the arm, and a look that was meant to warn him that Peter was not to be trusted with the grand secret of all—the secret of the murder!

"I will go with Peter," she said, "and see if any one is killed or hurt. It is a sad thing that thieves will thrust themselves into danger. Come, Peter, get a light."

"All's right," said Peter; "but you see the wind sets this way, and if I get another light, it will share the same fate as this one just now brought in here, and which has gone out. Let's go by the front door and take a look."

"Yes—yes, that will do."

"Of course it will," said Peter. "You either hit somebody or alarmed 'em, father-in-law. If the former, they can wait our leisure, I take it; but if the latter they are off far enough by this time; so, you see, there is no hurry at all."

Peter, either from fear, or from philosophy, was not at all disposed to hurry himself in the matter, and was rather slow in getting another light. Oxley was too curious to find out who he had hit, or too cowardly to be left alone, to stay in the cottage, so he followed Peter into the garden, and Mrs. Lerew, gathering up the skirt of her dress over her head, to protect her from the inclement weather of that night, walked by the side of Oxley.

"Now, father-in-law," said Peter, "where was the trespasser when you took that shot at him?"

"There," said Oxley, "close by the corner of the house where that pear-tree is growing. Just there."

"Very good."

Peter looked carefully over the spot, but nothing in the shape of either a dead or a wounded intruder was to be found on the spot.

"*Non est inventus*," said Peter.

Mrs. Lerew stooped down, and looked carefully upon a tree of holly that grew close to the spot.

"Blood!" she said.

"No—no," cried Oxley, "don't—that is —where is it?"

"Hem! Look for yourself. You hit somebody, Oxley, but whoever it was has been able to escape, notwithstanding."

Oxley groaned.

"Oh, what did I say, what did you say, what did Peter say—what did we all say that might have been heard to our great detriment by some one from the window of the room next to that in which we sat?"

"Be under no alarm," said Mrs. Lerew. "There was nothing said that any one could understand. What do you think, Peter?"

"I think with you there, mother. I don't know that there was anything said that we need be afraid of. And, after all, it was more than likely to have been some tramp looking out for what he could pick up. I think father-in-law, you are a little too hasty with a gun.'

"Too hasty?"

"Yes; some day or another, I shouldn't at all wonder but you will be shooting somebody you had much better have left alone."

Oxley shook dreadfully at this; but he tried to laugh, although it was in such a dreadful manner that Peter begged of him as a particular favour to put a stop to it.

Mrs. Lerew was getting chilled, and insisted upon a return to the cottage, which was by no means an unwelcome step to Oxley, for in addition to being chilled to the very marrow by the cold night air, he was full of all sorts of fears, natural and supernatural, and was right glad to find himself in the room again of the cottage.

"I tell you what it is," said Peter; "it strikes me, that being here, especially at this time of year, is deuced slow; now I wish you would be so good as to bring affairs to a conclusion as quickly as possible."

"They shall be brought to a conclusion," said Oxley. "Rest content. I come now to act wholly and entirely in this affair, and we will to-morrow set about it in earnest. Your old friend and employer shall be our man of business in it. The evidence shall be all arranged, and I yet hope to see you Master of Bloxdale."

"If I ever am such," said Peter, "you will see what a jolly life I will lead. I don't believe that one half the people that have money know how to use it. Oh, lor! my meerschaum is done for. Confound it! father-in-law, don't be trampling about among the pieces of my pipe."

———

CHAPTER LI.

MORRIS COURTLEY IS PLACED UPON HIS TRIAL FOR THE MURDER.

THE coroner's inquest brought in a verdict of "Wilful Murder" against Morris Courtley. It was quite impossible that twelve men met together to carry out such an inquiry, and with the sort of evidence that had been brought before them, should be able to come to any different conclusion.

You or I, reader, must have condemned Morris Courtley guilty, if we had known nothing of him or the circumstances which we really do know all about, and if the case had just been brought before us upon its bare merits.

There he was, in the mind's eye of those who had to judge him, with everything against him.

A dependent, although in a respectable situation in the family, and certainly not a domestic, aspires to the hand of the daughter of an earl—the family find out the affair, and disgrace and discharge follows, as things of course—the young lord takes the initiative in such proceedings, and is murdered—the secretary is acknowledged to be the last person seen in his company—his coat is found thrown over a hedge close to the scene of the murder—the cuff of the coat is in the grasp of the dead!

The gun with which the deed was done had hung over the chimney-piece of a room through which Courtley had to pass to go to the meeting with Lord Francis, which he himself admitted had taken place. The story of the footsteps in the soot told against him, for everybody would presume that they had been his.

Such was the case as against Morris Courtley.

Was it then a wonder that the coroner's jury returned a verdict of "Wilful Murder" against the accused?

In those times, too, although not very far distant, questions affecting the lives and the liberties of Englishmen were not so wisely considered, as they are now. It is one of the good things of our present age, that nothing is considered to be so sacred as human life, and no man can possibly be convicted of such a crime as murder while there is any natural supposition by which he may be acquitted.

The care with which evidence is sifted, and the elaborate nature of our present investigations, in such cases, reflect the highest honour upon the state of civilization of our country. But this is recent only. Even fifty years ago there was a much greater amount of intolerance upon such subjects.

To be sure, after all, the case as regarded Courtley was but a slender one—that is to say, it was not full of incident; but when people said to each other—

"If he did not do the deed, who did?"

they felt puzzled to reply in any satisfactory manner to such a question.

And so it was that gradually, hour by hour, and day by day, the guilt of Morris Courtley became a matter of more and more plausibility to the minds of the public, until he was all but condemned by the popular voice before his trial came on.

To be sure, there were people who stoutly asserted his innocence; but they formed a very small minority, indeed; and they laboured under the disadvantage of being, as it were, set to prove a negative, since all that was acknowledged by them, and by Courtley, to be true, seemed to point towards a substitution of his guilt.

There was Roots, and there were most of the servants of the hall—there was every one who had known Courtley in his youth; and last, although not least, there was Fanny.

Yes, Fanny never swerved for one moment from the opinion that she had at first expressed—

"Morris Courtley did not do the murder! Morris Courtley could not do it!"

Such was the answer of Fanny when the subject was broached to her, and she was even gradually working upon the mind of her father in the matter, until he began to doubt if it were possible such a contradiction in nature should exist as the will to murder in such a disposition, otherwise, as Morris Courtley possessed.

But the day of trial rapidly approached. One week only had elapsed since the night when the death of Lord Francis Bloxdale had created a sensation throughout England, which was long in being forgotten, before the assizes for the county were held at Southampton, as they were then, and not at Winchester as they were afterwards removed to.

Such was the state of things, then, on a Friday morning, while the snow still lay thickly upon the ground, and there was every appearance of the winter yet continuing for a considerable period of time.

Fanny had had an interview with Mrs. Courtley. It was too painful for her to think of having another while the fate of Courtley hung, as it were, in the balance of circumstances; but what a gleam of light it was, amid the murky obscurity of the sadness by which she was surrounded, to Mrs. Courtley to find that Lady Fanny believed in the innocence of Morris!

The poor mother fell upon her knees, and blessed the gentle spirit that, despite all that could be said to her to the contrary, still clung to its faith in the being she loved.

After this interview, Mrs. Courtley had a much better hope that all would go well with Morris. That Fanny should believe in his innocence seemed to be so much in his favour. She thought, too, that Fanny would be able to make her father share with her in that belief; and if such were the case—if those two who were the nearest and the dearest to him who was now no more, should think Courtley innocent, who would dare to condemn him!

This was going a little too far, though, for the earl could not come to a conclusion one way or the other; and up to the very night before the trial, he replied to Fanny that he only prayed to God that right would be done.

On the Thursday—that is to say, the day before Morris Courtley was to be tried for the murder—the bodies of Lord Francis and of his mother were committed to the family vault. The ceremony was conducted in as private a manner as possible by the earl; and when it was over, he felt as if a load had been lifted off his heart; for he seemed as if he had, by that act, consigned to Heaven his son, who never erred much, and his wife who had gone so much astray, but in whose repentance, late though it was, let us hope there was that virtue which still opened for her the gates of Paradise.

The letter that Morris Courtley had written in the library upon that dreadful night, which had produced such changes at Bloxdale, was found in the pocket of Lord Francis, and had been delivered to him, and then re-demanded of him to form an element in the judicial inquiry.

Those who were learned in such matters were at issue whether that letter was in favour of Morris or against him.

Some would have it that it was written merely as a scheme to make him look innocent. Others again decided that it was greatly in his favour, for that it bore the impress of truth about it.

The diary of the young murdered nobleman was found, and in it the last entry that he made concerning Morris Courtley, which went to confirm the fact that he had an appointment with him upon that night. There was some questions about the sum of money that Lord Francis had with him in his pocket-book, which it will be remembered Courtley had refused to take. That money and the pocket-book in which it had been contained were nowhere to be found.

And now it is night at Bloxdale—a blustrous winter's night again, and along the picture-gallery there glides a thin, wan, and wasted figure, all attired in black. It is followed by another figure, likewise in deep mourning—the latter bears a lamp.

Let us look at them well.

The first of these two figures is a young girl. More winters than summers appear to have passed over her young heart, and sered and blighted it, she was so thin—so very pale. Her beautiful hair was gathered up, and all but entirely concealed beneath a silken net, instead of floating about her neck and shoulders as it had used to do—her eyes looked much larger than usual; but that was owing to the shrinking of the flesh of the cheeks. Oh, how pale she was, and how thin and transparent the little hand was that held a shawl tightly around her neck and shoulders!

This is Fanny—yes, this is the once young and happy Fanny. One week has made all the change. She is still beautiful, but she is nearly as sad to look upon as death, and she moves along the old picture-gallery like a ghost.

Every few moments there is a strange catching of the breath with her, as though some deep sigh were only stopped in its full utterance by the will to impede it. Alas! what must that young creature have suffered? It is too fearful to dwell upon her looks.

Following her is our old friend, Ann, and she is very pale, too, and looks very ill. With a devotion that only pure affection could have made her acquainted with, Ann had been everything in that house. What the earl and what Fanny could have done without her Heaven only knows!

Fanny is proceeding to her father's room, for she has something to say to him about the morrow—that dreadful morrow which is to place Morris Courtley upon his trial.

"Ann—Ann, dear?"

"Yes, Fanny?"

"Does the snow still fall?"

"Yes, Fanny dear, it does, indeed! Are you very cold?"

"No—no. Thursday night, and to-morrow Friday—Friday. Oh, God! why is it on Friday?"

Ann knew too well, and so did Fanny, that the trial was fixed for Friday, with the strong opinion of the officials that the prisoner would be executed, and that, consequently, he would have a day longer to live, as Sunday would not be counted in the twenty-four hours that would be by law given him to prepare for eternity.

"Oh, my dear Fanny," said Ann, "do not weep."

"Weep? Oh, no—no."

"I thought you were crying."

Ann burst into tears herself.

"Happy Ann," said Fanny, as she pressed her hand upon her breast as though a sudden pain had come over her. "Happy Ann, you have tears—I have none. I have been so wishing for tears all this day, but I cannot weep. I think they are all gone—all gone."

"Oh, do not speak so, Fanny," sobbed Ann. "It is wrong of me to cry, but I cannot help it at times—I know it is wrong of me, because it distresses you; but I cannot help it, and when I catch a glance at your dear face, and see what it is, and think what it was, and what it ought to be, I—I——"

Ann was too overcome to speak further, and she sobbed aloud. A slow and solemn footstep came towards them.

"Hush, Ann," said Fanny, "some one comes."

"It is your father," said Ann, through her tears. "I will sit here."

As she spoke, she crept into a window seat, which was within the deep embrasure of a bay window, and sat down sighing and sobbing.

The Earl of Bloxdale slowly approached, and when he saw Fanny he quickened his pace a little, and tried to smile. It was so very faint a smile, though, that it could barely be called one.

"My darling," he said, "you will be cold in this part of the house. Why do you wander here! And alone, too?"

"No, father; Ann is with me. I was coming to you."

"Then come now, dear one. I was just about to take a little exercise in the gallery, but I will return with you, my dear."

"Ann, will you wait for me in my room?" said Fanny.

"Or come with us?" said the earl.

"I will wait," said Ann. "I am not cold, dear, I am not, indeed."

"But," said the earl, "you must not wait here, Ann, and by the window, too, on such a night as this. Come, now, be persuaded, and go to Fanny's room, or come to us. We cannot afford to let you get indisposed, you know."

Ann rose and thanked the earl, and went to Fanny's room, and then Fanny and her father walked slowly to an apartment which the earl usually sat in now, and which contained many of the papers and documents of the family. Hill, the valet, was there, making up the fire for the night, as his master usually now sat late by it, and he respectfully placed chairs for Fanny and her father, and then bowed himself out.

The air of that room was warm and soft, and grateful to the feelings of poor Fanny. Her father drew his chair close to hers, and took her hand in his, and looked in her face as he said—

"My darling, you look but poorly. We must have change of air for you, my Fan. I must return the roses to those cheeks."

It was evident that the earl was making a great effort to speak as though he had recovered from the blows that fate had of late given to him.

"You are ever good and kind to me, father," said Fanny—"too good, and too kind; but—but——"

"But what, darling?"

She clung to his arm convulsively, and placed her hand upon her heart, as she said in accents of deep affliction—

"To-morrow—to-morrow, father! Oh, God, to-morrow!"

"Hush—hush! Oh, Fanny, do not give way thus! Be calm, my child!"

"Yes, father, I will, indeed. I will be calm and good—I will, indeed! But, to-morrow, Morris Courtley comes to be judged —not by God, for if that were the case I should, indeed, be calm and happy, but by mortal, erring man. Oh, father, father, he did not do the deed of which they accuse him!"

The earl sighed deeply.

"Father, father, you must save him!"

"Fanny, Fanny!"

"You can—you will, father—you must say in all truth and in all sincerity that he did not do it! Heaven only knows who is guilty, but it is not Morris Courtley! Oh, no, no, no!"

The earl was greatly alarmed at the frantic vehemence of Fanny's manner. It was quite evident that she had worked herself to almost a pitch of frenzy to say this much to her father.

"My dear," he said, "it would have been as well if you and I had not made this sad affair a subject of discussion; but, as it is so uppermost in your mind, let me implore you to speak calmly concerning it. Now, Fanny, you know that I love you dearer than my life."

"Yes, yes, I know you do, father."

"Well, my child, be advised by me, and say not another word upon this subject till after to-morrow."

"To-morrow—to-morrow?"

"Yes, after to-morrow. It may be that Courtley may stand acquitted of the crime laid to his charge; but whether or not you should remember one thing, Fanny, and that is, that I am not his accuser. If those who place him upon his trial consider that he is guilty, I have no power, by the mere expression of opinion, to snatch him from any doom to which they may condemn him. Do you not understand that, my dear child? The crime with which he stands charged is against society, not against me or against you. Society will not listen to any parent's voice upon the matter. I may forgive, but society will punish."

Fanny looked rather confused.

"Surely, my dear," added the earl, "you have not been labouring under the delusion that I had any power in the proceedings?"

"No power, father?"

"None whatever. If I had such, and while a doubt could possibly remain of Morris Courtley's guilt, I should say to him, 'Go, for I leave you and your guilt or your innocence to be judged by God.' I would not have upon my soul the responsibility of a decision upon either; but I have no power to do that, Fanny. Under all the circumstances, not feeling convinced of the guilt of Courtley, I can but hope that he will be acquitted."

"You are not then convinced of his guilt, father?"

"Certainly not. The evidence is circumstantial; but that is liable to error, and so I cannot be convinced."

"Blessings on you, father, for that word; but—but—I am convinced that he is innocent. Oh, father, will you be angry with your child if—she—asks you a great favour?"

"No, darling."

"I have written a short letter—to—Morris."

The earl started.

"It is here, father. Do you think that

you could send it to him? Do you think that it would be wrong to send it?"

The earl felt much relieved. He thought from what Fanny said that she had sent the letter, but now he found that she had it in her bosom.

"My child," he said, "if you say that you wish that letter to go, despite all that I can urge to you against it, I will send it; but I wish you to forego such an intention. It is better not to send it."

"Alas, poor Morris!"

Fanny took the letter from her bosom, and held it towards the flame of the fire, but her father arrested her hand, saying—

"Will you let me see it?"

She handed it to him, and the earl found that it only contained these words—

"My Morris, I know that you are innocent. God help and bless you. I would not send you this if I had a doubt; because if you were guilty, it would stab you to the heart."

"I will send the letter," said the earl, as he kissed the pale cheek of Fanny.

CHAPTER LII.

THE EARL RECEIVES RATHER A CURIOUS LETTER ON THE MORNING OF THE TRIAL.

AN unknown donor had sent to Mrs. Courtley the sum of five hundred pounds in an envelope. The only words that accompanied the gift were—

"For the defence of your son."

Such a sum at once put it in the power of Mrs. Courtley to do all that could be done for Morris under the circumstances; and the judges were rather surprised at the amount of legal talent that appeared for the prisoner upon his trial.

Of course all this was done without in any way consulting Morris himself; for, in all probability he would have said—"Keep the money, mother, and let me stand or fall by my own acts." Such, however, was not the case; and although the attorney-general's ex-officiate came down from London to prosecute, the counsel who appeared for the prisoner were men of the highest standing in that branch of the profession.

We will state at once, as there is no occasion for keeping it a secret, that the money we have mentioned came from the Earl of Bloxdale, who was resolved that Courtley should have every chance of proving his innocence that the first talent in the country could give to him.

If Fanny had known of this impression of her father's, she would, indeed, have blessed him for it; but the fact was, that she never thought for a moment of any legal difficulties being smoothed away by money. Born and bred up in the very lap of luxury and plenty as she had been, the last thing she was likely to think of was anything connected with money.

Mrs. Courtley had taken a lodging in Southampton for herself and her family, and there she awaited the trial of her son.

We dread to think of what were the feelings of the mother on that dreadful Friday. It would be quite impossible for any person to depict them, and quite wrong to do so, if possible. There are feelings of the human heart which it would be too fearful a task to probe too deeply.

The morning was cold and cheerless, as it slowly broke over Southampton on that Friday which was to place Morris Courtley at the bar of the court to plead for his life. The account of the trial had brought people from far and near to witness it, notwithstanding the inclement character of the season.

From London had come quite a host of people, and the town of Southampton, which at that time could not boast of much more than one half of its present dimensions—for there was hardly a house above the Bar —was in a state of general commotion.

The witnesses, few in number as they were, were all in readiness; and the prisoner, perhaps, was the only person connected with the important concern of the day who slept soundly on the night before the trial.

Morris Courtley felt his own innocence to be so complete that he could not be said to have fairly awakened to the danger that he was in. It appeared to him so very improbable—so outrageously out of all rule, that a man so perfectly free from guilt as he was should be sacrificed upon weak and inconclusive circumstantial evidence, that he never fairly thought himself in any real danger.

This feeling, of course, could only be, to a great extent, in the mind of Morris Courtley alone. He only *knew* that he was innocent —that is to say, he and Oxley—but all those who loved him, and who believed him innocent could only believe it, and a person may believe what they do not know.

The coolness and calmness of the prisoner quite surprised the officials of the jail at Southampton, for they, with the instinct of their calling, always believed the man who was accused of anything to be guilty. They were so accustomed only to see the guilty in their custody, that the possibility that they were depriving an innocent man of his liberty, and subjecting him to all the indignities and all the systematic rules and regulations which may well apply to the guilty, never struck them.

To be sure, they knew that the inmates of the jail were often, when put upon their trial, for different offences, acquitted and set free; but then the officers and turnkeys of the prison thought that they only "got off," to use their own phraseology, and they did not consider that the question of their guilt or innocence was very much affected by the verdict of acquittal.

As Morris was accused of a capital offence, and as they all looked upon him as a man

LORD FRANCIS SHOT IN BLOXDALE PARK BY OXLEY.

whose hours upon this earth were numbered, they certainly felt rather induced to treat him with a sort of distinction; but all that was lost upon Courtley, as he did not know what constituted special civility to him, and what was the ordinary rule.

"Now, sir," said the governor of the prison, as he intruded himself upon Courtley at his breakfast, "you are ready, I hope?"

"Certainly," said Courtley.

"Here is a letter that I have been directed to give to you. It is from the lord Lieutenant of the county.

It did not, at the moment, occur to Courtley that it was Lord Bloxdale who was Lord lieutenant of the county; but when he saw the well-known Bloxdale seal, a flush of colour came over his cheeks, and he tore the letter open.

A small piece of paper fell to the ground, and when Courtley picked it up and read it, he kissed it twice, and placed it in his bosom.

It was Fanny's note to him.

"A new start that, Bill," said one of the turnkey's to another in an under tone.

"Oh, very!" said the other.

"The idea, now, of a feller kissing a bit of paper! Oh, my eye!"

"I am quite ready, sir," said Courtley to the governor. "I shall always consider that, as far as was compatible with your duty, you have treated me with kindness."

"Thank you—thank you! I'm sure I'm sorry you are here at all."

Courtley smiled sadly as he replied—

"And I, too; but I suppose there will be no occasion to come back after the trial?"

"Back?"

"Yes. To return here—when I am acquitted I mean?"

"Oh!—ah!—hem! We shall see. Of course you are quite right, Mr. Courtley. When people are acquitted they need not come back here."

"I shall demand my instant release, even in court," said Courtley, as he followed the governor.

"Well," said the turnkey, "what do you think of that, Bill? Ain't he about the coolest hand at this sort of thing that ever you seed?"

"Rather!" said Bill. "But, I say, Joe."

"Well, what now?"

"I've been a thinking."

"You don't say so! I wonder you didn't take off your coat and waistcoat afore you took to that hard kind of work."

"None o' yer jokes. I say I have been thinking that, arter all, perhaps, he didn't do it. Perhaps he's innocent."

"Perhaps he's what?"

"Innocent! My wife can't believe as he did it."

"Oh, indeed! Well, then, I tell you what—you don't know what you are a talking about. Innocent! Oh, lor! Wery innocent and like a baby a man must be as is brought here. Vy, what's this here place?"

"The old jail, to be sure."

"And what's it for?"

"For holding prisoners, to be sure."

"To be sure. Well, prisoners isn't prisoners unless they does things as they shouldn't ought to do. This is a land of liberty, ain't it?"

"Yes, but——"

"There ain't no but's in it. You are a fool. Don't say no more about it. You don't know what you are a saying no more nor a babby, that you don't."

While the head turnkey, Bill, was thus putting down his subordinate, Mr. Joe, upon the question of Courtley's guilt or innocence, poor Morris, with that strange confidence in his utter guiltlessness which never forsook him, so far as it tended to convince him that he could not be convicted till he found that he really was so, followed the governor, and was placed in a hackney-coach, with a guard of yeomanry around it, and so driven to the town hall, where the judges held their court.

It was now ten o'clock in the morning of that eventful Friday, and the streets literally swarmed with people, for the court was not opened, as the judges had not taken their seats

It was with the greatest difficulty that the mounted yeomanry could clear a passage for the coach through the dense mass of spectators that crowded around it, and Courtley was glad, at last, when he was fairly under cover in the court-house, and out of the mob.

The doors were then opened, and in the course of seven or eight minutes the court was crowded to excess in every part of it. A notice was pasted at the judges' entrance that the witnesses would be allowed to enter by that way, and if such had not been the case, it was quite clear to every one that they would not have got into the court at all upon the occasion, the pressure was so great.

It took all the exertion of the officers, before the judges appeared, to induce the mob within the court to be quiet; and the sheriff had to rise and assure them that the judges of assize had a discretionary power to order the court to be cleared instantly if there were any continued disorder, before the people were at all restored to quietude.

Even then, the whispering of so many voices made up a strange sound, which was very perplexing.

It was half-past ten when the judges, attended by the mayor of the town, and some of the civic authorities, and the high-sheriff, made his appearance upon the bench, and took his seat.

One glance at the crowded court induced the judge to whisper silently to the sheriff, who shook his head with a look of despair.

"We shall never get on," said the judge

"It's a good thing it is not a summer assize," said the mayor.

"We should be melted if it were so,' said the sheriff.

Silence was now produced in court, and then from a private door there came the witnesses, who were allowed to seat themselves with the attorneys, so that, whether they were honest men or not, they, at all events that day, got into very bad company.

"Silence!" cried the usher of the court. "Silence!"

The judge spoke in a low, distinct voice.

"I perceive," he said, "that the court is inconveniently crowded. I don't mean to say that any one could prevent such from being the case; but I warn all those who are here as spectators of the proceedings of this day, that what inconvenience they may suffer from pressure or otherwise is of their own seeking, and that they must either endure the same in silence or leave the court. The business of the assizes cannot be interrupted; and the officers have very strict orders now, without favour or partiality, to take into custody, and remove at once, any person disturbing the court."

This little notice of what he intended to do was spoken by the judge in a tone of voice that could not be doubted, as regarded the earnestness of it. Some fifty or sixty people, who were wedged into odd corners where they could neither see nor hear, accordingly made efforts to get away.

There was a considerable confusion consequent upon their getting out of the court, but the judge, as he saw what it was, paid no attention to it, feeling that after they had gone he would have a better chance of controlling those who still should remain.

The judge now slightly inclined his head to the clerk of the arraigns as a request to commence proceedings, and the usher raised the monotonous cry of—

"Silence—silence!"

There was a movement among the crowd, and the attorney-general, with the prisoner's counsel made their appearance, and took their places. The counsel at the table nodded and smiled at each other, as though they had met on one of the most ordinary of all ordinary occasions, and as though the life of a fellow creature did not hang upon the balance of the proceedings of that day.

"The gentlemen of the jury," said the clerk, "will please to answer to their names."

The jury all answered, and some tittering was commenced in the court at the difference in the tones of the voices that responded to the names as they were called over.

CHAPTER LIII.

THE TRIAL OF MORRIS COURTLEY AT SOUTHAMPTON.

A SUDDEN darkness now spread over the court, and the judge looked up to the skylight.

The snow was coming down in such a dense mass, that it was covering up the glass as if a coating of felt were placed over it.

"We will have lights, my lord, if you please," said the sheriff.

"I really think we must," said the judge.

It took some time to light the court, and then it had a strange effect, for here and there the snow, after collecting to a great thickness upon one of the sloping windows, would suddenly slide off like an avalanche, and then a strange yellow fog-like light from the outer day would struggle in to make war with the lamps in the court.

"Silence!" again shouted the usher.

All eyes were turned towards the dock. A constable appeared and placed himself by the side of it. A shuffling of feet was heard, and then the door that led from the dock to the other portion of the court-house was held open by another constable.

The accused was coming.

No—no. It is the governor of the gaol. Now he comes—no, it is the chaplain. They all look back. Another moment, and the tall, graceful figure of Morris Courtley appears.

He paused a moment as he met the sea of upturned faces, and a flush of colour mantled his pale cheeks. He then turned to the judge, and stepped to the front of the dock.

He was noticed to plunge his hand into the bosom of his clothing, and to keep it there. Some fancied he had the means of self-destruction in his grasp; but no—it was Fanny's letter that Morris Courtley held by as the anchor of his hopes.

The appearance of Morris Courtley, even as he occupied so unfavourable a position as that in which he stood in the dock at the court-house at Southampton, was very much in his favour.

It was quite impossible to look at that calm, intellectual face, without being prepossessed in the favour of its owner.

Then, again, there was the youth of Courtley—the peculiar circumstances under which he, one of the people, had become the associate of the highest and the noblest of the land—the love that Lady Fanny Bloxdale felt for him, and which now was quite notorious—and the lingering doubts, after all, of the possibility of his guilt, all conspired to invest the secretary with a tremendous interest.

It will not do in this world to judge wholly and entirely by looks, or we may make the most serious mistakes. It would do, perhaps, quite well if we were sufficient judges of the physiognomical expression always to arrive at correct conclusions regarding it; but we are not, and, therefore, it will not do to judge by looks; yet there was not a living soul in that court-house, who bent a long and steady gaze upon the lofty and placid brow of Morris Courtley, and looked at the feminine and sweetly-formed mouth, and marked the contemplative and benignant glance of his eye, that could feel that such a man could commit a murder.

The impression that the prisoner made

quite innocently—for it was a thing he never thought of—was immensely favourable to him; and, in the course of a few minutes, even those who had been the most impressed with a sense of the enormity of the guilt of whoever had murdered Lord Francis Bloxdale, might have been heard muttering to themselves—

"Surely this cannot be the man."

Well, we like to think that nature does not act so much by contraries as to stamp the impress of an angel upon the countenance of a fiend. The mind will be, to a great extent, reflected upon the face.

It is a favourite idea of many, and, indeed, it is the popular idea with by far the greater number now, that education will do everything, and that why one man is a philosopher and another man a criminal, is solely owing to the different circumstances in which they have been brought up; but with all due deference to these gentlemen, we entertain a different opinion. We think that no two minds are equal in what may be called raw material; and, therefore, that although education may do a great deal, it cannot do everything.

Why, or wherefore, vicious and intractable brains are created, is a question, the difficulties of which we are not bound to solve. It is sufficient if we are convinced of a fortunate phenomenon of nature. We are, by no means, compelled even to have a theory regarding its why and because.

But to return to Morris Courtley, who stood by the front of the bar, and who, after a few moments, took an earnest glance around the court.

It was a joy to him to see some friendly faces, and among them, the honest, weather-beaten countenance of Roots, who had the greatest difficulty in the world to control his feelings sufficiently to prevent himself from crying out some words of encouragement to poor Courtley.

The proceedings of the trial, however, soon engrossed the whole attention of the prisoner at the bar.

The judge had said something to the high-sheriff, and the high-sheriff had sent a message to the governor of the jail, who, stepping up to Courtley, said to him—

"What is it that you have got in the breast of your apparel, sir, that your hand is grasping?"

"A letter. You brought it to me this morning."

"Oh, is that it?"

"Certainly. Behold!"

Morris Courtley drew out the crumpled piece of paper and showed it to the governor, who nodded his head, as he said—

"The judge and the high-sheriff thought it might be something else. It's all right, sir."

This little episode was not at all understood by the spectators, who looked excessively curious concerning it; but although they asked each other what it could be, no one could give any explanation at all concerning it.

But now the jury having been sworn, the clerk of the arraigns rose with the indictment in his hand, and commenced—

"Know you, Morris Courtley, clerk, and all men concerned, &c., &c."

The indictment charged him, amid all the verbosity of such documents, with killing and slaying Francis Beauclerc de Rochford, commonly called Lord Francis Bloxdale, against the peace of our sovereign lord the king, &c., &c., &c.

Courtley listened intently to the reading of this document, and tried in vain, amid the tangle of its composition, to extract the sense of the whole of it.

The difficulty, though, of finding what had no existence, namely, the sense of the document, was insurmountable; so the prisoner was compelled just to assume that that was the proper mode in which he was charged with the murder of the man, in whose defence he would have interposed his own heart.

"Prisoner at the bar, do you plead guilty or not guilty to this charge?"

Courtley started, as the question came upon him rather abruptly; and after the pause of a moment, during which you might have heard a pin drop in court, he said, in a voice that struck upon every heart like a chord of music, for his voice was pre-eminently sweet—

"Not guilty, so help me, Heaven!"

Every one breathed more freely, and there was that noisy shuffling of feet, and changing of position among the people that generally succeeds some great excitement, during which the attention has been greatly enslaved, and the bodily comfort forgotten.

"Silence!" cried the usher in his monotonous, drawling tone. "Silence in the court!"

There was now some confused jargon about the prisoner being tried by his peers, &c. spoken by the clerk of the arraigns, and to which no one paid any sort of attention; and just before the attorney-general rose to open the case for the prosecution, Lord Bloxdale entered the court by a door that led him on the bench.

The judge bowed to him, and the earl returned the salute courteously, and then took his seat.

The Earl of Bloxdale was deadly pale; but he wore his uniform as lord lieutenant of the county. There was an expression upon the faces of all present of great sympathy with the bereaved father; but they could see he had conquered the violence of his grief, and that, so to speak, his deep sorrow had retreated to his heart, there to remain out of the sight of human eyes.

The earl had scarcely been seated a moment, when one of the officials of the court handed him a letter, saying—

"If you please, my lord, this has been placed in my hands for your lordship; and the man who did so went away before I could say I would or I would not deliver it; but as it is addressed to your lordship, I thought I had better do so."

"I thank you," said the earl. "You have exercised a sound discretion in the matter."

Upon the outside of the letter was the word "Important;" and so, while the attorney-general was arranging his papers, the earl broke the seal of the letter, and, somewhat to his surprise, read as follows:—

"Gray's Inn, London.

"To the Right Honourable the Earl o Bloxdale, &c. &c. &c. &c.

"My Lord,—I am instructed by a lady (Countess of Bloxdale) to call your lordship's attention to circumstances occurring some twenty or twenty-five years since, which the lady aforesaid (Countess of Bloxdale) has not thought proper to allude to until now, from motives of delicacy and consideration to your lordship; but having a son (Lord Peter Bloxdale), the lady aforesaid feels that it is incumbent upon her now to assert her rights as your countess.

"The lady aforesaid (Countess of Bloxdale) asserts her previous marriage with your lordship to your union with the individual who for so long enjoyed the title of Countess of Bloxdale, and who is recently deceased.

"To your lordship this circumstance will not be ambiguous; and your lordship's attention is requested to the subject (to prevent exposure) by your lordship's most obedient and very humble servant,

"Lilos Jacobs, (Solicitor)."

Lord Bloxdale looked at this letter with rather a bewildered expression of countenance. It was the opening of the campaign against him and against Lady Fanny by the Lerews and by Oxley.

"What on earth," thought the earl, "can this mean? Some maniac has written it."

The voice of the attorney-general, as he said, "My lord, and gentlemen of the jury," recalled Lord Bloxdale to the scene before him. Hastily thrusting the letter into his pocket, for future consideration, he turned his whole attention to the investigation before him, and which, to him, was one of the most painfully interesting character.

The attorney-general spoke in rather a subdued tone of voice; but it was so well modulated that it was distinctly heard in every corner of the court with the smallest attention. We need hardly say, that every word he uttered was listened to with an attention that bore no sort of flagging.

"My lord, and gentlemen of the jury—

"The subject of inquiry which will this day engage our attention, is one which, under all circumstances, is of an exceedingly painful nature; but it will happen at times, that from the peculiar circumstances attendant upon some particular case, those circumstances will, in their distressing incidents, far transcend all others.

"It is so, I grieve to say, with the present case.

"I do not mean to assert, gentlemen of the jury, that the guilt of the prisoner at the bar, if it be proved—and God forbid that I should prejudge him, or any man—is greater than that of any other human being who transgresses that dread command, which says to us—'Thou shalt not kill;' but yet there are circumstances connected with the case which render it at once awful and mysterious.

"I would wish you, gentlemen of the jury, yet to approach the investigation of this terrible act, with which the prisoner at the bar stands charged, with the most patient care, and with the most complete forgetfulness, if that be possible, of all that has been trumpeted forth concerning the case by the voice of popular rumour.

"The duration of time has been but short, since the commission of the crime, to investigate what we are here this day assembled to do; but it has been long enough to provoke all those lively imaginations, who prefer a good tale to truth, to exercise their vocation to an unlimited extent.

"Therefore, gentlemen of the jury, what you have to do, solely, is to weigh the evidence against the prisoner at the bar that will be fairly and upon oath brought before you this day; and should you not think it sufficient to convince you beyond a likelihood of a doubt of his guilt, no one will rejoice more than I shall at his acquittal.

"Allow me now, my lord, and gentlemen of the jury, to give a brief narration of what occurred upon the night in question, with reference to the murder of Lord Francis Bloxdale.

"A little after one of the clock upon the night in question, it appears that there was heard the report of a gun, fired in the immediate vicinity of the mansion at Bloxdale Park, not far from this town, and which is the abode of the Earl of Bloxdale and his family. Shortly after that, a cry of 'Help!' and 'Murder!' was raised, and the whole household became alarmed. Something like a careful search in the garden ensued, without a result; when, as the hall was crowded with the alarmed servants, and the family of the earl, the prisoner at the bar came staggering into it, bearing the lifeless body of Lord Francis Bloxdale.

"The statement of the prisoner was, that he had had an interview with the deceased in a little field or paddock, outside the park wall of Bloxdale, and that they had parted, and he had got some distance before he heard a gun shot, and upon returning back again to the spot upon which he had left Lord Francis, he found him lying upon the snow, and weltering in his blood.

"The prisoner then states, that it was he who called for help, but finding that help came not, he took the body upon his shoulders, and hastened with it to the hall.

"A judicial investigation took place at the

hall, which resulted in a suspicion of the guilt of the prisoner. A coroner's inquisition ensued, and a verdict of wilful murder was returned against him. After that the magistracy committed him for trial, and he stands here to answer for the offence.

"These, gentlemen of the jury, are the circumstances precisely as they took place before the eyes of numerous witnesses; and as they were heard by more than half a dozen persons, so these may be considered to be the notorious features of the crime about which there can be no possible dispute.

"It will be, now, my duty to detail to you more at length what can be given in evidence upon the matter, with relation to antecedent and subsequent occurrences connected with the murder. Of course what I in this address allege to you, I expect, and believe, will be proved by competent witnesses on oath before you this day.

There was now a general look of intense expectation upon the faces of all present, and even Morris Courtley himself seemed to feel a degree of curiosity to know in what way the advocate would strive to account for the supposed crime committed by him.

The most profound stillness now reigned in the court, so that, although, in truth, the attorney-general spoke in rather a low tone, every word that he uttered was distinctly heard.

"The prisoner at the bar, gentlemen of the jury, up to the very day, or, rather, as we may say, up to the very night of the commission of the murder, for which he is arraigned this day before you, held the position of secretary or librarian to the Earl of Bloxdale, and he was considered to be a kind of protegé of the Bloxdale family, and highly esteemed by all, with the exception of the late countess.

"It would appear that the countess, who is now no more, must have had some suspicion that the conduct of the prisoner at the bar was not such as it ought to be; for you will hear it upon oath this day, that upon more than one occasion that lady requested the earl to discharge the secretary, but without effect. What special reason her ladyship had for making such a request, we may, in the course of the inquiry guess, although she is no longer in this world to depose to these facts herself.

"A glance at the position of the Bloxdale family at, or about the period just antecedent to the murder, will very materially help us to an appreciation of the circumstances connected more directly with the dreadful deed."

At these words from the attorney-general, the paleness of the countenance of the unfortunate Earl of Bloxdale visibly increased, and he wore a look of distress that none could fail to comprehend.

"I hope," added the attorney-general, "that in what I have to say, I shall be able to exercise sufficient tact and prudence to avoid wounding the feelings of those whom we must all commiserate and respect."

This was so evidently intended to refer to the earl, that he slightly bowed, and then the attorney general proceeded:—

"It appears that Lord Francis Bloxdale, the unfortunate victim of whosoever committed this murder, was absent for a considerable time from the parental roof; and it was to a greater degree unfortunate, that during that time the health of the earl did not permit him to engage actively in the investigation of what was taking place around him. It was, then, under such circumstances as these, that the prisoner at the bar conceived the scheme of allying himself by marriage to the noble house of which he was a dependant.

"Gentlemen of the jury, the first intimation that the heads of that house received of such being the fact, was through the steward, Mr. Oxley, who made an accidental discovery to that effect, and the consequence was, a degree of hostility upon the part of the prisoner towards that individual of the most rancorous character."

"That is false," said Morris Courtley.

———

CHAPTER LIV.

PUBLIC OPINION WAVERS ABOUT THE GUILT OR INNOCENCE OF MORRIS COURTLEY.

THE tone in which Morris Courtley uttered these words produced a vast sensation in court.

The attorney-general looked astonished, and sat down on the moment—the people swayed to and fro with excitement—and the judge held up his hands to command silence, as he said,—

"Prisoner at the bar, you will receive from all here concerned a fair and patient trial—it is my special duty to sit here and see that such is the case; but if the proceedings be interrupted by you or by any one else, it will be, surely, obvious to you upon reflection, that it is very doubtful if they will ever be concluded."

"My lord," said Morris Courtley, "I acknowledge the justice of your reproof, and will be silent. It was an impulse that I could not at that moment resist that made me speak."

The judge inclined his head, and then said,—

"Mr. Attorney-general, pray proceed."

The attorney-general rose again.

"After the interruption I have received," he commenced by saying; but the judge interposed, in an under tone remarking,—

"I think that the least that is said of that, now, will be the better."

"No doubt you are right, my lord; I will not allude to it further. The prisoner at the bar, then, conceived, for I presume that is not direct, the idea of uniting himself with Lady Fanny Bloxdale. How far he had succeeded in making that very young lady a party to his plans, it is not our business to inquire: suffice it to say, that it was Mr. Oxley who discovered that such a state of things existed, and communicated as much to the Countess of Bloxdale, who carried the communication to the earl; and, finally, by some means or another, which it is needless to state, it reached the ears of Lord Francis, who had returned from abroad.

"It appears, however, that the prisoner at the bar had, in the clearest possible manner, threatened the steward, that if he made known what he had seen, he would get him discharged from the establishment. Gentlemen of the jury, as you know, the steward did make known the fact, and he is discharged.

"It is not for us to enter into the inquiry as to how far the sympathy of the sister of the murdered man with the prisoner at the bar, has influenced the discharge and the disgrace of any one whose existence appeared to be inimical to his interests in this matter.

"We now, gentlemen, get to a further step in this unhappy piece of business. It appears that Lord Francis discharged the secretary upon finding that such very ambitious hopes and feelings had entered his mind; but to avoid the unpleasantness of such a proceeding, he agreed with him to meet him at the hour when, no doubt, the murder was committed, and then take leave of him and give him a large sum of money.

"The diary of the murdered young nobleman is sufficiently confirmatory of those facts.

"And now, gentlemen of the jury, we come to the consideration of the events of the evening. Lord Francis Bloxdale went out of his paternal mansion to meet the prisoner, and he returned to it no more in life. All we have of a direct testimony regarding the fact of the murder consists of this:

"The prisoner at the bar was the last human being in his company. In the grasp of the murdered man is actually a portion of the apparel of the prisoner; and upon the hearth-stone of the great hall at Bloxdale—no doubt but that they were obliterated by some one, with a friendly feeling for the prisoner—have been found the marks of his footsteps as he reached above the old chimney-piece to take down the fatal weapon with which the deed was done.

"The evidence that I shall call before you, then, will consist of, firstly—

"Mr. Oxley, the steward—secondly, I shall put in the diary of the deceased nobleman—thirdly, I shall produce a servant who saw the secretary, that is, the prisoner at the bar pass along towards the park on the night of the murder—fourthly, I shall produce the gamekeeper, with whose gun the deed was done; the surgeon, too, will be examined, and a man who found clutched in the hand of the deceased a portion of the cuff of a coat—that man is Mr. Roachford, the respected magistrate of the county; then a servant will be produced who found the coat to which the piece of cuff belonged thrown over a hedge close to the spot where the murder was done; and, lastly, it will be found that that coat belonged to the prisoner at the bar.

"By this course, my lord and gentlemen of the jury, I regret to say, that we shall in the first place, find a good and sufficing cause to a wicked and diabolical mind for the commission of a murder; and then by such evidence, circumstantial though it be, as no human being can reject, we shall perceive that all the probabilities go towards the proof of the actual deed being committed by the prisoner at the bar.

"If it be possible, gentlemen of the jury, after all this, for you in your consciences to acquit the prisoner at the bar of the dreadful offence laid to his charge, no one will be more truly delighted at the result than I."

The attorney-general sat down.

There was an impression in the court that he had rather, as he went on with his address, played the part of a partizan against the prisoner than stated what he had to say fairly and dispassionately, but he might not have meant that. There was one new feature in the case, though, that the friends of Morris Courtley did not expect, and that was the appearance on the scene of John Oxley as an important witness for the prosecution.

No doubt if Oxley had not been in so summary a manner discharged from Bloxdale, he would have known nothing, and kept himself aloof from the whole affair; but his rage at the earl, at Fanny, and at Courtley, became so great after his ignominious dismissal, that he could not abstain from making the attempt to do them all the harm he possibly could.

If he could do nothing else, he knew that he had it in his power to wound their feelings most severely by the mode in which he would give his evidence.

"Call John Oxley," said the junior counsel for the prosecution.

There was a slight stir in the court, and the steward, dressed in a suit of black, and otherwise in the deepest mourning, made his appearance. At that moment it is likely enough that Oxley repented of the temerity with which he came forward to give evidence, and would have compounded with his desire to do injury to the earl's feelings for liberty to forego the being examined at all; but it was too late now.

Oxley was placed in the witness-box and duly sworn. He took a white handkerchief from his pocket and wiped his eyes; and then affecting to see the earl for the first time, he bowed profoundly, and said loud enough for every one to hear him—

"Ah! I will not cease yet to respect my poor deluded and misguided master. God bless him!"

"Now, Mr. Oxley," said the junior counsel, to whom the attorney-general deputed the task of conducting the examination of the witnesses. "Now, sir, we do not wish to hurt your feelings at all, but you will be so good as to answer the questions I shall put to you."

Oxley only bowed.

"What are you?"

"I may call myself steward to the Earl of Bloxdale, although I have been discharged; however, I feel convinced that as the truth, sooner or later, always triumphs, my dear master will take me on again when he finds that I am right."

"Well—well, with that we have nothing to do. You will be so good as to state to the court if you did or did not make a communication to the Countess of Bloxdale regarding Lady Fanny Bloxdale and the prisoner at the bar?"

"I did."

"What was it?"

"I would rather not say."

"You must say it. Recollect, sir, you are here on your oath."

"But surely a man is not bound to hurt the feelings of those he loves and is most anxious to serve? I assure you this has nothing to do with the murder. I appeal to the judge."

"It is not for me to say at this stage of the proceedings," said the judge, "what has to do with the case or what has not. I should hardly think that the prosecution would go out of its path to ask irrelevant questions."

"Certainly not," said the attorney-general. "Our instructions state that this person can give important evidence, and we must have it."

"You had better speak freely," said the judge; "no one can blame you for telling the truth."

"Then I submit," said Oxley, with a sigh.

Morris Courtley was rather curious to know what could possibly be the evidence that the steward was so anxious to give—for Courtley measured his anxiety to give it by his pretended reluctance so to do.

The most breathless attention was in the court as the examination of Oxley proceeded; but before we go on with that part of the trial we may call our readers' attention to a little circumstance, which being kept in mind, will show more fully how Oxley was falsifying facts.

It was Peter Lerew who, from the secret door in the gallery of the library, had heard enough to convince him of the mutual attachment of Lady Fanny and the secretary; but in so hearing, he had heard nothing that was inconsistent with honour and purity.

We shall now see how Mr. John Oxley, on his oath, in that court of justice, with a thousand eyes upon him, had the audacity, knowing that he was protected by the law, to make a monstrous conclusion from that slender fact, for the purpose of avenging what he considered his wrongs upon the earl, Lady Fanny, and Morris Courtley.

"Now, Mr. Oxley," said the counsel, "you will be so good as to tell us clearly and distinctly what you know of this matter as regarded any disagreement between the prisoner at the bar and the deceased nobleman."

Oxley coughed slightly, and then, in quite a meek and amiable tone of voice, he said—

"It sometimes happened that I had to go to the library to get a book or some letter-paper or pens for the countess, who was a most amiable lady; and upon one occasion of that sort, towards dusk, I rather abruptly entered the library, but yet I was so noiseless in my movements, owing to wearing a pair of list shoes, or the parties in the library were so much occupied, that they did not hear me."

"Who were those parties?"

"Lady Fanny Bloxdale and the prisoner at the bar."

"Where were they?"

"By the fire-side. You will excuse me saying more."

"We must hear all you have to say."

"Well, then, I heard Lady Fanny say—'My brother's opposition to our union will never cease,' and then she cried, or pretended to cry, and the prisoner at the bar said—'You may be tranquil upon that head, for I know a mode of bringing your brother's opposition to an end, which will be most effectual; so dry your tears and be happy.'"

"What else did you hear?"

"Nothing."

"What did you do?"

"I got out of the library as quickly as I could, for I could not but feel that I was an intruder there, and nothing in the world will induce me to say what I saw upon that occasion. I will not blot for ever the fame and name of a young lady, who, no doubt yielded to the seductive influence of the prisoner at the bar. No, I will say no more."

The judge looked at Mr. Oxley, as he said—

"You were not asked to say what you have said."

"Thank you, my lord. Any commendation from one holding your lordship's position is truly valuable."

"I did not commend you, sir."

Oxley pretended not to hear that remark. The counsel looked puzzled for a few moments; and then, after a whispered conversation with the attorney-general, he said—

"We have nothing further to say to you, Mr. Oxley. My learned friend who is for the prisoner may wish to ask you a question."

"Oh no," said Courtley's counsel. "Not a word. We do not insult the jury by even the supposition that anything this man has said can be true."

Oxley, with a faint smile, glided out of the witness-box.

CHAPTER LV.

THE TRIAL OF MORRIS COURTLEY CONTINUES,
AND GOES AGAINST THE PRISONER.

OXLEY was quite satisfied that he had done
all the possible mischief he could, and as he
slunk from the witness-box, he cast beneath
his shaggy and overhanging brows one glance
of triumphant malice at poor Morris Courtley,
who had been condemned to hear such false
hoods of her whom he loved, and whom he
knew to be as pure as unsmeared snow.

This was certainly the greatest possible

triumph of temper that Morris Courtley
could possibly hope to obtain—to hear Fanny
so spoken of, and to preserve silence. However, he preferred such a course rather than
by any long justification of her purity and
honour keep the matter before the thronged
court. Coming from that incarnate fiend,
John Oxley, it sadly wounded the feelings
of the young man to hear his Fanny, whom
he knew to be the essence of everything
that is good, spoken of disparagingly; but
if the insinuations had come from any
source of greater weight than Oxley it
would have been impossible to refrain from
vindicating her.

We can hardly, however, say that what
John Oxley had urged and maintained
against Lady Fanny Bloxdale had much, if
any, effect upon the thinking and educated
portion of the auditory, and it had none whatever in the way he, Oxley, had intended
it should, upon the judge and the official
personages connected with the trial.

Oxley was a tolerable actor in a part
where his own passions and interests were so
much interested as in the one in question;

but, then, even the best actors will overdraw a character, and the villain had shown, by several too clever touches, how very anxious he was to do all the damage he could to Lady Fanny Bloxdale.

The feeling towards Oxley, even in the body of the court, must have been pretty evident, when the spectators around him shrunk from contact with him, and left him the centre of a little circle, which was, by no manner of means, an ordinary one.

All these things might have reconciled Morris Courtley to the temporary pang which the words of the false steward had given him in the name of that fair and innocent being whom he loved so well.

After a pause, now, of some five minutes, the attorney-general put the diary of the late Lord Bloxdale before the court, and there appeared the entry with which the reader is already acquainted, to the effect that he had to meet Morris Courtley upon the night in question.

No remark at all was made by the counsel for the prisoner concerning the diary. The fact was, that there was so much of truth in all the details brought forward by the prosecution, that it was not possible to say much, if anything, indeed, during the progress of the trial. It was the monstrous conclusion drawn, or attempted to be drawn, from all those facts, that he, Courtley, was the murderer of Lord Francis, that was the thing to quarrel with in the matter, and that had not yet been arrived at.

"Call Thomas Shaw," said the counsel for the prosecution who acted under the directions of the attorney-general.

Thomas Shaw merely deposed to the fact that he was sitting up on the night in question, and saw Morris Courtley in the grounds of the mansion, going towards the spot where the murder was evidently committed.

No questions were asked of him. He only deposed to one of the little incontestable facts which made up the string from which the false declaration was drawn.

Roots was the next witness.

It was well know that Roots was favourable to the prisoner at the bar, and, indeed, the bold and good-hearted game-keeper took no pains to conceal that fact. It did not seem to strike him as reasonable that any one could imagine he would falsify a fact upon that account.

But, really, what Roots had to depose to was of no great consequence. He could merely swear that it was with his gun the bullet had been fired that deprived Lord Francis Bloxdale of his life. Both gun and bullet were produced in court.

"Where did you leave the gun on the night in question?" asked the counsel of Roots.

"Over the old chimney-piece in the great hall."

"Do you know anything of certain footsteps being seen in a thick coating of soot, that the snow and the cold rains had brought down upon the old hearthstone of the hall?"

"Nothing further than that I stopped John Oxley from going to tread them out; but some kind friend of his did so for him before we could get them."

"You do not know that," said the judge.

"Oh, yes, my lord, I do."

"Not of your own knowledge; you mean, you think it. You cannot know what you cannot see."

"Oh, that's it? Well, my lord, I admit that, and a little more: One don't always know what one does see."

"That is true enough."

Roots was told they did not want him any further, so, after casting a deeply compassionate look at poor Morris Courtley, he cried out—"God bless you, Mr. Courtley!" and then left the witness-box.

There was so much frankness and noble bearing about Roots, that the mere expression of his opinion in favour of Courtley had its effect, and the popular feeling was decidedly favourable to Morris Courtley up to that point.

The next witness was the surgeon, who merely deposed to the nature of the injury received by Lord Francis, and to the fact that death must have very speedily taken place, as the consequence of such a wound as he had received.

There was now one of those ominous pauses that occur when a something of more than usual importance is about to take place; and the attorney-general said in a low tone of voice—

"Call Mr. Roachford."

With a slow step, attired in deep mourning, and with the traces of either illness or deep affliction upon his face, Mr. Roachford stepped into the witness-box.

The fact was, that Mr. Roachford had during the time pending between the committal and the trial of Morris Courtley suffered a martyrdom of anxiety. He knew and felt that it would be upon his testimony that Morris Courtley, if found guilty at all, would be convicted—he knew that without what he had to say there was no case as against the prisoner, and he knew that what he had to say was to him, Courtley, of the most awful significance.

And yet there was at the bottom of the heart of the magistrate a terrible doubt of the guilt of Courtley. He had heard and read of extraordinary circumstances, pointing, even as the circumstances he had to detail, to all the presumption of guilt, and yet being all false both in facts and in conclusions, and he dreaded to think it just possible that he was the innocent instrument of some terrible imposition, which might end in the destruction of a man who never even conceived the commission of the dreadful crime for which he was arraigned.

Oh, how devoutly the magistrate wished that some one else had found the bit of cloth in the hands of the corpse, so that he might have been left at liberty to form a more independent judgment of the fact. But it was his lot to have to say what he had come to the court that day to swear to, and, notwithstanding all the mental suffering that was visibly depicted in his face, say it he must.

A death-like stillness pervaded the court as the attorney-general himself rose to examine the magistrate.

"Mr. Roachford, you are a magistrate of the county, I believe?"

"I am, sir."

"Will you tell us what you know of this fearful piece of business?"

"It is a fearful piece of business. I reached Bloxdale some time after the body of Lord Francis had been brought in by Morris Courtley; and it was lying on a table in the hall. The servants shrunk from it with a natural fear, but I did not. There was nothing that came over me in the shape of strong feeling but pity and horror. I approached the corpse, and in the cold clenched hand I found a piece of cloth, which I took from it, and placed in my pocket."

"Have you that piece of cloth with you?"

"The sheriff has it."

The sheriff produced a small sealed packet. It had upon it the seal of Mr. Roachford as well as that of the sheriff. The packet was opened, and there appeared the little piece of torn cloth which had, for poor Morris Courtley, such a terrible significance.

"Is that the piece of cloth, Mr. Roachford?"

"It is."

"You can have no doubt about it?"

"None whatever."

"What further occurred?"

"During the examination of the prisoner a man named Walsh, came into the hall, and produced a coat that had been found near to the scene of the murder. That coat I examined, and found that the cuff of it was torn. The piece of cloth I had taken from the hand of the corpse, was evidently the piece that had been torn from the coat."

"Did the prisoner make any remark?"

"Yes. He requested to look at the coat, and then without any hesitation, declared it to be his."

"We need not trouble you further, Mr. Roachford."

The magistrate cast a look of deep compassion at Courtley; and then he glanced a the judge and the jury, and in a voice tremulous with emotion, he said—

"God help us all this day in the judgment that will be come to upon a fellow creature!"

"Amen!" said a deep, loud voice in the court.

"Call Joseph Walsh."

The servant who had found the coat in the paddock made his appearance, and distinctly swore to finding it.

Both the coat and piece of cloth were handed to the judge, and then to the jury, to examine. A couple of servants then came forward to swear that the coat belonged to Morris Courtley, for his own evidence would not be received, as he had pleaded not guilty at the trial. All this, then, went on quite smoothly and evenly; and then there was a terrible pause, after which the attorney-general said—

"That is the case."

The people looked at each other in dismay —the case was so much shorter than they had expected it to be; and yet how awfully conclusive it seemed to be! The facts seemed all to cry out, "Guilty!" while opinion and supposition only remained to whisper the bare possibility that Courtley might be innocent of what was laid to his charge.

"Are there any witnesses to be called for the defence?" said the judge.

"Yes, my lord," said the counsel for Courtley. "I have, in the first place, to put in this letter, which we found on the body of the murdered man. That letter we now place before the court. It runs thus:"

In a clear voice the counsel read the letter which the reader will not fail to recognise as that which Morris had written and asked Lord Francis to deliver to Lady Fanny.

"The Library at Bloxdale. Eleven at night.

"MY OWN FANNY,—I have made a promise to your brother, and I have made one to you, and I have made one to myself. The promise to your brother is, that, as I am not noble, I will leave Bloxdale to-night.

"The promise to you, dear one, is, that while this life remains to me, I will love you.

"The promise to myself is, that I shall yet be able to raise such means as will enable me to come back and say that I can confer reputation upon her whom I so dearly love, and who stooped from her high estate to love me when I was but the poor secretary.

"Ah, my Fanny! this is a pleasant dreamy thought. It is the principle which upholds me in the fight against the adverse circumstances that have made, for the time being, our love an affliction. Do you, too, put on that corslet of the affection, sterner than burnished steel; and do you, too, feel that in the thought that we shall meet again, you are armed against all the trammels and all the trials that the world can have in store for you.

"And, my Fan, I have a hope that you will live in calm peace until I come back again. Your brother loves you, and he will protect you. Cling to him, Fanny, as to your guardian angel. He can powerfully support you, while I can give you nothing but my prayers.

"Do not mourn my departure. It is for the best, dear, dear Fanny. But, oh, believe, present or not, I am still ever and ever,

"Your own,

"MORRIS COURTLEY."

While the letter was being read you might, to use a common simile expressive of intense stillness, have heard a pin drop in the crowded court; and at its conclusion everyone drew a long breath, and the sentiment of every heart was, "Can the man who wrote that be a murderer?"

The letter was handed to the jury.

"The handwriting of that letter," said the judge, "can be proved, I presume?"

"Yes, my lord. We purpose calling the waiting-maid of Lady Fanny Bloxdale, who will be able to swear to the handwriting, as well as to depose to the perfectly good understanding there was between the deceased Lord Francis Bloxdale and the prisoner at the bar."

There was a slight bustle near the door of the court, and then poor Ann, in mourning, appeared, and looking very ill and pale, took her place in the witness-box and was duly sworn.

She deposed, in answer to the preliminary questions, that she was the personal attendant upon Lady Fanny Bloxdale; and then, when Morris Courtley's letter was placed in her hands her eyes swam in tears as she solemnly declared that she could swear it was in the handwriting of Morris Courtley.

"Of that you have no doubt?" said the judge.

"Oh, no — no — none whatever. It is quite impossible to have a doubt upon the subject. Poor Morris! Oh, no—no—no!"

Ann burst into tears.

"What do you mean by those violent negatives?" said the judge.

"I mean, sir," said Ann, struggling with her emotions, "I mean that Morris Courtley did not, and could not do the deed with which he is charged. Lady Fanny loved her brother dearly, but yet she knows the innocence of Morris Courtley, and has charged me in the open court to tell him, and you, my lord, and you all here present, that she believes him innocent and sends to him her love and her blessing!"

This bold and altogether unexpected testimony in favour of the prisoner created an immense sensation in the court. Morris Courtley raised his arm and uttered a cry of agony, and then covering his face with his hands he leant upon the edge of the dock and wept long and bitterly.

This message of love and tenderness from Fanny had at once overcome him, and he felt then as if his heart were breaking.

It was some time before the court could proceed with the business in hand, and then it was in a voice of emotion that the counsel for the defence proceeded to question Ann.

"Do you know upon what terms the deceased Lord Francis was on with the prisoner?"

"Oh, yes, the very best."

"Did you hear of the discharge of the prisoner from his situation as secretary?"

"No, but Lady Fanny expected and feared that he, Morris Courtley, would, out of the abundance of his love and his delicate wish not to encumber her fortunes with his presence, go from Bloxdale upon the first intimation of the displeasure of Lord Francis at their intimacy.

"Then you consider the prisoner might have staid?"

"Oh, yes; and but for this cruel murder he would have staid."

"How do you mean?"

"I mean that Lord Francis loved him too well to let him go, and he must have called him back. Lord Francis always knew that his sister would be happy with Morris Courtley, but it was the pride of birth that stood in the way a little, and that was a feeling that was melting away before the affection and the reason of Lord Francis."

"Have you any proof that it was the prisoner who discharged himself and not Lord Francis who discharged him?"

"No—no, I have no proof. But Lady Fanny wrote a letter to Mr. Courtley, and she has given me leave to bring it to this court, and let it be read, as it shows what she no longer cares to conceal, namely, that she loves him, and that she thinks him worthy of that love, and that it was her opinion he would leave the mansion when he need not have done so."

"Have you that letter with you?"

"Yes, it is here, sir."

Upon this poor Morris looked up again, and when Ann handed the letter to the counsel, he kept his eyes rivetted upon it, and evidently considered it the most precious piece of paper in the world, except that which contained the few lines of consolation and love that Fanny had sent to him before the trial.

The counsel read the letter in a low voice—

"Bloxdale.   Eleven at night.

"MY MORRIS.—I can hear the rough winter's wind surging past my window, and the snow is falling thickly, yet I am up and thinking of you, and only of you, dear Morris. I have told you that I love you; why, then, should I hesitate to write it? for if you are not true to me, it is as well that you should break my heart utterly as not.

"You must not go from Bloxdale, Morris. My brother loves you well, and when he has had time to familiarize himself to the idea of your loving me, I think and hope his objection will vanish. He has my happiness, I know, most at heart.

"And now, Morris, above all, do not quarrel with Francis. I don't know why I write this, but it came to my mind at this very moment, although upon further thought I do not think it at all probable—I rather think, that what I wished to say was, do not agree with him over much.

"I mean, dear Morris, that you should not, in your quiet way, say—' Yes, my lord, you are right; I will leave Bloxdale'— because it is not at all right you should do so.

"I have been crying, Ann says, and the

eyes you were pleased to think the brightest in the world are but dim now with tears. Morris, I can write no more; but I know that you love me, and I would not barter that consoling thought for all the world;

"And so, my dear Morris, I am, as you know well,

"Your ever-constant, loving

"FANNY."

Every one who heard this letter read were deeply affected at its contents; and when it was finished, Courtley said—

"I have but one request now, and it is that I may be permitted to see that letter."

The letter was handed to him, and after pressing it to his lips, he placed it in the bosom of his apparel, and clasped both his hands over it as a priceless treasure.

CHAPTER LVI.

THE JUDGE SUMS UP THE CASE, AND THE JURY RETURN A VERDICT.

NOBODY seemed inclined to object to his retaining the letter, and as Ann had said all she could say, she was permitted to withdraw; and then, to the surprise of all in the court, the Earl of Bloxdale slowly rose, and walked from the bench to the witness-box, and was sworn.

"I have but few words to say," he said, "and they are just these, that in all matters whatever I have ever found the prisoner at the bar the very mirror of honour and generosity. During his service with me, he has given me the most unlimited satisfaction, and I give this public testimony to his high character. Whether or not he—he——"

The earl was too affected to proceed, and letting his head drop upon his breast, he suffered himself to be led back to his seat.

"That is all we have to say,' said the counsel for the defence.

The judge looked at Morris Courtley, and said—

"Now is the time, prisoner at the bar, for you to speak, if it shall seem fit for you to do so."

Courtley cast a steady glance around him and then in that soft and musical voice, which he possessed in so eminent a degree, he said—

"My lord and gentlemen, I stand here, it seems, charged with the commission of a crime my soul abhors—the crime of murder; and that murder, too, supposed to be perpetrated upon the person of one whom I loved and honoured.

"If I am guilty, there never yet appeared before an earthly tribunal so great a criminal: if I am innocent, which God in Heaven knows I am, there never yet appeared before you so injured a man.

"My feelings have been outraged, and my heart has been lacerated this day, by the introduction, in the painful inquiry, of the name of a young lady whose thoughts and feelings I would have kept sacred from the public observation; but since so much has been said, I may say more.

"To look upon Lady Fanny Bloxdale—to listen to her voice—to hear of her many virtues and to feel that she was as near an angel as possible, consistent with her human trammels, was impossible without loving her. I did love her—I do adore her. I felt, though, that the difference in our artificial condition was such as to interpose obstacles in the way of our union; and in my interviews with Lord Francis Bloxdale, I never attempted for a moment to ignore that fact.

"Lord Francis Bloxdale, who has been by some one foully murdered, was my friend—my companion—my patron—my benefactor. It would be impossible for me to convey to the court, let me use what language I may, anything like the grateful feeling that I had to him while living, or the reverence I bear for his memory now that he is no more.

"Let it suffice that he became acquainted with our mutual attachment—that is, the attachment between Lady Fanny and myself. She herself told him, and he spoke to me calmly and dispassionately about it; and, it was agreed between us that I should leave Bloxdale for a time, and see how I sped in the great world, while, at the same time, my absence would be a test for the feelings of Lady Fanny.

"All was agreed in friendship, and in mutual confidence; but if I had spoken what I might have spoken, Lord Francis would have yielded and held me to his heart as a brother. I did not think I ought so to speak, and so I was content to go.

"All that I have further to say is simple and clear. We had an appointment to meet by the park wall after midnight. We met, and I took with me the letter which has been produced in court. We parted with every expression of friendly feeling, after I had refused money from him, and then—even then, he called me back; but I lingered a little, and there was a struggle in my breast. I then heard the report of a gun, and upon turning back to the spot I found the bleeding form of Lord Francis on the snow. I called for help—I shouted murder. No one came, and I lifted the body, and carried it to the hall.

"My lord and gentlemen, I know no more than this. The coat produced in court is mine. No doubt the cuff of it was in the grasp of the dead, but I had not worn that coat for some time, and to the best of my belief it was left hanging in my chamber at Bloxdale on that night. I never was very cautious. Any one might go into my room at almost any time. God help the man who has by this frightful deception brought me into this peril, for the time will come when he will need God's mercy.

"My lord and gentlemen, I am innocent!"

Calm and tranquil as Morris Courtley was throughout this address, it had a great effect upon all hearers; and his counsel nodded with satisfaction at the conclusion of it.

All eyes were now upon the judge, who slowly arranged his notes; and then in a voice which sufficiently indicated how deeply moved he was by the doubts and fears that oppressed him, he summed up the case.

"Gentlemen of the jury—

"The prisoner at the bar stands charged with the wilful murder of Francis Bloxdale, commonly called Lord Bloxdale. It appears that the prisoner held the situation of secretary and librarian to the Earl of Bloxdale, and that he was greatly esteemed by the family, and admitted to familiar communications with them.

"The result of these familiar communications seems to be admitted on all hands to be an attachment between the prisoner at the bar and Lady Fanny Bloxdale, the daughter of the respected earl of that name, and sister of the murdered man. There is nothing, gentlemen of the jury, in evidence —there is nothing by implication in the smallest degree to cast a shadow of a stain upon the honour and fame of that young lady. Gentlemen of the jury, I say this emphatically."

A murmur of applause ran through the court; and John Oxley, who then found that the judge did not believe a word of his machinations against Fanny, felt sick and faint. Oh, how devoutly he wished that he had believed that the Bloxdale family suffered enough without the attempts he made at the trial to increase that suffering!

The grateful look that Morris Courtley gave to the judge for saying those words of Fanny was truly beautiful to see.

The judge continued—

"It appears that after the return of Lord Francis Bloxdale from the continent, the fact of the attachment between the secretary and his sister became known to him, by what means is of no consequence; and thereupon there ensued certain communications between him and the prisoner at the bar, resulting in the arrangement by which he, the prisoner, was to leave Bloxdale.

"The case for the prosecution, then, so far as motives to the commission of the crime goes, resolves itself to this: That the prisoner, finding the deceased lord so great an obstacle to his continuance at Bloxdale, and his enjoyment of the society of the sister, and his ultimate hope of making her his wife, foully murdered Lord Francis.

"After this, gentlemen, come the events of that night — events which are only mysterious as regards the simple fact of whether they lead in an undeniable manner to a supposition of the guilt of the prisoner at the bar, or do not do so.

"There seems to be no dispute about all the facts deposed to; and under such circumstances, it is for you to draw your own conclusions.

"The prisoner at the bar has an appointment to meet a man at a very unusual hour, and at a very strange place. How this appointment was brought about we have no evidence direct. It may have been the suggestion of Lord Francis himself, to get the prisoner away without any show, or it may have been that the prisoner suggested the plan, and the hour of meeting, on some pretence or another, in order to get his victim to such a spot at such a time.

"One thing is certain, that there and then the murder was committed by the prisoner or some one else. Then we have the evidence of the respected magistrate of the county, Mr. Roachford, respecting the finding the portion of the coat of the prisoner at the bar in the grasp of the murdered man. It seems as if some struggle had taken place between the victim and his murderer, and that in that struggle the coat had been torn. We are irresistibly led to that conclusion.

"It is my duty to tell you, gentlemen of the jury, that the evidence against the prisoner at the bar is circumstantial merely. No one saw him do the deed with which he stands charged; but if he did not do it, some one must have been cognisant of the appointment between him and Lord Francis Bloxdale, some one must have taken possession of his coat, some one must have passed through the hall where the gun hung, and which it is pretty clear the prisoner passed through, and so, dogging his footsteps, and fathoming his almost every thought, the real murderer, if it be not the prisoner at the bar, must have, with consummate tact, made it appear to be him.

"Gentlemen of the jury, I say again, it is for you to decide upon all the questions which will naturally arise in you minds in this truly disastrous affair. It is fitting and proper that you should place due account upon the high character which the prisoner has received from the Earl of Bloxdale this day. It is fitting that you should take into account his own bearing and appearance at this bar, and given him the advantage and the full benefit of any doubt that may arise in your minds regarding his guilt; for better is it for twenty guilty men to escape— ay, a hundred, even, than for one innocent man to perish."

The judge ceased, and then, as the jury rose to retire, the counsel for the defence said—

"I feel that it is rather irregular, my lord, but I would submit to your lordship this memorandum."

The judge took the paper presented to him, and after reading it, he said—

Heaven forbid that we should, upon any point of regularity or irregularity, omit anything which is calculated to throw a light upon a case jeopardising the life of a fellow-creature. By this memorandum it appears that a pocket-book has been found containing the sum of money that Lord Francis Bloxdale intended to give to the prisoner, and which he states he refused. It is clear, then, that the prisoner did not possess himself of that money. The pocket-book has been found behind a picture in the gallery at Bloxdale.

"A gentleman wants a glass of water," cried a voice. "Here he is."

All eyes were turned upon Oxley, who looked like a ghost, or like a ghost is popularly supposed to look, so far as complexion is concerned.

"No—no," he gasped, "I'll go!"

The crowd made way for Oxley, and he staggered out of the court and fell down in a faint at the threshold.

The judge placed his hand over his eyes and appeared lost in thought for a few minutes, and the jury whispered to each other. Then, rousing himself, he said—

"Gentlemen of the jury, you will please to consider your verdict on the case."

There was now a strange, suppressed kind of murmur in the court, and the people moved to and fro like the heaving of the sea. All eyes were fixed upon the jury, with the exception of the few who felt so deeply personally interested in the fate of Courtley, that he was the principal object of their regards.

Courtley himself looked very pale; but he did not betray any agitation. As the trial had advanced, his own feeling had been that of a man in a dream. He could hardly bring himself to believe that it could all be real.

Every now and then, though, he kept feeling in the breast of his apparel for Lady Fanny's letter; and as often as he placed his hand upon it a glow of satisfaction would light up his countenance.

The excitement now upon the countenance of Roots, the gamekeeper, imparted to it quite a glow. Lord Bloxdale, too, after trying in vain too keep up, was compelled to ask the assistance of the mayor of Southampton to help him from the court.

The bereaved father was followed by a commiserating murmur from all present. The noble manner in which he had stepped forward to say what he could say in favour of the prisoner had won him golden opinions from all sorts of men.

Suddenly, now, the foreman of the jury, with a very agitated look, turned towards the judge. The rest of the jury left off whispering, and the stillness as of death was in the court.

The clerk of the arraigns rose, and looked at the foreman, who nodded his head.

"Gentlemen of the jury, have you considered well and true your verdict?"

"We have."

"What say you, gentlemen of the jury—is the prisoner at the bar guilty or not guilty?"

The foreman shook like a man in an ague, and his voice seemed to stick in his throat for a moment. The clerk of the arraigns

bent forward, and put up his hand to his ear to listen. The answer came at last—it was but one word—

"*Guilty!*"

CHAPTER LVII.

MORRIS COURTLEY IS LEFT FOR EXECUTION, AND HIS HOURS ARE NUMBERED.

THE people in the court swayed to and fro, as if actuated by some mighty feeling, when the verdict was announced; and there was a terrible rush of many persons to carry the news to those who were without, and who were so anxiously expecting it.

Perhaps the most unmoved person in reality in all that living throng of persons was the prisoner himself, Morris Courtley, who felt that by that verdict he was, as it were, hovering between life and death.

And yet what a woeful and a terrible thing it was for him so young, and feeling himself so innocent, to die in such a fashion! What a terrible end was that to all his bright aspirations—to all his knowledge—to all the pains that he had taken to raise himself from a lowly condition to be on a level with the highest and the best through the majesty of mind!

Well might he tremble; but he did not do so outwardly. The eyes of the multitude did not see how the proud heart shook within the apparently calm and placid bosom.

It was many moments before, with a solemn "Hush!" the crowd was awed into silence now, and the eyes of all wandered for a moment from the prisoner to the judge, and then back to the prisoner again.

Twice the judge tried to speak, and the words seemed to die away upon his lips; and at last, when he did find power to give them utterance, they were faint and low.

"Prisoner at the bar, having been found guilty, have you anything to say why judgment of death should not be passed upon you?"

Courtley started at this appeal, and holding up his hand, he cried out—

"Have I anything to say? Oh, yes, much! How much ought he to have to say who is falsely and ignobly condemned?—how much ought he to have to say who is told that, with all the pomp and circumstance of law, he is to be judicially murdered?—how much ought he to have to say who stands upon the brink of that eternity to which his fellow-creatures would bring him in fearful mistake, while he feels that his soul is innocent of a stain?"

These words were uttered with an indignant emphasis that made them ring again through the court; but with them the feeling that had dictated them had passed away, and in a tone of ineffable sweetness, Morris Courtley added—

"My lord, and you, gentlemen of the jury—God forgive you, for you know not what you do—I am innocent of the crime laid to my charge—not innocent by any quibble or evasion, or by any play or emphasis of words, but broadly and truly innocent in thought, word, and deed. God forgive you, I say again, if you send me to death. It will be murder: but you know not what you do!"

He ceased, and the spectators could see that the judge trembled like a man in an ague, as he placed his hand beneath his desk, and after a moment produced a small velvet black cap, which he placed upon his head.

A shudder ran through the court.

"Morris Courtley, you have been duly convicted of the wilful murder of Lord Bloxdale. At this awful time, I do not feel that I can say anything from my own judgment regarding the verdict which has been passed against you, nor is it necessary for me so to do. My duty is, to pronounce the sentence of the law against one in your present condition."

The judge paused for a moment or two, and then in so low a voice that it was quite an effort to catch it, he added—

"The sentence of the court is, that you be taken from this place to the common jail, and that from there you be taken to the place of execution, ordinarily appointed in this county, and there hanged by the neck until dead; and may the Lord have mercy upon your soul."

"Amen!" said Courtley, solemnly.

The judge slid from his seat on the bench, and fell in a faint to the floor.

The greatest confusion prevailed in the court, in the midst of which the governor of the prison touched Courtley upon the arm.

"Are you ready, sir?"

"For what? Death?"

"Oh, no—no. To come back with me to the jail, that is all. You have time before you, sir. Monday morning, you know, is some distance off yet."

"Monday morning? Well—well, I am ready, sir."

Roots sprang forward, and grasped Courtley by the hand.

"No—no, Mr. Courtley, they can't and they shan't hang you. You didn't do it, you know you didn't, and so do I. Why, the very stones of the old town of Southampton would rise against your murder. It would be murder!"

Courtley could only press the honest hand of the gamekeeper for a moment, and then he was hurried off from the dock to the jail again.

How like a dream it all was! Morris Courtley could scarcely yet believe that it was real. That condemned cell—the diabolical evidence that had been brought forward against him—the sea of faces that had for hours met his eyes whichever way he turned—the fainting judge—the sentence—Roots—the black cap—all seemed blended together in his mind in one mass of confusion.

"No—no," he said, "it is not real—it is not real!"

"Sir—sir?"

Courtley started. Some one had entered his cell, and was addressing him. It was the chaplain of the prison.

"Did you speak to me, sir?"

"I did. Your feelings are worn and harassed—you are fresh from the court in which you have been found guilty: at this moment let me implore you to do an act of mercy."

"An act of mercy? I an act of mercy? What mean you?"

"I will explain to you. Do you pity the Earl of Bloxdale—the bereaved father?"

"From my soul I do."

"It is to him, then, that I would have you be merciful."

"Alas! sir, it may be that what you say is plain and comprehensible enough, and that my brain is too much bewildered by all that I have gone through this day to enable me to understand you; but to me you seem to speak in riddles."

"Listen."

"With all the attention and reverence in the world, I will."

"There is but one thing that could add to the agony of mind that the Earl of Bloxdale has already suffered in the death of his only son, and in the deep grief of his daughter, and that would be that this frightful domestic tragedy was consummated by your sacrifice, you being innocent. I implore you to spare him that pang, and if you be guilty, to say so now; and by so doing, to make the only faint reparation in your power for the past."

"Oh, Heaven!" cried Morris Courtley, "this is worse than all. Hear me, sir, since it seems to be necessary that I should make this declaration. By all that I hold sacred as connected with that Divinity, not to adore whom betrays a want of mind, I declare that I am innocent of the death of Lord Bloxdale. Oh, how much rather would I have died for him!"

The clergyman shrank back; and from near the door of the cell, where it had been hidden by the gloom, there emerged a tall figure wrapped in a cloak. This was the Earl of Bloxdale.

Approaching Courtley, he held out his hand, and said in a voice that was half choked by emotion—

"Morris, I believe you!"

With quite a cry of joy Morris Courtley flung himself upon the breast of the earl, who affectionately embraced him.

"You do—you do, indeed, think me innocent?"

"As Heaven judges of all hearts, I do, Morris."

"And—and—and——"

"I know what you would say. It is of Fanny you would speak?"

"Yes—oh, yes!"

"She, too, thinks you innocent. She wanted but this one last test. Oh, Morris, you could not *play* such a part as this!"

THE CAVALIER'S RETURN TO THE HUT IN THE FOREST.

"I could not, indeed. I am—indeed I am innocent."

"I feel that you are so, and this gentleman feels likewise that you are. Have hope—have much hope, Morris; there is ample time. Within one hour from now, Fanny and I post for London. It will be my duty to seek an interview with the king. Surely, when I am satisfied of your innocence, no one else ought to say a word."

"And Fanny, too?"

"Yes, and Fanny. She will go with me. I promised her that I should see you, Morris, and I am happy that I did so. As for my poor boy, he is with his God. It is we who remain behind who suffer. But you shall not be sacrificed. In my old age, Morris Courtley, you shall fill up the place of my lost Francis, and in the happiness of you and Fanny I shall be able to recover some of the serenity of resignation, if not of joy."

Morris wept bitterly.

"Oh, my dear lord," he cried—"my honoured patron—my friend! death has now, even if it should come to me, lost its sting—the grave has, indeed, lost its victory!"

"Be of good cheer, Morris. The innocent seldom, I hope, suffer in this country. It is a grievous mistake when such is the case; but, surely, you will not be an instance of such a social calamity. I will but see the judge, and then I will go to London."

"And Fanny!"

These words—"And Fanny"—were ever on the lips of poor Morris Courtley. The blissful idea that she thought him innocent, and that she intended herself to procure a recognition of that fact, was, indeed, balm to his wounded feelings. How fain he would have asked to see her; and yet, when he thought of where he was, and of what others might say if she were to visit his cell, he repressed the wish, although it cost him a pang to do so.

Nothing in the world could be so consolatory to poor Morris Courtley as this well-timed visit of the Earl of Bloxdale. It had taken place, too, just at that moment when one might expect that Courtley's mind, if it gave way at all, would do so as a consequence of the reaction that would be certain to take place after the great excitement he had gone through during the day.

But, like some gentle sedative, this kind visit soothed his excited nerves; and when the earl and the chaplain had left him, it was with a gentle, quiet smile upon his lips that he lay down to rest.

"I say, Jem," said one of the turnkeys to another, who was amusing himself by tossing a hot potato from one hand to the other to warm them, for the jail was very cold—"I say, Jem, that chap as is to be scragged on Monday takes it easy?"

"As how?'"

"Why, I'm blessed if he hasn't been and gone to sleep like a precious babby as never was."

"Ah! has he?"

"Yes, to be sure, stupid. What do you mean by amusing of yourself with a 'tater in that way? You are old enough, and ugly enough to know better."

"There's nothing like a 'tater," said the other, casting up his eyes in a philosophical manner to the ceiling—"there's nothing like a 'tater. But as regards this chap as did the scragging job, it's nothing his going off to sleep. They always does it; and atween you and me, and the—and—the 'tater here, it's rather a stale secret how that 'ere is done."

"What do you mean?"

"Why, haven't you heerd of fellows as is going to be hanged in the morning always sleeping quite comfortable over-night?"

"I has," said the other, regardless of grammar—"I has."

"Well, the doctor does. He gives 'em a what-do-you-call it in something as they takes for supper, that's it."

"You don't say so?"

"Yes, I does."

"Well, now, I didn't think o' that; but, cuss you, why don't you put down that 'tater?"

"'Cos, I'll tell you, I was in the army once, you know, Bill."

"So I hered—drive on. What has that to do with a 'tater?"

"I'll tell you. I was with General Gage in Upper Canada, and it was so precious cold there, that one day, when the parson said that if the men didn't behave better they'd go where there was never such a jolly fire, the fellers all grinned and hoped as they might soon."

"Oh, oh!—gammon!"

"It's a fact. But as I was saying about 'taters,—one day we had all—eight hundred on us, infantry—to keep in line for more than four hours, at the skirt of a wood where we expected the French and the Injins to come by, and it was so precious cold that if they had come, I'll warrant there wasn't half-a-dozen men as could have lifted their muskets to their breast."

"Lor!"

"Well, there was a sergeant-major of our regiment who was an out-and-out clever chap, and he got a few sticks, and made a fire at the end of the line, and it blazed up pretty well. We all stood at ease, mind you, just then, for the colonel, who was a stamping and walking to and fro with the major, didn't like to order us to pile arms for fear of the French and Injins a coming."

"Oh, go on. What a while you are."

"Well, as I was a saying, the sergeant-major lights a fire, but one fire wasn't no good for eight hundred men, only two deep; but he got one of the camp-kettles, that holds, a tidy lot, and then he went round to the men and asked 'em, 'Have you a potato?' Well, our chaps had a good many in their haversacks, for they used to lay hold of 'em when they could, and cook 'em when convenient."

"Werry good."

"Well, he got together about fifty 'taters—nice large round ones—regular whackers—and in he pops a lot of snow into the camp-kettle, for water there was none, and in he pops the 'taters, too. In about twenty minutes or so there was such a biling of 'taters as you never did see, and then the sergeant-major, he pokes in the end of his sword and out he takes one, and he says to the fellow on the extreme left as was next to him—

"'Take this and pass it on. Give the word to pass it down the line as quick as you can.'

"'Yes, sir,' says the fellow.

"Then the sergeant-major does the same with the rear rank man."

"Oh, lor! You don't mean it?"

"Yes I do. The 'taters were deuced hot surely, and the fellows quite danced agin when they got hold of one, and everybody was so mighty anxious to pass it on to his neighbour; but the sergeant-major kept them at it, and plied the man next him with 'taters till the whole lot was a going down the line, and there was stamping and swearing, and laughing at such a rate, till the colonel cries out—

"'Tention! What is all this about?'

"Then the serjeant-major steps up to him, and tells him, 'Sir, the men are all nice and comfortable now, if you please, sir, and it's all owing to a camp-kettle of potatoes.'

"Well, the colonel laughed, and stepping up to the line, he took one of the 'taters, and hot it was, and no mistake. 'D—n it!' says the colonel, 'here, take this, major.' 'Confound it,' says the major, cutting a caper, 'take this, captain!' and so it went all round among the officers, and the men roared and laughed, till tap, tap, tap, went the drum, and up came the French and the Injins, and didn't we walk right into 'em, and no mistake; and it was all owing to the 'taters."

"Oh, gammon—gammon!" cried the other turnkey.

"Well, you may say gammon as long as you like; but facts is facts, and no mistake, and the longer you live the more you will learn—leastways, if you ain't too stupid, which may be for all I know to the contrary."

CHAPTER LVIII.

MR. OXLEY REPAIRS TO HIS FRIENDS TO REPORT PROCEEDINGS.

WHEN the trial was over—when the innocent man was condemned to die, and when the crowd had departed to spread the news, Oxley rose to leave the court.

With trembling steps, and shrinking from every little knot of men that he saw collected in the streets, lest they should suddenly turn round and call out—"This is the real murderer, after all," he made his way to the hotel, where the worthy and accomplished Miss Wicks had taken up her abode, and where she had made up her mind to wait for him.

Oxley had, in his own mind, settled completely the fact, that Miss Wicks was to be put out of the way; but the how and the when were questions that he had not quite decided. He hoped that something would take place in the course of his interview with her to enable him to say to himself something more decisive upon these points.

If, however, Oxley had but been quite sure that Wicks knew all that she now really knew, he would probably, at almost any risk, have made short work of it; but he did not suspect that Wicks's information went quite so far.

That she not only suspected him of the murder of Lord Francis Bloxdale, but that she might be said to know that he had done that deed, was pretty clear to Oxley's mind, for there were many little circumstances only known to Wicks which he felt must conduce to such a result; but there he thought that the information of the waiting-woman stopped.

Oxley did not think that he run any risk in consequence of Wicks suspecting, almost to the verge of proof, the fact that he was the murderer of Lord Francis. He knew her unscrupulous disposition too well to think that from any love of justice or horror of the deed that he had done she would deceive him.

But if Oxley had had any notion that Wicks was aware that there was such a person as Mrs. Lerew in the world, he then would have trembled to think upon what the enraged waiting-woman might do.

As it was, he was in happy ignorance of his danger, and he slunk along the streets of Southampton towards the hotel where Wicks had gone to play the fine lady, with his mind full of all sorts of vague conjectures.

Now Wicks did know that there was such a person as Mrs. Lerew, from the fact that she had seen Oxley at the cottage, and had listened to much that had been there said; but, although Wicks had heard enough to convince her that Oxley was a welcome visitor there, and that some strange intrigue was going on, she had not heard enough to settle the fact in her mind that the woman inhabiting the cottage was Oxley's wife.

It scarcely occurred to Wicks that such could be the fact. It seemed to her that Oxley, mingling as he did with terrible crimes, would scarcely have had the folly to make himself so intimate with her, at the risk of her discovering his actual intimacy with another.

But then Wicks reasoned upon Oxley's affairs as people usually do upon the affairs of others, namely, without knowing the full particulars, and often without the most important particulars of all.

She knew of his falsification of accounts—

she knew of his hatred to Morris Courtley and his desire for revenge—she knew that he detested Lady Fanny, and would be glad to involve her in misery; but she did not know of the little plot regarding the title and estates of Bloxdale, which had been the main cause by which Oxley had been induced to so closely mix up his interests with those of Mrs. Lerew and the delightful Peter.

Thus, then, we may say that these two wicked and highly criminal people, Oxley and Wicks, met each other, knowing much of each other's crimes, but not knowing all, and they made many mistakes accordingly in the treatment of each other.

The hotel at which Wicks had put up was one rather famous for adventures, for it was one at which the noodles who go to that coast and exhibit their nationality in fancy nautical dresses and get dreadfully sea-sick in yachts put up frequently.

But Wicks intended that Oxley should pay, so she was not at all particular as to the bill she run up at the hotel.

The mode of life, and the behaviour of Wicks at the hotel, was an imitation of Lady Bloxdale during the worst and most selfish period of her existence.

Reclining upon a couch of crimson satin was Wicks, holding some long narrow bottle of essence to her nose, as though the ordinary atmosphere of the hotel was much too common for her delicate nervous organization.

When Oxley had shut the door of the gorgeous room, and glanced for a few moments about, she smiled languidly, as she said—

"Well, I have heard the news."

"Oh, have you?"

"Yes; but what are you staring at?"

"This room—it is the best, that is to say, the most expensive in the hotel."

"To be sure."

"To be sure, do you say? Is it quite prudent, do you think, to make so much display at present?"

"As far as I am concerned, as long as it is paid for, it can't matter to me."

"Oh, indeed!"

"Not in the least. I am not aware that I am in any danger. I have done no murder, you know, Oxley."

"Peace, wretch!"

"Wretch, indeed! Oh, beware, John Oxley: you are in my power. You had better be careful. I am in possession of proofs."

"Proofs of what?"

"Of your guilt. Come, John, we have often approached this subject, but never got so close to it as now. I don't see any use in disguising it any further; you know it was by your hand——"

"Oh, hush—hush! Walls, they say, have ears. But, my dear Wicks, you spoke of proofs—what—what——"

"Ah, how you would like to know that, would you not?"

"Well—I—that is——"

"But you won't."

"I do not really see, if we are to be confidential at all, why you should refuse to let me know the nature of the proofs you have."

"I intend to keep them to myself, so it is of no use your saying more about it, Oxley. What I want to know is when a certain interesting event is to take place."

"Interesting event? What do you mean?"

"Our marriage."

"Oh, yes, my dear Wicks, certainly. But it must be after the execution, you know, of Morris Courtley. Then, when the excitement has all subsided—when all is quiet, and when no prying eye is on the alert to watch our every movement, I hope to have the pleasure of calling you my own."

"Well, be it so."

"We will then go to London, my dear Wicks, and I hope that neither you nor I will ever set eyes upon Southampton again. I have no love for the place."

"Nor I," said Wicks, "for, however we may feel bold and strong, and try to outface even anything and anybody, still it is not worth while, when we can go elsewhere, to remain in places which surround us with disagreeable associations."

"How very true. Then after the ceremony of the hanging shall come the ceremony of marrying, and we shall be quite comfortable."

Oxley rose from his chair.

"What!" cried Wicks. "Are you going?"

"Why, a—yes—I have several things to do. I have to circulate a report that Courtley has fully confessed his crime and the justness of his sentence. I hope to get it into print that he begs pardon of the respectable Mr. Oxley for his treatment of him while at Bloxdale; but that will not be difficult."

"When do you return?"

"As soon as I possibly can, my dear Wicks; and you ought to think that it would be just as well that we should not be seen too much together in so public a place as a hotel."

"Oh, that is of no consequence. I have told the landlord that you are my husband. I thought it better to do so to avoid scandal. They call me Mrs. Oxley here."

"Mrs. Oxley?"

"Yes, and why not? You know I shall be so soon."

"Oh, yes—yes! Of course you will. Only I think—well, well, it don't matter; I will return to you as soon as I possibly can; and, in the meantime, I hope you will make yourself quite comfortable, Mrs. Oxley. Ha! ha! Good-by—good-by! I am not quite sure that I shall return to-night, but if I can I will, Mrs.—Oxley!"

Despite the great effort he made to appear quite cheerful and pleasant, Oxley could not help speaking in a terribly gloomy tone of voice to Wicks; and as he descended the stairs of the hotel, he uttered some terrible imprecations, with which her name was associated.

It was just dark by the time Oxley left the hotel, and he left it with the determination in his mind of taking the life of Wicks, and with the settled fact in his mind that all he had now to think of was the best way of doing the deed so as to avoid any evil consequences to himself by it.

While Oxley walks slowly across the platform at Southampton, and is making his way towards the Itchen ferry, we will glance at what Miss Wicks is about.

No sooner was she satisfied that he was really descending the staircase of the hotel, than she ran into an adjoining room, and with great speed, and really wonderful dexterity, put on an old grey cloak and bonnet, and then with her hands hidden in a muff of capacious dimensions, she left her room, and ran down the stairs, and through the hall of the hotel in a moment.

She had an idea of what direction Oxley was going to take. That cottage on the Bloxdale property where she had before watched him was, without doubt, his place of destination now; so Wicks at once cast her eyes to the left, and just saw him as he was creeping along the platform.

Once having her game in sight, Wicks found no difficulty at all in keeping it so. With great tact she stooped, so that she shortened a good six inches of her height, and so different did that make her whole figure and appearance, that it is probable, in the dim light of that winter's evening, she might have passed quite close to Oxley without being discovered by him.

In this way, then, she dogged the footsteps of the guilty man to the ferry, and she went over it in the same boat with him. Then keeping at a cautious distance, she followed him to the cottage where Mrs. Lerew had her head-quarters.

Wicks was quite resolved, if possible, to find out, upon this occasion, the precise nature and extent of Oxley's intimacy at this cottage; but yet, in all her thoughts upon the subject, the only one which was the real truth, namely, that he was actually married to Mrs. Lerew, never came across her mind at all.

Perhaps that was too virtuous and proper a proceeding for Wicks to think of. Intrigue was her passion, and the idea of a man visiting his wife was one of the things that her lively imagination was not in the habit of suggesting.

Oxley paused at the great gate for a few moments, and glanced around him, and then hastily opened it, and walked towards the cottage.

———

CHAPTER LIX.

MISS WICKS FINDS OUT THAT LISTENERS HEAR NO GOOD OF THEMSELVES.

MISS WICKS had taken especial care to keep out of sight of John Oxley as they neared the cottage.

She had two reasons for doing so.

In the first place, every step that Oxley took in that precise direction tended to convince her that that little building was his destination, as she had in the first instance guessed; and, therefore, it was not by any means so necessary for her to keep close upon his heels.

In the second place, she knew that as he approached his destination his caution would be greater, and that he would naturally look about him all the more carefully to see that no eyes were upon him; so she took good care that when he did so look about him he should not see her.

This Wicks knew a thing or two, certainly.

Hidden among some old trees, the thick trunks of which afforded her a good shelter, although there was no foliage to cast an extraordinary shadow over the spot, Wicks remained till Oxley had fairly entered the cottage, and then she emerged.

The former visit of Wicks to that spot, upon the occasion when Oxley had favoured her by the discharge of a gun in the direction she had seemed to be in, had made her sufficiently acquainted with the spot to seek it without much difficulty.

Opening the gate, as Oxley had done, Miss Wicks walked over the little flower-beds instead of the gravel-walk, because she conceived that the latter might, by the sound her feet would make upon it, betray her, while the former would not. She made her way by the back of the cottage to the same window at which she had before stationed herself.

It would not have been a very easy thing for Miss Wicks, or for any one, in fact, to overhear from the window at which she was situated what might transpire in the cottage, if the listener had not had such abundant reasons as Wicks thought she had for wishing to come at the truth with regard to the connection between John Oxley and the inhabitants of that little residence.

Sharpened, then, as the senses of Miss Wicks were by rage and by jealousy, she listened intently; and in a short time she managed to catch the sound of voices, but they were too indistinct for her to hear well. Disdaining the danger that might occur from such a proceeding, she fairly climbed in at the window.

The room in which Wicks now found herself was small, and in some portions of it very much choked up by all sorts of lumber, so that if occasion had arisen for such a course, there is very little doubt but that Miss Wicks would have found some mode of hiding herself in the place from even the scrutinising eye of John Oxley.

Soon, though, all her attention and all her thoughts were engrossed in what she heard from the room adjoining the one that she was in.

The voice of John Oxley speaking with great apparent bitterness of spirit to some one, struck upon her ears.

"It is truly provoking," he said, "that Peter, for whom we are doing really so much, should take upon himself to be at all disagreeable about the means by which it is done. It is quite inexplicable to me, Mrs. Lerew, what he can be thinking about."

"I will trouble you, John," said the lady, "whatever may be your opinion of Peter, to call me by my right name. I am your wife, John Oxley, as well you know."

Wicks very nearly screamed; but what she most wanted to hear, was Oxley's reply to this little assertion.

"So you are, Maria," he said—"so you are; but you know as well as I do that prudence dictates that the fact of our union should be kept a secret; and if I get into the habit of calling you Mrs. Oxley, I don't know but I may do so at some stray moment when it might prove very injurious, indeed, to our plans."

Wicks held her breath very tightly.

"You have always some specious reason or another for what you say you must do," said Mrs. Lerew, "and what you say you must not."

"My dear, I have a good reason. I am very much afraid, do you know, that the old hag of a waiting maid that belonged to the late Countess of Bloxdale suspects something of the truth regarding Lord Francis's death, and the only thing that keeps her quiet, I do believe, is the hope of inducing me to marry her."

"Where is she?"

"At Southampton; but, between you and me, it would be prudent to send her on a journey from which she is not likely to come back again. You understand me?"

"I think I may take upon myself to say that I do. If you decide upon such a course of action, it will show some sincerity upon your part; for I tell you, I shall not be at peace till you have got rid of that woman."

"You may be so," said Oxley, in a tone of muttered deep purpose, "for as soon as to-morrow's sun will rise, I will have her life."

"That is quite satisfactory," said Mrs. Lerew. "When you look in that sort of way, John Oxley, I am quite content to believe that you will have some one's life."

"It will be hers. I tell you, Maria, that we have both of us more to fear from the evil passions and the disappointed ambition of that cursed woman than from anything else besides."

"Indeed?"

"It is so. My own belief is"—here Oxley decreased his voice to a whisper—"my own belief is, that on the night of the death of Lord Francis——"

"The murder, you mean."

"Well—well, what need you and I cavil about a word, so long as we understand each other?"

"Not at all, John Oxley. Only let me warn you, that if you once begin to be afraid of a word that you will soon get into a very uncomfortable condition of mind. I should not have said murder, if it had not at the moment struck me that you were afraid to say it."

"Let it pass, then. What was I about to tell you?"

"Something about this hideous woman, Wick's conduct on the night of the murder."

"Ah—ah! true. Well, then, my candid opinion is, that during the whole of that night she had her eyes upon me."

"Watched you?"

"Yes, I think she did."

"Then, your life is in her hands."

"In a manner of speaking, it is."

"Oh, Oxley, is this like you? Why did you let that woman live another day after you had such a suspicion? But why do I call it a suspicion merely! I suppose, in truth, it amounts to more than that?"

"It does."

"Kill her, Oxley—kill her!"

"Hush! don't speak so loud. I did hope that we had had enough killing. There will be a killing on Monday morning, and that will be the worst of all."

"You really and truly think that they will hang the secretary?"

"I do."

"Well, you were at the trial, and you ought to be a good judge. I suppose it is better for us, and for our plans that he should die; but though he is going, do not have any pity upon the woman, Wicks."

"Pity? I hate her."

"So do I. She dies, then?"

"My life upon it, she don't live another week."

"I am satisfied, John, with that assurance. And now about Peter: do you know, I am really very much afraid that Peter begins to have some suspicions——"

"Of what?"

"That all is not what he calls right. How strange it is that he should feel and know what is right and what is wrong, and do one wrong thing and not another! If he did but fancy for a moment that Lord Francis Bloxdale had come by his death by your hands——"

"Hush—oh, hush!"

"There is no one near."

"But, my dear Maria, you cannot be too cautious. I would not whisper such a fearful secret to the winds."

"You are too much afraid; but, however, caution can hardly in that way be carried too far; but I was going to say, that if Peter was but sure of what I am inclined to think he suspects, I feel pretty clear that he would desert us."

"What! and desert all the chances of his position—all the hopes of being the Lord of Bloxdale? Surely he would not do that?"

"He would."

"This is the most perplexing thought of all. Oh Maria, you must try your best to manage Peter. The suit concerning his claim to the Bloxdale estates, as heir to the present earl, must be carried out. It is the gem for which we have risked much, and we must win it."

"So say I. The whole affair is pretty well arranged; I don't think there will be any difficulty in getting the necessary evidence, and it will then be of such a character that the earl will not be able to fight up against it. In all likelihood, he will die of shame and vexation, and then all will be ours."

"And Lady Fanny is a pauper—ha! ha! How I do hate that girl, to be sure!"

"So do I, of course; I hate all of her kind," said Mrs. Lerew, with an air of intense bitterness.

"Well, well," said Oxley, "let us have some supper, and a bottle of the old Madeira, and another of champagne. I do not by any means take a gloomy view of the affair; but it will not be advisable to make the least movement, now, till after Monday. In fact, I think that the very best thing I can possibly do, is to keep myself quiet, and all but concealed."

"It is so. Why not stay here till you are certain the execution is over? and then you will find that your mind is free to act against Wicks."

"Be it so."

There was a slight bustle now in the room, and Wicks, to whose greedy ears every syllable of the foregoing dialogue had come, did not think it worth her while to stay longer, for if they were to go on conversing for the remainder of the night, she did not believe that they could by any possibility say more to the purpose than they had.

With noiseless steps she left the cottage, and again took her way along the little garden in silence.

The soft snow on the flower-beds made no perceptible sound under her feet, and Wicks scarcely dared to breathe till she got to the open roadway off the domain of Bloxdale, and at some distance from the little cottage.

Then it was that, with a fearful howl of rage, she raised her clenched hand and shook it in the direction of the cottage, exclaiming—

"Murder me, will you?—murder me! Ha! ha! Oh, but we will see about that— we will see about that! I, too, will wait till Monday has come and gone, and then we will see about that—wretch, beast, monster that you are!"

"Hilloa!" said a voice, "what's the matter, my good woman?"

Wicks started as though she had been shot, and turning hastily she saw, by the dim night light, what in London we should call a gent, smoking a cigar, and wrapped very comfortably up in a capacious great coat.

"What's the matter, eh?" said the gent. "You seem to be put out of your way, old lady!"

There was nothing in this address, finishing as it did with the words "old lady," that was very flattering to Wicks; but an idea took possession of her regarding this individual which she hastened to carry out.

"Your name is Peter?" she said.

"Eh? Well, so it is. How came you to know that?"

This was, indeed, Peter Lerew. It was but a guess upon the part of Wicks that it was he, but his answer put that all to rights.

"Oh, I know you, sir," she said.

"Do you? Well, you have the advantage of me."

"Yes, sir; I have been waiting for you. There is a young lady in Southampton, aged seventeen, rich and lovely, and she has seen you and fallen in love with you."

"Dem it, you don't say so?"

"Well, I don't see that there is anything very extraordinary in it."

"Why, a—a—nor do I—for I rather think I am what they call the cheese, and all that sort of thing. When I do come out strong, I do the thing slap up and no mistake. If you saw the waistcoats that I have, you would say they were stunners, rather, old gal."

"No doubt of it; and there is one thing that I am very glad of, and that is, to find, for the young lady's sake, that you are a gentleman of so much sense and ability."

"Oh, thank you; pretty well for that, as the world goes, I daresay. I don't set up for a Solomon."

"I think you would do well not to do so."

"No, I don't intend But, I say, now about this gal. Where is she? It isn't a sell, is it?"

"Far from it. If you will come to the Royal Hotel on Monday evening, and ask for M. W. you will see her."

"Monday evening—M. W.? Well, I'll come. There can't be much harm in going to the Royal Hotel, Southampton. I'll come, old lady, and here's half a guinea for your trouble."

"No, I don't want it. The young lady will freely give me a hundred times the amount for the intelligence I bring her that I have met with you; so now good night. Make it eight o'clock when you come."

With these words, Miss Wicks gathered her cloak more closely about her, and darted off in the darkness towards the Itchen ferry.

"Monday evening at eight," said Mr. Peter Lerew to himself. "Upon my life, this is something like; only seventeen, too! Well, whoever she is, she is resolved to begin in good time. But she has seen me, and that has done it. Oh, Peter, Peter, you always were a devil among the girls. Now there is that little enchantress that I used to meet in Piccadilly; I daresay she is breaking her heart about me; but I cannot help it—I really cannot help it. What am I to do if they will run after me, the dear, soft, nice, delightful creatures? Ha! ha! 'Pon soul I cannot help it."

With this comfortable assurance, Peter made his way to the maternal residence, little dreaming that Wicks was making him a tool for the accomplishment of her vengeance against Mrs. Lerew and John Oxley.

"Morris Courtley may be hanged," said Wicks, to herself, as she crossed the ferry at the Itchen. "Morris Courtley may be hanged and welcome. I hate him, and I hate Lady Fanny; so let him die. Then for Oxley. I will see Mrs. Lerew, and I will see Peter. They will both aid me—not from a wish to aid me, but from motives of revenge against Oxley; and from some secure retreat I shall learn, and enjoy the confusion of them all. This woman, Lerew, shall, and will be the accomplice of Oxley. They will hang her with him—ha! ha!—they will hang her with him."

Wicks made her way back to the hotel, and passed such a night of dreams as made her in the morning look a perfect hag; but still she was steadfast to her purpose of revenging herself upon John Oxley, whom she now considered in no other light than as an enemy who must be destroyed at any sacrifice.

"He shall die! He shall die!" Wicks kept continually muttering to herself. "Let Courtley die, for I hate him, but that shall make no difference in the fate of Oxley."

Little did John Oxley, when he congratulated himself upon affairs going on pretty steadily, think what was passing in the mind of Wicks.

CHAPTER LX.

THE EARL OF BLOXDALE IS UNSUCCESSFUL
IN PLEADING COURTLEY'S CAUSE.

LET us now take a glance at the proceedings of the Earl of Bloxdale, who went upon a mission to London in favour of poor Morris Courtley.

Before starting upon that mission he had applied to the judge, in order to get from him a letter to the effect that he considered the judgment against the prisoner might be respited without hindrance to the due course of justice.

The answer of the judge was to the following effect:—

"With every possible feeling of respect for your lordship, and deep sympathy with the sufferings of yourself and family, I regret that I can do no more than I have done. I have made an official report to the Secretary of State, in which I set forth the fact that the prisoner, Morris Courtley, has been convicted upon purely circumstantial evidence alone; but I cannot stultify my judgment sufficiently to say that I have any very genuine doubts of his guilt."

After this, it was out of the question to expect any help from the judge, and the chance of saving Morris Courtley from the fearful death that hung over him decreased by one half at the least.

The hopes of the Earl of Bloxdale just resolved themselves to this: That he, being the father to the murdered man, and having had such ample and numerous opportunities of witnessing the character of Courtley, might reasonably be expected to come to a clearer and more correct opinion regarding the probabilities of his guilt or innocence than any one else; while if is mind were to be swayed in either direction by any other consideration, it would more likely be to the detriment of the supposed murderer of his son than in his favour.

Then, again, the personal character of the Earl of Bloxdale, it was well known, stood very high with the king, in consequence of the earl having been many years before a warm advocate for some matters in the Upper House of Parliament which it was well known the king favoured.

For this reason the earl thought that his simple request to spare the life of a convicted man ought to do it.

We shall see how very much mistaken he was in any supposition that was founded upon the gratitude or the humanity of George the Third.

The journey from Southampton to London, with the resources of the earl to make it quick, was, notwithstanding the inclemency of the weather, performed in eight hours; and, on the morning of Saturday, at about twelve o'clock, the Earl of Bloxdale drove to St. James's Palace, where the royal family were passing the cold, dreary months of winter.

A nobleman of the rank of the Earl of Bloxdale may, according to the constitution of this country, demand an audience of the king; but, of course, there was no necessity to do other than ask it in his case, for the king was readily enough available to those who might serve him, and concerning whose position in life there could be no doubt.

The Earl of Bloxdale was told that the king would see him, and was shown into one of the antique, but yet magnificent old rooms of St. James's.

It was a strange position that the earl was in to be the advocate of the supposed murderer of his son; and it could not but strike him forcibly, as he there waited for the king, that his motives might be greatly misconstrued, and even his judgment largely misrepresented in consequence.

But the earl had thoroughly convinced himself of the innocence of Morris Courtley, and the impression had been for some days stealing over him that the real murderer was to be looked for in his household yet. The figure of John Oxley had always risen before the eyes of the bereaved father when he asked himself in the agony of his

THE EARL OF BLOXDALE'S APPLICATION TO THE COURT OF ST. JAMES'S.

heart—"Who is it that has taken my son from me?"

In the course of a quarter of an hour the king was ushered in.

"Ah, Bloxdale." he said. "How are you—very well? Glad to hear it. Come and see the queen—eh—eh? The queen recol-lects you quite well, come along and see her."

"If your majesty would pardon me for arranging first the business that brings me to London, and which, next to my duty to your majesty, is the uppermost thought in my head at this moment."

"Business—eh? What is it? Business

Dear me! pleasure first, don't the proverb say, and business afterwards?—no bless me, business first—no, pleasure—which is it? I know it is one or the other. Go on, my lord."

"I have a great boon to ask of your majesty."

"A what— a great what?"

"The life of a fellow-creature."

"God bless me, my Lord Bloxdale! what do you mean? I don't at all comprehend you—your family quite well, eh?—yes; glad to hear it."

"My son, Francis, is murdered. He who was accused of the crime is condemned to die. I think him innocent; and I come to you with the hope that you will exercise your royal prerogative, and pardon him."

"Murdered—your son? And you want to pardon the fellow that did it?"

"No, your majesty, I think he did not do it."

"Eh? Let me think. Dear me, Landerdale was saying something to me about a man at Southampton. Hilloa! Lindsay!—Lindsay!"

One of the pages appeared.

"Send for Landerdale. We will hear what he has to say. And you don't think, after all, that your son did murder the man, Bloxdale, eh?"

"It was my son that was murdered, your majesty."

"Well, I said so. That is no reason why you should be hanged for it. Come and see the queen—eh, eh?"

"If your majesty would condescend to settle this matter first, I should esteem myself much your majesty's debtor."

"To be sure. Business first—no pleasure —no, that ain't it. I know it's one or the other, though."

There must have been good speed made in summoning Lord Landerdale, the then secretary of state, from his residence in Spring Gardens, for in an incredibly short space of time that nobleman was announced, and made his bow to the king, and to the Earl of Bloxdale.

"Well, Landerdale," said the king, "here is my friend, Bloxdale, here, come to get somebody hanged."

"Somebody hanged, your majesty?"

"Pardon me," said the earl, "I have come to beg the exercise of his majesty's royal prerogative of mercy in favour of one Morris Courtley, who now lies under sentence of death at Southampton; and who, if the execution be not staid, will suffer on Monday."

"You, my lord?" said the secretary of state—"you come to plead for the—the—murderer of your son?"

"Gracious Heaven, no; but from my soul I believe him to be innocent."

"There," said the king, "you hear him. That's what he says. Have you a report of the case, Landerdale?"

"I have, your majesty. It is here. I am very sorry to say that I do not see the slightest ground for sharing with the Earl of Bloxdale his belief in the innocence of the convict."

"That is the death-warrant of Morris Courtley," said the earl; "I trust, as a personal favour to me, his majesty will pardon him."

"There were three men hanged last Monday for stealing a sheep," said Lord Landerdale.

The king shook his head, and in a low tone said—

"I cannot hold human life cheaper than mutton—Eh? eh? I am very—very sorry; but I can't, indeed."

"Hear me yet a moment, your majesty," said the earl. "I have known this Morris Courtley since he was a boy—I have well watched his career—we all know him well at Bloxdale—he loved my son dearly. As I hope for mercy in Heaven, I believe him innocent!"

The king looked at Lord Landerdale, who only kept his lips very firmly closed; and then shaking his head, the king turned to the earl, saying—

"I am very sorry; but I dare not. Don't ask me again."

The earl bowed, and sighed deeply; and then, as he sank lower and lower, he at length reached the floor, and swooned away.

The king was terribly alarmed, and shouted for the pages, who quickly made their appearance; but Lord Landerdale begged his majesty to leave the earl to him, and he took the unhappy father with him in his carriage, and had him placed in bed.

Some of the first physicians in London were sent for, and all they prescribed was what the earl could not get—serenity and rest.

"No, no," he said, "I must go back! My child—my poor child!"

The Earl of Landerdale thought that he alluded to the murdered Lord Francis; but it was Lady Fanny, with her white, sad, tearful face, that was uppermost in the mind of the Earl of Bloxdale.

Contrary to the injunctions of the physicians, and the friendly advice of the secretary of state, the unhappy nobleman entered his travelling carriage again at four o'clock on Saturday afternoon, and posted to Southampton, having completely failed in his mission to London.

"Poor Bloxdale!" said the secretary of state, when he had gone. "It was said that he had got quite well of that mortal blight which had come over him; but I see that such is not the case, or he could never have come to London to plead for the life of the man who has been clearly convicted of the murder of his son."

It was midnight on Saturday when the Earl of Bloxdale's travelling carriage dashed into Southampton. The snow was falling in a drifting cloud, and the wind was howling around the prison of the innocent, but doomed Morris Courtley.

CHAPTER LXI.

**REFERS THE READER TO A PREVIOUS PART
OF THIS MOST VERACIOUS HISTORY.**

WHILE the Earl of Bloxdale is pacing his library to and fro in a state of mind of the most miserable character—while Lady Fanny is lying upon a couch in her chamber in a deep swoon—and while John Oxley is turning hot and cold by turns, as he calculates or miscalculates the chances of his position, we must refer the reader to the first portion of this story, in which will be found detailed the execution of Morris Courtley.

It would be by far too harassing to the feelings of the reader if we were to attempt to relate the interview between the Earl of Bloxdale and Fanny, at which the aged and bereaved father had found it necessary to tell her that there was no hope for Courtley.

Suffice it to say that the result of that communication to the fair and gentle girl was to throw her into a kind of stupor, from which it was much feared she would not emerge with her mind intact.

But, perhaps, after all, it was a mercy that she was in such a state; for what if she had been up and stirring, and counting the hours, and then the minutes, and then the very seconds that separated Morris Courtley from eternity? What if she had been able to tell herself with shrieking agony—"Now they seize him—now they strangle him!"

Yes, that swoon was surely a great mercy, for it saved poor Fanny a world of agony.

* * * * *

Those who will turn back to that opening portion of this sad domestic story, in which Morris Courtley's sufferings at the place of execution are detailed, will, by perusing that part of the narrative, find that after the frightful judicial murder upon Southampton Common the body was hung in chains.

They will find, too, that the faithful Roots, whose faith in the innocence of Morris Courtley had never for a moment wavered, came in the night and took down the body, accompanied by his friends, and that he took it in a boat, with some peril, across the Southampton Water.

We left Roots and two of the hardy smugglers he had with him at the verge of the New Forest, carrying the body of poor Courtley swiftly and silently into the depths of the wood, amid the snow and the roaring wind of that terrible night.

And now let us plunge far into the depths of the New Forest—let us reach that little cottage home in which the younger days of poor Morris Courtley were spent; and if the picture be not almost too painful a one, let us look at what is going on beneath that roof.

A couple of candles are burning upon a table in the front room of the cottage—a wretched fire of half charred wood is upon the hearth, and in one corner the bed is made and over it all is laid a sheet.

In the middle of the place is a mass of something, all in black, lying huddled up in such a way that it is difficult to say precisely that it is a human being, and yet it is. That is the mother of the victim—that is poor, heart-broken Mrs. Courtley, waiting for the body of her darling son. Roots has whispered to her that he would bring it, and there she waits for it. Oh, horrible thought! She asks herself repeatedly if she is going mad.

In the chamber above is the sister of Morris. The hand of sickness is upon her, and she seems to be hastening to meet her brother in a better world; but she does not know what preparations the mother has made below, or it would kill her. She does not suspect the visitor that is coming. Mrs. Courtley felt that it would be too dreadful a thing to tell her.

Poor Ned, the young brother who so idolised Morris—who looked up to him as to the perfection he himself might hope to reach in the course of time, is with Roots and the party who have gone to the common to get the body.

Nothing but force would have kept Ned from partaking in what he considered that duty; and yet it had nearly killed him, for the cold and the intense excitement of the scene had prostrated him for a time.

Sob after sob came from the breast of the mother, as she knelt upon the floor of her hut. She tried to pray, but she could not. There was a something at her heart which seemed to choke up the avenue of prayer; and in the wild restlessness of her spirit, when she tried to utter words of submission, and of reliance in God's mercy, she found herself arraigning that mercy and that justice for allowing her Morris to be murdered.

Tap—tap—tap! came a slight sound upon the floor above, and Mrs. Courtley slowly struggled to her feet. She knew that her sick child was calling to her.

With trembling steps the mother made her way to the foot of the little stairs leading to the room above.

"Mother! Oh, mother!" cried the sick girl. "Come to me!"

"Yes, darling! I come—I come!"

Mrs. Courtley did her best to get rid of the appearance of weeping that she wore, and she then crept gently up the staircase.

"What is it, dear? I thought you tapt?"

"Yes, mother, I did; but I have seen brother Morris!"

"Oh, God!"

"Why do you tremble, mother? Indeed, you should not, for you know that brother Morris loves us all so dearly. I thought I saw him, or could it have only been a dream?"

"A dream—a dream!" said Mrs. Courtley.

"Perhaps it was; but I thought that he came to the side of the bed, and with such a sweet smile upon his face that it warmed me like sunshine to look at it, he said—'Dear sister, we shall all be so happy, for this is only a cloud that is passing away;' and then I tried to speak to him, and when

I uttered a sound he seemed to float away—away—oh, so far, and I could not see him."

Mrs. Courtley made a great effort to control her tears, as she took a cup from the table in which was some drink for the sick girl.

"Drink," she said, "you are feverish and restless, my dear. Drink of this, and then try to sleep again."

"I will—I will. Kiss me, mother, and take away the light. It seems to me that Morris is more likely to come to me again if all is dark. I will shut my eyes and try to see him."

The mother could not answer, but she kissed the young creature on the cheek, and then, looking more like a ghost than a living being, she tottered down the stairs, and once again she sunk upon the floor, and sobbed, and tried to pray.

The latch of the cottage-door stirred, and Ned Courtley, as he was familiarly called by all who knew him, staggered into the little dwelling.

"Mother—mother! it—is—coming!"

Mrs. Courtley suppressed a shriek, and sprang to her feet, clasping Ned wildly by the arm.

"No—no! they did not—they could not kill my son!" she said. "He was so brave, so good, and so beautiful! Oh, God, no!"

Ned staggered back, and dropped upon his knees close to the door through which, as it swung wide open, the cold blast came blowing with gusty violence. He held up his clasped hands, and his very lips were white with his soul's agony.

The mother clutched by the table for support, and in a whisper she muttered—

"Now—oh, God, now have mercy—now grant me only a little strength. Oh, God! Oh, God!"

The snow drifted in at the open door, and was scattered along the floor—the flame of the candle waved to and fro in the blast, and the corner of the sheet that lay upon the bed flapped like a living thing as it was stirred by the wind.

Something huge and dusky appears upon the threshold. A voice says—

"You go first! Now turn!"

"God! Oh, God!" wailed the mother.

Another moment, and through the open doorway comes Roots, bearing the head and shoulders of the body of Morris Courtley. The two seamen follow him carefully.

"On to the bed," said Roots.

The rough weather-beaten men did not speak, but they laid their burden on the sheet; and then Roots lifted that portion of it that hung over the side of the bed, and flung it over the face of the corpse.

Mrs. Courtley could sustain herself and her feelings no longer. With a shriek she rushed forward, and clasped the body in her arms.

"My son! my Morris! my joy! Oh, God, my life's hope—my boy—my boy!"

The perspiration stood in drops upon the brow of Roots, and he breathed hard through his clenched teeth. He nodded to the two men, and they left the hut and closed the door.

Ned still knelt close to the entrance, trembling and clasping his hands together; and then, gliding down the stairs like a spirit came the sick girl, and stood before Roots.

"What is it—oh, who was that that screamed? Speak! What is it?"

"Go it," said Roots—"go it all on you, and drive a fellow clean mad—go it. I know'd you would—I know'd you would!"

He sunk into a seat; and there, for once in his life, sat Roots completely overcome, and sobbing like a child.

"Mother—mother!" said the sick girl—"oh, mother, speak to me! What is that upon the bed?—why don't it move? Let me look—let me look!"

"No—no, sister," shrieked Ned, as he rushed across the floor, still on his knees, and caught her round the feet—"no, no—oh, don't!

"Yes—yes: I must—I must. What is it?—who is it?"

Mrs. Courtley fell off the bed on to the floor as if dead; and as she did so she dragged the sheet off the face of the corpse.

"Morris—Morris!" shrieked the sister. "My brother Morris! Dead, dead! Oh, Morris!"

"Go it," said Roots; "that's the way to do it—go it. I know'd you would—I know'd it! I'm a ass; but I know'd you'd all drive a fellow mad."

The door of the cottage was abruptly opened, and a tall figure appeared on the threshold, holding a horse by the bridle.

"Can any one here direct me to Lyndhurst? It lies somewhere hereabouts on the borders of the forest, I think."

The horse neighed and stamped upon the ground, and shook the snow from his mane.

Roots rose and went to the door. Without a word he pointed to the right, amid the darkness.

"Is that the way?" said the stranger.

Roots nodded.

"Why, my good fellow, what is the matter with you? Can't you speak? Ain't your name Roots? Why, what's this?"

In choking sounds Roots managed to say—

"Nothing—nothing. I don't know you, sir. Go—go."

"Not know me? Don't you remember getting a couple of slugs in your shoulder about four years ago, and coming to me to take them out?"

Roots made a dash at the table, and then brought one of the lights, and held it up to the stranger's face. It was but for a moment that he saw his face, for then the wind blew out the flame; but that moment was sufficient.

"You are Doctor Pierce, sir?" he said.

"Yes, my good fellow, I am, and I have lost my way in the forest. The snow has covered up all the usual tracks, and I don't know how I shall get home to Lyndhurst."

Roots stepped outside the hut, and, to the surprise of the doctor, took his horse from him, and then he called—

"Ned! Ned! Up, boy, up!"

Ned crawled out to Roots.

"Put the horse in the old barn, Ned. It will be something for you to do, boy. Litter him down a bed. Now, doctor, come in here—come; you have a heart, I know. There, now, I have shut the door, and you can see about you—Oh, do something for these poor creatures! Look, doctor, that lying on the floor is the poor mother—that on the chair there, looking as if she had been half way to Heaven and come back again, is the sick sister—a kind, good girl, bless her; and—and upon the bed here—Look! look! there is poor Morris! You can't help him now; but you may put a little life into the others, and you may say a kind word or two to them. Will you, doctor?"

"What is the meaning of all this? Whose body is that, and who are these people?"

"That," said Roots, as he dashed his hands over his eyes, and pointed to Morris Courtley's remains—"that, doctor, is the body of one of the best and bravest, and most innocent of God's creatures; but they have done for him, for all that. It is Morris Courtley."

"Morris Courtley, who was hanged this morning?"

"Yes, yes, that's him! My friend, Morris. Well, it's done now—it's done; only look at him, doctor; and that's his poor old mother, and that's his sister—and that's his little brother that has your horse, and here's a great stupid Roots, that could not help him, though they murdered him before my face; and now you know all about it."

"I do, indeed. God help them all! Roots, I am glad I lost my way in the wood."

"So am I."

"That's right, Roots. Make up the fire."

"I will."

"Light that other candle."

"Done, doctor. There's a bed-room up stairs where the girl sleeps; but she heard her mother shrieking over the corpse, and so down she came."

"Very good. Light me, Roots."

"I will."

The surgeon carried the sick girl tenderly up stairs, and placed her in bed. He then came down, and lifting Mrs. Courtley in his arms, he likewise carried her up and placed her by the side of her daughter.

"The mother has fainted," he said; "but we will soon get her to rights. Some water, Roots."

It was quite a sight to see how Roots promptly did whatever he was told by the surgeon, so that in a little time Mrs. Courtley was herself again, and by the advice of the surgeon she remained with her daughter.

They were mingling their tears together when Doctor Pierce and Roots went down stairs again, and there they found Ned, kneeling by the corpse of his brother Morris—his idolised Morris!

"He knows me yet," said Ned, quite innocently. "I have called to him, and he knows me yet, does my brother Morris."

"Knows you?" said Roots. "What do you mean, boy?"

"I kissed him on the cheek, and then as the light fell upon his eyes, they gave a kind of flutter, and so, you see, I knew that he was aware that his brother Ned was with him."

Roots staggered back to the wall of the cottage, and there stood like a statue. The surgeon, with a quick, noiseless step, reached the side of the bed, and laid his ears flat upon the heart of the corpse. There was an awful silence for a moment or two, and then Doctor Pierce said in a strange voice, as he shook from head to foot for a moment—

"Get some hot water, Roots, as soon as you can, and bar the cottage door."

CHAPTER LXII.

A FORTUNATE ARRIVAL AT THE COTTAGE IN THE FOREST.

ROOTS opened his mouth thrice before he could utter a word, and then it was with a suppressed shriek that he said—

"Doc—doc—doctor! you don't mean to say—no, no, you wouldn't deceive a fellow; you don't—oh, sir, you don't mean to say that—that the blessed life is not—not quite gone?"

"He lives!"

Ned clapped his hands, and would have made a rush to the staircase, and yelled out the news, but Roots stopped him by clapping his hand over his mouth, and saying—

"Peace, Ned. You young villain, what do you mean? Doctor Pierce, say it again."

"I say that there is life in him yet. It is but a spark, but it may be fanned into a flame. Roots, I implore you to obey me explicitly in whatever I direct you, and you, my lad, do the same. We shall all have, perhaps, enough to do. Thank God I am here to-night! Now, Roots, for the hot water."

"You bar the door, Ned."

Ned placed the wooden bar across the door of the hut, as Roots seized upon a chair, and dashed it into pieces in a moment, and piled it on the fire. The dry wood soon made a cheerful blaze. Hot water was procured in great abundance, though they had to melt ice to get it. A blanket was warmed and folded round the body of Morris Courtley—the feet were placed in hot water; and while Roots held the still apparent corpse in his arms, Doctor Pierce opened an artery.

Poor Ned, he could do nothing. He only knelt in a corner with his head buried in his hands, and trying to stifle his sobs.

Oh, what an awful half-minute was that which now ensued! At first there came a thick, half-coagulated drop of blood—then another—and then another—and then a little stream. A shudder passed over the body, and with a gasping sob, Morris Courtley opened his eyes!

The tears gushed from Roots's eyes, and Doctor Pierce was much affected. Another ten minutes, and Morris Courtley lived again. The surgeon took from his pocket a small phial, the contents of which he gave to Morris in some warm water, and then they gently laid him in the bed, and wrapped the hot blankets round him, and he fell into a deep sleep. Morris had recovered, but he had not spoken a word yet.

*   *   *   *   *

The old grey morning is making its way through the trees of the New Forest, and gently creeping through the little latticed windows of the cottage that was the abode of the Courtley family.

Roots was lying down in one corner of the room, Ned was asleep close to him, and Docter Pierce sat by the side of Morris Courtley, with his watch in one hand, and the fingers of the other slightly pressed upon the wrist of the slumberer.

"He will do," said the doctor, in a low voice to himself. "He will do yet. They must have bungled the execution very much to leave any life in him. He will soon re-cover now."

The doctor rose and paced the room for some few seconds, and then he stood at the foot of the staircase, and listened attentively.

"The opiate I gave to the two females," he said, "has done its work. If they had come down here, and interfered with the flutter-ing amount of life that was left to this poor fellow, he must have gone. How near to death he has been twenty times, at least, since I came beneath this roof."

The doctor approached Roots, and touched him with his foot.

"Roots?—Roots?"

"Yes, doctor?"

"Were you asleep?"

"With one eye only; but since you told me that he was all right, and getting on pretty well, I have felt a little drowsy, that is all."

"Well, my good fellow, get up now. I want to consult you about what is to be done."

"To be sure, sir. What, are you awake, Ned, too?"

"Yes," said Ned, as he rose, and then pointing to the still form upon the bed, he added, as he looked in the face of the doctor—

"My brother will live to speak to me yet, sir?"

"He will. That is to say, Ned, I hope he will, for I have no right to say it so pointedly. Look to the fire."

"Another chair, Ned," said Roots, as he broke one up, and put it on the fire. "Now, sir, what are we to do?"

"When Morris awakens I want some-thing to give him. What is there in the house?"

"Horse-chestnuts," said Ned.

The doctor shook his head.

"I must have something better than that for my patient, Ned."

"I don't think there's anything but some brown bread, sir. I can go to Martin's farm, and gets some milk. We shall want some to make sister's arrow-root and gruel with."

"Arrow root and gruel? Dou you mean to say that you have such things in the cottage?"

"Oh, yes, sir. Lady Fanny sent us such a lot of all that kind of thing, and preserved fruits and meat, done up in such tidy little canisters, all out of the store-rooms at Bloxdale."

"That will do. Now, Ned, do you under-stand how to make the arrow-root? for if you do not, I do, you know, so don't say so if you don't."

"I do, though, sir. I often make it."

"Then set to work, while Roots and I have a little talk together. Now, Roots, admitting Morris Courtley recovers, what is to be done with him?"

"Done with him, sir?"

"Yes, how is he to be secreted?"

"Lor, sir, they wouldn't surely go for to hang him again?"

"I don't know that."

"If they do, may I be——well, well, I don't mean that; but it didn't strike me before, you see, sir, that there was any danger. Why, we will get him away to-night."

"No—no, not for some days; but do you think that there is no likelihood of any visitors here for that time?"

"Visitors, sir? Lor, sir, do you think that visitors ever come to such a place as this? Oh, dear, no, sir. Such as you, sir, may come, but there ain't many of your sort, I can tell you, sir. He may stay here for a month, and nobody but us crosses the threshold of the place."

"Stop a bit, while I think of it. Is any medical man attending the sister?"

"No, sir; while she was able she went to Southampton to the dispensary, and since she has been too weak and ill to stand the cold, why she has done the best she can without the doctor, no offence to you, sir, but I rather think she has done much better."

"No offence at all, Roots. I can easily believe it, my good friend; and so, after what you have told me, I should say, keep Mr. Courtley here till he is strong and well. Do you think, now, that the Earl of Blox-dale would befriend him? I hear that he went to London to try to get his pardon of the king."

"Ay, sir, that he did; and I'm sure that it will be like heaven to the old man to hear that Morris Courtley breathes again; and as for Miss Fanny—oh, lor! what will she say? I think I see the pretty little creature, sir, with her sweet eyes, lifting her hands up, and saying——"

"Here's the arrow-root," interrupted Ned.

A faint moan from the slumberer on the bed attracted the doctor's attention, and he was by the side of it in a moment.

Courtley was awake.

"Mr. Courtley, be calm," said the doctor "and all will be well. Don't speak if it is any pain to you, or much exertion to do so; but if you feel that you can do so easily, you can, you know."

"God!" said Courtley. "Fanny!"

"Be calm—be calm!"

"A long dream, sir. Is all ready?"

"For what?"

Courtley shuddered,

"Eight o'clock," he muttered, "the crowd! I tell you I am innocent—innocent! Oh, Heaven, I loved him as a dear brother!"

"Mr. Courtley, will you listen to me? I think that it is safer to tell you your true condition, than to leave you to all the vague and dreamy suggestions of your imagination."

"I know all, sir. I am to die!"

"Not so. Come, attend to me while I hold your hand."

So slowly, and with such a mild, quiet voice, did Doctor Pierce now communicate to Morris Courtley what had happened, that the communication, strange and startling as it was, did not prove to be anything like the shock that it might have been to Courtley.

At its conclusion he moved his hands up and down for a moment or two, and then burst into tears.

"Good!" said the doctor. "Now he will do, indeed."

We need not go through all the details of Courtley's recovery. Let it suffice that Ned made the arrow-root to perfection, and that his brother partook of it, actually sitting up in bed; and then, as the doctor heard a movement in the room above, he crept softly up, and tapped at the door.

Mrs. Courtley answered him, and he entered the room, and found the poor mother clasped in the arms of her daughter. They both looked the picture of intense suffering.

"Sir," said Mrs. Courtley, "I think, as well as I can recollect, that we have much to thank you for, although how we came, both of us, to sleep so soundly as we did, is to us both a mystery."

"Never mind that," said the doctor. "There are more mysteries in the world than that. Are you a strong-minded woman, Mrs. Courtley?"

"Ah! no, sir."

"Because, if you were, I should tell you what was down stairs."

"I know! Oh, God! I know! My boy—my Morris!"

"My dear brother!" sobbed the girl.

"Just so," said the doctor. "You both

have been rather ill. I doubt, now, if you could bear joy at all."

"Sir, we shall never be put to the trial of that."

"I don't know that. Now, I will tell you a story. The other day I called upon a family, quite unexpectedly, who lived in a little cottage in a forest as this might be, and—you will pardon me for referring to such a case, but the dear and idolised son had been hanged for murder!"

"Sir?"

"Nay, madam he was innocent, I do think. His body lay upon a bed, and when his mother and sister were set to sleep by means of an opiate that I gave to them, I had the curiosity to examine the body, and, to my surprise, I found that life was not extinct. Indeed, after a whole night of patience I recovered him! Silence, madam! Silence, on your life!"

Mrs. Courtley half sprang to the door of the room, but the stern way in which the doctor spoke resisted her. In a moment or two he added, in a kind tone—

"Any great excitement would endanger his recovery still. Go to your son, and may God restore him wholly to you."

We cannot attempt to describe the scene that followed in the cottage—it is far beyond human cognizance; but there was smiles and tears, laughter and deep sobs, and prayers and thanksgiving to God; and even the rude winter's wind appeared tempered to sunny beauty as it ruffled past that cottage in the old forest.

CHAPTER LXIII.

MRS. LEREW CALLS UPON LORD BLOXDALE AND THE MAYOR OF SOUTHAMPTON.

"Now," said Miss Wicks, as she sat sipping a glass of something rather exciting to the world in general, but only, from long habit, pleasantly sedative to her, "now that Morris Courtley is hanged, and that Lady Fanny Bloxdale is, no doubt, going into a galloping consumption, and the old earl is going out of his wits they say again, and everything is quite comfortable, I will attend to Mr. John Oxley."

Wicks rose and paced to the hall of the hotel, where a glass coach awaited her sweet pleasure.

"To St. Mary's Church," said Wicks, and she was driven at once to the vestry of that establishment.

"I wish," said Miss Wicks, addressing a little bald-headed man who came bowing to know her wishes—"I wish a certificate of marriage of a couple who were united at this church about three months ago."

"The names, if you please, madam."

"Show me the register and I will point them out to you."

"Certainly, madam. This way, if you please—this way."

Miss Wicks soon had the parchment-covered volume of the registry before her, and she placed her finger to one of the entries there, saying—

"I want a regular copy of this, if you please."

"Yes, madam. Hem! Certainly, madam. I will prepare one in a moment."

Miss Wicks took out her purse, and laid a guinea upon the table, as she said—

"You will be so good as to write it in pencil, if you please. That is to say, you will fill up one of your regular printed forms in pencil. Yes, I prefer it much in pencil, and there is your guinea fee."

The words, your guinea fee, banished the scruples of the clerk, and Miss Wicks walked off with one of the printed forms of certificate of marriage having been duly solemnized at St. Mary's Church, Southampton.

"To the hotel again," said Wicks to the driver of the glass coach.

"Yes, ma'am."

Wicks was soon in her sitting-room at the hotel—a piece of indian-rubber removed the pencil marks upon the marriage certificate, and in their place she wrote, "Annabella Wicks, spinster, and John Oxley, bachelor."

"That will do," said Miss Wicks, and again she descended to the glass coach, which dutifully awaited her at the door.

"To the Itchen ferry," said Miss Wicks.

"Yes, ma'am."

"Let me see," said Miss Wicks, as she lolled back in the coach in quite a cosey, comfortable sort of way. "Within this next hour that idiot, Peter, will call according to appointment at the hotel and ask for M. W.; of course, they will tell him they know of no such person, and after most probably staying to partake of something at the bar, he will just consider that he is hoaxed, and there's an end of the whole affair. So much for Peter! Within this hour, too, John Oxley will call at the hotel, for I have written to him so to do, saying that I have something of the greatest importance to communicate to him. Perhaps he will meet Peter there. Well, that don't matter. They will neither of them meet me at the cottage of this woman, Lerew, whither I am bound. So much for John Oxley!"

The glass coach stopped at the Itchen ferry.

"You will return to the spot in half an hour," said Wicks, "and if I am not here then, you will wait for me."

"Yes, ma'am."

The sweet Wicks crossed the ferry, and then through a shady lane—shady even in winter-time, for there were tall fir-trees whose thick black foliage resisted the "winter's flaw"—she made her way to the cottage in which resided Mrs. Lerew.

Before turning out of the lane Wicks felt in one pocket for a knife, and in the other for a pistol which she had loaded there, for she did not think it quite prudent to venture into the immediate presence of Mrs. Lerew quite unarmed, after the kind manner in which

that lady, upon her last interview with Oxley, had recommended that she, Wicks, should be put out of the world.

"All's right," said Wicks, "and now, my dear madam, I think I am something more than a match, even for you."

Wicks rang loudly at the gate bell of the little cottage.

Now Mrs. Lerew, for reasons of weight, kept no servant. Now and then only an old hag, that Oxley recommended, came to the cottage to do a little work, and it so happened that she was there upon this occasion, and came hobbling down the path to speak to Wicks.

"Open the gate," cried Wicks in a tone of authority.

"Who do you want, ma'am?"

"Mrs. Lerew."

"She ain't at home, ma'am."

"That's a lie. She told me she would be at home at eight to the moment, and this is the time. There is half-a-crown."

"Oh, ma'am, if she told you she would be at home, ma'am, that's quite another thing, in course, ma'am. Pray walk in, if you please; you will find her in the parlour, my lady."

"Thank you," said Wicks. "It has only cost one-pound-six as yet. How cheap it will be to hang John Oxley for such a sum! and I do think it will do it."

Without any ceremony Miss Wicks opened the parlour door, and confronted Mrs. Lerew, who looked the picture of astonishment at the interruption.

"Pray, who may you be?"

"I may be, for all you know, anybody; but I am Mrs.—hem! I will not be precipitate—hem! I have the pleasure of addressing Mrs. Lerew?"

"And what if you have, madam?"

"That is a sufficient answer, I am a woman, and I don't like one of my own sex to be deceived by a man, if I can help it. It is of no use to ask me how I got my information, because I won't tell; but I have got it, and it is to the effect that John Oxley has married you, or intends to do so."

"John Oxley?"

"Yes; late steward of the Earl of Bloxdale. He has not married you yet, but he may——"

"Yes, wretch, he has! I am his lawful wife."

"Only last month, though."

"There you are wrong again; it was two months ago to-morrow."

"Indeed. Read that."

Miss Wicks deliberately unfolded the certificate, and placed it before Mrs. Lerew, who glared at it as though it had been a basilisk."

"Are you satisfied?"

"The villain! Your husband, and over three months ago."

"Just so."

"I will have his life!"

"I would."

THE OPPORTUNE ARRIVAL OF DR. PIERCE AT THE COTTAGE IN THE FOREST.

"And you are the Miss Wicks whom he always abused so much to me?"

"Yes; and you are the Mrs. Lerew whom he always abused so much to me."

"I—am; but he said you were the greatest wretch he knew."

"He told me you were the vilest of your sex, and that it saved him the trouble of taking an emetic if he ventured only to look at you. He said, when I last saw him, that he was only waiting for a convenient opportunity to smother you. Good day—good evening, I should say. Rather fine for the time of year after the dreadful weather we have had for the last month, ain't it?—Good evening."

"Stop!" shrieked Mrs. Lerew—"stop!' but Wicks was gone : she had completed her mission, so she had nothing else to stay for. One look into the eyes of Mrs. Lerew after she had read the certificate was quite sufficient to convince Wicks that all her revenge against John Oxley might be left to her with safety.

Wicks was certainly one too many for Mrs. Lerew.

"She is gone!" gasped Mrs. Lerew. "His wife! a former marriage, too! To deceive me in such a way! The villain—the wretch! And so he thinks I am such a poor fool that I may be made the mere tool of his purposes! Oh, I will be revenged! He shall die for this!—yes, he shall die for this! Let me think—oh, let me think! How can I manage it?—Yes, I must think deeply. There must be another hanging on Southampton Common for Lord Francis Bloxdale. What shall I do? What can I do?"

Mrs. Lerew remained for some time in deep thought, and then she muttered to herself—

"He has the gold watch and seals that belonged to Lord Francis Bloxdale, and which he had in his pocket on the night of the murder. I have letters of his in which he more than hints at the deed. The shoes he wore are soaked with blood, and he owned to me that he hid them in a cupboard in his own room at the hall, and left them there, as he had not the courage to take them away, or even to look at them again. He is doomed—doomed! If he be accused, he will be in that fright that he will at once condemn himself: that is certain. The mere words,—'John Oxley, you murdered Lord Francis Bloxdale,' will so act upon his coward spirit that ten to one but he confesses all. What will become of me?"

This was rather an important question.

"Ah! what will then become of me?"

Mrs. Lerew trembled at the thought that something might, by a possibility, become of her that would be not very pleasant to reflect upon.

Pacing the little cottage room to and fro, she deeply thought over this part of the affair; and then, after a time, she considered of a plan of operation which would not only help her to her revenge against Oxley, which

had now certainly become the innate passion of her mind, but enable her to escape from any of the consequences of the ruin which she intended should fall upon his head alone.

"I will give up," she said, "all the plot about installing Peter in Bloxdale as the son of the earl. I see, that with such a man as Oxley—a man so full of deceit and treachery that it would be quite out of the question ever to hope to bring such a plot to a successful issue. He has deposited with me a large sum that he has from time to time pilfered from the hall, and which he is afraid to place anywhere else ; but the question should arise of how he became possessed of it."

Mrs. Lerew smiled to herself as she uttered these words, and it was clear she meant to avail herself of the misplaced confidence of John Oxley, and to walk off with his money.

"Susan!" cried Mrs. Lerew—"Susan!"

"Yes, ma'am."

"Is Mr. Peter at home?"

"No, ma'm. He went out and said he shouldn't be home, ma'am, till to-morrow morning, as he was going to make a night of it with some gents in Southampton, ma'am ; and then he said as they were going to cross the water, ma'am, to the other side, and going to have something there, ma'am, as he called a spree."

"Oh, very well. If Mr. John Oxley should call here before I get home, you can say that I shall not be very long."

"Yes, ma'am."

Mrs. Lerew wrapped herself up in a rich cloak, lined with ermine. It had been the gift of Oxley, and he had procured it from Wicks, who had stolen it from the wardrobe of the poor, wretched, deceived countess.

There was a look of determination about the countenance of Mrs. Lerew that, if Oxley could have but got a glance at her, he would have at once suspected boded to him mischief.; and, as she sallied forth from the cottage, her eyes flashed again with the anger—the positive rage that was working in her soul against that man who had deceived her, as she believed he had.

It was strange, though, how such a woman as Mrs. Lerew, knowing what sort of man John Oxley was, should fall into the error of thinking that, being as he was, false to all, he should be true to her; but such was the fact.

Not far from the cottage there was one of those little lanes that run from the interior portion of the country thereabouts down to the brink of the Southampton Water, along the bank of which there is in summer-time a pretty enough walk upon the loose shingles. At that time of the year, though, that walk was anything but in an agreeable condition.

At the end of the lane there was a few rough piles driven into the water ; and some cross pieces of timber overgrown with weeds, and blackened by long exposure to the weather, made a little landing-place for a few wherries that usually plied there for hire.

It was towards this spot that Mrs. Lerew now bent her steps with what sped she could muster.

The evening was still young, so that there was no chance of not finding a boat there. When she reached the spot, a rough voice called out to her—

" A boat, ma'am ?"

" Yes; but not now," said Mrs. Lerew. " I shall want a boat in about two hours from now—say ten o'clock."

" Ten, ma'am ? Couldn't you make it half-past ?"

" Why ?"

" Oh, it would be more convenient, that's all, ma'am, as I shall have another fare, you see, to attend to. Where do you want to go, ma'am ?"

" To the Isle of Wight."

" Well, that will do, too. There will be a nice little breeze, I think, and we can hoist a bit of canvas, and get over capitally; but make it half-past ten, ma'am."

" Be it so. I will pay you well. There is half a guinea in advance. It is to ensure your being here at the appointed time. You will get as much again upon landing me at the island."

" All's right, ma'am."

" That will do, then."

Mrs. Lerew left the little landing-place, and went up the lane again towards the open country. When she got to a cross-road that in one direction led to Bloxdale Park, and in the other to the ferry over the river Itchen, she paused for a few moments, and it was quite clear that she was passing through some mental struggle. Suddenly, then, she took the road to Bloxdale, at a rapid pace.

" Why should I hesitate ?" she said. " He has deceived me, and he shall die for it ! John Oxley, your doom is fixed !"

The cold night air, which was all the more chilling from the proximity of the water, ruffled the cloak that Mrs. Lerew wore, and at times there came a slight drift of snow or sleet with it which beat upon her face like so many needles ; but the intense desire to revenge herself upon Oxley kept her to her purpose, despite all disagreeables, and she reached the domain of Bloxdale as a distant clock struck the hour of nine.

" An hour and a half," she muttered, " that is the time I have. Well, it is ample, and the man will wait for me with his boat if I am late."

CHAPTER LXIV.

THE INNOCENCE OF MORRIS COURTLEY IS MADE APPARENT.

WE will now take a glance at what is passing at Bloxdale Park, while Mrs. Lerew is gliding along the grand avenue towards the mansion.

In an apartment which went by the name of the small drawing-room, and which was certainly, for winter occupation, one of the pleasantest in the whole range of apartments on the ground-floor, there blazed upon the hearth an ample fire.

The furniture of this room was rather antique, but the massive old oaken chairs and settees with their Utrecht velvet coverings, gave promise of great comfort at that period of the year when all without was so cold and so sterile.

A chandelier of burnished silver hung from the roof of this room, and sent from the dozen wax candles it carried a clear and sweet light into every corner of the apartment.

A couch was drawn in a slanting direction close to the fire ; and, propped partially up by pillows and cushions that belonged to the couch, there lay upon it the sickly and faded form of Lady Fanny Bloxdale.

The young creature looked like some sweet summer bird ruffled by some rude wind ere it could expand into all the beauty that it had promised.

So pale, so wan—so wasted and so weak was poor Lady Fanny, that Ann, her faithful attendant, who was with her, and who scarcely ever left her, could not bear to look at her without tears.

Fanny held a book carelessly in her hand, but her eyes were bent upon vacancy ; and it was only now and then that, with a kind of shudder she drew her breath that she gave any sign of vitality at all.

Ann had been trying to stifle her tears, and now she crept up to the side of the couch, and sitting upon a little footstool that was close to it, she looked in the face of her young mistress, and spoke to her gently—

" Fanny—dear Fanny ?"

" Yes, Ann—yes, dear ?"

" You will, for his sake, when he comes, try to look calm and to seem a little better ?"

Fanny uttered a gasping kind of sob, and nodded her head. It was some moments before she could speak, and then she said—

" I recollect, Ann ; my poor father has prevailed upon me to see a physician from London. I will be as calm as I can."

There was a tap at the door of the room, and a slight flush came over the pale face of Fanny, as she said—

" They are here, Ann. I will, indeed, seem to be hopeful. Kiss me, Ann."

Ann did so, and then she opened the door, and three persons entered the room. One was the Earl of Bloxdale, the other was the Mayor of Southampton, and the third was the physician who had come from London, at the request of the earl, to see Lady Fanny.

The old earl staggered to the couch, and took the white, thin hand of his daughter in his own, and looked in her face, but he could not speak. His heart was nearly broken.

"I am better, father," said Fanny. "Indeed, and in truth, I am."

They all started at this moment, for amid the stillness that reigned in that house, there came the sound of the great hall bell announcing a visitor. It was a sound which, under ordinary circumstances, at Bloxdale, would not have been heard at all; but of late the silence in the mansion had seemed to have something awful and solemn in it, and the servants that remained, for many of them had left, walked about on tip-toes, and if they met each other they only conversed in whispers.

Thus it was then, that, the sound of the hall bell came so plainly to the ears of all in that room.

"News!" said Fanny, holding up her hand. "I dreamt it. Oh, God!"

She fell back upon the couch, and while her father looked at her with alarm, and the physician with curiosity and professional interest, there came a gentle tap at the door of the room, and a servant then opening it, said, in a very subdued voice—

"Mrs. Lerew, my lord."

"Who?" said the earl.

"Mrs. Lerew. She says your lordship expects her, and that you would be angry if not informed at once of her arrival, let you be ever so much engaged."

"I do not know any such person."

With a sudden push, that went near to sending him on his back, Mrs. Lerew, who had followed the servant from the hall, sent him out of her way, and entered the room.

"My lord," she said, "you know me! Look at me!"

The earl started.

"That will do," added Mrs. Lerew. "I don't care how many witnesses I have to what I have to say to you. John Oxley murdered Lord Francis Bloxdale!"

Fanny uttered a shriek and fainted.

"John Oxley murdered Lord Francis Bloxdale!" added Mrs. Lerew. "He has in his possession the watch of the deceased. Here are letters confirmatory of his guilt. In a cupboard in his room you will find the boots he wore on the night of the murder. Morris Courtley was falsely accused, and falsely convicted and murdered. The woman, Wicks, who was waiting-maid to the late countess, is Oxley's wife. She is equally criminal with him. Good-night. Out of the way!"

A blow upon the face of the astonished servant made him clear the doorway, and Mrs. Lerew was out of the house, and away they knew not where in the darkness, before any one could cry out, "Stop her!"

She had thrown a small packet of letters upon the table in the room that happened to be nearest to her.

The earl staggered to a seat.

"Oh, Heaven!" he cried. "What does all this mean? If it be true, it is too late. Oh, God, too late!"

The mayor was as pale as death, but re-covering in a few moments to a sense of his duty, he said—

"My lord, will you allow me to act in this matter?"

"Yes—yes! Too late—too late! Oh, Courtley! Oh, my son!"

The agony of mind of the earl seemed to be such that the return of that mental torpor which had afflicted him for so long, and from which he had so happily recovered, appeared to be all but a certain result. Poor Fanny lay like one dead.

Although immediate orders were given by the mayor to stop Mrs. Lerew, no one could find her; for those who ran out in the first excitement of the moment into the darkness after her had not the least idea of which way she had gone. But the search in Oxley's room was effected. The shoes he had worn on the night of the murder were found, with the most unmistakable marks of blood upon them. The letters that Mrs. Lerew had left on the table in the drawing-room, more than hinted at the dreadful crime that their writer intended to commit, both for the purpose of avoiding the further examination of his own false accounts, and the destruction of Morris Courtley.

It was two hours before Fanny recovered from the swoon into which she had fallen, and then she found her father kneeling by her side, and she stretched out her arms to him, and burst into tears, saying—

"Morris—my Morris is innocent. Father, they have killed him, but he is inno-cent."

The earl wept aloud.

The father and daughter remained together till the cold light of the coming winter morning shone in upon them in that chamber; but during the time that they had spent in mutual confidence and in prayer, some rather important events had taken place.

When Mrs. Lerew left the mansion at Bloxdale in the precipitate manner that she had thought it advisable to do, she proceeded at once to her cottage, and in the space of a quarter of an hour succeeded in packing up in one small parcel all the ill-gotten gains of John Oxley that he had confided to her care, and likewise such little valuables as she did not wish to leave behind her.

The intention of Mrs. Lerew was to go to the Isle of Wight, and thence from it in the morning to find a conveyance to Portsmouth, and from there she fully intended to proceed to London, having, by making that little circuit from Southampton, thrown, as she considered she would, all persons who might be too curious in inquiring for her off the scent.

Some five minutes before the appointed time, she reached the landing-place by the side of the Southampton Water, where she had ordered the man with the cutter to be in waiting for her.

"All's right, ma'am," said the man; "step in. That's it, ma'am. We shall have rather a fresh passage, but nothing to hurt."

" Be quick."

" Yes, ma'am, we will be quick. My boy is going with us, ma'am, you see. Now, Bill, come aboard."

For some reason or another, that Mrs. Lerew could only conjecture concerning with alarm, the boatman evidently delayed his departure, until she rose and cried out in anger—

" I will leave the boat. I will not remain here any longer. I will seek some other mode of conveyance."

" Hold hard, ma'am, it's all right. Here he is."

" Who—who ?"

" Why, ma'am, there's a gentleman as wants a passage to the island at just this time, so I thought it would do no harm to take him."

" How dared you, after I had hired you and your boat."

" It wasn't after that, ma'am. The plain fact is, that when you came to hire me, I was hired by him for the same hour, and to go to the same place, and I thought he might not object to you, so I didn't say no to you."

Mrs. Lerew bit her lips with vexation, and her first idea was to give up her passage in the boat rather than have a companion in it ; but when she saw the cloaked figure of rather a young-looking man, as well as she could judge by the dim night-light, she altered her mind, and drawing the crimson-lined cloak she had on right over the lower part of her face she turned her back to the stranger and determined to go.

The stranger paused upon seeing some one in the boat already, but the sailor said to him in a low tone—

" It is only an old woman, sir, who is going home to her friends in the island. I didn't like to say no to her as she wanted a passage."

" Oh, if that is all it don't matter," said the stranger, as he took his seat in the boat, as far from Mrs. Lerew as possible.

The passage as far as Calshot Castle was rather a boisterous one ; but when the little vessel felt the swell of the sea upon the island off that point of land, it was tossed to and fro at such a rate that the gentleman passenger catching a sea, as it is called, which covered him from head to foot with salt spray, suddenly threw off his cloak, and uttered quite an unmistakable feminine scream.

Mrs. Lerew turned in a moment and uttered a scream, as she shrieked—

" It's Wicks—it's Wicks !"

" Lerew—Mrs. Lerew !" shrieked Wicks, for it was, indeed, no other than that lady, who accidentally had adopted the same mode of escaping from the fallen fortune of Oxley that Mrs. Lerew had.

In an instant they flew at each other like two mad cats. They rocked to and fro in each other's embrace, and then, before the sailor could resolve upon leaving the helm

to separate them, a heavy sea struck the boat—she gave a lurch, and over went Mrs. Lerew and Wicks into the bubbling surge.

There was a smothered cry mingled with the howling of the wind and the flapping of the sails of the boat, and then all was over with those two bold, bad women, who had been at last the destruction of each other.

" I say, Bill," said the sailor to the boy that was with him. " We couldn't help it could we, Bill ?"

" No how," said Bill. " It's a coming on to snow, it is, blowed if it ain't. "

CHAPTER LXV.

THE CONCLUSION.

THE events that have so rapidly changed the fortunes of the principal personages in our story naturally now herald it to a conclusion. The sword of justice hangs over the head of the guilty Oxley—Miss Wicks, and that kindred spirit, Mrs. Lerew, have gone to their account.

The dawn of the winter's morning is spreading itself over Southampton, and Mr. Oxley is cautiously making his way to the cottage where he thinks Mrs. Lerew may still be found. He has no conception of the strange events that have taken place within the last few hours.

After calling at the hotel for Miss Wicks, and waiting there a very considerable time, and, during it, imbibing certainly more than was good for him of port wine, Oxley had fallen asleep, being exhausted both in body and in mind ; and it was not until the dawn of the morning that he shook off a deep slumber which, for once in the way, was dreamless, and made his way to the cottage.

There was a crisp and pleasant freshness in the air upon that morning, and the sun was beginning to peep over the tops of the distant forest across the Southampton Water as Oxley reached the little gate leading to the garden of Mrs. Lerew's abode.

There he paused for a few moments and looked about him, and a strange feeling came over him that made him tremble, but which he could not account for.

" Now," said he, " if I were a believer in presentiments, which I am not, I should say that something is about to happen which would really affect me in my prospects ; but I fancy that it is but the keen morning air, which is a little too much for me after all. I wonder if Mrs. Lerew is up."

If Oxley had but known that Mrs. Lerew lay amid sand and seaweed at the bottom of the Solent, he would have quickly enough fled from that spot.

Lifting the latch of the little gate, he walked slowly through the garden ; and as he glanced at the cottage, he saw that a thin mantle of blue smoke was curling up from one of the chimneys.

" Ah ! there is a fire alight," he exclaimed

"that is a comfort, at all events. I did not expect to find one at so early an hour as this."

Oxley had a key to the street door of the cottage, if we may so term it; and after some fumbling in his pockets he found it, and attempted to open the door, but, before he could do so, it was suddenly opened by some one from within, and, to the surprise of Mr. Oxley, a strange man confronted him in the passage.

For just a moment Oxley thought it possible that he had mistaken the house; but it was only for a moment that such a supposition could find a home in his breast, for the sight of several well-known articles of furniture in the hall confirmed him in the opinion that he was right, and that it could be no other than the cottage of Mrs. Lerew that he had reached.

"Good morning, sir," said the man.

"Good—that is—who are you?" said Oxley.

"Walk in, sir. Your name is Oxley?"

"Well, sir?"

The man smiled and gave a sort of nod with his head, and then a heavy hand descended upon the shoulder of Oxley, who, upon abruptly turning round, saw standing close to him another man of rather portentous aspect.

Oxley gasped for a moment as though something impeded his breathing, and then he said—

"What—what—is—the—the meaning of this?"

"You are my prisoner, John Oxley," said the man who had placed his heavy hand upon his shoulder. "You are my prisoner on a charge of murder!"

"Murder!"

"Yes, you can say what you like, or leave it alone."

"The—the murder of—of—whom?"

"Lord Francis Bloxdale! Jem, the handcuffs."

Oxley spun round upon his heels, and fell to the ground fainting. The suddenness of the charge, combined with the awfully ominous manner of the officer, and the place in which he was taken, which, to his mind, seemed convincing of the fact that Mrs. Lerew must have betrayed him, all combined to overcome what little strength of mind and body Oxley possessed; and he lay upon the threshold of the door dead to all sensation for a time.

When Oxley recovered, he found himself in the old jail at Southampton, and a couple of turnkeys with him.

It was at that same hour in the morning, and just as the officer laid his hand upon the shoulder of Oxley, that a costly and roomy barge, well covered in, and which belonged to the corporation of Southampton, pushed off from the quay nearest to Netley Abbey.

In that barge were several persons besides the rowers. One of the persons was the Earl of Bloxdale—another was the magistrate, whose evidence had been so fatal to Morris Courtley, and who had been so deeply affected at having to give it against him—another was the Mayor of Southampton, and another was poor Fanny Bloxdale.

The young creature had herself ventured upon paying a visit to Mrs. Courtley at her own cottage in the New Forest; and the London physician had told the earl distinctly that she was to be thwarted in nothing that she desired that was at all practicable.

In the barge, too, was Ann, who knew the way to the cottage, in consequence of having frequently visited there, and who was to act as guide to the party.

An old-fashioned sedan-chair, that stood usually in the hall at Bloxdale, was brought in the barge for Fanny, in case she should feel unable to walk, and the watermen of the barge were ready to carry her through the glades of the forest.

As the barge neared the shore there was seen a man with a gun in his hand, standing close to some old trees, and looking with intense interest upon its progress. This man's apparel was faded and torn. Upon his head he wore an old seal's skin cap, and his leather leggings showed that he was accustomed to make his way through the tangled brakes of the forest.

A green bag over his shoulder looked as if it contained something that had rewarded his early exertions amid the old leafless trees, notwithstanding the scarcity of game at that time of the year.

The attention of the party in the boat was attracted towards this solitary-looking man; and the earl, upon looking at him, said to Fanny—

"My dear, I can see our old acquaintance, Roots, on the shore. He will be the most efficient guide we can have to Mrs. Courtley's; and, besides, he will be able to tell us how it fares with her."

Fanny nodded quietly, but her heart was too full to permit her to speak. She was thinking of her murdered lover, for all had been told to her now, and the innocence of Courtley was apparent to every one in the barge.

"Now, by gun, and trap, and pitfall," said Roots to himself, "if there is not the Earl of Bloxdale! What can they want here? Bother take them, I can't pretend not to see 'em. I only came out to pick up a bird or two to make poor Morris a drop of soup, and if they are bound for the cottage it will be a hard thing to give them notice of the visit; and if Morris should happen to hear the voice of that little bit of an angel, Fanny, I wonder what will keep him quiet, as the doctor said he was to be kept?"

The earl waved his hand to Roots.

"Ah, they see me," said the poacher, for such, indeed, he was now, in the full sense of the word. "It won't do to fly from them; that would look shabby. Well, I must do the best I can. Mayhap they ain't coming to the cottage at all, but are going to see some of the fine gentry out away by Lynds hurst. Ah! that's it, I'll be bound, so there' nothing to fear for Morris, poor fellow."

Roots strode close to the water's edge, and lifted his cap to the party in the boat.

The boatmen knew Roots, and called to him to help them, which he did by catching at the coil of rope they threw to him, and in a few minutes the party safely landed. Fanny leaned upon her father's arm, and declared that she could walk, and the earl, addressing Roots, said—

"Our errand here is to call upon Mrs. Courtley. You, no doubt, can take us by the shortest route to her abode."

"I can," said Roots — "Hem!—Poor woman!"

The earl was silent for a moment or two, and then he said—

"Since the innocence of poor Morris Courtley is now fully established, his death will weigh heavily upon me for the few years I may yet have to live. The villain, Oxley, is by this time in prison, and it is perfectly clear that he, and not Morris Courtley, was the murderer of my son."

A flush of colour came over the face of Roots, and for a few moments he could only stare at the earl, with his mouth made up to the expression of a whistle, but in silence.

"You don't mean, my lord, that it's all found out?"

"It is."

"And old Oxley did it?"

"There can be no doubt."

"Oh! oh! I — that is — nothing!—God bless you, Lady Fanny, I shall live yet to see the sunshine of one of the old smiles upon your pretty face again."

Fanny shook her head, and the tears gushed to her eyes.

"Come," said Roots, "I do know the nearest way to the cottage. Come after me. Ha! ha! Oh, gracious! Come along!— Come—ha! ha!"

The earl looked at Roots with a suspicion that he was mad; but, with Fanny upon his arm, he followed him, and in the course of half-an-hour they all reached the little cottage of the Courtley family. Mrs. Courtley met them at the porch, and the earl started at the sight of her, for she wore no mourning, and there was such a look of placid joy upon her face that it was quite at variance with what he had expected.

"Here's the earl and Lady Fanny, Mrs. Courtley, come to see you," said Roots. "Its all found out, and old Oxley is in gaol for the murder, and Morris is innocent, as we all knew he was. Come in, my lord— come in, Lady Fanny. Oh, dear, what a day this is, to be sure!"

Mrs. Courtley staggered back into the cottage, and looked ready to faint; and the earl, as he gazed around him, said—

"I am glad to see that resignation has usurped the place of grief here."

"Oh, my lord—I—I—dear Lady Fanny— what shall I say?"

"You should have been my mother," said Fanny, as she burst into tears, and knelt by the side of poor Mrs. Courtley, who had sunk into a chair—"if our poor Morris had not been murdered."

Tap! tap! tap! came a sound upon the floor above.

"He wants the goat's milk," said a voice, and Ned popped his head into the room.

"Listen!" cried Roots, as he stood out in the middle of the cottage floor, with his head nearly touching the roof. "I loved Morris Courtley. I watched over his welfare when a boy. I followed him to— to—"

"Hush!" said the earl, as he pointed to Fanny.

A smile came over the face of Roots, as he, too, pointed to her:

"My lord, does joy kill?"

"Joy?"

"Yes. Look at that young fawn. Bless her! do you think, now, that you could kill her with joy?"

"You are mad."

"No, no, my lord—no. Listen. There was a man hanged—don't start—hanged for murder; but he didn't die; and the great God held him up, and when his friends took what they thought the clay-cold corpse to his mother's home, they found life in it — the blessed life that God had given it—and— and they prayed, and did better still than that, for they fed and nursed him, and treated him, and—"

"Roots, what do you mean?" cried the earl.

"He lives!" cried Roots, holding up his arm above his head, and speaking in a voice of deep emotion, "he lives—Morris Courtley lives!"

"Oh! no, no!" shrieked Fanny. "This is cruel. Oh, God, say it again!"

"He lives!" God, he lives!"

Roots staggered to a chair, and covering his bronzed face with his hands, he wept aloud.

"Morris!" cried Fanny, "my Morris— my own true love! Oh, God! they have not killed him! God has saved him for me— for me!"

She flung the clustering ringlets from her face—she cast one glance around her, and then seeing the little staircase that led to the upper room of the cottage, she reached them in a moment, and flep to the upper apartment.

There was a cry of joy, and then, for some minutes, all was still. Fanny held in her arms her lost lover, and the world had not another joy for her that could compare with the delight of that moment.

It would be difficult, indeed, to give to the reader anything like a perfectly just and true picture of the scene that took place in the little sleeping-chamber of poor Morris Courtley when that, to him, and to all who knew her, vision of beauty and goodness, Lady Fanny Bloxdale, made her way into it.

It is a debt, however, that we owe to the reader of this narrative, who has followed us thus far in our details of the fortunes of persons for whom, we hope, we have awakened something like a friendly interest, to attempt to record the few and brief expressions of joy and thankfulness with which the hearts of the young couple overflowed.

The condition of Morris may be in a very few words explained.

From the moment that the doctor had found out that the supposed dead body of Morris Courtley really had life in it, he had felt the very deepest interest in the case in a professional point of view; and, quite irrespective of any other feeling, there can be no doubt but that he would have night and day have paid attention to the condition of Morris.

When, however, he came to know all that had taken place—when, step by step, he was able from one and from another to trace the whole course of those strange and romantic events which had apparently terminated in the death of Courtley, and in the triumph of the malignant spirit of John Oxley, a feeling of reverential awe came over him at the thought that the finger of divine providence was surely most manifest in the affair.

Along with this religious feeling, which, under the circumstances, was very natural, indeed, there came another; and that was one of great pride and thankfulness that he could be selected as the instrument of carrying out the scheme by which the innocent Morris was yet to be preserved to the world, despite all the resources of the blackest treachery and false testimony that had been brought to bear against him for his utter destruction, so far as regarded his human existence.

With confused feelings, then, of this character, it can scarcely be wondered at that the surgeon gave up all other considerations than the all-absorbing one of the recovery of Morris Courtley.

Under such circumstances, with youth and all the fine and rich resources of a good constitution, aided by the most profound art, it is not to be wondered at that, notwithstading the severe shock that Morris Courtley's system had undergone, he completely recovered from the effects of the hanging; and nothing remained but a degree of debility and nervousness which the surgeon felt that care would completely overcome in the course of time.

Of course Morris felt that it was the accidental breaking down of a portion of the gallows at the moment when he was being turned-off that had really saved him; for if he had had all the fall intended, a dislocation of the neck would certainly have ensued, and then nothing could have restored that poor, inanimate form to life again.

As Courtley had gradually—very gradually, we may indeed say, gathered strength, all that had occurred since his trial and condemnation and execution so far as it was known to those about him was important to him.

There was one hope though, more than any other, which came like a sweet balm to his heart, and tended much to his recovery, and that was that his dear Fanny might yet be his, and that through good report and through evil report, she had still, with a noble and endearing confidence, clung to the conviction that he was innocent of the crime for which he had suffered.

Morris would lie in that little chamber with his arms crossed upon his breast, and his eyes closed, while all was stillness in the cottage, because they had peeped at him and thought that he slept, and pictured to himself the joyful moment that might yet come in after years, when he should be permitted to let Fanny know that he lived, and have the joy of again looking into her eyes.

Little did he suspect that that happy moment was so near him, as in good truth it was.

The bustle below stairs had come upon his ears, and he had listened to catch, if he could, some of the words that were spoken; but, although he had heard a confused murmur of voices, nothing distinct had come to him.

His brother, Ned, had been reading to him in a low voice, and after fancying that Morris had gone to sleep, he had leant back upon the old arm-chair in which he had sat by the bedside, and gone to sleep himself—for Ned's devotion to his brother was such that he had kept himself day and night at his service, and it is a fact that Ned had not had his clothes off above once since Morris had come home.

When the voices came from below, Morris, who had only closed his eyes, but who had not slept, had heard them, but Ned had not.

After a time, then, the idea had crept slowly over the mind of Morris that possibly there might be something amiss below; and then, just as there commenced a flutter at his heart upon that account, the unmistakable tone of Roots' voice came upon his ear, and there was nothing in the tone to indicate anything but pleasure and satisfaction upon the part of the sturdy and kindhearted forester.

"Roots is pleased," thought Morris, "so all is well. If I tap on the floor with the stick he has left by the side of the bed he will hear me, and come up and tell me the news."

Upon this inducement, then, was it that Morris Courtley gave the taps upon the floor which had come so strangely and suddenly upon the ears of the party in the little lower room of the cottage.

But the taps not only attracted attention below, but they awakened poor Ned, who even in his sleep might be supposed to be listening for them, inasmuch as he was in the habit of being aroused by them to attend upon his brother, Morris.

OXLEY IN A FELON'S CELL.

"The goat's milk—the goat's milk, yes, in a minute, brother Morris," said Ned, as he hurried to the little dressing table under the old fashioned latticed window with its mass of ivy nearly excluding half the light which otherwise would have found its way into Morris's neat little chamber; poor Ned had been so much in the habit of running for the goat's milk of late whenever his brother stirred that it is no wonder, that being just disturbed from an unrefreshing slumber, his mind should immediately revert to what his brother so often required.

"No, Ned, thank you," said Morris, "it is not the goat's milk that I want this time. I heard sounds as though many people were talking in the lower room ; and I also heard Roots laughing more merrily and heartily than since our misfortunes began ; something of importance is taking place below I feel convinced : it was my calling for Roots, Ned which awoke you, and I'm sorry for it, for you have not had much rest of late. Try to compose yourself again, Roots will be with me directly."

While he was speaking he raised himself

into a sitting posture in his bed, and then Fanny clasped her arms around him.

"My Morris! my own—own living Morris!—oh, God! how can I ever thank you for this mercy! Morris—Morris!—oh, speak to me, and tell me, indeed, that you live!"

"Fanny—Fanny!" was all that Courtley could say, but he clasped her to his heart, and the tears—tears that he had not shed since the time when they had last met, gushed from his eyes.

For the space of about five minutes, now, neither of them could speak a word, but they both wept; and then Fanny smiled, and kissed his eyes, and his cheeks—oh, how pale and thin they were!—and his forehead, and then she wept again, and called him her Morris, and looked so happy, that he cried out—

"Oh, God! if this be a dream, let me not awaken from it, but in mercy let it last for ever!"

"Morris, it is no dream."

"Are you sure, dear one?"

"Quite, Morris: I am your own Fanny. Oh, Morris, don't you know me too well to think me a mere vision? Look at me now, Morris. Are not these tears real?"

"They are—they are!"

"But they are tears of pure, pure joy."

"Oh, how richly am I repaid for all that I have gone through! Fanny—Fanny, you never had a thought—a doubt, even—it never came across your mind that I raised my hand against poor Francis, your brother! You could not look at me as you do if you ever had the remotest thought that I could be guilty!"

"Oh, no—no, Morris, I never had such a thought—never, oh, never! Do not you think for a moment that I had."

"And your father?"

"He, too, knows and feels that you are innocent."

"I thank Heaven!" said Morris. "Let those now still instigated by John Oxley do their worst: I can suffer death again, now that I have held you once more in these poor arms; and with the hope that we shall meet again in Heaven, I will suffer patiently, if fate so wills it."

"But, Morris, there is no danger now."

"Oh, yes—yes, love! You know it not. There is danger, although you, in your consciousness of my innocence, think otherwise."

"No—no, Morris! It is all discovered, and John Oxley is now known to be the guilty one. You are in no danger now. All who know you will hail your appearance in life with delight. Those who condemned you upon the testimony of such a man as Oxley are already covered with shame and reproaches. There is no danger, indeed, now for you, Morris; but all the world will hold your name in veneration, and I most of all."

Morris was almost stunned by this intelli-

gence, and he looked in the eyes of Fanny as though he had a doubt whether she were not deceived herself in some way by such apparent good news.

"It is true, Morris—all true."

"Then, indeed, I live again! Oh, Fanny, what have I done to deserve so much joy as this?"

"You have done all that should deserve it, my Morris—you have, under circumstances of difficulty and of danger, done what your heart told you it was right to do. All who, from the lips of my father, have heard your story, have been struck by sudden admiration of the nobleness of your conduct—I have, too, felt that it is time to banish all reserve, and to let the world know how nobly you behaved to me when you knew that I loved you."

"Cease—oh, cease, Fanny! it is you who behaved so nobly in allowing yourself to love the poor secretary."

"Nay, my Morris, not so."

"Yes, dear; our rank in life was so different."

"Indeed, Morris?"

"Was not your father noble, and were not you noble?"

"And were not you, too?"

"Me, Fanny?"

"Yes, Morris. God has a nobility among his creatures as well as man, only the nobles of God's making are his own, with hearts and souls of true nobility, and will inherit heaven; but those of man's making, my Morris, are the creatures, too often, of intrigue and of accident; so you see, my Morris, I will have it that it is you who were noble, and who confer honour upon me by offering to me your pure and excellent heart."

"Ever kind and good!" said Morris Courtley, as he covered with kisses the little hands that he held in his. "Oh, do not leave me!"

"But you are not strong yet, Morris; and who knows but that even by thus long talking with you I may have hindered your recovery much?"

"No, no—a thousand times no! It is true that I was not strong, Fanny, but I am now. This blessed interview with you has given me new life, and I feel so happy that I cannot be otherwise than well. Joy, you may depend, is a good physician."

"It is, Morris, for I now feel again the glow of health and youth in my veins, which I have not felt for many and many an hour. Oh, Morris, there is but one thing wanting now."

"And what is that, dear one."

"My poor brother!"

"Oh, forgive me! How selfish, after all, the best of us are in our pleasures. I had indeed, and in truth, forgotten him. But reflect, Fanny, that, after all, he is with his God, and that

" 'After life's fitful fever he sleeps well.'

We will pray by his grave, and will strew with spring flowers, for, in good truth, there never was a better heart ; and well and truly he loved both of us."

"He did—he did!"

"And, after all, dear Fanny, it is well that joy should have about it some shadowing of sorrow, to temper the pure sunshine, or else we should be too apt to forget that we, too, are mortal."

"That is true, Morris. Let me draw this little blind aside and look at you, for the room is so darkened that I cannot see those dear eyes so well as I could wish."

Morris smiled as the young girl drew aside the small blind that was at the chamber window, and then he turned to the light, and she placed her hands upon his shoulders, and looked him in the face till the tears trickled from her eyes.

"My poor—poor Morris !"

"Do not weep, Fanny."

"I must take such care of you. None will tend you as I will. You shall soon be well again ; quite—quite well. But now you are so pale, and so sad-looking."

She could say no more, but fell into his arms in a paroxysm of sobbing ; but how happy was Morris to hold to his heart that fair and beautiful being whom he loved so well, and without whom life to him would have been but

"An unweeded garden."

* * * * *

John Oxley was executed on the tenth of January, and had to be supported to the scaffold by the police, for he had made two attempts to destroy himself while in prison.

On a sweet May day, when all nature was in one of its happiest aspects, Lady Fanny Bloxdale and Morris Courtley were married, and need we say that they were happy ?

Roots lived long and happily at Bloxdale. The old earl died when Courtley's eldest son was ten years of age ; and by interest that was exerted with the Government, the title of Bloxdale was conferred upon Courtley at the earl's death. Mrs. Courtley and Ned and the sister of Morris all resided at the mansion in peace and serenity.

Peter Lerew disappeared, and nobody ever heard of him again.

Ann lived comfortably at Southampton, and was well looked after by the Bloxdale family, in the archives of which, with his own hand, Morris Courtley wrote the strange story of the " Secretary ; or, Circumstantial Evidence."

THE END.